10|19

Stay and Fight

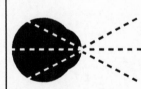

This Large Print Book carries the
Seal of Approval of N.A.V.H.

STAY AND FIGHT

MADELINE FFITCH

THORNDIKE PRESS
A part of Gale, a Cengage Company

GALE
A Cengage Company

Farmington Hills, Mich • San Francisco • New York • Waterville, Maine
Meriden, Conn • Mason, Ohio • Chicago

LIBRARY OF CONGRESS CIP DATA ON FILE.
CATALOGUING IN PUBLICATION FOR THIS BOOK
IS AVAILABLE FROM THE LIBRARY OF CONGRESS

ISBN-13: 978-1-4328-6808-6 (hardcover alk. paper)

Published in 2019 by arrangement with Farrar, Straus and Giroux

Printed in Mexico
1 2 3 4 5 6 7 23 22 21 20 19

To Ann, Liz, and Linden
May our families continue to make a way
together

And to the land

■ ■ ■ ■

PART I
STINGING NETTLE

■ ■ ■ ■

1

Helen

One winter, Rudy got an infection in his testicles while he lay out drunk on coal company land in a one-room shack that didn't belong to him. When the corruption began to smell, he washed his balls with creek water and put some plantain on the infected place. He wrapped it up in duct tape, and kept the whiskey bottle by the bed. He lay on his bunk until his dick turned black and started bleeding out pus, at which time he found he could no longer walk. He couldn't even get up to light the fire. When he started hallucinating, he knew he would die if he didn't get up, so he forced his feet to find the floor, and he forced his body upright. He made it to the road, where he began, somehow, to walk. He knew his only hope was a ride. But it was the middle of the night, and it was February, and he was miles from town, and no one came by. Rudy would count out fifty paces and then collapse. Each time he passed out, he tried to do it in the middle of the road so that any car that came would have to stop for him. He kept himself moving like that most of the night. Finally a truck passed, some poachers coming back from a run. They pulled him up into the cab despite his odor, and they drove him the hour into town, speeding the whole way. He stank like he'd dug himself out of his own grave, shit and piss, the high smell of white worms and the paste of decay, and the hunters hauled him into the emergency room and left him there, and he fainted away on the floor.

"What happened then?" I asked my boyfriend, the night before he left me.

"They put Rudy in a hospital bed," he said. "He was dead to the world for three whole days."

"And then?" I asked.

"And then? Well, I guess then he woke up," my boyfriend said.

"But what happened after he woke up?" I asked. We were lying in our narrow camper bed, not touching, but maybe about to.

"Come on, Helen," he said. "That's not the point of the story."

"What's the point of the story?" I asked.

"The point is that I'm quitting," he said. "I can't take working for Rudy anymore. He's crazy. He's spent too much time alone. He's a first-rate blowhard. He's impossible. And besides that, he's sexist. All women are his mother, sister, girlfriend rolled into one. Every waitress, he says she wants it. Ranks them one through ten, that sort of shit. Like I'm gay if I want to talk about anything besides tits and ass, if I consider women to be human beings. He hates women and he's obsessed with them."

"Are you sure you're not being too sensitive?" I asked.

Oh yes, he was a fine man. And yes, I drove him away.

I met my boyfriend the week after my thirty-first birthday, when he hired me on to his landscaping crew in Seattle. Some people might have called him two-faced but when I met him I noticed his wavy hair and how he smiled at me all the time, whether or not he meant it. It annoyed me right up until I couldn't do without it. He had ambition. I didn't. I'd barely graduated college, never really got around to dating. He wanted to leave the city, to get some acres and live off the grid, not that a person could expect to buy land in the Northwest at those prices, not that he'd managed to save much money, not that he had any credit. After we'd fumbled around for a few months, he said, In the Southeast you can get land cheap. The Southeast? I asked. Appalachia, he said. Never been there, I said. He said, Didn't your uncle leave you some money?

The only thing keeping me in Seattle was my aunt, who was walking dogs and selling vintage clothes online, barely making the mortgage, busy grieving my uncle. What was I busy doing? What I'd been doing since college: seasonal work, mostly outside, circling around the city hoping my uncle wouldn't get sicker and now he was dead. I thought my aunt might want me to stay, but how she put it was, Thirty-one's not old, but you might as well see if you can hold on to that man. I really didn't know him that well. I still wasn't sure what he was smiling at me for. But I'd been waiting for my life a long time.

It was March when I followed my boy-friend to the oldest slope, not quite West Virginia but right there on the border. In a hill town with a land grant institution, a hardware and salvage store, an IGA, a diner, and thirty bars, we searched the nickel ads and went for a drive. After six miles we saw a FOR SALE sign scribbled on a paper plate.

The paper plate was stuck to a mailbox. The mailbox was stabbed into the bank of a creek. Behind it, twenty acres of raw wooded hillside. A gravel driveway spiraled up.

We climbed it, maybe seven hundred feet but felt like a quarter mile. At the top, I looked back the way we'd come, but the road below had disappeared. You couldn't even hear it. The driveway went nowhere, but ended in thorns, soggy husks, wide-faced grasses, trees that I didn't take seriously at first, because out West forest means evergreen. No houses, no structures, nothing but mud, rocks, and not-quite-wilderness. What about neighbors? I asked. My boyfriend studied a map. He said, We're surrounded by coal company land. Miles of it. Coal mines? I asked. Isn't that dangerous? The industry moved on a long time ago, my boyfriend said. They left the land to itself. Untrammeled forest, he said. Post-trammeled, I said. He said, It's cheap to buy around here. I said, I had this professor once who said that private property is a totally problematic concept. My boyfriend said, We can start from scratch. We can hack some trails. Clear some trees. Build our way. He pointed into a thicket. Do you see that? Buried in the roots of an elderberry bush, a cast-iron kettle spilled muddy water. A freshwater spring, he said. We'd be fools not to. I used my uncle's money to make the down payment.

We bought a camper so small that the two of us could push it up into the woods, where we cleared a sugar maple, an ash tree, and a red oak. I learned their names as we cut them down. With a shovel and a grub hoe we dug out enough space to prop up the camper on a stack of sandstone so it was level. Only the barest bit of light came in the windows past the orange spray-painted declaration scrawled across them, THE MC-CANN'S: STEP AWA, someone else's feud.

April, May, and most of June, my boyfriend worked up north in one of those new boom industries, drilling whatever, so we could pay off the rest of the land. Meanwhile, I was supposed to stay home and get shit done. But it was me against the land and I was in awe. No one was watching me all day but god, and I didn't believe in god. I didn't know how to get started. I wasn't sure I wanted to. It was cold and it was raining. I put on a poncho. I dug out the spring, buried a plastic bucket beneath the cast-iron kettle, called it a refrigerator. I strung a tarp, put another bucket under it, called it an outhouse. I tried to plant some onions, not knowing how much sun they needed, not knowing they were heavy feeders. Mostly, I waited for my boyfriend. I biked the gravel roads until I had enough signal to call him. He didn't pick up. I biked to the bar and stood under the air vent, asked the bartender to turn up the heat. I played pool against myself. There were men in canvas, caps pulled low, college girls wearing miniskirts in the pouring rain, fuzzy boots to make up for it. No one found out that I was a good conversationalist. No one talked to me. I charged my phone. Tried my boyfriend again. At night I lay in the camper, figuring I'd get murdered or a tree would fall on me. I told myself I could always head back to Seattle and find another landscaping crew. Instead, my boyfriend came back with ducklings in a cardboard box. What did you do while I was gone? he asked. I gestured toward the buckets and the tarp. And I played pool, I said. There's this bar in town. It rained a lot. You should have been planting, he said. I planted onions, I said. But peas, he said. Kale. Or I don't know chopping wood. What would I chop wood for? I asked. It's going to be summer soon. You've got no ambition, he said. We took down a hickory, pried apart some pallets, and built a duck shed.

That summer, Rudy hired my boyfriend

to run his ropes. Who's Rudy? I asked. Just one of these assholes, said my boyfriend. A tree trimmer. I saw him up in a maple on the way into town, so I asked if he needed a hand. It's not forever but it's a job.

When my boyfriend came home from work each evening, I was desperate for company, but he wasn't much for chatting. Me, I could talk all night. We would get in bed, and I would begin. When I began talking, the raccoon crept by, and when I finished, the woodpecker hammered its spring-loaded head into the ash tree outside our window. I jiggled my boyfriend's arm to keep him awake.

We almost made it to September.

The night my boyfriend quit working for Rudy, he was finally in the mood to talk. He'd come home with a cut on his face, but he didn't want to talk about that. He wanted to tell me the story about Rudy's balls. "It's not that I'm sensitive," he said. "The guy's a mess and that story proves it. I mean, what the hell kind of man trespasses on coal company land to hide out and cure himself with whiskey and duct tape? Just ask yourself that."

"But what are we going to do for money?" I asked.

"We'll think of something," he said. "What

about your aunt?"

"They're about to foreclose on her house," I said.

"What about your college degree?"

"What about it?"

"There's a college in town, maybe you could I don't know be a professor or something," he said.

"You can't do anything like that with a college degree, the only thing you can do with a college degree is get another degree," I said.

"I could go back up north to work," he said. "Plenty of money up there."

"And leave me alone here again? I'll die."

He told me that I wasn't going to die, and so I said, Okay but I want to die, and he said, No you don't, and I said, Okay but I want to kill you. He opened his eyes then, but he didn't say anything, so I told him that I was going back to Seattle. He told me not to leave, and I told him to give me one good reason.

"It's not right that you should go," he said. "I'll go. I'll find someplace else. I'll go in the morning."

That was how he outsmarted me.

After my boyfriend left, I packed up, too. But I'd spent all the money from my uncle on that infernal slope. I couldn't even pay for a bus ticket home. I went to the bar and stood under the air vent. I charged my phone and called my aunt, ended the call before she picked up. I didn't want to admit defeat. I knew she'd made some outlandish equation that if I would just get married all her struggles would be worth it. But now I was alone with a leaky camper, a flock of ducks, twenty acres to care for, little firewood, and no income to speak of. My aunt's number blazed up on my phone's screen. She was calling me back. I canceled it. The air vent blared. I went through my contacts, the guys my boyfriend had known, who'd been up north with him, or worked construction in town. Called Frank. "You know I can't hire you onto my crew," he said. "Why don't you try Rudy? I hear he's desperate. Your man left him high and dry."

"Why can't you hire me?" I asked.

"I've never seen a woman could work a full day like one of my men," Frank said. "The economy's too hard right now to do it out of sympathy. Besides, what would my wife think?" To be helpful, I told him that his crew was primarily made up of pill heads and drunks, that I could work circles around them, and that, as far as I could tell, he had never asked his wife what she thought about

18

anything before, so why start now? These people believed strongly that the world was coming to an end soon because of solar flares and the shifting of the poles, not that they ever mentioned climate change, relentless war, or industrial capitalism, but he had hung up.

So I shifted my bike down to its lowest gear and I rode up to Tanner's Corner, where Rudy was clearing a half acre of yellow pine. Tangled red ponytail sticking out from underneath his hard hat, pink safety goggles, hairy face so full of sawdust it looked like he'd been breaded. He had his Husqvarna 362XP gnawing out the hinge on a fifteen-foot stub when I leaned my bike up against his truck, but he let it idle when he saw me.

"If you come any closer, I'll take it you want to be killed by this tree," he yelled above the motor. I stood back while he made the back cut. We watched it fall. Rudy turned off the saw and lifted his goggles. "You expecting your man back anytime soon?" he asked.

"Seems like you're having a hard time holding on to ground crews," I said.

"Must be due to my bad attitude," he said.

"I don't think he'll be back," I said. "But I need work."

"Any experience?" he asked.

"Landscaping, tree planting, firefighting, flagging, clearing debris. I've taken down my share of trees," I said. "And I have a college degree."

"Oh my," Rudy said. "Slumming it with the hill folk." He knelt and began to oil his saw, judiciously dripping it from an unmarked plastic bottle.

"I'm saving money to go back to Seattle," I said.

"What did you go to college for?" he asked.

"I don't know," I said.

"Sounds like you got scammed," he said. "Do you know your knots?"

"Of course I do," I said.

"I'll probably yell at you. It's not that I'm proud of it, but that's just how I am."

"If you yell at me, I'll walk off the job," I said.

Rudy screwed the lid back on the bottle of chain oil and stood up. He wiped his hands on his shirt. He pulled wood chips from his beard. Coarse red hair crept from his cuffs and his collar, laced with sawdust. He reached in and scratched. "Might as well start today," he said. "It doesn't appear that you have anything better to do." I stashed my bike. He handed me a hard hat.

While I watched, Rudy set his climb line on another yellow pine, and strapped on his spurs. Then he threw his body upward, making his way up the tree by launching himself up into the air, an eel, gaining inch by inch up the rope. He moved as a current, sending his Blake's hitch up ahead of him, until he reached the lower branches, twenty feet up. Then he dug his spurs in, hugged the trunk like a bear cub, and went higher, using the small handsaw in his holster to cut twigs and small branches out of his way. Finally, he looked down at me. "Turn a quick-hitch on my climb line and send me up the Echo for limbing," he called. So I sent him up the little saw. I tied on the bull rope, and he hoisted it up. "Come-along's hooked onto a cherry tree," he said, swinging in his harness and pointing into the woods. I took the highway of a fallen pine and found it.

Fifty feet up, Rudy tied his bowline, then drew back and launched the end of the bull rope. A long white arc, it sailed through sun and shade, snaking down into the forest. I went for it, pulled it out of a greenbrier. I hooked it up to the come-along by wrapping a klemheist three times around, then yelled up to Rudy, and waited to hear his saw begin working. When I heard him knock out the wedge, I fit the steel handle into place, and cranked it hard as he made the back cut. Three clicks forward, two clicks back, then two, then one, rowing it to and fro until it was almost too heavy to pull. Rudy dug his saw in again, while I heaved back, and then the rope went nearly slack, and I cranked hard and fast and looked up to see the top of the tree moving. Far up in the sky like it had nothing to do with me, the fringe of green began to flinch and duck, and I dropped the handle and got the hell out of there. I skidded sideways down through the saplings, then turned to watch it go. The pine toppled, dizzy and slow in the first moments, then picking up speed. It hit like a trampoline, the matted pelt of branches and trunks leaping up together, then shuddering back to earth, crushing one another, making new hollows and hiding places beneath the boughs.

Rudy whooped, and I whooped back. That was to tell each other we were alive. Then I unhooked the come-along and hiked back up, pulling the bull rope out with me.

"You didn't kill me," Rudy said, stepping out of his spurs. "Maybe you really do know your knots." He went to the cab of his truck and came back with a gallon jug of water and a bag of super-spicy red-hot Cheetos, the bold hue of artificial cinnamon. He passed me the bag.

"What about you?" I asked.

"What about me?" he said.

"Where did you learn your knots?" I asked.

"My dad," he said. "That motherfucking cocksucking piece of shit. He taught me everything I know about tree work."

"Are you from around here?" I asked.

"What is it with you fucking anthropologists, you want me to speak into the mic? Of course I grew up around here. My family's been here since 1840. Basically stole their land directly from the Shawnee." He teased some Cheetos from his beard, tipped them into his mouth. "But that's over now," he said. "No family. No land. Lost it all to the coal company." He took a long drink, then stretched out on the ground with his head resting on his hard hat. He reached into his tool bag and brought out a thick book, opened it to a folded page. When he caught me looking he waved the cover at me. *The Count of Monte Cristo.*

"You want to say something to me, college girl?" he said.

"I've never read it," I said.

"Philistine," he said. "It's the classic tale of revenge. I read it at least once a year.

Come on, English major."

"Liberal studies," I said.

"Well, mind your own fucking business," he said. "I'm taking a break. And I'm not paying you to ogle the locals."

I worked for Rudy most days twelve hours. Each morning, he waited for me in his truck at the bottom of the driveway. At dark, he paid me in cash and dropped me off at home. According to Rudy, the big-animal vet only called him up to work if her husband wasn't home if you get my meaning, and according to Rudy, a group of sorority sisters from the college had asked him in for a beer after he dragged a maple out of their yard with no shirt on if you catch my drift. He'd had a steady girlfriend, he said, but things had ended poorly between them because she had two-timed him. When I asked why she had two-timed him, he told me he didn't know but she sure liked to talk about her feelings a lot, and one day she found someone else to talk about them to.

From what I could see, most women wanted nothing to do with Rudy, yet I noticed that he maintained something of an association with a couple who lived on the Women's Land Trust out near Scupper Ridge. Lily worked at the hardware and salvage store, and her partner Karen was a nurse at Community Health. I had seen Karen giving people spinal adjustments in the IGA parking lot, so that they cried out in pain, tears of gratitude running down their faces.

Rudy was one of those men whose feelings were hurt by the very existence of lesbians. He was furious because Lily was pregnant, which Rudy insisted just wasn't fair. Still, Lily and Karen sent him on all manner of errands, and requested numerous favors of him, which I never knew him to resist. Once, we dropped off a trailer load of wood chips at the top of their driveway. "For their fucking new moon garden or some shit, you expect me to know?" said Rudy. Another time, he put an extra bar on his Bailey's order. "The one with the mustache says her saw finally bit the dust. You think that's my problem? Jesus. I should give her shaving tips," he said, dialing in the order from the front seat of his truck.

One morning, as I untangled Rudy's throw line, he said, "We've got to knock off early today. One of those dykes needs a ride home. She gets off at five."

All day he talked about it, continuing to check his watch. "Don't know how it's even possible for me to give her a ride home, seeing as men aren't allowed on her piece-of-shit land. Of course I wouldn't set foot there even if they expressly invited me. Which they have. Oh, it was rich when they brought me onto their land to take out that ash tree. That's feminists for you. They still want men to do the heavy lifting."

"How did you meet them?" I asked.

"Like I said, me and your man cleared an ash for them," Rudy said. "He didn't tell you?" He looked at me strangely.

"No," I said. "He never told me. So, what? So men are allowed on their land after all?"

"It still proves my point," Rudy said. "They don't need men until they need men. And now one of them is pregnant. It doesn't make a bit of sense. Goddamn, have you seen her? She must be as big as a house by now. But I've still got my standards," he said. "I'll give her a ride, but I won't stop the car all the way to let her out. I'll just open the door and let it roll. I have to show them I have some self-respect. They always think they can get the best of me." He shook his head. "Goddammit," he said. "She's as beautiful as god himself."

That afternoon at the hardware and salvage store, I followed Rudy toward the back, where a pregnant woman in overalls lay with her head underneath a jacked-up cabinet. Her belly domed above her. Lying there, she could have been a snake eating an elephant. Rudy stood blushing behind his beard, chewing on the end of his matted ponytail. She kept working. No one said anything.

"Are you Lily?" I finally asked.

"We do everything here," her voice came from under the cabinet. "Scratch-and-dent. We fix it up, sell stuff out back. Hardware in front. You need something?" She pulled herself out from under the cabinet, but stayed on her back, holding a screwdriver in one hand, her long black hair spilling out from under a baseball cap.

"Rudy," she said, "would you mind putting this stuff away for me?" She pointed her chin at the tools strewn on the floor.

Rudy scooped them all up and disappeared down an aisle. Lily closed her eyes and put her hands on her belly. She seemed to be sleeping. I wasn't sure what to do. Then she opened her eyes and looked at me a long moment. Carefully, she mentioned my boyfriend.

"He left," I said.

"I know," she said. "How are you getting along?"

"Just fine," I said, to see how it sounded.

27

She continued to lie there, her sharp white chin pointing up at me. "It can be hard on your own. Especially when winter comes," she said.

"I won't be here that long," I said.

"Are you selling your place?" she asked. I hadn't thought about that part of it yet, so I just shrugged. She turned over onto her side, pushed herself to hands and knees, laboriously rose to her feet. Rudy rushed over and tried to take her elbow, but she shook him off. She clocked out.

We squeezed into the truck, me with my knees up over the gearshift, Lily's belly pressed against the glove compartment.

"How's working for Rudy?" she asked, like she already knew.

"Fine," I said, glancing at him, but he kept his eyes on the road, except when we hit a bump. Then he would look around me to see how Lily had taken it. She never noticed.

"When are you due?" I asked her.

"January," she said. "Karen's home right now figuring out how to hook up a pump so we can have hot water in the birthing tub. It's a real pain in the ass. Our cabin's only sixteen by sixteen. Karen built it. We got hot water just for the birth. We moved a propane water heater into a little shed out back."

"You're not going to the hospital?" I asked.

"Where they'll treat Karen like she's just some stranger, and all that hassle?" Lily said. "No. We'll just do it ourselves." She smiled and closed her eyes, leaned her head against the window.

"Fuck the hospital," Rudy said, and stuck his ponytail in his mouth again.

Lily opened her eyes and raised her head. "Has Rudy ever told you the story about how his balls almost rotted off?" she asked me.

"My boyfriend told me that one," I said. "He said Rudy got to the hospital just in time."

"Is that what he said?" Rudy said around his hair. "I guess he didn't tell you what happened next."

"I wondered about that," I said.

"Lily's already heard it," Rudy said.

"I don't mind," Lily said. "I like the way you tell it."

Rudy grinned straight ahead, chewing. Then he spit his ponytail out and said, "They asked me, Why didn't you come in sooner? Why did you get this infection? I said I got a wound and I tried to stitch it myself, but it went bad. Where do you live? they asked. I told them I slept on a rock, or

29

in the shack when it was too cold, but mostly on the rock if it was clear. Where? they asked. On my family land, I said. Address please, they said. There's no fucking address, I said. It's the coal company. It's just everywhere. It's everything. Acres and acres. Then the pain shot up through me again, and I groaned, I howled, Oh, I want to die, I hope I die, I'll do away with myself, give me an implement, I'll do it! I woke up in the psych ward. The note they wrote said I'd threatened to harm myself, and was acting unreasonable, attempting to perform surgery on myself and living outside the bounds of civilization. Put me down for vagrancy, trespassing on private property, et cetera. They brought pills. They said if I took them I would calm down. They came around every afternoon at the same time with those same pills for everyone. They wouldn't quite tell me what was in them. I won't take your fucking pills, I said. I've been through all that. I don't take pills anymore. And they marked me down as paranoid and noncooperative."

Lily nodded. "So then he called us in the middle of the night, and Karen was pissed. She said, Rudy, if you think you might be crazy there's no need to tell the people who can put you away for it. But we went down

30

there and brought him some Cheetos and carrot juice. I'd never seen his beard without sawdust in it."

"My boyfriend left out the part about the psych ward," I said.

"There was always something off about that guy," Rudy said. "He had an angle. You could never quite tell where you stood. Someone should have told him you can't please everyone."

Lily took off her hat, and twisted her black hair once around her wrist, then tucked it up off her neck, resettled the hat over her eyes. I could see her take me in sideways. "Me and Karen have been thinking about you up there," she said. "Twenty acres and just you by yourself? You got any animals?"

"Ducks," I said. "We got them for laying, but they haven't laid yet."

"Are you sure they're ducks? Have you sexed them yet?" she asked.

"Not yet," I admitted.

"Have you ever done that before?" I hadn't, but I didn't say so. She laughed. "Could be that you've got drakes," she said.

"So I'll kill them for meat," I said.

"Duck killing's hard with just one person," she said. "Takes a long time to pluck them, all those pinfeathers. Rudy, you could help her."

"I could," Rudy said. "But I'm trying to keep things professional." I have to admit, it stung.

"It's all right, I can manage on my own," I said. Lily didn't say more, just closed her eyes and reapplied her cheek to the window.

Rudy pulled onto Scupper Ridge and idled the truck across from the Land Trust driveway. He got out and walked around to open the door for Lily. She reached for his arm and pulled herself up, then walked down the long driveway toward her mysterious separatist land. Even to me it was mysterious. Even to me, a woman. I knew I could never be allowed there, because I still thought about my boyfriend. Why couldn't I hold on to him? If I didn't want to be alone in the woods, why was I alone in the woods?

Rudy chewed on his ponytail in silence until he turned back onto the main road. Then he thumped his fist on the wheel. "Shit, I want to have a baby so bad," he said. "Sometimes I hear a baby crying and saliva rushes into my mouth."

"Oh, it does not," I said.

"You mean that doesn't happen to you?" he asked.

"No," I said.

"Well, it will," he said. "It's been worse

ever since the dykes started doing it. She's like the fucking earth or something."

"Don't make me throw up," I said.

"Maybe it's my age," he said. "I'm thirty-five. About the same as you, right?"

"Thirty-two," I said.

"You probably know how it feels, now that your man left. Your hormones are probably talking to you real loud right about now."

"You don't know a thing about it," I said.

"What about me and you?" Rudy said. "We could have a baby."

"Real professional," I said.

"What do you want?" he asked.

"I want to go back to Seattle," I said.

"What's so fucking great about Seattle?" asked Rudy. "You act like you own the fucking Space Needle or some shit."

"There's nothing so great about it," I said. "But it'll be winter soon. What am I supposed to do, hibernate?"

"That's what I do," Rudy said.

"What, just hole up in my camper? I don't even have electricity."

"You've got twenty acres and ducks," Rudy said. "No one to tell you what you can and can't do. No one to bother you. Goddamn. There's no pleasing some people."

■ ■ ■ ■

Rudy dropped me at the bottom of the driveway just as the rain gathered itself and became a storm. I climbed the hill, fed the ducks, shut them into their shed for the night. They made one downy animal of themselves all plastered together, heads tucked down. I burrowed into my sleeping bag. In the night, the camper sprang new holes, the wind and rain coursed through it. I could hear water rushing and roaring down the gullies all around me, the wind beating against the slope, and behind me in the forest, beech trees snapping, smacking the ground.

In the morning, I came out to face the calm. The ducks climbed into their drinking trough, dipping and splashing in the rainwater. The drainage ditches sent runoff down toward the creek. After all, my place didn't get hit too hard. It was hiding behind bigger hills, deeper valleys. The big weather passed it over. It was good that way, my place. I was starting to know it.

I wondered how high the creek might be, so I went down the long driveway. I saw a small orange turtle, spotted like a frog. I saw a black rat snake stranded and slow in

34

the cold morning, flung out of hiding somehow. I saw that the persimmon tree had dropped some chalky fruit, and at the bottom of the hill, above the high creek, Lily and Karen leaned against Karen's pickup, two bright orange traffic cones on the ground at their feet. Karen, her long frame zipped into a big hooded sweatshirt, a loose braid falling out from beneath her hat, stepped forward and stuck her hand out. "We came by to see how you made it through the storm," she said.

"Fine," I said, shaking her hand. "You?"

"Not too bad." She looked around. "You're living right on the pipeline," she said, thumbing toward the cleared easement, fifty feet wide, that careened down the hillside and met the driveway. My boyfriend and I had never bothered talking about it.

"Do you know much about it?" I asked.

She shrugged. "Probably the same one runs near our place," she said. "I know it runs all the way from East Texas to northern Ohio. Supplies gas to houses up north. Or used to. A lot of these old lines are abandoned. Though maybe this one's not. Looks like they still mow it."

Lily said, "My grandma told me she sat on the bank of the creek and watched them bury this line the same year they buried John F. Kennedy. Those steam shovels turned up arrowheads by the dozen. Grandma filled her pockets with them. By law the line's supposed to be buried four feet, but you can see it surface in places. Cast-iron."

"Damn," I said. "What if it explodes?"

"What if the world explodes?" Karen said.

Lily laughed. "We can help you sex the ducks," she said.

"Or slaughter them if they turn out to be drakes," said Karen. "It's no problem. Might as well do it today, before it gets colder."

"Thanks, but I don't have a place to keep the meat," I said.

"I already thought about that," said Lily. "You can borrow our pressure canner. Jars and lids, too." She turned to lift it all from the bed of the truck.

What was I supposed to do? The sun was coming out, and steam rose up off every jutting muddy piece of the land, which sparkled in a great show of democracy. A discarded truck bumper shone just like the sandstone, just like a scrap of metallic insulation and the white of yarrow flowers and the flash of blue jays' wings, a coil of chicken wire, an old license plate half

36

entombed in mud. Karen picked up the traffic cones. Lily handed me the canner and shouldered the bag of jars. We went up the hill.

"What are the cones for?" I asked.

"You'll see," Karen said.

"I hear you're a nurse," I said.

"I hear you're from out West," she said. "City girl."

"But I've been outside a lot," I said. "I mean, I've worked outside."

"Sure," she said. "I was in Seattle once. Hitchhiked there after I picked apples in Wenatchee when I was young and stupid."

"What did you think?" I asked.

"There wasn't much to see besides too many goddamn mountains," she said. "But Lily told me you're going back soon."

"Probably," I said.

"If it suits you," she said. "Me, I was glad to come home."

"I've seen you at the grocery store cracking people's backs," I said.

"It's true that I do that," Karen said. "But I'd rather you think of me as a whittler."

"What do you whittle?" I asked.

"Useful things," Karen said.

"And not so useful," Lily said. "You should see it. She can't just carve a spoon without she has to put a captive ball in the handle."

"What's that?" I asked.

"Whittling's just subtraction," Karen said. "Start with the spoon handle, then carve out a case for the ball to fit in, carve the ball at the same time, last thing you do, you wick off the tiny piece holding the ball to the case, watch it rattle around inside. Seems impossible when you see it, like elves made it or some shit." She set down the traffic cones and took a knife from her pocket, pulled the short blade from the cork it was plunged in. "That's what you call a sheepsfoot blade," she said, holding it out to show me.

"Karen's a perfectionist," Lily said. "She spent hours carving a tiny thimble-size skull out of cherrywood, and then she gave it to me for my birthday."

"She lost it," Karen said.

"I put it in a safe place," Lily said.

"How can you lose a skull in a sixteen-by-sixteen cabin?" I asked.

"Oh, you can," Lily said. "You can lose anything anywhere."

Back up the hill, I knew enough to get the propane burner going full-bore, and to fill my largest pot with spring water. Lily and Karen went to the duck shed and picked out the drakes. It's only the female ducks who quack, Karen told me. Drakes make a choking whistling sound. They held each bird and listened to it, then Sharpied each duck with an *X* on her beak. It turns out I had seven drakes and only four ducks. Soon the water roiled and steamed. Karen took a utility knife from her belt and sawed off the top of each traffic cone, letting the stubs fall like candy corn near the firepit.

I took a chance. "You're the first people up here since my boyfriend left," I said.

"Do you miss him?" asked Lily.

"He was a pretty good boyfriend," I said. "But I talked too much. I didn't know when to shut up and leave him alone. And now I'm on my own."

"You think he left because of something you said?" Karen said. "That's horseshit."

"And he said I wasn't ambitious," I said.

"That might be true," Karen said. "But that's not why he left."

"I didn't really know how to get started out here," I said.

"If we're going to do this, we'll need buckets," Karen said.

"At night, sometimes, I bet it's hard," Lily said. "I wouldn't want to sleep out here all alone."

"Buckets," Karen prompted.

39

I found some, and Karen rigged a long line and suspended the traffic cones like funnels over them. She held the drakes until they were calm, and then two by two we lowered them upside down into the cones, so their necks stuck out the narrow end. They did not struggle but opened their beaks and gazed at the woods, the firepit, the razor knife. We slit their throats at the jugular.

The sun grew hot and the yellow jackets came. We sat by the firepit and ripped feathers out by the fistful. It was true that to get all the pinfeathers out was nearly impossible. The hot smell of boiled feathers and blood choked the air. We cleaned the drakes. We set up the pressure canner. We rinsed everything down. I hoped that Lily and Karen wouldn't leave.

"Do you want to go swimming?" I asked. "It might be the last warm day. And we're covered in gore."

"Where?" Karen asked.

"We could get in the creek," I said.

We pushed down through the woods until we found a place where the elderberry bushes dipped into the high water. There was a honeybee hive on the far bank, the bees gone sleepy and slow this time of year. Lily and Karen peeled off their clothes and plunged in, scooping handfuls of water over Lily's belly, whooping at the cold. I stripped down and followed them. Together, our bodies showed the marks of elastic waistbands, of chigger bites and peeling scabs, stretch marks, birthmarks, ingrown hairs, generous ripples of fat around thighs, jellied parts, furry belly buttons, sunburnt clavicles. Caked with grime, our toenails were sharp and filthy as hooves.

After, we sat on the bank.

"Why do you live at the Land Trust?" I asked.

"Because that's where Karen is," Lily said.

"I needed a place to stay while I went to nursing school," Karen said. "They said I could build out there."

"But why land that's women only?" I asked.

"I used to think my trouble was that I didn't want to live around men. That place brought relief for a while," Karen said. "Now I'd just as soon not live around women, either. It turns out my trouble might be that I don't want to live around anyone at all."

"Even me," Lily said. She laughed. Karen didn't.

"My boyfriend said too much solitude is what drove Rudy crazy," I said.

"Do you think Rudy's crazy?" asked Karen.

I thought about how to answer. "I trust him with my life every single day that I work with him," I said.

"That counts for a lot," Karen said. "Maybe for everything." She spat a wad of sticky saliva into the water, watched the current carry it away. Lily leaned back onto her elbows. Stretch marks traveled from her pubic hair to her belly button, pressed inside out.

"How long have you known Rudy?" I asked.

"Karen went to high school with him," Lily said.

"Not really," Karen said. "Neither one of us ever went to class."

"How can you be friends with him?" I asked.

"We're not friends with him," Karen said.

"Well, we sort of are," Lily said.

"We're associates," Karen said.

"I don't think he has anyone else," Lily said. "Except maybe for you."

There was silence, and I thought, What am I doing? What am I doing inviting these two women down to the creek? Setting up insurance? Is it appropriate to spend time with people so that later you can call them from jail? So that they will miss you if you lie out on the coal company land too long? If Rudy was isolated and weird, so was I. To map it out: Karen and Lily sat side by side in their small square cabin, waiting for no one but their unborn child. A few ridges away from them, my camouflage camper was as far away as a comet, spectacularly wrecking itself in outer space.

They must have known it. They must have known it much better than I did. Why else would they have come to help me with the ducks? But if that's what Karen and Lily thought of me, they did not see a need to say it out loud, and maybe it was then that I began to love them.

"We know about the names Rudy calls us," Karen said. "We know about his bad attitude, but we have a certain relationship with him."

"It's because of that day with the ash tree," Lily said. "That changes things between people."

"I don't know what you're talking about," I said.

"The ash tree," Lily said. "Oh Jesus, Shane really didn't tell you why he was leaving?"

"Lily, stop it," Karen said. "Don't gossip."

"What? You think I should just keep quiet?

43

Is that it?" said Lily, going red.

"You're emotional because you're pregnant," Karen said, stone-faced.

"Oh good," Lily said. "The diagnosis of a medical professional!" She sat up and plunged both feet in the water, splashing Karen and me. Her voice rose to a shriek. "Fuck! What's this tumor growing out of my stomach? Why is it kicking? It's alive!" Her chin crumpled and her lips were wet. She turned to me. "Why do I put up with this?"

"It's not gossip," I said. "Or it is gossip. Tell me."

Lily began to cry, gulping in air. On the far bank the honeybees took slow laps around the yarrow. Everything was doing what was built into it, and would keep on until it died. Karen started talking.

"Rudy and Shane showed up at the Land Trust one morning," she said. "Me and Lily were at our place. I was whittling. Lily was weeding. It was a workday. We heard the chain saw going back there at first, but then we heard shouting, a lull, then buzzing. A low whine, something shrill, I can't say what it was. But I stopped whittling. And then Shane came out of the woods, white in the face, a gash on the side of his head. He didn't say anything. He just stood there."

44

"Didn't you ever see that gash?" asked Lily, passing the backs of her hands over her eyes.

"He came home with his face cut up," I said. "But he said it was nothing."

"Right. For him it was nothing," Lily said.

"Lily, stop interrupting," Karen said. Lily began to cry again, quietly, but Karen kept talking. "Where's Rudy? I asked him. Rudy, Shane repeated. Tell us, I said. Where's Rudy? Then I just dropped my knife and took off at a dead run through the woods. Rudy was back there on the ground. He was out. There was vomit all down his beard, a blue and red bruise at the front of his head. His shoulder was pinned beneath an ash branch. I pushed at the branch, but couldn't move it. Shane had followed me, but he just stood there with his mouth open. He said, I dropped it on him. I killed him. It was an accident."

"But he didn't kill him," I said.

"Nearly did," Lily said.

"Why didn't he roll that branch off Rudy?" I asked.

Karen looked at me, long and cool. "How should I know why your boyfriend does things or not?" she said. "All I know is I tried to push that branch off Rudy. He's not dead, I told Shane. You have to help

45

me. I can't move it on my own. I can't, said Shane. You have to, I said. Okay, he said like he was waking up. He knelt down and heaved on that branch, and it rolled off into the leaves. You could see the marks up and down Rudy's chest. He wasn't breathing."

"What did you do?" I asked.

"I started breathing into him," Karen said. "Finally he breathed back. He came to. The first thing he said was, No hospitals, no doctors, no nurses, they'll put me away again. I'm a nurse, you stupid idiot, I told him. He turned over and threw up again."

"And my boyfriend? Where was he?" I asked.

"Shane left," Karen said.

"He walked right past me as I went into the woods," Lily said, wiping her dripping nose on the back of her hand. "He looked right through me. I found Karen back there, and she and I carried Rudy out of there. We don't know where Shane went."

"He came home to me," I said. "He came home to me and told me he quit. He said Rudy was crazy. He said he couldn't bear to work for him anymore."

"Well, now you know it wasn't quite the way he said it was," Lily said. "I always liked your boyfriend, though, really. Hard not to, he was so nice."

46

"Nice," Karen said. "That's one way of putting it. You could see he cared a lot what people thought of him."

"What about Rudy?" I asked. "Did you take him to the hospital?"

"We kept Rudy on the land overnight," Karen said.

"Isn't that against the Land Trust rules?" I asked.

"We drew the curtains, is all," Karen said.

"Do you know where Shane is now?" asked Lily.

I could hear up to the tops of the beech and sycamore. I could hear the flapping of turkey vultures. I knew how to answer. "Somewhere that no one really knows him. Somewhere that he can be new," I said. We gathered our clothes and headed back up through the forest.

Winter came hard, and tree work ended for the season. Rudy gave me my final pay and said, "I'll see you in the springtime, if I still have a liver."

"I probably won't be here in the spring-time," I said.

"Don't be so fatalistic," he said. "Most people make it through."

"What are you going to do?" I asked.

"What do you think I'm going to do?" he

47

said, starting up his truck. "I'm going to go dormant with whiskey." I watched him drive away.

I told myself I could leave anytime. But first, I taped an extra layer of plastic in the windows of my camper. I sealed the door of the woodstove with new rope, and I cleaned creosote out of the pipe. I can get a bus ticket as soon as there's a thaw, I thought. But when the thaw came I didn't bike to the bus station. I didn't even bike to the bar. I biked to the public library and checked out some books with pictures of local animals and trees, encyclopedias of primitive skills, accounts from old home-steaders that must have been scrawled when they were hungry or irritated. At night, alone in my camper with a headlamp, I hunched in my sleeping bag and read every page. I took notes in the margins. I never returned those books to the library.

By the end of December, I'd eaten my way through the drakes. I'd boiled the bones. I checked my notes and went outside. I took the .22 my boyfriend had left. I aimed. I shot. I missed. I dug roots from the frozen ground, ate bark, set snares. I began to recognize tracks. I began to follow them.

In January, I heard from the mailman that Lily climbed into the tub and gave birth to a boy, which meant that they would have to leave the Women's Land Trust and start over someplace new. According to the mailman, boy children were only allowed on the Land Trust until the age of five. The mailman told me that Rudy celebrated the birth by inviting someone at the bar to punch him in the teeth. He spent one warm night in jail, the mailman said. But I didn't see any of them that winter. I didn't see anyone, really, unless you count the mailman.

In February, after not speaking one word out loud for two weeks, I wrote a letter to my aunt. I wrote that I'd be home soon. I crossed it out. I wrote it again. I meant to mail it, but I didn't have stamps. Then the ducks began to lay small misshapen eggs. They tasted like wet feathers but still I wanted more. I was hungry. My aim with the .22 improved. Following shadowy diagrams, I took apart and cleaned small animals. Mostly what I could catch were raccoons and possums. One tasted much like the other.

By March, I was so lonely I considered eating snow until it drowned me. One cold day, I was looking a raccoon in the eye. Its eye was dead and I was skinning it, and I knew I should go visit Karen and Lily.

Those women had told me that my boyfriend had not left me, that he'd simply left, and I had stayed. I'd made it through the winter on the strength of it. You could say I was proud of myself. You could say, in fact, that I wasn't myself, but someone new, someone newly ambitious, and if crazed, if disturbed, if hungry and desperate, then so much the better. I gave up pretending I was going back to Seattle. But I'd had enough of being alone. I looked at the dull raccoon eye and decided to remind Lily and Karen that I had twenty acres. There was a place for them and their boy if they wanted to try it.

2

Lily

Some people take to their life with joy, but not Helen. Instead, she was passionate. That's how it looked to me. The winter had changed her, either back into what she was before Shane, before I'd known her, or into someone else again. She'd proved she could handle working for Rudy. She'd proved she could slaughter drakes. She'd proved she could make it on that piece of land on her own. Finally, when winter was nearly over, she set her sights on us.

It was very soon after Perley was born. His birth had been easy, no big deal, except for the pain so bad you couldn't even call it pain, it was just my life, me begging for drugs, and Karen holding my hand, saying, You don't need drugs, Lily, you can do this, you're strong, just think about what your grandma would have done, and me screaming, You don't know shit about me and you

51

don't know shit about my grandma, I'm praying to her right now and she's answering my prayer, she's telling you to shut the fuck up, and then one more long push and then Karen caught the baby. Green shit and blood plumed into the tub. The three of us crawled into bed and laughed and bled a little more and rested, baby Perley coated with white mud from inside me. We left it on him, just rubbed it into his skin, like my grandma would have done. We didn't want him to catch cold. There was no way you were going to touch our boy with water.

Karen and I spent long days next to the woodstove in our snug cabin at the Land Trust. We passed Perley between us, watching his shit turn from black to yellow, his umbilical stump fall off, his wizened face grow rosy. He was all out of size, enormous testicles, miniature toenails, eyes two-thirds the size of his head, no neck to speak of. Our baby. We witnessed his long hours of sleep and long hours of wailing, stared into his open mouth, lost ourselves down the tiny black pit of his throat. Sometimes we looked at each other, but hardly recognized the one who looked back at us across that baby, the one who'd gone from lover to coworker overnight. My coworker fed me bowl after bowl of stew or casserole or meat pie. She kept the fire stoked. She whittled a spork, a lopsided top, four cubes that she marked to make a set of dice. She reread her old *ElfQuest* comic books, holding the pages up before Perley's unfocused eyes. We ate and slept and washed diapers and hung diapers to dry over the stove.

The Helen we'd met in autumn was a lopsided top, spinning off-center. I could hardly coax her to string three words together, let alone to admit she could use our help or our friendship. She'd insist she was going back to Seattle, then just stand there looking at us to see what we'd say. She didn't know what she knew. But now here she was barging into our cabin, didn't call ahead, just showed up swinging a Dutch oven of raccoon stew, talking like talking and breathing were the same thing. Her hair was cut blunt and uneven in the front, tucked back long behind her ears. One deep line right between her eyebrows. She looked like she hadn't seen mirrors much. She'd lived off the drakes, she told us, but when the meat was gone, she'd used her .22 to shoot raccoons and possums. She set the stew to warm on our stove, then wedged herself in to take measure of Perley, who stretched out naked and red on Karen's lap, his feet curved into each other, his eyes attempting to focus. Helen looked long and hard.

"He's certainly a baby boy," she said.

"You can hold him if you want to," I said.

"Thanks for the offer, but no," Helen said. Then she got right to the point. "Look at those testicles," she said. "You'll have to leave this place. The Women's Land Trust doesn't allow those."

We knew it way better than Helen did. We knew the bylaws. We knew the board. They were obsessed with anatomy, with who was in and who was out. We knew we'd soon be on the out list. Karen and I had placed a vague bookmark there in the days after Perley was born, but it was hard to remember the reality of anything other than sleeping, nursing, and thick white spit-up.

"If I were you, I'd get out now," Helen said. "Why wait?"

"There's no rush," I said. "The Land Trust bylaw says that we can stay until Perley's five."

"Heavy burden for a five-year-old," Helen said. "He asks why you have to leave the only home he's ever known. You tell him, It's your fault, boy. It's because of your balls."

"Where would we go?" I asked, but I might have guessed that over the course of

54

that long winter, Helen had learned the answers to all the questions, and she was more than ready to share them.

"Come live with me," she said, unsmiling. "I've got twenty acres. Plenty of room. My boyfriend's not coming back. And I'd be glad to have you. I need some help. You need some help. It could be a good arrangement."

"You want to be our landlord, is that it?" asked Karen.

"Karen," I said.

"Let's just call it what it is," Karen said.

"I don't want to be anyone's landlord. I want to own the land in common," Helen said. She kept her voice even, tried to make it sound like it didn't matter to her one way or the other, but you could hear that she'd already decided: she had a plan, and we were it.

Karen heard it, too. "Can't afford to own land," she said, touching Perley's nose so that his eyes crossed.

"But thank you anyway," I said. "It's wonderful of you to invite us."

"The land's paid off," Helen said. When Karen raised her eyebrows, Helen said, "My boyfriend earned money working up north, up in one of those man camps."

"So it's Shane who owns the place?" asked Karen.

"We never got around to putting his name on anything," Helen said. "Just mine. I put the money down to start. But we could put your names on it. We'll pay the land taxes together. You won't owe me anything." It got my attention, and I could see Karen was listening, too. In our four years together, Karen and I had never lived anywhere we weren't just renting. Even the Land Trust, with all its talk about sisterhood, owned the cabin Karen built. We were probates. We paid. Not much, but enough that we couldn't afford to have both of us home with Perley much longer. We were already a month behind, as Deirdre and Janice gently reminded us at weekly land meetings. Still, I reached out and put my hand on Helen's arm.

"Slow down," I said. "What's this about?"

"What do you mean?" she asked.

"Why us?" I asked.

The stew spat, sizzled. Perley farted. Helen looked hard at the ceiling.

"I don't really know any other people," she said. Karen looked at me like, Danger, danger, but my eyes were already full.

"I thought you were going back to Seattle," Karen said.

"And just walk away from that piece of land?" Helen asked, voice like she'd swallowed wet fur.

"There's no place to live out there but that camouflaged camper," Karen said. "Which is smaller than this place, for Christ's sakes."

"Move onto my place in the spring, and we'll build a house this summer," Helen said, herself again.

"Can't afford to build a house," Karen said.

"We'll salvage material," Helen said, as if butting heads with Karen was the final ingredient to her resolve. "Frank's selling me the seconds his crew demos. They're replacing some professor's roof next week and giving us the old one."

"Us," Karen repeated, shaking her head.

"Hardly a thing wrong with it," Helen said.

"When are we going to have this house finished by?" asked Karen.

"We'll move in next fall," Helen said.

"Next fall? Better be a small house, then," Karen said.

"It'll be the perfect size for three," Helen said.

"Four," I said.

"Right," Helen said.

"Since when do you know how to build?" asked Karen.

"I half know how to build, so if you half know how to build, then that makes one whole carpenter," Helen said.

"Half know how to build? What the hell does that mean?" Karen asked.

"You built this cabin, didn't you?" Helen said.

"I'm half of nothing," Karen said, and caught Perley's waving hand. But then she smiled a little, or glared, depending on how you looked at it. Her wait-and-see smile. I could tell she was beginning to consider the thing.

We hadn't known each other long when Karen said these two sentences in a row: You should know I'm bound to be alone. I want to provide for you. I'd laughed. How can both of those things be true? I'd asked. To find out, I began to sleep in her bed on the Land Trust so often that I lived there. I put up with her never-show-you-like-it, her wait-and-see, her storms. When she said, I want to have a baby with you, I'd answered, I want to have a baby with you. I couldn't help but add, That's the opposite of being alone, you know. She just gave me that smile again. In bed at night, Karen held her comic books up to Perley's silly face, whispered,

58

"We are a wolf pack." To live with Karen was to watch the daily fight unfold. Stranger or provider. Loner or wolf pack. Wait and see.

Helen couldn't take it. Into the silence, she said, "I figure we'll eat mostly what we can grow or hunt. Or gather from the woods."

"Sounds like you have it all figured out," Karen said.

"I've been learning a lot about wild foods," Helen said.

"Who from?" asked Karen.

"I've been reading," Helen said.

"I might have known it," Karen said.

"Karen's into wild foods, too," I said. "She's always boiling down elderberries for medicine and drying nettles for soup and tea."

"But I didn't learn it in a book," Karen said.

"I can do without that stuff," I said. "Reminds me too much of lean times growing up."

"You just have to know the right way to do it," Helen said. "Mushrooms, huckleberries, hickory nuts, acorns. Especially acorns. It takes some work to process them, but that's the way to get calories."

"Have you done it?" asked Karen.

"I've calculated the amount we'd need to get all of us through next winter," Helen said.

"Calculated," Karen said.

"Did you know there's seventy native trees in this bioregion?" Helen asked.

"More than that," Karen said.

Oh lord, Helen was hard to take, barreling in from some West Coast city with her college degree, not knowing a thing, needing our help, then emerging after a hard winter a self-styled sourdough, flaunting her newfound skills to us, who'd always lived here. I could see Karen weighing the whole force of Helen against the possibility of providing for our family. Her bootheel rapped the floor. It could fail, of course it could. But what Karen liked best was a project likely to fail. My love never could resist difficulty, and I never could resist her.

Karen looked at me. "Well, Lily?" she asked. "What do you want to do?" But it wasn't a matter of what I wanted to do. I'd already synchronized myself like a watch to her desire. Perley searched Karen's thigh for a place to nurse, so she scooped him over to me with one hand because he was that small. I took his nothing weight and I held my left breast like feeding my boy a sandwich. Karen was ready, and I was ready to please her. I agreed to throw our lot in with Helen Conley.

Perley was three months old in April, when we moved to Helen's land. Three months old, holding his head up, demanding to be held facing forward so that he wouldn't miss a thing. We didn't bring much with us because we didn't have much to bring. All our clothes and all Perley's diapers fit into two big garbage bags. Besides that, we brought Karen's toolbox, brimming with chisels. Our rubber boots. A splitting axe and a hatchet. Two shovels, one flat-bottomed, one sharp. *The Encyclopedia of Organic Gardening,* by J. I. Rodale and Staff, 1970 edition. Karen's stack of *ElfQuest.* Packed it all easily into one truckload and drove the five miles to Helen's place and confronted the long driveway, and at the top was Helen, eager and trying to hide it.

There wasn't much up there, not at first. You could see the freshwater spring seeping from beneath the roots of an elderberry, someone's effort to catch it in a cast-iron kettle and a plastic bucket. Besides that, there was Helen's tiny camper up in the woods, and the duck shed in a clearing below it. The firepit, where we'd slaughtered drakes the previous fall, had now become some kind of processing area for small game, the traffic cones we'd left there stacked neatly near a flat stone and a five-gallon bucket. The ducks met our truck, falling all over one another, beating their wings and cackling. "Laughing at us already," Karen said. I unpacked Perley from his car seat and he swung his arms at the ducks, who quieted to pick for bugs in the gravel. Karen stuck out her hand to shake Helen's, but Helen's hands were full. She'd already unloaded both of our garbage bags and was lifting out Karen's toolbox, the first volume of *ElfQuest* balanced on top.

"Didn't take you for being into escapist literature," Helen said to Karen.

"You should read them," Karen said. "You're so into living by your wits, survival skills, you might be inspired."

That first night, Helen cooked for us at the firepit, dandelion greens and duck eggs mixed together in one pan. "To family!" she toasted, bypassing any mention of friendship, of basic compatibility. What followed were heady times, wine and gin. For a week straight, we stayed up late around the campfire each night, singing Perley to sleep with his raucous lullaby, the one about the shipwreck where everyone drowns. Karen sanded and polished her set of dice, and we gambled cheaply. We rolled and called out. Snake Eyes, we called. Dog Paws, the Necklace, Cut Moon. We set up target practice with the .22. Helen's welcome was as single-minded as everything else about her. At dice, she bought us all in. Each night, she cooked dinner at the outdoor burner. She insisted we move into her camouflaged camper, with its graffiti from some forgotten feud. Meanwhile, she climbed past the camper up to the ridge, where she set up a wall tent to live in.

We hauled in truckloads of compost. Uphill from the firepit we cleared trees and stair-stepped the hillside with deep black garden beds. In the afternoons while Perley slept in the shade of a dogwood, I planted peas, onions, potatoes, carrots, and kale. My grandma had loved asparagus, and her patch still came back every year right where she'd planted it by the front steps of her trailer, long vacant. On Helen's land that spring, I started an asparagus patch, knowing full well that when you plant asparagus you don't eat it the first year. If you're smart, you don't eat it even the second year. When you plant asparagus, you're making a bond, to be there when it's time to harvest it, at least three years on.

■ ■ ■ ■

While I planted, Karen and Helen planned the house we'd build. They located a place for it, a nearly flat spot close to the firepit, just below the garden. In fact a swamp, but Helen said it didn't matter because we'd build the house on piers. She said it was better than up on the ridge because we wouldn't have to haul lumber so far. Karen didn't say much. She drew pictures: one large room, a kitchen and living room connected, and a second story, a loft with two bedrooms, separated by a partition. Post and beam. Two hundred and sixty square would be the footprint. Only slightly bigger than the cabin Perley had been born in at the Land Trust, but this one would be ours. Ours and Helen's.

In May, we borrowed a generator from Frank. Helen bought a cheap set of power tools. We were getting everything used, on the cheap, or borrowed. I hadn't been to work in three months, but my boss at the hardware and salvage store raised an eyebrow and gave me the employee discount. Still, Karen and me were getting low on funds, not that we ever talked to each other about it. I don't know if she remembered that we still owed a month's rent at the Land Trust. I waited for her to bring it up, but she acted like life began and ended on Helen's slope. She hadn't talked about the clinic since the baby was born. Me, I couldn't see leaving Perley, not yet. He still wanted milk every forty-five minutes. Besides, who would I leave him with? Karen and Helen were too busy building the house to look after him, so I got busy, too. The sooner we had the place finished, the sooner we could think about other things. With Perley strapped to my back, I dug post holes, hauled lumber, and drove nails. Perley didn't mind me hammering. He'd swing his legs back and forth against my hips as I knocked nails in. He and I stood back while Helen and Karen mixed concrete and used the circular saw.

I noticed right away that Helen acted as lead carpenter, which didn't make sense. Rather than half knowing how to build, I saw that, as with many things, Helen wouldn't allow any part of herself not to know.

I dug holes for the piers, while Karen mixed concrete in a wheelbarrow. She tossed me a tape measure. "Make sure those holes are deep enough. Remember we have to get below the frost line," she said. But

Helen took the tape measure. "They're deep enough," she said. "Can't be perfectionists about every little thing. Not if we want to get this thing up before winter." I looked at Karen, but she became busy with the concrete, trying to mix more water into a dry crumbling heap that Helen had declared ready to be poured.

By June, the frame was up, and we'd wrapped the place in used billboard canvas, so an enormous pixelated hamburger stared us in the face. We tacked plastic up on the walls. We were still waiting for siding that Mike from the gas station said he could get cheap off this guy once he helped him take down a barn. Helen hauled garbage bags of cellulose insulation up the hill, wheelbarrowed them down the trail to the house site.

"Just what is that?" asked Karen, turning off the generator.

"It's the latest," Helen said. "Eco-friendly. Way easier than spending all day cutting up foam boards. Read the package. It says we just blow this stuff in."

"Blow it in with what?" asked Karen.

"We'll rent a machine," Helen said. "Trust me, this stuff is cutting-edge."

"You're supposed to wait to put that stuff in until the siding is up," Karen said, but Helen shook her head.

"We'll insulate first, then get to the siding later on," she said. "Don't worry about it. It's industry standard."

I waited for Karen to say, What the hell do you know about industry standard? but Karen, usually so tough, had lately turned meek. The only ferocity she showed was in pulling the cord on the generator so hard she almost broke the damn thing. Then she went back to work.

We blew the cellulose insulation into walls that were out of square. The floors weren't floors, but tamped earth. We worked together through July flooding and storms and weeks of dry weather. The windows, set into cockeyed frames, were shimmed in with spongy bits of elm wood. Without siding, the cellulose insulation sank into its plastic sheeting, leaving large gaps at the ceiling. But it wasn't until the heavy upsetting heat of August, after we set the pallet floor right on the ground, screwed plywood to it, and coated it in polyurethane, that I took up the unspoken subject with Karen. We lay nose to nose over Perley's head, and I could feel Karen's thick toenails against my shinbone. It was close quarters there with Perley drooling between us, but it wasn't clear yet whether Karen and I would really touch again the way we used to do. I reached for her as best I could.

"Helen's no carpenter at all," I said. "Not even half of one." I felt Karen stiffen. "But you are," I said. "That cabin you built at the Land Trust will probably be the only thing left standing after the apocalypse." I ran my hand down her shoulder. She shrugged it away.

"So what?" she said. "So what if I'm a better builder than Helen? You're a better builder than Helen, too. Perley's probably a better builder than her."

"Why don't you tell her that?" I asked.

"Why don't you?" she asked. I didn't answer. "Exactly," she said. "You know why. This is Helen's place."

"That wasn't the deal," I said. "Helen says she wants things equal. She wants it to be our place, too. We're not her employees."

"Do you believe that?" asked Karen.

"She's very welcoming," I said.

"Right," Karen said. "She's very welcoming. She's so fucking welcoming it's like we're not even here. Her welcoming takes up the entire twenty acres. No room for anyone else." She cupped Perley's heel, looked at me hard. "Do you want to stay here?" she asked.

"I planted asparagus," I said.

She nodded. "This is a good place," she

said. "The spring, the creek, the garden, the ducks. And the forest. We can stand on the ridge and only see one light. All that coal company land between us and them."

"You want to stay," I said.

"I want to stay," she said. "Helen can say what she wants about things being equal. But you see how she is. She wants things her own way. Notice she hasn't rushed to put our names on anything official. I'm not going to push it. Helen thinks she's in charge, but if we play this right, we'll still be right here after she burns out. I'll fix what needs fixing later." She managed to turn her nose from mine so that she faced the low ceiling. She removed her toe from my shin. "If you've got a better strategy," she said, "then you can stand up to Helen yourself."

But I never found a way to say word one to Helen, who, while gazing past us to the ridge beyond, had told us that we were her emergency phone number. That we were the people she'd call from jail if she had one phone call. That she loved us. She'd told us the story of where she came from. She'd always done what someone told her to, went to college when they told her to, wrote letters to one widowed aunt who didn't understand why anyone would live

69

without a man out of view of the Puget Sound, let alone live with those kind of people, by which she meant us. What kind of people are we? I asked. Not lesbians, Helen said. She's not homophobic. Then what? I asked, but Karen said, She means rednecks, and Helen blushed. Helen said that when she'd been with Shane, her aunt was proud of them for striking out on their own. It seemed like a grand adventure. But now that she was single it was uncharted territory, she said, and to most people it just seemed unfortunate. The aunt sent her gifts, which she passed on to Perley: paints, bright slippers that were child-size, lip gloss that came in the shape of chocolate truffles. Helen said, It might be different if my uncle was still alive. Him, I could talk to. But my aunt is unaware that I'm a grown woman.

As if building the house wasn't enough for her, Helen rose at dawn, buzzing, humming, learning, managing, bursting with good ideas that Karen and I didn't want to hear about. She put a pot on to boil, then went to collect duck eggs, so the bottom boiled out of the pot while she'd already got onto another task, pulling bent nails from used lumber, or salting a hide. She culled cabbage leaves for sauerkraut, but uprooted the plants, killing them. She saved a deer stomach to make blood sausage, but then turned her attention to drying red clover, so the stomach went to black slime. She ricocheted back and forth between Appalachian apprentice and holier-than-thou outsider, casually slipping in shit she must have picked up from some college class, spouting opinion as fact. Of course she didn't notice that Karen was the better builder. She wouldn't even notice if the house fell down. Still, Karen and I wanted what most people want, to harvest and eat our own asparagus. If you eat the raw shoots in the springtime, your blood thickens like a warrior, is what my grandma told me.

By the end of summer, the three of us were so tired at the end of the day's work that we no longer cooked meals together. We ate separate sandwiches and went to sleep. We'd stopped making toasts. We'd run out of wine and gin. We didn't buy more. We tried not to buy anything. We still hadn't talked about money. In town, I dodged Deirdre and Janice so I wouldn't have to tell them, Soon, soon, about that last month of rent. My boss at the hardware store said my job was still mine when I wanted it, and I held that in the back of my mind. After work hours, Helen disappeared up into the woods to gather food, and she came back with baskets full of dusty and dark plants, buckets of fur and feathers, flesh and intestine. The first few times, she invited Karen to come with her, but Karen declined. One evening at twilight, as Karen and I silently ate our peanut butter and jelly sandwiches, Helen strode into camp with two squirrels slung over her shoulder.

"Figured you might be hungry," she said, letting her squirrels drop onto the pallet she used for processing. "I haven't seen either one of you buy groceries in a while." Karen squeezed her sandwich crust.

"We need to save money if we're going to be able to finish the house by winter," I said. Since we'd arrived, it was the first time that word — money — had been spoken aloud.

"Don't worry, I'm happy to feed you," Helen said, and that was what finally did it. That's what brought Karen back to herself.

"I'd be surprised if this house even lasts through the winter," Karen said, pitching the crust over her shoulder.

"What is that supposed to mean?" asked Helen.

"It's shameful," Karen said. "It's an embarrassment."

"What is?" asked Helen.

"You heard me," Karen said. "The house.

72

It's a ringing example of poor craftsman-ship."

"And whose fault is that?" asked Helen, as ready as if she'd rehearsed.

"Yours," Karen said.

"Karen," I said.

"You know it, too, Lily," Karen said. "You've known it all along. We should have said something earlier. But Helen never stopped talking." Perley leaned off my nipple to watch her. He was nearly seven months old, but he hadn't yet seen this Ka-ren. The Karen he knew kept her head down and held her tongue, let Helen have the last word. But this woman, the one scowling up at Helen, was the Karen I knew well, who spoke plainly, who was happy only when she was angry and fighting.

Helen began talking fast. "It's your fault, Karen, because you should have been the lead carpenter. You should have been the lead carpenter, but you're trying to make me feel good about myself or you're afraid of me or something."

"I'm not afraid of you," Karen said.

"But you wouldn't speak up," Helen kept on. "You wouldn't speak up, and how do you think it felt for me to make mistakes, so many mistakes, with you watching me make them? How do you think that made me feel?"

"This isn't about your feelings, Helen," said Karen. "This is about two things only."

"What two things?" asked Helen.

"Running out of money and not having any shelter for the winter," said Karen.

"We have the camper," I said. "And you could go back to work at the clinic."

"Please shut up," Karen said.

"Just stay out of this, Lily," Helen said.

Karen turned back to Helen. "And I don't care if you feel good about yourself. I just want to know who's in charge. Is it me because I'm not full of shit and I actually know how to build things or is it you because this is your place?"

"This is not my place, it's our place, our place, our place, okay?" Helen said. Karen smiled. Helen said, "If you don't believe me about that, it's never going to work out here. Who's in charge? I don't know who's in charge. Why does someone have to be in charge? Why can't we work together?"

"The house is a piece of shit," Karen said.

"It's not that bad," Helen said. "The roof doesn't leak."

"You don't know that," Karen said.

"I'm nearly one hundred percent sure," Helen said.

"Is that the same as you being half a carpenter?" asked Karen.

"Maybe it's time to ask for some help," I said. "Why don't we ask Frank to come over and take a look?"

"I told you to shut up, Lily," Karen said, and I was almost happy to see Helen turn to me with the same poisonous face, because it meant that she and Karen were finding something in common.

"I'd sooner die than ask any of these ass-holes around here for help," Helen said.

"It's bad enough that we had to borrow Frank's generator," Karen said.

"Okay, well then what about Mike?" I said. "He gave us that siding almost for free. I'm sure he'd be happy to help." Karen and Helen rolled their eyes at the same time.

"What's so bad about asking for help?" I asked.

"Trust me," Helen said. "You ask any of these guys around here for building tips, they'll tell you how to hold a hammer."

"They'll tell you what a goddamn tape measure is," Karen said. "I'm not doing it."

"But we don't know how to build a house," I said. "This house is more like a kid's fort."

"We're not asking for help," Karen said.

"Right," said Helen, and they breathed

75

again in each other's company.

But it was the beginning of something that's run between them ever since. Who's in charge? And it was the beginning of something else, too. It was the beginning of the two of them versus each other, and the two of them versus me.

The sun went down, and we sat around the campfire together for the first time in weeks. No one said anything, but I wanted to mark the calendar. It felt like a celebration day. Our first fight, and Helen hadn't kicked us out. Instead, here we all were. Perley nursed. Helen squatted on her pallet, her knife out, skinning the squirrels. Karen whittled. Helen asked Karen what she was making.

"Tools for Perley," said Karen.

"Tools? You mean toys?" asked Helen.

"No time for toys. The boy needs to learn practical skills," Karen said. "He needs to be prepared out here."

Helen nodded, wicking blood efficiently into the flames. "That's right. Practice and prepare," she said.

"Prepare for what?" I asked. They looked at me like they'd just remembered I was there.

"For the future," Helen said gently, as if speaking to a small child. Then she looked at our small child. "For Perley's future." Perley, hearing his name, turned to let his eyes catch the firelight, graciously accepting fealty.

"I think we're pretty self-sufficient," I said. "I mean, more than most people."

"Ha. Most people," Karen said with contempt, and Helen, too, shook her head. Karen said, "Most people think we're ready for anything out here, but we're not. Not yet."

"But what about the garden? And Helen's wild food?" I asked.

"We're basically hobby farmers," Helen said.

"It's true," Karen said. "If we couldn't go to the grocery store, we'd starve."

I'd grown up in town, or nearly, where my grandma was the only one I knew who could knit a sweater, bake bread, build a chicken coop, and keep an engine running. My parents never had their own place long enough to plant flowers even, and most people of my generation went for a double-wide if they could get one and minimum wage if they could get that, too. When I was sixteen, I tried leaving. New York City was the place people talked the most shit about, so that's where I went, and it only took a day on the bus. I was proud of myself at first, but the main thing that city taught me was that I have a home. It's where everyone knows whose granddaughter I am. It's where I know every tree. It's where, when the mayapples blossom, I know which animals are going to get to the fruit before I do. So I came back and got a job at the hardware and salvage store. I kept it for five years before Karen walked in, rangy and loose in old work clothes, her messy braid unraveling beneath her mesh ball cap. She was a woman with skills, courage, strength, a woman who was good, so good with her hands. She was older than me. When you're twenty-two, thirty sounds wise. She'd hitchhiked all over. There were all kinds of ways to live, she said, but none better than what we could make right here. She scoffed at New York City. She scoffed at talk of minimum wage, of double-wide if you're lucky. She insisted we live in the cabin she'd built at the Land Trust, solid as a bomb shelter. She knew how to process roadkill. She insisted that we birth Perley at home. She insisted that we do for ourselves, and I hadn't met anyone like her since my grandma passed. Karen had told Helen that she hadn't learned her skills from books, and it was true. She'd learned them from the old folks, just like we all did. But she left out the fact that she measured our lives against *ElfQuest,* going on about the elves' self-reliance, discipline, skill at hunting, wood carving, healing. I gave those comic books the once-over and noticed right away something the elves had that we didn't: magic.

Karen whittled fast enough to make the shavings fly and spark into the flames, and Helen pierced a squirrel with a sharpened stick, thrust it out over the heat. At my nipple, Perley clamped down with his gums. I shifted his latch. I looked from Karen to Helen. I could feel their excitement build.

"But we haven't been to the grocery store in two weeks," I said, thinking of the single box of macaroni on the shelf, the five-pound bag of oats, the half loaf of stale bread, the jar of peanut butter dwindling each day. "We don't have the money for it. Maybe one of us should go back to work soon."

"No time to go back to work. We've got to build the house. And Perley needs us here," Karen said.

"Anyway, I've got money," Helen said.

"You do?" I asked.

"I saved plenty of money working for Rudy last year," she said. "He wanted me back this season, too, but I told him not

79

until the house is finished."

"You have money?" I asked. My stomach felt vacuumed clean.

"We don't need Helen's money," Karen said.

"It's not about that," Helen said.

"It's about practicing and preparing," Karen said.

"Right," Helen said. "We can do better. We can certainly do better than we've been doing."

"If one of us has money, then I think we should go to the grocery store," I said. "I'm hungry. We're almost out of peanut butter."

"But what if there was no grocery store? That's the point," Karen said.

"I wonder how long we'd last," Helen said.

"I'm breastfeeding, Karen," I said.

"But what would we do if you were breastfeeding and there was no grocery store?" Karen said. "That's what we need to be thinking about." Helen nodded.

"I'll go," I said. "I'll go to the store tomorrow. Let's make a grocery list."

"Lily, stop it. You don't have to go to the store," Karen said.

"Okay, you can go," I said. "I don't care who goes. Why don't we rock paper scissors to see who goes? Or we can roll the dice."

"That's it!" Helen said. "We'll roll the

dice." With relief, I watched her produce the pouch of dice from where we stored it in the toolbox. She emptied the four dice into her hand. I was already picturing bread all squishy in its plastic bag, a brick of cheese, maybe even butter and milk, cold cuts, when Helen said, "From now on, when it's time to go grocery shopping, we roll the dice. If we roll doubles, we go to the grocery store. If not, we subsist on what we have stored, and what we can get from this land."

"Survival Dice," Karen said, her eyes glowing. Their fight was forgotten. Who cared about the shitty house when we could starve together? I put my arms around Perley and held him to me until he wriggled and twisted, trying to turn himself to the fire. He liked to stare into the flames — like every other primate, Karen said — but I screwed my eyes shut. I hoped for Dog Paws, Snake Eyes, the Necklace, for the Squid. I hoped hard for doubles, and when I opened my eyes again, Helen had rolled double sixes, the Full Moon.

I drove to the IGA in town the next day, but the stakes were high, and I hardly knew where to begin. Perley was just starting solid foods. Perched regally in the shopping cart, he swung his arms out for pickles and olives, anything briny. But I was there for staples. I filled the cart with oil, rice, flour, beans, cans of tomatoes, cans of fish, a box of powdered milk, bouillon cubes. Back at home, Karen and Helen said I was cheating.

Cheating or not, I was glad that I had such foresight. The odds were against us, and as August wore down into September, we rolled doubles only twice, once Snake Eyes, once the Necklace. We spent most weeks working our way through what we had on the shelves. We developed a new taste for crawdads dug from the murky garden paths, bluegills netted from the creek, chickweed, the cattails that grew at the bottom of the driveway. But it was impossible to get enough. The crawdads and the bluegills were mostly bone or cartilage, the chickweed and cattails flared fast inside us and then went out. The meat we could get, possum, raccoon, or squirrel, we would savor, knowing it wouldn't last. Helen's passion for wild food didn't match her skill in getting it. Most of what we had planted in the garden was either low-calorie or low-yield. We looked forward with urgent vigilance to the potato harvest, only to find that we'd grown enough to feed us for only a few meals, and not enough to store. The green beans, on the other hand, were so plentiful that for most of September they were nearly all we ate. I was ravenous, much hungrier than I'd been when I was pregnant. I came to love only two things deeply, Perley and fat. I woke from dreams of fat, thought of fat while I was driving in nails, caught myself admiring the crease of fat behind Perley's knees. I dreamed of fat, and I ate what I could, and what I ate Perley drank from my body. As he grew, I shrank. But no matter what, I nursed Perley. No matter what, I saw to it that Perley thrived.

Karen and Helen might not have been getting much nutrition, but they were thriving, too. Thriving on self-satisfaction. They could barely contain themselves.

"It's a good lesson," Karen said. "We'll learn to store food better."

"We'll learn to get more wild foods," Helen said. "We can get acorns."

"We'll get a couple of deer and have venison all winter," Karen said.

"What about Perley?" I said. "Soon he'll be eating more food. I want him to be healthy."

"It's not healthy to be feasting all the time," Karen said. "This is better. This is better for Perley. He'll be hardy. He'll be ready for anything, right from the beginning of his life. And he's got you. You'll nurse him as long as he'll let you. Right, Lily?" But I could see how happy she was, so I could see that she didn't need me to answer.

They could agree on Survival Dice, but when it came to the house, the truce between Karen and Helen was bound to fall apart. After all, the truce was based on starvation, a condition whose first symptom is irritability and whose second symptom is poor decision-making. The house continued to go up but it didn't get any better. The first September rain, the roof leaked and water blew in through the walls. We had to wait for a dry day to do anything about it. Grim, Helen bought caulk, grout, and spray foam insulation. Pale, she climbed a ladder and patched the roof. Tight-lipped, Karen sprayed foam into the gaps in the walls. I rested beneath the dogwood with Perley. He was almost crawling by then, tipping himself forward onto all fours so that he could reach out and share the last tin of kippers with me. Karen and Helen stopped for lunch, and Helen divided a songbird in half.

"I divide, you decide," Karen said.

"But I divided," Helen said.

"Right, so I get to decide," Karen said.

They ate their swift in tense silence.

"We need to move the woodstove in soon," Karen said. It had been sitting beneath a tarp at the top of the driveway all summer. It weighed four hundred pounds.

"We should borrow a dolly," Helen said.

"A dolly won't work," Karen said. "It's too heavy and the ground is too uneven."

"A dolly will work fine. We can borrow one from Frank," Helen said.

"I'm telling you a dolly won't work," Karen said. "And I'm sick of borrowing things from Frank."

"Then you figure it out. Is this my job? To come up with ideas so you can shoot them down?" asked Helen.

"Do you want some kind of award for coming up with bad ideas that won't work?" asked Karen.

"Anytime something goes wrong with the house it's my fault, and anytime anything goes right it's because you're a genius," Helen said.

"You're hungry. Finish your sparrow," Karen said.

"I'm not hungry, you're hungry. And it's not a sparrow, it's a swift," Helen said.

"I'm not hungry," Karen said.

"Let's have a housewarming party," I said.

They looked at me.

"So people can help us move the wood-stove," I said.

"I don't want to have a bunch of people up here to look at the shitty house we're building," Karen said.

"I don't want people to help us," Helen said.

I took Perley and walked away. I walked up through the garden and into the forest. I waded through the damp tangle of early autumn, the blackberries dying back, the grapevines, the flowering nettle and red clover turning brown and spongy. I was weak, and I was dizzy, but I made my way straight up to the saddle below the ridge, and I found a place to be alone with Perley. It was a sheltered place between a tulip poplar and a beech tree, where the dry leaves were cooked to brown and yellow. If I looked, I could see down through the trees to the garden, firepit, and house site, but they were far away, too far away to matter much. I swung Perley off my back and settled him in my lap, and he latched on to nurse.

No one was asking me, but I was beginning to answer. I was beginning to see that I lived with two women who were against things. They were against things, and I was one of those things. They were against each other so that they couldn't see how alike they were. Helen liked telling people what to do. Karen didn't like being told what to do. As for me, I liked being told what to do. But sometimes I couldn't do it.

My grandma had been dead more than ten years, and I could hear her. What in the hell are you doing, girl? You take that baby and you leave. But leave and go where? I didn't want the double-wide. I didn't want the minimum wage. Or at least that's not all I wanted. There was no room for me in the usual way, never had been. I'd known that as soon as I knew I loved women. Karen gave the usual script the once-over with that skeptical eye of hers, then she handed it back and insisted that life could be lived from scratch. We were hungry and angry, but we'd agreed to seek our fortune together. So far, she'd chosen wolf pack over stranger. She's my pack, I told my grandma, and I can't say that I would be any better off without her. I love Karen. More than that, Grandma. She reminds me of you.

Perley made his small steady nursing noise, his chug chug. He fixed me with his whale eye, that large peering marble next to my nipple. He gazed at me with — well, I guess I thought of it as trust, but not simple trust, more like don't-fuck-this-up trust. Do you respect me? he was asking. I whispered into his face, I respect you. I respect the mystery of you. He laid his hand against my cheek and pinched. He reached up and touched his index finger to my eye, and he pressed hard. With Perley's finger buried in my eyeball, stupid names came to me. He was my Lumpy Bundle, my Thorny Lamb, my Silken Puppy, my Fruit Bat, my Monster Rat, my Velvet Piglet.

I reached into my overalls and I took out the bottle of cooking oil that I'd smuggled from camp. I unscrewed the top and drank from it for ten full seconds before taking a breath. The golden oil coated my insides. It was meat and milk and cake and bread. Fat.

I rocked Perley and drank deeply. I looked down the hill. Through the leaves, I could see Helen and Karen far below at the house site. One of them dropped the nail gun and the other bent over to pick it up. I saw, but didn't hear, a sheet of plywood crash to the ground. Helen climbed a ladder. Karen steadied it. With their bright faces under the sweep and gleam of the dogwood, they could have been mistaken for the best of friends.

3

Karen

I spent my twenties traveling and watching. A woman alone, it wasn't hard for me to get rides, and it wasn't only men who offered them. Families with a protective streak pulled right over. I watched them. I watched the people who let me camp out in their yards, watched the people who hired me to do odd jobs, carpentry or electric work or apple picking. I watched families at diners and in bus stations. I watched parents all over this great land being bullied by their toddlers over soda and TV and bedtime. I watched them bribe their own kids to do simple chores. I watched them hand their kids over to strangers who'd stick them behind a desk for six hours every day. Even on my lonely days, the days I didn't know if I was fit for human company, I knew I could do it better. I certainly knew I could raise my kid better than the way I was raised. My mom coming at me with endless platters of white and yellow food so that I hid in the woods at the sound of the dinner bell. My dad, who I'd swear went on disability just so he'd have more time to roam around the county and brag. Deirdre used to talk about coming out to her family like it was some big thing, but what about when your family doesn't hear you when you talk? I hardly noticed when my dad's mind started to go, because the only thing he'd ever remembered about me was my whittling, probably because he was the one gave me my sheepsfoot blade. At my mother's bedside, and then at her funeral, I whittled my first skull. I gave the carving to my dad, and, just like Lily, he lost it, like I knew he would. The only good part of growing up was how much time I'd had to spend in the woods, alone with my knife, my wood, and my comics.

It took almost three years of planning and trying before Lily was pregnant with Perley. The day we found out, on the Land Trust, we dragged our mattress out beneath the sumac tree at the edge of the pasture. In those days we rushed to close any air between us. We lay there and talked about what kind of parents we wanted to be. It felt good. It felt like love.

"I want to be taken for granted," I said, holding her. "I want it to be news to the kid that my feelings could be hurt, that I even have feelings at all. To be boring, that's the real trick. Let the kid be the exciting one."

"What else?" she asked.

"I want to be the provider," I said.

"All right," she said. "But you also want to be alone."

"It's not that I want to be alone," I said. "It's that I am alone. Sometimes."

"Well, I don't want to be alone," Lily said. "That's not what I signed on for."

"We're a wolf pack," I said. "Don't worry."

"My breadwinner." She sighed, burrowing close.

"Not the breadwinner," I said. "The provider."

"What's the difference?" she asked.

"I want to provide education, skills, and structure," I said.

"Structure?" Lily asked. "You mean a house?"

"A house," I said. "And stability. I want to be so There that this kid doesn't even know what There is because the kid's life is defined by There. I want to be so There that I'm not there."

I put my mouth into Lily's hair, sucked a strand, pushed with my nose. "What about you? What kind of parent do you want to be?" I asked.

She touched her belly button, which was still concave. She was only six weeks along. "I can't really imagine being a parent," she said. "All I can imagine is this baby. When it comes out of there I'm going to get a bottle of Elmer's glue, and I'm going to glue it to me. I'm going to love whoever it is until its head pops." She turned in my arms, her body beginning to generate quarts of new blood. Twined together, we upset the sumac. It dropped its berries to smear our bodies the color of rust.

By mid-October the house was pretty much finished, even though Helen had ignored every single piece of building expertise I offered, treated me like goddamn free labor. But still, there it was, basically livable. Osage orange posts held up the porch roof, which leaked. Three large pieces of sandstone, pulled from the hillside, led down to the front door, which let daylight in above and below. Despite all its flaws, I'll admit it wasn't bad to look at.

It was hard to know just who to invite to the housewarming party or how to invite them. We could think of a few people we knew, sure, but we weren't certain we wanted to see them, or that they wanted to see us, or that they wanted to see one another. We hadn't seen these people having a good time, and we weren't sure we wanted to. But Lily insisted that moving a woodstove was the perfect party for people who hated parties, so we temporarily called off Survival Dice, went to the grocery store, bought a case of beer, some packages of hot dogs, and three bags of chips. Lily showed up at the register with a bag of avocados, no matter she was the one always so worried about money. At home, Lily set up a folding table in front of the garden. She put the food on it, but couldn't wait and ate two avocados right there, ate them as if they were apples, just peeling them and chewing them right through to the pit. The green paste encircled her mouth. I built a fire, even though it was humid as hell. The guests were invited for six o'clock.

I sat near the fire, smoothing Perley's eyebrow as he kicked on my lap, an issue of *ElfQuest* open next to me. Helen mashed avocados in a bowl. Lily looked at me like the avocados she'd already eaten might not stay down. She said, "Karen, I think that's enough smoothing."

"Everyone's got a rough eyebrow," I said. "You've got it. I've got it. Even the elves have it." I nodded toward my comic. Lee-tah, the beautiful elfin healer, stared up at Lily from the glossy page. She had one eyebrow tuft out of place. "But Perley, he's got a chance," I said, licking my thumb, smoothing Perley's brow again and again. "If I smooth his eyebrow every day, he won't have that fuzz, that sprout. With me and you and Helen, no one cared. No one who loved us got to us in time. But Perley will be perfect."

"You know those comics are totally problematic, right?" Helen said, mashing.

"Please, enlighten me," I said. "Just don't charge me for the college credits."

"For one thing, the elves are basically meant to be some kind of advanced race who show up to be worshipped by primitive humans as gods. It's imperialism all over again."

"You're way off," I said. "The elves are outcasts. They're misunderstood and trying to get by on their own terms."

"Not to mention the way they draw those female elves, it's obviously some kind of sex fantasy for men," she said.

"It's not for men," I said.

"I'm just saying," she said.

"You haven't even read them," I said.

"I've skimmed them," Helen said. She

watched me lick my thumb, smooth. "And what you're doing is certifiably obsessive. Might as well get the kid a nose job."

"Nobody asked you, Helen," I said, flipping *ElfQuest* shut, and handing Perley up to Lily. He glared at Helen, his odd eyebrow slick with my saliva. Sometimes I worried he preferred her. He scowled at her with a single-mindedness that could be adoration. All I could do was scowl back at them. At six o'clock, the ducks warned us that our guests had arrived.

Deirdre and Janice from the Women's Land Trust came. They brought a guitar and sang rounds at the campfire, to stave off any attempts at conversation. The mill operator came, with her handsome young boyfriend. They brought us a sack of flour as a housewarming present, which Lily received with tears in her eyes. Mike from the gas station came, bringing us a quart of maple syrup from his trees. Frank came, with his wife and their six gap-toothed daughters, all of whom, except for Frank, wore lace-trimmed long skirts and checkered flannel shirts. Rudy came, his orange beard dyed a shade brighter by Cheeto dust, wearing several strands of Mardi Gras beads around his neck, which he gamely distributed to Frank's children. As a rule he hated all socializing, so he'd prepared for the party by waking up early to drink. He stood near the campfire, swaying along to Deirdre's rounds until Janice asked him to stand a little farther away. Lily's manager from the hardware and salvage store came, built like a shagbark hickory yet so persnickety that she sold acne cleanser by the register. She presented us with an economy-size bottle of hand sanitizer. "Happy housewarming," she said, but Helen wouldn't take it from her.

"This crap is exactly what's wrong with the world," Helen said. "I'd put it in the trash, but there's no safe way to dispose of it. It's not fair to sanitation workers."

"But thanks so much for thinking of us," said Lily, taking the bottle.

The mill operator kissed her boyfriend with tongue right there in front of everyone. Lily elbowed Helen. "When are you going to date again?" she asked.

"Leave me alone," Helen said. "Perley needs a maiden aunt."

I passed around the guacamole, chips, and beer. I caught our guests glancing over at the new house. I braced myself, but they took their time commenting on it. The kids took handfuls of chips down onto the porch and sat around blowing across empty beer bottles. They didn't ask to go inside. Instead,

by way of conversation, Frank told us what
he'd heard on what he called the news.
Chewing the wrong kind of gum could
make all of his children go instantly brain-
dead. Then Mike started in on fluoride in
the water, and Lily's manager joined in.

"It messes with proper hormone messaging," she said. "And that's just the beginning."

"Sounds like that orangutan thing," Helen
said.

"What orangutan thing?" asked Lily.

"In some orangutan communities, there's
only one male, and he can't stop growing,"
Helen said. "He grows giant flat cheeks and
a big fat throat. It's called a flange. It's all
about hormonal messaging. Everyone in the
medical community is talking about it.
They're wondering what kind of implica-
tions it has for humans."

"I've never heard of that," I said.

"Sure you have," she said.

"No, I haven't," I said. "And I'm a nurse."
I was a nurse, but I hadn't talked to another
nurse since Perley was born. There were no
nurses at our party. I hadn't invited them. I
couldn't bear to hear their plans for improv-
ing Perley: shots, doctor visits, regular bath-
ing, combing out his cradle cap. I couldn't
bear to be around people who thought of

my son as just another body to be managed. Now that I knew Perley, I'd stopped believing in the ordinariness of humans, or at least didn't want to be made aware of it. I didn't want to know about other bodies, other baths, other wiping, other chapping and applications of ointments and administering of medicines. All these duties that I'd been proud to see to, now I wanted to reserve only for my son. When the clinic number showed up on my tiny screen, I held my breath until it disappeared. Still, everyone in the medical community? Everyone?

"This is bullshit, Helen," I said.

"Why does the flanged orangutan get so big?" asked Lily, shifting Perley to her other hip.

"He's the only male," Helen said. "There's no other male in the vicinity to compete with, so his hormones are unchecked."

"And is he the strongest?" asked Lily.

"No," Helen said. "That's the peculiar thing. He's not that strong. He's got a weak heart and he doesn't live very long."

"We have to do something," Lily said.

"About what?" I asked.

"About Perley," Lily said.

"What does this have to do with Perley?" I asked.

"He's the only male in the vicinity," said

Lily. "What if that happens to him?"

"It's the hormonal message that's important," Helen said. "You just need to get his brain to send the hormonal message."

"So we need Perley to, what, smell men?" Lily asked.

"I think that would do it," Helen said. Perley looked into all of our faces and laughed, kicking Lily in the stomach. Our neighbors just watched us, respectful as cable TV. I took Perley out of Lily's arms, against his squirming. "He's my kid, Helen, and I'm telling you to back off," I said. "This is ridiculous."

"But what if it isn't?" asked Lily.

From the moment I met my son, blue as a cave troll, coated in vernix, gasping in the new air, my mission became to not undo all he was born with. To watch him develop habits was painful to me. I resented each neural pathway as it was blazed in his brain. These made him more familiar to me, and I wanted him to stay choose-your-own-adventure. We'd been given a perfect thing, a wild animal, ours to domesticate and diminish. He didn't need our intervention.

But sometimes I couldn't stop myself. I couldn't stop myself from smoothing his eyebrow. I watched his tiny tucked-in face, his nose pressed on, the way that his nostrils curled in like parentheses, small gleams of oil in the corners, eyelashes rising and falling on his cheeks, crease of eyelids folding back toward his temples. I put my hand to his heart. I felt that steady unlikely rhythm. If I couldn't believe in its reliability, then I couldn't believe in anything.

"Rudy," I said. "Can we borrow one of your shirts?"

Rudy stepped forward, red-faced and puffed up with generosity.

"This is a very good decision you're making," he said. He peeled off his T-shirt, and his wiry hair sprang forth. The shirt he handed me had possibly once been white. It gave off a smell of yeast, onions, pine needles, sawdust, beer, and sap. I draped it over my shoulder. "I've been waiting for this moment," Rudy said, scratching his furry belly. "A boy needs a father. I've said it all along."

"You're not his father," I said.

"A father figure, then," he said.

"You're not his father figure," I said.

"I'm happy to do it," he said. He leaned down into Perley's face. "You and me, kid," he said. "You and your old uncle Rudy. We're going to be good pals. I'll teach you how to use a chain saw. I'll teach you how to drink."

"He's not your uncle," I told Perley.

Perley said, "Ah!" and punched Rudy hard in the nose, sending him off-balance.

"Motherfucker!" Rudy said, holding his nose.

"No hitting, Perley," I said.

Lily said, "But did you see that? My Velvet Piglet is incredibly strong!"

"You little scamp," Rudy said to Perley, still holding his nose. "You think you're stronger than your old uncle Rudy. But someday we'll have a real fistfight, and then you'll see."

"Can we switch this shirt out for a fresh one next week?" Helen asked. "I mean a fresh dirty one?"

"Babysitting, diaper changing," Rudy said. "Anything I can do, just let me know."

"Let's see this woodstove," Mike said.

We all, even the children, even the ducks, went up the path to the head of the drive-way, where the woodstove lay in wait next to the scrap metal pile. We approached it as if it were a wild animal. We were cautious yet firm. I shifted Perley into the crook of my arm, used my free hand to yank off the tarp. The stove looked like the portal to hell, its double door a gaping maw, its clanking dials extending on iron antennae that cranked open and closed, its small windows flashing darkness.

Helen brought the dolly. "You kids get out of the way," Frank said. The children chased the ducks back toward their shed, and everyone pressed forward. The women from the Land Trust quietly but firmly shouldered their way in past Rudy and Mike, the mill operator rolled up her sleeves, her handsome young boyfriend took off his shirt and stuffed it in his back pocket, the hardware store manager counted off, and they heaved. Frank pushed the thing too fast from below so that the rest of the group called out in protest. They rested. They swore. Then Frank's wife took Perley, and I got in there, too, shoulder to shoulder with our neighbors. Mike counted off again, and this time we levered the woodstove onto the dolly, and then we walked that thing down the uneven gravel path, past the duck shed and the elderberry bushes and the spring, careful not to tip it into the ditch. We dodged the folding table, and stopped to rest at the campfire, just up the bank from the new house. Frank's daughters cleared a path across the porch, moving the beer bottles and empty guacamole bowl out of the way.

"What next?" asked Lily.

"What next? We put it in the house, is what next," Rudy said.

"Will it fit in the door?" she asked.

"We'll make it fit," Frank said. Then Janice rose up and gave one of her lectures about feminist lifting techniques, and Rudy responded with a passionate speech about manning up. Then there was no talking but a lot of grunting as we walked the thing down one sandstone step and then another, inched it across the porch, upended it to get it through the door, and finally the woodstove was inside, taking up a third of the kitchen.

Frank's wife handed Perley back over to me, and he gummed Rudy's T-shirt while Lily refilled the guacamole and brought out another six-pack. Everyone stood around the woodstove, breathing and smiling and looking over our new house, which barely had room for all of us. We had to stand close together, Land Trust women cozied up next to mill operator and her boyfriend up against Mike leaning on hardware store manager nestled into Rudy's hairy back stepping on Frank, children clustered on the floor. We didn't even have any furniture yet. Our guests couldn't have been comfortable. They sipped beer and craned past one another to look the place over. Shame choked me. But no one said, Pretty damn small for four people. No one said, Are you planning to fill the gaps? No one said, The rim joist isn't flush. No one said, Is this floor made of pallets? Is it built directly onto the ground? When I set my beer down on the woodstove, the tilt to the liquid was clearly visible, but no one said, The floor isn't level. No one said, This house is already sinking by degrees into the wet orange clay. No. Instead Frank clapped me on the back and said, "Look at that. Finished well before winter."

"You women surely are ants, not grasshoppers," Frank's wife said.

"There goes the neighborhood, you fucking yuppies," Rudy said, raising his glass. I swallowed my beer.

Deirdre brought out a sage stick. "If you don't mind, I'd like to do a cleansing ceremony to drive bad spirits from the house," she said.

"We do mind," Helen said. "The last thing we need is more white people co-opting Native American spirituality." Mike, the only person at the party who wasn't white, laughed. Deirdre looked hurt.

"Thanks anyway, Dee," Lily said, frowning at Helen.

"Actually, I'm pretty sure I'm part Indian," offered the mill operator's young boyfriend, still shirtless.

"Oh, of course," Helen said. "A royal line, I'm sure."

"I don't know about him," Mike said, "but when my great-grandparents came up from down South they settled with the Wyandot, married, children, everything. That was around 1820 or so. The way my grandma told it, those slave catchers were too scared of Indians to come looking for folks there."

The hardware store manager said, "My great-grandma told me that when she was a little girl in these hills, the Shawnee would come down out of the woods because they were hungry, and our family would feed them."

"That's a beautiful story," Frank's wife said.

"But why were they hungry? That's a fucking crime," Helen said. "Right, Mike?"

"Do you ever think of something to say, and not say it?" I asked Helen.

"There aren't enough hours in the day," Helen said.

Rudy opened another beer. "You know what's a fucking crime is private property," he said to no one in particular.

"That's what I'm always saying," Helen said.

"Private property is what this country was founded on," Frank said.

"Fuck what this country was founded on," Helen said.

"I'll drink to that," Rudy said, and did.

Mike said, "Now, hold on. If they try to come on my land, I've got my Smith and Wesson."

"You're right about that," I said. Perley turned his head to the side, and fit his mouth around my collarbone, trying to suckle. "If they try to mess with Perley or Lily —"

"Wait a minute. Who is They?" Lily asked.

"I don't care who it is, I'll do whatever it takes," I said.

"But who is it that you're so worried about?" Lily asked.

"Do you really have to ask?" I said.

"Let's all drink to that," said Rudy, and we all did.

Lily knew as well as I did who They were. Sardined there with our neighbors, I didn't choose to say, According to the state, I'm not here. According to the state, I'm gone, I'm nothing. Lily is Perley's only official parent. Neither Lily nor I liked to say it out loud, not even between the two of us. We didn't want to make it more true. And if sometimes I felt myself hovering near invisibility, if fear made me fragile or turned me tyrant, if fear made me want to flee, well so what? I wasn't going anywhere, not anytime soon. I was bound and determined to parent Perley within an inch of both our lives.

Maybe Helen was right about all the shit she said to people, maybe she wasn't, but I couldn't see how her jabbering changed anything. It didn't change anything to stand there and talk. It didn't change anything to talk about who They were. It definitely didn't change anything to talk about this land, about why we were on it, who'd been on it before, and why they weren't on it. It didn't help to think about being kicked off of it or kicking other people off of it, or to figure ourselves as heroes. But Helen would have said not talking about it wouldn't change anything, either. We stood around the stove with our neighbors and tried in vain to feel like we had something in common. When we got along at all, it was when we moved a woodstove together. It was when we pictured ourselves standing together against outside threats, instead of threatening one another. We preferred to imagine ourselves on the right side of things, including history. We preferred to stand side by side, thinking despising thoughts about people who were long dead and the mistakes that they'd made, instead of thinking despising thoughts about one another and about the mistakes we were right now making each moment. Then one of Frank's daughters pointed down behind the woodstove and said, "Snake!"

The black rat snake slid from beneath the stove until it showed itself five feet long, and Frank's daughters, all six of them, set up a delighted shrieking. The snake froze in place. It grew rigid and crimped up all along its length. It gave off a sulfur-and-onions smell, the fairy godmother crashing the party.

"You're scaring it," I told the shrieking daughters. "Black snakes kink up like that as an anxiety reflex. They only smell like that when they're afraid." But they continued shrieking.

"Be still!" Frank commanded. And they were still.

"We're just playing," the oldest daughter said. "It's just an old black snake, we ain't scared of them."

"I am," the youngest daughter said. "I am and I bet he is," and she pointed at Perley. But Perley opened his mouth wide and made a happy screech, imitating the girls' noise. I held him under his armpits, crouched down so he could get a better view. "Meet your new friend Snake," I said, as he goggled and drooled. "This snake lives here, too."

"Da!" Perley said. "Da!"

"Say snake," Frank's oldest daughter said. "Snake, Perley, snake."

"Na!" Perley said.

"That's enough," Lily said, grabbing for Perley, but I swung him up to my shoulder.

"What do you do about a black snake in your house?" Lily asked the room.

"You feel lucky," Frank said.

"I got them at my place, too," Mike said. "They're not venomous. And they'll eat mice and copperheads."

"Come on, Lily," I said. "You grew up around here. You know about black snakes." Perley gripped my braid and pulled.

"Not about having them in my house. And I grew up in town. Not so many snakes in town," Lily said.

Rudy said, "Black snakes are territorial. If they've decided to live here, it's next to impossible to get rid of them. This is the time of year they move in, too. Autumn. When it's getting cooler at night."

"They?" Lily asked. "As in more than one?"

"You might get a lot of them," her boss from the hardware store said. "They're loners, but they all like the same thing. So if you've got a good habitat, they might all move in at once."

"They need somewhere to hibernate," the mill operator said. "A hibernaculum. Someplace warm to spend the winter."

"A house full of snake experts," Lily said. "So snakes need a place to hibernate. Fine. I don't see why it has to be our house."

"Good a place as any," I said.

One of Frank's daughters squatted down for a closer look, and the snake fled into the wall via one of the gaps we'd failed to seal, so that only its tail was showing. Perley laughed and tried to lunge out of my arms.

"They're harmless, Lily," I said. "Even Perley can see that."

Lily closed her mouth on whatever she planned to say next. Deirdre fingered her sage, but the snake was better than any hijacked ceremony. The snake made me feel like our fucked-up house had been chosen.

"Black snakes in the walls are much better than having flying squirrels in the walls," Frank's wife said.

"Now, that's true," Mike said. "Or what about these red beetles?"

"The hornworms this year," Frank said. And so the talk turned to the many disappointments and hardships of the lives we were living, and how once you got rid of one thing, another thing was sure to turn up, and how this succession of pests, irritations, and unfairness would surely last until we were too weary to move, and so lay down on the lush water-laden land, lay down to rest, just to rest, lay down and died.

4

Lily

The first snake lived in the wall behind the woodstove. The second snake lived among the pile of dish towels under the kitchen counter. The third snake lived in the drawer with the rolling pin and the measuring cups. The fourth snake lived on the bookcase, fourth shelf up. When I left for work at the hardware and salvage store each morning, a snake filled my right rubber boot with its coils. I used the broom to overturn it, watched it slink into a knothole in the floor-board.

The house was livable for the animals that moved in, and it was livable for us. Snakes, mice, spiders, wasps, even once a raccoon. Year by year, we got used to it, or, in the case of the raccoon, we killed it and ate it. In the summers the house molded. We washed the floor and the walls with vinegar every week. In the winters, the wind found all the gaps, all the places where the insulation had sunk. It blew in above and below the front door. But we kept the fire hot. We played Survival Dice. The house sank into the clay, but it wasn't completely swallowed. It leaned, but it didn't capsize. Our garden grew each year, so did our ability to bring in wild food, and so did Perley.

When Perley was one, he sat in my lap and reached out to grasp the fifth black rat snake, the one that took up residence along the back of the sofa. "Nake!" he said. When he was two, he said, "Snake!" and went down on hands and knees to hiss in delight at the black snake that lived behind the front door. When Perley was four, he jogged up and down on the sofa next to Karen and said proudly, "I am Friend of Snake!" as the black snakes slowly overtook our house.

"We were up to ten snakes last time I checked," I said. "I think it's time to do something." I'd said this before. Karen was whittling, which didn't seem quite safe to me, blade so close to bouncing boy, but I'd said this before, too. Helen leaned over the kitchen counter, writing furiously in the three-ring binder, a to-do list that she'd been keeping for the past year. We could see that it grew each day, that she carried it with her everywhere. It was obvious that she

113

wanted us to ask her what was in it. But we had our own to-do lists, and at the top of both of our lists was the same item. To do: Don't look at Helen Conley's to-do list. Sometimes, accomplishing that task could take the whole day.

"Nothing to do except get used to them. It's their house, too," Karen said. "Where people make their biggest mistake is in thinking they can control everything." The wood shavings flew. Perley bounced next to her, kicking off his socks, then pulling them back on and doing it again.

While I worked, Karen stayed home with Perley. The first time Perley had thrown a ball right-handed, Karen had brought the ball back to him and closed his left hand around it. It was the same thing when he learned to eat with a spoon, or to dig with the shovel she'd carved for him. When she caught my look, she said, "In the future we're preparing for, ambidextrous people will be needed."

She saw to it that Perley only ate from the garden, from the forest, or from my breasts. I pumped three times a day to keep my supply up, so Perley would have milk even when I wasn't there. No bread. No grain. No sugar. She gave him bones to chew on, made sure that Helen saved all the organ meat from the animals she found, spooned groundhog liver into his mouth. "I don't want him to lose his taste for bitter," she said. "We have to fight the endless monotony of salt and sweet."

When Perley learned to walk, Karen frowned at me when I carried him. "Never do for a child what he can do for himself," she said. She whittled tools that were just Perley's size, a rake and a shovel, a pitchfork, a pick, a mallet. He wanted her to play with him but she said, "You're better than that, Perley. You can work with me." In the spring, we harvested nettles side by side. I tried to keep Perley from the patch, but Karen said, "Let him try it if he wants to." He cried when the nettles stung him, and milk rushed to my breasts. I folded him in my arms. But Karen beamed with pride to watch the rash tendril down his chubby arms. She called it proof of his vigorous circulation. She declared that he'd never be sick a day in his life.

Karen said we should leave everything to wildness, including our son. But if she wanted to let things go, it didn't make her more relaxed. Practicing, she called it. Preparing. The way she saw it, wildness took work.

■ ■ ■ ■

I watched Karen whittling what looked like a chain, for what purpose I couldn't say. At least it wasn't another spoon. We had a kitchen full of those molding away, little wooden marbles rattling around in their handles. I watched Perley next to her, jumping up and down, like he was training for some contest. I watched the black snake on the windowsill behind him flick its tail. Lazy. Satisfied. Helen snapped her binder shut.

"Finished!" she said, then looked thoughtful. "Actually it'll never really be finished," she said. "We can keep adding to it forever. But it's ready to be shared."

"Oh, rejoice," Karen said.

"Sharing! Rejoicing! Sharing! Rejoicing!" Perley said. He put his socks on his hands and kept bouncing.

"And it's not really a to-do list," Helen said. "Or, it started out as one, but now it's a gift. It's a gift from me to this land. To our family." She held up the binder so that we could not help but see what she'd written across its cover in permanent marker: Best Practices.

"Best Practices?" Karen asked. "What is

this, some kind of corporate retreat?"

Helen looked hurt. "It's helpful," she said. "It has everything in it." She held it out to me.

Reluctantly, I took the binder, opened it to the first page, which read, "A Compendium of Helpful Strategies and Methods for Optimum Daily Living." Karen set aside her whittling and came to look over my shoulder. Perley kept up his sofa exercises, making what he thought of as the sound of a motor.

"Optimum?" Karen said. "Where do you get this shit?"

I turned the page.

The Best Practices Binder seemed at first to be a how-to-homestead guide, an imitation of the books that Helen had studied. There was a page about the proper procurement of roadkill. Best to get a deer that wasn't there when you went into town, but appeared on your way back out. That way you know exactly how long it's been lying there. There were instructions on how to kill tree of heaven. Don't bother trying to uproot it or cut it down. Instead, scrape its bark off in a circle all the way around the trunk. There was a page about duck slaughtering, a page of notes on knife sharpening. Drawings of edible mushroom varieties, with notes about each one. Look for morels in the creek beds, near clusters of mayapples. Oyster mushrooms smell like anise, can be found along aspen logs. A page about acorn gathering: Two fifty-five-gallon barrels should get a family of four through the winter, but just barely. For higher calorie count, gather the acorns from the ground so that you get the ones with grubs in them. Kindling: Preferably poplar or ash, never elm, never red oak. Firewood: Remember that the old-timers brought in wood two years ahead of when they planned to burn it. There was a recipe for pickling nasturtium seed, a diagram of an effective drainage ditch, rocks and pebbles lined up according to size. Helen had done it all on lined notebook paper in a tidy cursive hand.

"Useful," I admitted, but Karen tapped her foot, annoyed.

I kept turning pages, and the Best Practices Binder began to change. How to Press the Coffee: Fill to brim, wait three minutes, press slowly so that any coffee that spills can be caught in a porcelain mug. What to Do with Bananas: Only peel one if you are ready to eat the whole thing. Butter Knife: Lick it clean so as not to attract ants. Where to Park the Truck: Use the empty oil drum and the scrap metal pile as markers. Tea:

Boil only two cups of water rather than filling the whole pot. Tea Bags: Reuse. Water: On cold nights, leave it at a drip, but so that you can see only two drops fall per minute, no more and no less. Dishes: Consider giving your dirty dish to someone who hasn't eaten yet to save time on dishwashing. Shit: More than two squares of toilet paper is excessive. Don't pee in the shit bucket. Cover shit completely with sawdust. Empty bucket when two-thirds full.

Karen got evil. "Best practices, huh?" she said. "Who is this for?"

"It's for Perley," Helen said.

"It's a present for me because it's my birthday," huffed Perley. He flopped upside down on the sofa and beamed at Helen.

"It's not your birthday," Karen said.

"It's so that he'll know how to do things the best way," said Helen. "There's so much we try to do out here, and there's no one to tell us how to do it. There are things we can't imagine about the mind-set of old-time homesteaders. They worked much harder than we do. They had no expectation of personal happiness. Things are different for modern people. We think we can have it all."

"That's such horseshit," Karen said. "You know even less than I do about these so-called old-time homesteaders. It wasn't even homesteaders who came up with that acorn shit. The homesteaders just came along, found all the acorns the Indians had stored for the winter, and stole them."

"Fascinating," Helen said, making a note of it. "Local knowledge."

"And me, I didn't grow up with anything. I left nothing for nothing," Karen said.

"In the city, no one even thinks about these things," Helen said. "There's a right way to do nearly everything. If someone had been here ready to teach me when I first got here, I'd be so much further ahead of where I am now. I'm giving Perley a head start."

"Perley can't even read yet," Karen said.

"I can read," Perley said. "I am Friend of Snake, and I can read Wolfriders," which was what he called *ElfQuest*.

"You're not really reading them yet," Karen said. "You're just looking at the pictures."

"Then read them to me," Perley said.

"Not right now," Karen said.

"You'll learn to read when you go to school someday, Perley," I said.

"Over my dead body is he going to school," Karen said. Perley wriggled to right side up, took his socks off his hands, and reached up to the shelf above the sofa. He found his comic book and lay back with it, resting his head on the sofa's arm. The black snake above him extended its tongue. Perley laughed.

"The Best Practices Binder is something all of us can use," said Helen.

"I don't need you to tell me what to do," Karen said.

"I don't want to tell people what to do," Helen said. "It's exhausting. Now that it's written down, I don't have to be so bossy. I can just refer you to the binder."

I kept reading. How to Get Rid of Black Snakes. Fill gaps. Humane traps. After that, a question mark. I looked up at Helen. "You actually think we can get rid of the black snakes?"

"I've got some ideas," she said.

Karen pushed her breath out through her teeth. "The black snakes aren't disturbing anything," she said. "They just lie there."

"It was all right when it was just one or two," Helen said. "But they're really out of hand."

"They don't even smell bad," Karen said.

"They do smell bad," Helen said.

"They do. They smell like rotten eggs," I said.

"They only smell like that when they're

scared. You should stop scaring them," Karen said. "Anyway, they're what we get for building a shitty house."

"That's not fair," Helen said. "We're perfectly comfortable."

"Okay, fine," Karen said. "We're comfortable. Cozy, homey, drafty, easy access. There's plenty to eat. Of course other animals besides us want to live here. I don't blame them."

"But where do you draw the line?" Helen asked. "We can't just let the wild descend upon us. What did we build a house for?"

"Look," Karen said, "if we plan to live on this land by sterilization and destruction, then it's going to be an uphill battle. We'll never get a moment's rest. Have you noticed how fertile this place is? Have you noticed how much other life there is besides our life? The quickest way to live here happily is to learn to adapt."

Helen met my eyes over the top of the Best Practices Binder.

Karen caught us looking at each other, and I could see she knew what day it was. It was a special day. I felt light pour in, an iron glee. It was Helen and me versus Karen.

"Fine," Karen said. "Good luck. Humane traps. Ether. Best practices." She actually laughed. "Good fucking luck."

She stuffed her wooden spoon into her coat pocket, pushed her knife into its piece of cork, and grabbed the comic book from Perley's hand.

"Give it back!" he said, swiping for it, but she raised it out of his reach. He looked at me. "Make Mama K give my Wolfriders back," he said.

"Yours?" Karen said. "Those are my books. I'm just letting you borrow them."

"Mama L!" Perley appealed to me. I gave him our special look of, It's out of my hands.

"Come on, Perley," Karen said. "First we'll muck out the duck shed, and then I'll read you Wolfriders."

"I don't want to muck out the duck shed," Perley said.

"I don't care," she said. He inched his way off the couch, still looking doubtfully at Helen and me.

"Go on," I said. "We've all got our work to do." Lip out, he followed Karen through the front door.

Before I left for work, Helen and I scooped the snakes up with shovels and put them outside, but they were back by the time I got home. Next, we patched the holes where the snakes were getting in, but there were too many holes. Still, Helen greeted us and the black snakes with a fresh and hopeful smile each morning. When Karen smirked at her over breakfast, she pretended not to notice.

Karen mostly stayed away, patching the driveway where it was rutted, stacking firewood, fetching propane in town. She tried to enlist Perley, but he drifted back to Helen and me, fascinated by our fight against the wild. He always went right for the snakes, hissing at them, or giving them a thwack to make them kink up and send up their sulfur smell.

"You've got to stop him doing that," Helen said.

"He's being friendly," I said.

"He's frightening the snakes," Helen said. "The smell is horrible."

"What can I do?" I said.

"Tell him not to hit the snakes," Helen said.

"Hitting is Perley's form of love-patting," I said.

"What is love-patting?" Helen asked. "That's just something that you made up." So I love-patted her. Like a sort of a soft slap with a caress at the end. She shrank from it.

"I don't like that pat," she said. "And

124

that's not what Perley's doing. He's trying to hit the snakes. Like how he hit Rudy. Like how he hits you when you don't give him chocolate."

"Well, maybe it means he needs chocolate," I said.

"I need chocolate," Perley said.

"But don't tell Mama K, right, Piglet?" I said, slipping him some chocolate chips.

"You can't hit snakes, Perley," Helen said. "It's dangerous."

"But aren't they harmless?" I asked.

"Not if they're provoked," Helen said. "I'd fight back if someone hit me. Wouldn't you?"

"Perley, gentle touch," I said.

"I am Friend of Snake," Perley said, swinging *ElfQuest* at the snake on the sofa.

For a long time, Helen stayed undaunted. She took notes in the Best Practices Binder. She crossed strategies off the list. She added new ones. We moved to humane traps. We found one at the feed store, a metal box to place a mouse in. We bought an extra trap to catch live mice to use as bait. "Not so humane for the mice," observed Karen, baring her wait-and-see smile. Helen bit her lip and didn't respond. The traps actually seemed to attract more snakes. It was like word got out that we were providing captive mice for free, and every black snake from miles around came to see if it was true. It was true.

Once I found Perley, in his dinosaur footie pajamas, squatting near the trap, elbows on knees, head down to peer into the slotted window. "One, two, three," he said.

"One, two, three, what?" I asked.

"One, two, three snakes in the trap," Perley said, so I got down next to him to look, and there they were, three snakes writhing together in a ball, fighting over a mouse that had long since been reduced to tail and speck of innard. "Three snakes," said Perley. "Zero mouse." That was how he learned to count.

In their trap, we carried the snakes all the way to the bottom of the driveway. We carried them across the creek and released them. We tried to get them hopelessly lost. But theirs was a tale of courage and bravery, a tale of homecoming. They always found their way back to us.

Karen's final victory came one morning when I woke up to Perley laughing softly next to me in bed. He lay on his side spooned into me, his back to my belly. He was playing with something against the wall, something I couldn't see.

"Good morning, my Piglet, what have you got there?" I asked.

"My snake came home," Perley said, and raised his arm to show me. A black snake coiled twice around his arm. I went for it, swiped that snake down Perley's arm like taking off a bracelet, then swung my baby out of bed and onto the floor, falling headlong over Karen. She woke up.

"What the fuck, you're crushing me," she said. Perley and I knelt on the floor beside the bed. Sulfur engulfed us. The snake fled to the far corner of the mattress, stiffened into crimps. Karen sat up.

"It was in the bed with us," I said.

"What was?" she asked.

"The snake," I said, pointing. The snake, as if ashamed, seethed down into the crack between the bed and the wall.

"Perley, did you bring that snake into the bed?" asked Karen.

"When I woke up my snake was next to me," Perley said. "Mama L said gentle touch."

Karen grinned at me. "I thought you and Helen got rid of the black snakes," she said. "Don't tell me the humane traps haven't worked."

"What are we going to do?" I asked. I ignored her satisfaction.

"Snakey's cold," Perley said. "He wants to go under the covers."

"Perley, snakes don't belong in our bed," I said.

"Actually, Perley, you're exactly right," Karen said. "The snake doesn't make its own body heat. It's cold-blooded, so it wants to get near us, into our clothes and even into our beds, to keep warm. It's natural. And it's not going to hurt you."

We climbed down the ladder to breakfast, and Karen took such pleasure in telling Helen about the snake in the bed that I felt sorry for Helen and her feverish can-do attitude. "What did I tell you? This is a habitat," Karen said.

"Our habitat. Not the snake's habitat," Helen said.

"I think what we've learned," Karen said, "is that our habitat and the snake's habitat look very much alike."

"Do you have any new ideas, Helen?" I asked. Karen laughed.

"This isn't over," Helen said. "I just have to think about it."

Who doesn't love a common enemy? The snake in the bed should have made us pull together. The snake in the bed should have forced us to make common cause. But the snake in the bed didn't. We were pushed over the edge, all right, but not into action. Instead, the snake in the bed divided us into defiance, avoidance, competition. Of course, those words are just ideas. And ideas are nothing against an actual black snake in an actual bed.

Helen didn't exactly admit defeat. But she picked up more tree jobs with Rudy and was gone most days. When she was home, she paid less attention to the snakes, and she tanned hides, planted ginseng deep in the woods, sprinkled diatomaceous earth on the pantry shelves to keep the ants away, pressure-canned venison. She stored the Best Practices Binder on the shelf near the stove. "Easy," Helen said. "Right there for whenever you need a quick tip."

"Thanks," I said. But I didn't use it. Helen added to it every day, watched us to see if we were watching her. I looked away. Karen never opened the binder, not once.

The snake in the bed stayed. Night after night, it stretched itself along the headboard or cascaded down into the comforter. It slept near our bellies, where our cores glowed hot. The snake preferred the bed, so I moved Perley to a camping mat on the floor, tucking him in with one of Rudy's smelly T-shirts, which he'd delivered freshly dirty each week since Perley was a baby.

"I miss Snakey," Perley said.

"This is just until we figure out how to get the snake out of the bed," I said.

"But where will Snakey sleep?" Perley asked. "He'll be cold."

Karen smiled.

On the floor, I nursed Perley and sang him his shipwreck lullaby until his head fell back off my nipple, milk pooling into Rudy's shirt. Then I turned to Karen.

"Perley's not one of your projects," I whispered. Through the thin partition, we could hear Helen turn over in bed.

"Project?" said Karen. "You're the one who got all worked up over that orangutan thing, and we're still stuck with Rudy's shirts."

"That's just a precaution," I said. "But you're too hard on him. He's not one of your elves with some kind of snake magic. He's a kid. You don't even let him play."

"Is that where he learned the word play?" Karen asked. "From you? I was wondering where he learned that concept."

"Don't force him to be perfect," I said, abandoning the whisper.

"But he already is perfect," Karen said. "It's my duty to see that he doesn't shrink down to averageness the way the rest of us have."

130

"Maybe you should go back to work, too," I said. "We could use the money."

"Who would stay with Perley?" Karen asked.

"When's the last time you talked to anyone at the clinic?" I asked.

"It won't be hard for me to pick up shifts when I'm ready," Karen said. "They're always shorthanded. Don't worry." But she wouldn't look at me.

"I just want you to have something else to focus on," I said. "I want you to have fun. And I want Perley to have fun, too."

"Fun. What is fun?" Karen asked. I waited, then tried to laugh.

"I'm not joking," Karen said. "What's fun? Fun is the last thing on my list. Fun can suck it."

"We used to have fun," I said. "What about when we met? Remember the sumac tree?"

"That wasn't fun," Karen said. "That was something else."

I got that itchy feeling in my ears, my nose was warm, the tears spilled over, but Karen wouldn't relent.

"This isn't a game," she said. "We've got important things to prepare for. We have a chance out here. We have a chance to make sure Perley gets the proper training. We aren't going to be around forever to protect him. You think things are going to last the way they are? Not likely." We heard Helen sit up. Then, under the gap at the bottom of the partition, her light came on. I tried to stifle my sobs with the pillow.

"You want my opinion?" Helen asked, sounding as if she were there in the bed with us.

"No," Karen said.

"Lily overindulges, and you overtrain," she said. "What the kid needs is to be ignored. Just leave him alone and let him figure things out for himself."

"I don't overindulge," I said.

"Oh please," Helen said. "You won't even tell him not to hit people. You reward him when he pinches you. You've been giving him chocolate chips on the sly, not that it's any of my business."

"Childless people always think that the secret to parenting is to leave your children alone," Karen said to the partition.

"It's worth trying," Helen said. "He loves it when I do it."

"You're dreaming," Karen said.

Perley had a name for Helen: Mean Aunt. It was true what she said. She mostly ignored Perley and he loved it. He followed her around all day. When she'd go into the woods to collect wild foods, he'd hurry along with his rolling baby walk, trying desperately to keep up. But she'd disappear up the goat path to the ridge. Perley was soon swallowed by sedges and sassafras saplings, unable to see his way back to camp. Karen trailed behind, hoping he'd turn to her. Instead, Perley waited for Helen, making a game of hitting a tree with a stick to pass the time. If Karen approached him with a tool she'd carved so that the two of them could practice what she called a skill-based activity, Perley would wave his stick at her until she left him alone. When Helen came back down the goat path, her bucket full of whatever she'd harvested, she never greeted Perley, but he would screech with joy, abandon his game, and follow her back to camp. When I first heard Perley call Helen Mean Aunt, I felt a lurch of hope on Karen's behalf. But no. He said it as if he and Helen had an understanding, an inside joke. It was a title of pure affection.

"Mean Aunt," he'd say, hugging her around the ankles as she processed acorns, his eyes tenderly closed.

"Let go of me," she'd say. "I'm busy. Go hug your mom."

"Come over here," Karen would say.

"Come to me, Perley." But he wouldn't.

It's what Karen had wished for. Because it wasn't that Perley didn't like Karen. It was worse than that. Perley loved her. Perley knew that she would always be there, and so she wasn't there, except as part of the patient landscape. Oh, I could see it caused her pain.

I could never stay angry, not even about the snakes. "Don't worry," I whispered to Karen, as the light on the other side of the partition went dark. "Helen doesn't know what she's talking about." I climbed into bed. I couldn't sleep with a snake, but I also couldn't sleep without Karen. She was still my person, my warm one, my buddy, my pack, the woman with the sumac smeared on her thighs. Despite everything, I still wanted her to think that I was game, that I was up for this, the life we were making together from scratch, the life that other people might not understand. But fuck other people. It was each other we wanted. Us and our Perley and our preparations.

I lay on my back on the bed, hearing Karen breathe on one side of me and, on the other side of me, the breath of the snake. The breath of a snake is canceled sound. It's silence. It's the whine of the demon whose bone you've stolen. The demon who wheedles to come in. I lay awake and listened. I would swear that my eyes never closed. But I must have dropped off, because each morning I woke with Perley in my arms. He'd climbed back into bed with Karen and me sometime during the long fraught night.

PART II
WOLF TREE

5

Perley

The snake has strong beliefs. The snake has strong beliefs about territory my Mama K said when the snake began to sleep with us in our bed. We tried to ignore him, at least I think it was a him. He wasn't the biting kind, but he had a piss flinty smell which was hard for Mama L to sleep through. The snake considers our home to be its home. Who will say whose home it is? It's the same with the wasps. We let them nest up there in the rafters they are a bunch of grapes. They sometimes lose their grip and drop onto the sofa like anyone would. They sting you if you sit on them like anyone would. Who will say that this is their fault? What would you do if you were a wasp?

Most of the people I know are women except for the snake and me, we are boys. A small boy, Mama K said, he's small for his age so we can get rid of Rudy's friggin

139

shirts. Which we didn't. When my age was five I stopped nursing. When my age was six I climbed the tree and shook the acorns down onto the blue tarp. When my age was seven the yellow bus rumbled by on the road each day, passed right by the bottom of our driveway, but I didn't get on it. The thing about me that isn't like other kids at the IGA or the gas station or down along the road is that I am the only male in the vicinity and I have an extra mom. And I have a Mean Aunt who isn't fun or anything my Mama K says she's bitchy and she knows everything. They aren't like a lot of people but they are mine. My women are always working and I am always working.

This is what we do, me and my women. We hunt in the woods. We gather plants. We fry grubs in a skillet. We roll the dice. We know how to fight. We drill our reflexes. We practice lying down on the ground and then getting up really fast. We practice throwing spears and shooting arrows into bales of straw. Sometimes we get really hungry and then we make a big stew that is dark green and then we get our bellies full of iron my Mean Aunt says. When it is time to kill the ducks, we kill them and eat them, even the extremely cute one named Brownie Starlight. I named him that. We don't cry.

In the evenings in the summer and also when it rains and also when it snows I build a fire that my Mama K showed me how to build log-cabin-style, little stuff then medium stuff then big stuff then the bow drill. I blow on it so the Smoke Witch dies and the Fire Fairy comes out, and then we sit with our stew and Mama K asks for my report and then she whittles with her sheep-killing knife and I demonstrate everything I know how to do: bowline, klemheist, one-handed push-up, pickle a bean, cure a potato, process a hickory nut, four-strand braid.

A wizard chiseled from the very stone holding a crystal ball that is for sale at the gas station is what I'm not allowed to have. Also cereal from the IGA. Also anything from the mall on the way to the feed store. Also TV, sugar, and a dirt bike like the kids along the road. What I am allowed to have is lip gloss that came in the mail for the Mean Aunt that looks like you're supposed to eat it but don't eat it. What I am allowed to have is as many blackberries as I can pick, venison jerky, *ElfQuest,* and chocolate-chip pancakes secretly. What I am allowed to have is as many pet snakes as I want. That is what Mama L says even though I know she doesn't like the snakes. She says that because she doesn't want me to be afraid, but why would I be afraid? Mama K says the snakes aren't pets, they are wild. She says they are wild and I am wild. What does it mean to be wild? I asked, and she said, It means that you can make yourself invisible. When you are in the woods, no one can see you.

That's true. For example the mowed head kid along the road. I hid behind a sycamore and watched him catch the yellow bus and I knew the bus was going to school because the Mean Aunt told me. Were we alike or not alike? Was he real or was I real? We both had like a ton of freckles and winter-grass kind of hair I mean yellowish nothing color but mine kept falling into my eyes and someone had driven over his head with a tractor. The Mean Aunt saw me behind the sycamore and said, Don't worry about that kid, Perley. Trust me, Perley, you are the lucky one. But what's the point of being the lucky one if all those other unlucky kids along the road have each other and you have no one and are skinny and small and can't even have a chiseled wizard? The mowed head way looked pretty good. The mowed head way was to eat Twinkies and black cherry soda pop and to ride on a dirt bike which Mama L said was too dangerous. The mowed head way was to eat at the DQ on the road into town if there was a four-piece special, and then sit outside in the back of his uncle's truck. And if there was a wasps' nest in the mowed head house his dad sprayed it with WD-40 and he had a dad. Also he didn't use a bow drill but poured gasoline onto his campfire. That's toxic, said Mama K when I suggested it. Do you want to be toxic? she asked me, even though the answer was obviously hell yes. His dad burned a tire which turned all kinds of colors and his uncle was there with fireworks and his family would, it's hard to say, just mix more. Like with other people. They knew good songs with music you could move your body to. I thought I could be like that. I watched every day from the woods, skillfully like a Wolfrider with ultimate stealth, but the mowed head kid didn't see me and the mowed head kid didn't invite me over. If someone doesn't invite you over how do you get to go over? You have to go live with them. Or you have to go to school.

So I said, I want to go to school.

Mama K said, Christ, who put that into his head, Lily, was it you? And Mama L said, School, my Piglet? Of course you can go to school if that's what you really want,

143

but you missed kindergarten. I don't care I want to go to school with the other kids, I said, and the Mean Aunt said, I'm sure he could test into first grade no problem, and Mama K said, He's not going to school conversation over. And I said, Yes, I am too going to school. I'm going to go down there and get on that bus tomorrow and go where it takes me. And Mama K said, Oh, you are, are you? And Mama L said, My Perley, are you sure? And Mama K said, You know what they have at school? Useless bullshit brainwashing is what, and the Mean Aunt said, You know what they have at school? Other kids is what. Mama K said, You stay out of this you aren't his parent, and the Mean Aunt said, It's actually really problematic not to let Perley go to school. You see how he watches the neighbor kids, he hides behind the trees and spies on them it's not healthy, and Mama L said, Perley, you should go play with those kids, you don't have to go to school to do that, just go say hello, I'm sure they'll love you as much as I do. Mama K said, Who cares about other kids? There's more important things. I care about other kids, I said. I want to mix more. Mix more? said Mama L. Come here and give a cuddle and a nose kiss, and I said, No, and hid behind the sofa with the black snake who looked at me with silver eyes and who sent me this message, Stay true, Perley, stay true. The Mean Aunt said, What's going to happen is that he's going to be fixated on school the more you won't let him go there. You should probably just let him go to school and get it out of his system. And Mama L said, I think that if Perley really wants to go to school it should be his decision. Mama K said, Of course you do, Lily. You always think that Perley should get whatever he wants. But he's not going to school.

Mama L went down to enroll me and she stopped at the gas station on the way home to buy me school supplies which were a notebook and a pack of pencils but not the chiseled wizard even though I begged. Maybe for your birthday, Mike said. Maybe, Mama L said.

Then it was the first day, and I opened my eyes and looked through the crack in the wall to the light out in the woods, and I felt the snake at my belly uncoil. I sat up and the snake slid down into the wall. During breakfast Mama L cried, My Velvet Piglet, and Mama K sharpened my pencils with her whittling knife and she said, Oh, now you're crying, Lily? Well, just remember

I didn't think he should go in the first place, and I said, Mama K? and she said, What, Perley? What is it now? And I knelt down as Strongbow would and I said, Don't worry, I am prepared. You have trained me well. I will honor your training. I will return this evening and I will be ready to give you my report. She said, Get up. Let's just hope your report is that you don't want to go back to that horrible place, and she gave me my pencils. The Mean Aunt looked at the clock and said, If he's going, he'd better go, and Mama K said, I can't believe any son of mine wants, actually wants, to go to school, and Mama L lay on the sofa and wiped her eyes and the Mean Aunt took me by the hand and led me down to the bus stop so I wouldn't miss the bus.

In my lunch box there was a jar of pemmican packed in tallow and there was a jar of milk and there was a can of sardines with the tab I could pull and Mama L had put a square of chocolate in there, too, even though Mama K didn't know. The Mean Aunt marched me down the hill and pulled out some yarrow as she passed it. She chewed it furiously and gave me a fistful. Chew on this it has superpower, she said. It will shoot juice into your brain that will make you so brave. It's like she didn't even

146

notice that I was already brave. I was going to school which is where the other kids were. So I pulled my hand out of the Mean Aunt's hand just as we got to the roadside where the mowed head kid stood waiting for the bus. His eyes were crusty and he was eating something from a piece of cellophane with a cool animal on it in sunglasses. He looked at me real quick but then he looked away again and the yellow bus pulled up so that the sun went dark and I didn't wave goodbye to the Mean Aunt. I threw back my shoulders and I walked to the door of the bus and then I turned to the Mean Aunt, and I put my fist to my heart the way that a Wolfrider would, a noble salute of undying gratitude and respect.

On the bus everyone was laughing, and I loved laughing. It was one of my favorite things to do so I started laughing, too, except then I thought maybe we weren't laughing at the same thing exactly because the bus was full of kids, which was toxically cool, but they were all making the same sort of salute I had made to the Mean Aunt, the noble salute I gave so that the Mean Aunt would tell Mama K that I was steadfast and resolute. No one had ever laughed when I did the salute before. But when I saw all the kids on the bus doing the salute, I knew that it was funny. In fact, it was the funniest thing anyone had ever done and I was the one who did it.

I sat down next to the mowed head kid and the girl in the seat behind us put her fist on her heart and said, Hey, Bexley, aren't you going to say hi to your new friend? So then I knew the mowed head's name so I said, Hello, Bexley, I am Perley. We could be new friends.

Could be but ain't, he said. I've seen you.

I've seen you, too, I said.

Shut up, he said. You wouldn't hide like that behind the sycamores with your mouth hanging open unless you were touched, is what my uncle said.

I am an elfin spy with optimum fighting skills, I said. Part wolf. Maybe you are, too.

You're touched, he said. Or you're a baby. That's how come you need a grown-up to take you to the bus. He pointed out the window at the Mean Aunt, who stood scowling at the bus as it pulled away but that was just her face. Is that your mom or is that your dad I can't tell, said Bexley. The girl behind us laughed so I was helpful and said, Actually I don't have a dad that's my aunt.

You know what that makes you? said the girl. That makes you a bastard.

I don't think so, I said.

Yes, it sure does, said Bexley.

I have two moms and one mean aunt, I said.

Two moms? the girl asked, and I said, Yeah, Mama L and Mama K.

That makes you a faggot bastard, Bexley said. And I didn't know what either of those things meant because they weren't in *Elf-Quest,* and they weren't in *The Encyclopedia of Organic Gardening* by J. I. Rodale and Staff, 1970 edition, and my women had never mentioned them to me. I didn't know what they meant, but I knew I would have to remain extremely vigilant at school to find out.

It's a good thing I was prepared. It's a good thing I was ready for anything. It's a good thing I remained steadfast and resolute. Because even after the bus stopped and I went into my classroom things didn't turn out the way I had imagined them. I was highly skilled, my training was top-notch, and I thought that would make the other kids like me, but I didn't get a chance to show them how prepared I was or how much I had practiced.

When do I get a chance to make my report? I asked the teacher, who was a grown woman like a box of tissue at the IGA, that beautiful. I almost touched her, but I remembered Mama K had said, Don't touch anything, Perley, just don't. So I held my hands to my sides, and the teacher said, Your report? And I said, When do we show our skills? And she said, Right now is the time to show your skill on the tablet. Which is one thing I knew about because the elves had tablets, too, they were made out of stone. The teacher said, Class, it's time for Specials and from now on we are going to do our Specials on our tablets. It's an initiative, it's an initiative that each Appalachian child gets a tablet. Carved from the very stone, I said. No, you faggot bastard, said Bexley, but really quiet so the teacher didn't hear. She passed around books that weren't books and each and everyone else got started but I just waited for the tablet. Perley, you've got to turn on the tablet so that you can do your Specials, she said. Oh yes, I said, and that's how I knew that the book was a tablet not an elf tablet a school tablet it was made of plastic. It was like what my women had but bigger, a phone with a screen that they had to walk up to the top of the ridge to get reception, and they wouldn't let me touch it because they said it would rot my ear.

I love tablets, I said. That's good, Perley, said the teacher. Plastic is my favorite material, I said. So you should turn it on and get started, she said. That's okay, I just love to hold it, I said. But you've got to do the work, Perley, she said. You've got to do your Specials. I just stroked the tablet like it was a baby wolf and she said, Perley, the other children are getting started, what is the trouble? Nothing, I said. Fucking hillbilly, said Bexley, but still so quiet it was almost like he was sending to me with his mind like an elf would even though I was beginning to realize that there was no way Bexley could be an elf, or at least not a valiant one, definitely not a Wolfrider.

The teacher leaned down and pressed a button on the back of my tablet and the screen glowed up at me like opening a magic vault. There, she said. Thank you, I said. I love this. I love this tablet. Good, she said. I'll let you get started. She left me alone. I looked at the tablet. But I didn't know what I was seeing because I was a total fucking hillbilly. All the other kids were quiet, staring into the light and using highly skilled finger actions, but when I looked at mine, all the light from the vault went so fast that I didn't know where to look, and I didn't know where to put my hands. I knew how to read but it's like I forgot I knew how to read. So even though I loved the tablet, and even though plastic was my favorite material, I took a break and looked out the window for a minute. Just to check if I was missing anything out there, and I soon saw Leetah and Cutter through the oaks at the edge of the playground and they were riding on Nightrunner, the noble old wolf. Nearby were their children, Suntop and Ember, tumbling around with Choplicker, who was still only a pup. They were calling to me and I had to go. Also my leg had a cramp it felt like it was flexing itself. I'd never been inside for so long unless it was a total friggin blizzard. I stood up. Perley, what is it? asked the teacher. I knew that she wouldn't understand. She wouldn't understand that whenever I saw the wolves with their elfin riders I had to drop whatever it was I was doing and see how close I could get to them before they disappeared. I had to get close to them because one day they might carry me off and there was no way that I was going to miss that. I have to go to the bathroom, I said. It was my first lie. At home I told the truth and then watched my women fight it out. But I could tell school was different. Optimum strategy was called for, like when the elves match wits with the trolls. It didn't matter if I lied or not. What mattered is if I made it through. So the teacher gave me a hall pass which said hall pass and was a laminated piece of construction paper with some yarn on it.

I took the hall pass and I didn't go to the bathroom I went out to the playground but by the time I made it outside Cutter and Leetah were gone, and the wolves were gone, so I undid my pants and peed in a bush. Then I looked up at the school and Bexley was looking back at me through the open window and then the nice teacher's head appeared above his mowed head and then she came outside and took me by the arm to the principal's office.

Perley, said the principal. Sir, I said. You've just joined us, he said. Yes, sir, I said. This is your first day, he said. Yes, sir, I said. Don't call me sir, he said. Call me Mr. Anderson. Yes, sir, I said. He won't focus, said my nice teacher. He can't focus on the tablet. We're doing Specials and he won't do it. He went outside without permission. Think of the trouble I could get in. Also another child said he peed in the bushes not that I encourage tattletales. The principal was a good man I mean he was a good big man I mean his belly was big he was like a balloon with the nicest wig on top. The teacher said, I

153

have twenty-five other kids to look after, and he said, Go, Ms. Carroll, go on I'll take it from here. When she left he smiled sadly at me and I smiled sadly back at him and I had never smiled sadly before, not like that, and it felt good, almost as good as being an animal wearing sunglasses on some cellophane. Perley, the principal said, we can't have kids wander away what if you were hit by a car or a stranger kidnapped you, think what would happen to us here at this school think about it we are responsible for you. I thought about it. I smiled sadly. You have to focus, he said. You have to do what the teacher says. Don't you want to do your Specials? I said, Yes, sir, of course, sir. And he said, Why did you go outside without permission? And I said, My body did it my body went outside without permission, and he said, That is unacceptable, and I said, Yes, sir. And he said, Did you pee in the bushes you can tell me. And I said, The Best Practices Binder says, Don't pee in the bucket. Pee on a tree but instead I peed on a bush. I waited for the principal's sad smile to turn to a sad smile of understanding, but it didn't. Instead he asked, Don't you have a toilet at home, Perley? And I waited ten seconds. I waited exactly ten seconds I know because I counted and I looked out the window behind the principal and I saw that Nightrunner the wolf had come back and was winking his green eyes at me from behind the oak tree. I wanted to make the principal happy so I said, Yes, sir, you should see our toilet it has one of those automatic flushers with a flashing light, it's even more powerful than the one at the IGA. Which was my second lie.

I thought the principal was going to make me do like fifty push-ups or run laps or something where I could show my physical strength and endurance, but the principal just sighed and wrote something on a piece of paper and then he said, This is an adjustment period, Perley. You'll soon understand how things work around here. Remember our motto here is excellence.

He sent me back to my classroom but by that time Specials were over for the day and anyway no one cared about the skills I had and I could hardly even remember what they were because there was no place to try them out because we were always inside except for half an hour at recess. And later, when we opened our lunch boxes I realized that sardines were the funniest thing a person could eat. They were the funniest thing a person could eat and I was eating them and everyone was laughing.

I knew what my women would say, they'd say, Fuck Bexley, don't say fuck, and Mama K would point out all the reasons Bexley could never be a Wolfrider and was totally not noble. But they hadn't seen him mix. It was like Bexley built the school himself he was that easy inside it. He was like Winnowill, who was evil but was also beautiful and in charge. I wanted to know if Bexley's way could be my way. So I threw my hilarious lunch in the garbage and I stood against the chain-link fence and I watched. Bexley and the other kids did everything like they'd always known how to do it, like they'd known how to do it even when they didn't exist yet, even when they were just an energetic force in the universe which is what Mama L said I was before I was born. Even then, they were an energetic force that knew all about tablets and Specials and kickball and shoes that flickered and animals wearing sunglasses, and they had bubble gum instead of yarrow and they knew what was funny and what wasn't funny and they knew why.

And I saw that even though it seemed like all the other kids were one way and I was the other way, actually there were some other kids that were also the other way. For example, there was this one kid, a chubby kid, he was in the second grade, but the other second-graders avoided him, and this kid had round glasses and brown skin and curly hair that floated around his head, like only a few of the other kids at school did, like what the Mean Aunt said about Mike at the gas station, He is an oppressed minority, and Mama K said, Why don't you say that to his face? and Mama L said, Love sees no color, and the Mean Aunt and Mama K laughed meanly at her. But what I really noticed about this kid is that he wore red rubber rain boots even though it was definitely not raining and this kid collected acorns.

I watched him skirt the perimeter of the playground. He walked beneath the oak trees at the edge of the wood chips and he picked up a few acorns at a time and he put them in a pouch he made by tying the front of his T-shirt in a knot. No one else looked at him they just barreled past him screaming and throwing the kickball onto the roof of the school. No one else looked at him but I looked at him and then I followed him.

He took his acorns around the corner of the school building, behind the blue dumpster where there was an oak tree whose roots were tearing up the pavement. He checked to see if anyone was watching, so I hid behind the dumpster and he knelt down by the tree and then I saw that he had dug out under one of the roots and untied his T-shirt so that the acorns fell into the cave he had made there and he must have had hundreds stored away. I wanted to help him so bad so I sent to him with my mind like an elf or like a wolf but he didn't hear me so I stepped out from behind the dumpster and I said, We could do that together I am pretty good at collecting acorns I actually do it pretty much all the time with my Mean Aunt, but he said, Back off I have all the help I need, which was weird because he didn't have any help he was doing it all by himself. Which I told him and I said the Mean Aunt is toxic at acorns and I am toxic at acorns. Actually I'm part wolf. He said, Back off faggot bastard.

I backed off. But my motto was excellence. I stayed resolute and steadfast and I played a game with myself where I was his wolf acorn guard. I stood against the chain-link fence and made sure that no other faggot bastards tried to help him. And none did.

At home, when they asked me, I just said it was good. It's an adjustment period, but it's good, I said. Mama K said, Oh really, they

158

just have you sit there in a chair all day, getting all atrophied, and getting diabetes and becoming unskilled and saying the Pledge of Allegiance like a little robot and they make you call them sir, and Mama L said, Piglet, if you don't like it you don't have to do it, you don't have to do anything you don't want to do, Mama K can be your teacher or you can come to the hardware and salvage store with me and I can be your teacher or Helen can be your teacher, and the Mean Aunt said, I don't want to be his teacher, it's good for him to be at school it will help socialize him, and Mama K said, Oh, like how it helped socialize you? All those teachers care about is obedience, and I was like, No way, I love my teacher and I love the principal and I am making a lot of friends my own age. Which made them all shut up probably because they didn't have friends their own age and they were jealous. School is the best, I said. I love school.

What I loved was not having every single person know every single thing. What I loved was keeping a few things for myself. My home was the Holt the forest grove where the elves lived where Mama K was a tree-shaper like Redlance except with a knife, and no one at school knew what happened there. No one at school, not the teacher or the principal or mowed head Bexley or even the acorn kid, no one knew I could send to the elves with my mind and no one knew I was a wolf pup sometimes or how quick my reflexes were and no one knew I was Friend of Snake.

And just the same, no one at home knew what happened at school. Mama K didn't know and Mama L didn't know and the Mean Aunt didn't know. They thought they knew but they didn't. And nothing happened at school. Nothing except that I began to see what the problem was. The problem was that I had practiced and prepared for the wrong things. I was totally problematic. The problem was my mamas and the problem was the Mean Aunt and the problem was the way we all lived together outside without permission, with sardines and yarrow and faggots and stone tablets, and so the problem was me.

6

Helen

When Rudy began collecting buckets, I figured it was something to do with self-improvement. Fall was the season that Rudy traditionally vowed to get his shit together. He had tried hibernating the whole winter. He had tried fasting. He had quit drinking briefly. He had tried eating a pound of raw ground beef with cayenne and honey in it twice a week. He had tried swishing coconut oil around in his mouth for thirty minutes a day. He had tried Christianity. He had even tried simply announcing, when I showed up for work in the mornings, "Look at me. I am new and improved. I'm a better man."

Now buckets rolled around in the back of his truck, more of them every day. Five-gallon mayonnaise buckets, two-gallon buckets that were stained with deep green frosting, food-grade buckets that had once held potato salad, lemon meringue pie filling, nondairy whipping cream. I worked for Rudy nearly full-time that fall, repairing trees from summer storms, preparing them for winter ones.

"Why so many buckets, Rudy?" I asked him, when I could no longer see the chain saws underneath them. We were facing a spruce that day, its split trunk showing a keyhole to the sky.

"New business idea," he said. "Whenever we go out on a tree job, pruning, removal, I don't care what it is, we offer the client some fruit trees, too." He tightened his harness, unwound his throw line. "If everyone had fruit trees growing in their yards, no one could be pushed around. We'd be like, Fuck you, we have our own fruit, so stop trying to sell us your fucking Washington State apples and shit. We'll do for ourselves."

"Sounds like permaculture," I said.

"I don't care what it sounds like," he said. "If the hippies want a tree, fine. If they want to talk to me about culture, watch me kick some hippie ass."

"So you're planting an orchard?" I said.

"A nursery," he said. "That's why the buckets, or are you an idiot?"

"Where are the trees?" I asked.

"I've been cultivating rootstock out on the coal company land," he said. "But it's too much shade. The trees need eight hours of full sun. I've got to find somewhere better. I'm thinking maybe the pipeline easement runs down the side of your place. Plenty of sun. Lots of space."

"You ever worry about it?" I asked.

"Worry about what?" he asked.

"The pipeline," I said.

"Oh sure," he said. "Sure I do. You hear about accidents sometimes. But it's like getting hit by lightning. Could happen but no use fretting about it while you wait. Anyway, the mailman told me the company's selling out," Rudy said. "Abandoning their holdings."

"Is that good news?" I asked.

"I'm just passing on what the mailman told me," Rudy said. "All I know for sure is that the pipeline's a good place for fruit trees until I get something else figured out." He swung back and pitched his line, with its yellow weighted pouch, toward the uppermost branches of the spruce. The pouch missed its mark and plummeted back down to us. Rudy backed up and tried again.

In those first years, I had turned to Karen and Lily as a respite from Rudy, but the longer I lived with them, the more my time with Rudy had become its own sort of relief.

At least with Rudy I could put my ear protection on and shut up. I could let him do the talking. At home, there was no rest. When I had something to say, I said it. I said it until I was hoarse.

I knew a snake slept in the bed with Karen, Lily, and Perley. I knew black snakes didn't bite, but still, it didn't seem quite safe. We couldn't agree long enough to get rid of it. Perley had begun school and become secretive and pale, chatting to himself and laughing at nothing, spending hours alone in the woods, yet insisting each morning on hiking down the driveway on his own to get on that school bus. Nothing could stop him. Karen and Lily were at odds over it. As usual, no one listened to me.

As usual, my wild foods were keeping us alive. I worked all day with Rudy, then came home to send Perley up into the oak trees. He'd shake the branches so that the acorns rapped my hard head. We aimed to collect at least a hundred gallons that year.

Karen and Lily, absorbed in Perley and in each other, for once didn't object, when I mentioned that Rudy might tend his trees out on the pipeline. "As long as he doesn't think he's going to live out there," Karen said.

"Of course not," I said.

"I don't care to see him sweating out his hangover at my breakfast table," Karen said.

"Don't worry," I said. "It's only temporary."

As for my Best Practices Binder, I was the only one who ever brushed aside the cobwebs and mouse shit, opened the cover, and added to it: acorns, buckets, chain saws, fruit trees.

Rudy spent a week putting in a deer fence, sinking locust posts and stringing wire. When it was finished, he moved his infant fruit trees in by the bucketful. They didn't look like much, just some sticks with felted ears poking out, but Rudy said they'd get bigger. He said that planting them in the fall was best. The roots fortified over the winter to flourish when the spring came. There were Magness and Potomac pears, Lodi, Ginger Gold, and Idared apples, North Star cherries, Fellenberg plums, Saskatoons, even two varieties of peach tree, which did not do well in our climate.

"You've got to try," said Rudy. "You never know. You mind if I sleep over tonight?"

"You can forget about that, Rudy," I said.

"I mean in my nursery," he said. "I'll sleep out. I've got my sleeping bag and a piece of waxed cardboard. Jesus. Get your mind out of the gutter."

At seven thirty the next morning I was wrenched awake by what sounded like a fifty-car pileup in the sky. That or the end of the goddamn world bearing down on us, before it faded out to nothing.

On the other side of the partition, Karen and Lily's light came on. I already had my feet on the floor, was feeling around for my rubber boots and my overalls when I heard Perley's sleep-voice croak, "It's Madcoil. He's attacking the Holt," which was from one of his comics.

"Go back to sleep, Perley," I said to the wall. "I'm going to take care of it."

"Take the .22," said Karen. I lowered it down from the rafters and slung it over my shoulder. What would I do with it, anyway? Surely not aim it at someone. Surely not shoot.

Outside, tanagers and cardinals began to call one another. There was nothing else to hear. Our hills were honeycombed and hurt beneath the surface. Light crept into the sky. There was nothing else to see. I climbed up through the garden and headed out past my old camper, now used for storage, through the woods to the pipeline easement.

Rudy stood in his nursery wild-eyed. He wore a large gold-colored chain around his neck, with an enormous pendant representing Greek drama, the twin smile and frown gleaming up at me.

"Fucking helicopter," he said. "Scared the living shit out of me. Came down almost on my head. Like I say, they're always watching."

"Who?" I asked.

"Must be the fucking pipeline company," Rudy said.

Then the roar again, the whining blast. Rudy covered his head, I let go of my rifle and clapped my hands to my ears. We dropped to our knees, gaped upward to see the helicopter beat over the ridgeline again, blazing yellow like it was bringing the sun with it. It pulsed down low over the trees only a hundred feet up, maybe less, like it planned to land on us, or drop something, bombs, propaganda, who could say? It was so close I could almost make out the company man inside with his fly eyes. The trees waved and dipped to the propeller. We cowered, our teeth clacking in our heads, and the helicopter didn't land, it didn't drop bombs or any kind of paper. It tracked the path of the pipeline, lifted up over the opposite slope, cleared the next ridge, gone, leaving the frank morning in its wake.

Rudy squinted after it. "Doing another flyover, inspection or some shit, right?" he said.

"But this early in the morning?" I asked. "I never saw them do that before."

"I told you those assholes are planning something," Rudy said. "After all these years, they're finally checking on the line."

"If they're selling out, maybe they'll leave us alone," I said.

"Maybe," Rudy said. "Maybe not. Maybe what's next will be something worse. The devil you know."

Karen and Lily were on the sofa eating reheated acorn mush for breakfast when I replaced the .22 in the rafters. Perley sat on the high stool at the kitchen counter, murmuring to himself over a comic, his bowl of mush untouched beside him.

"Well?" Lily asked.

"The pipeline company sent a helicopter out," I said.

"How do you know it was the pipeline company?" asked Karen.

"Rudy says he heard it from the mailman," I said.

"What in the hell is Rudy doing out there this early?" asked Karen.

168

"He's camping on the pipeline," I said.

"He's living out there?" asked Karen.

"He wants to be close to his fruit trees," I said.

"This is exactly what I was worried about. That man will not rest until he's eating dinner with us every night," said Karen.

"And sleeping in our beds," added Lily.

"I don't think he eats dinner," I said. "He doesn't sleep in a bed. Did we get any mail from the company recently? About plans to sell or something? Mowing?"

Karen shrugged. Lily shook her head. Perley closed his comic book and sat with his hands in his lap, gazing out the window. Karen and Lily looked at each other.

"Come on, Perley, eat your mush," Lily said. "Mush is a treat! Mush is fun!"

Perley smiled gently.

"Oh please, Lily," Karen said. "Can you quit it with that? That is such bullshit."

"He needs to eat," Lily said.

"Food is not fun," Karen said. "Food is food. Why should food be fun? Isn't it enough that we need it? That without it we would die? Does it also have to be fun?"

Perley asked, "Do we fight?" and stopped them.

"Who?" Lily asked.

"You and Mama K," Perley said. Then he

added, "And the Mean Aunt. And me."

"Do we fight?" Lily repeated, setting down her spoon.

"Bexley said his parents fought all the time and that's why his mom took off," Perley said.

"Bexley?" asked Karen.

"Bexley Epps?" asked Lily. "His dad grew up just down the road. I thought he had a boy your age. Oh, Piglet, I'm so glad that you've made a friend." Perley stabbed a finger into his acorn mush. Karen looked at him.

"Is that right? Bexley's a friend?" she asked. Perley didn't answer, just gave a laugh like someone had clapped their hand over his mouth.

Karen put down her spoon. "Perley, I asked you a question."

Perley raised his eyes to the ceiling, put his acorn mush finger into his mouth. In the bowels of the sofa, the black snake squirmed. I could hear the industrious wasps building their homes in our walls. Karen and Lily leaned forward.

"Yes," Perley said. "Yes, that's right. Bexley's my friend."

Lily leaned back, exhaled. "There, you see?" she said. But Karen frowned, rapped her spoon once and twice against her knee.

I could see that, as usual, they needed my help. "Perley's only asking if we fight because he doesn't know what a fight is," I said.

"I know what a fight is," Perley said.

"And obviously he doesn't know what a fight is because he's surrounded by fighting all the time," I said. "It's like asking a fish what water is."

Lily said, "Perley, in this family, we all have a lot of important discussions. It's not really fighting."

"Yes, it is," Karen said.

"It is," I said.

"Okay, but even if we fight," Lily said, "we're not going anywhere."

"That's the point," Karen said. "That's what family is. The people who stick around to fight with you."

"Don't worry, Perley," Lily said.

"I'm not worried," Perley said, and he sat there looking at us. Even Karen couldn't think of any more useful life lessons. Perley said, "I'm going to miss the bus." He slid off his stool, stuffed his comic book into his backpack, and left the house.

"Do Karen and me really fight that much?" Lily asked, after he'd gone.

"Not much," I said. "It's just that you're in a lifelong disagreement."

"But we're close," Lily said. "Some people aren't close."

"We're close to what?" asked Karen. They sat together on the sofa, which was covered with hair and grit like always. Karen was tall, Lily was short, Karen pale, Lily rosy, Karen long, Lily round. Karen had just turned forty-one, Lily was thirty-three. From where I sat, they looked like nothing so much as conjoined twins.

"Were you including me in that thing?" I asked Karen. "That thing about sticking around to fight together?"

"There's no room for fighting with you," Karen said. "You don't think you know everything. You know you know everything. Which is probably one reason you're alone."

"Karen," said Lily.

"It's fine, Lily," I said, keeping my voice light to hide where she'd hurt. "It's true what Karen says, I do know a lot of things. I know that partnership doesn't suit me. So what?"

"But you're not alone, Helen," Lily said, her eyes filling with tears. "You're with us."

"I'm with you and I'm alone," I said.

I wanted to help. But there's no helping some people. Why tell Lily and Karen how soundly I slept, while the two of them hissed back and forth on the other side of the partition? I certainly didn't envy them. I certainly didn't miss my boyfriend. Not anymore. You spend your life figuring how you'll reckon with death, with losing everyone that matters to you, including yourself. You partner up to get some comfort, but there's no comfort. Instead, you have someone else's naked fear to contend with as well. Some people are forgiving of that fear in their partner, and some people are forgiving of that fear in themselves. But no one is both. Karen and Lily didn't want to hear what I knew: when you're alone, you're not creating that terrible equation, one plus one.

Now that Rudy was camping on the pipeline, I had a VIP pass to his slimy teeth, crusty socks, unruly body hair, sweat-stained long underwear, crushed beer cans. I left Karen and Lily squabbling on the sofa and found Rudy chain-smoking next to his sleeping bag, bootlaces loosened. The Greek drama pendant lay on the grass next to him, smiling and frowning up at the sky. "Work's canceled," he said. "I'd rather be in the nursery today. Are you going to help?"

"Until Perley gets home from school," I said. "Then he's helping me collect acorns. We've still got another barrel to fill before winter."

"You're eating acorns again? Hard times," said Rudy.

"They actually taste good, you know. You should try them," I said.

"I know how they taste, you fucking carpetbagger," said Rudy. "My grandpa used to eat them. Good isn't how I would describe it. Just because the old-timers did it doesn't mean it's made of gold. Old-timers did lots of stupid shit, just like everybody else."

We gathered buckets, shoveled soil into them, buried exposed root networks, swamped each tree from the rain catchment Rudy had rigged off the toolshed roof.

"You mind if I ask what the hell was up with the .22 this morning?" Rudy said as he Sharpied labels and I stuck them on buckets.

"I didn't know what I'd find out here," I said.

"You know how to use it or what?" he asked.

"Yeah, I know how to use it," I said.

"Didn't, though," he said.

"What did you want me to do?" I asked. "Shoot the helicopter out of the sky?"

"Warning shot couldn't hurt," he said.

"What about you?" I asked. "If you're so into guns, why don't you have one?"

"Have one but don't feel the need to go flashing it around," he said. He peeled up the piece of waxed cardboard, which was his mattress, and displayed a twelve-gauge shotgun. "Didn't need it anyway," he said. "I had my bling for protection."

"Your bling?" I asked.

He picked up the Greek drama pendant. "Like my forefathers," he said. "Celtic warriors liked to get naked and paint themselves blue. Scared the shit out of their adversaries."

"But no one in that helicopter could even see your bling," I said.

"Did you see how low they were flying?" he asked. He fingered the shotgun thoughtfully. "When it comes to guns," he said, "you can always use practice."

So we set up Rudy's empty Natural Ice cans, and we spent the rest of the day on target practice. I had other things I needed to be doing. I had acorns to rake, rabbits to snare, roots to dig, cattails waiting in the bog, but Rudy insisted.

"Your neighbors will hear it. That's always useful," he said. He sprayed one final round of shot, sending the beer cans flying into the woods. Far below us on the road, Perley's school bus pulled up in front of our mailbox and sighed open its door, releasing

175

Perley and Bexley. I stood up and waved. "Perley! Bexley!" I called, but at the sound of my voice, Bexley took off running across the road toward the Epps place. Perley came bobbing straight up the pipeline in his hopelessly oversize T-shirt, his dorky sweatpants. Skill is one thing, style is another.

"Mean Aunt," he said when he reached the top, "are you ready to get acorns?"

"Why did Bexley run off like that?" I asked, and he let out that new laugh of his, a mirthless one-note thing.

"That kid's been a shithead to you, isn't it?" said Rudy. Perley smiled at the ground.

"Bexley's my friend," he said.

"Just say so if you want me to kick his ass for you," said Rudy.

"You will not be kicking the ass of a seven-year-old," I said.

"Bexley's eight," said Perley. "He got held back."

"It's because you don't have a dad these little rednecks think they can say what they want," said Rudy. "I told you no good could come of it. Now you see what happens."

Perley, who still slept with Rudy's dirty shirts under his head, filled his cheeks up with air.

"Fuck dads," I said. "Perley, don't say fuck." I took Perley's hand and he let me lead him away from Rudy, over the ridge and down into the coal company land, where our best oak stood. Our climbing gear, our wheelbarrows, and our tarps for collecting were stowed beneath it.

Perley didn't remember, but I remembered that first year, when we hadn't gathered enough acorns. I remembered the second year, when we only gathered acorns from up in the trees, because the ones already on the ground were sure to have worms. I remembered those years when we rolled the dice and were hungry, and that memory drove me. Now, of course, we went for windfall first, prizing the stowaway grubs, their burst of protein. As a three-year-old, Perley had run behind me picking up the fallen acorns, his first real chore. He separated each nut from smartweed, oak leaves, moss, and coltsfoot, sorting them into the leeching sacks. At first I pretended not to notice him, but soon I couldn't deny that we were teammates. When Perley was six, I fitted him with a harness and sent him up into the trees to shake the branches. Lily brought in sweet potatoes and squash, planted garlic and coaxed along the winter greens, but Karen hovered around Perley and me, looking for a way in. Eventually she had to concede. Now that he was seven, it was understood that acorn gathering was for Perley and for me.

That fall, we'd already filled one barrel, fifty-five gallons, and we were working on the next. Harnessed in, Perley scrambled out onto a branch and shook hard, while I raked up the nuts below. I gathered up the tarp and unfurled it, letting the acorns beat into the wheelbarrow. Perley lay on his belly on the branch, peering down at me through the leaves. I knew he had more to say, but I knew my job was to act like it was the last thing on my mind. After I had spread the tarp out again, he said, "Mean Aunt, does it bother you that you look like that?"

"What do I look like?" I asked, looking up at him.

"A man with a mean face," said Perley. It had been some time, maybe years, since I thought about the way I looked. I felt best in rubber boots and a flannel shirt, a big canvas jacket over the top. I cut my hair with the kitchen shears, taking it short in the front to keep it out of the way, tucking the rest under a woolen watch cap. In the shadowy sliver of mirror above the sink I saw the way the weather had beaten me about the face and neck, I saw the wrinkles pressing in. I was thirty-nine that year. It made sense to me.

"Perley, name the men you know, and then tell me which of them I look like," I said.

"We don't know any men," he said. "That's part of the problem."

"We do know men. We know plenty of men. They just don't live with us. And I don't look like a man, I look like a rope," I said. "Or a reliable piece of leather. A good tarp. A well-tanned hide. A wheel with all its spokes."

"You're not listening to me," he said. "It's that orangutan thing you used to talk about when I was little. Everyone can see that I have a flange."

"Everyone at school?" I asked.

"Yes," he said.

"So now you've seen what school is like, maybe you don't belong there after all," I said.

"I do belong there," he said.

"But if the other kids are giving you a hard time," I said.

"They aren't giving me a hard time," he said.

"Perley," I said. "You're not an orangutan. That's not what we meant by flange."

"What's a faggot?" Perley asked.

"It's a bundle of sticks," I said.

179

"What's a bastard?" he asked.

"It's what you say when you stub your toe," I said. "If you're rude."

Perley reached out and shook a branch to make a drumroll of acorns against the wheelbarrow, the tarp, the rake, my boots, my skull, the forest floor. I knew a lot. I knew I was helpful. I knew I was an interrupter. I knew I could have talked to Perley more about what those words meant, why they might be used against him. But I also knew Perley hardly preferred me anymore. And I knew that sometimes I was the only one who could just let him be.

The principal lived in the middle of town. He lived directly across the street from his school. His house was a big old Victorian, newly painted. It reminded me of my aunt's house, the kind of place I rejected when I left the coast. The most recent letter I received from her, she was holding on to it, but barely. In the principal's side yard, a massive tulip poplar was ready to drop a limb right on the flash-new roofing job. I sorted gear in the driveway, untangled the bull rope, filled the saws with gas and oil. Rudy unloaded two Ginger Gold apple trees from the back of the truck.

"How much are we going to charge for

them?" I asked. Rudy looked at me like I was scum.

"No charge," he said. "We just give them away. Selling fruit trees is immoral."

"I thought you said it was a business idea," I said.

"It's my life path," he said. "Anyway, you get paid the same either way, so what do you care?"

Rudy climbed, I worked the Port-a-Wrap, we lowered the dead limb to the ground and bucked it up. It took three hours all told. When we were done, the principal brought us each a watery beer, not the kind of watery we liked, not Natural Ice. It was Michelob Ultra he brought us. He set the bottles down on the back step, and he carefully closed the door behind his back to make it clear that we weren't to go inside. Rudy asked him if he'd like a couple of apple trees.

"No," the principal said.

Rudy dug into his ear and pulled out the wax. "Say again," he said.

"No, thanks," the principal said. "All I wanted was that poplar trimmed. I don't have room for an apple tree, let alone two or three. Where would I put them?"

"Just about anywhere," said Rudy. "Take up some of your fucking lawn. When I see a lawn I just about want to shoot myself in the fucking head." The principal laughed, but not very hard.

"I don't know why you think that's funny," Rudy said. He stuck his ponytail in his mouth.

"You do good tree work, Rudy Gibbs. Let's just leave it at that," the principal said. He held out a check, and Rudy accepted it, and we climbed in the truck to leave, but not before it hit me. That laugh. Gentle, sad, sinister. It was what I had heard welling up from Perley's young voice box for the past two months, and it turned that warm day cold.

Four tree jobs that week, and no one wanted apple trees. No one wanted pear trees. No one wanted peach trees, plum trees, Saskatoons, or even cherries. Not Ginger Gold, not Lodi, not Potomac, not Idared, not Fellenberg, not Dwarf Meteor, not Dwarf North Star, not Red Haven. None of Rudy's clients wanted fruit trees. Not one.

I thought this would enrage Rudy, but instead I had never seen him so innocent, so unprotected. "Why?" he asked, sitting in the truck at the end of a hard day. I recited some of the standard answers. "Too much maintenance. No room. Doesn't go with their landscaping plan. Don't eat fruit." Rudy lowered his head gently onto the steering wheel.

"Drink some water," I suggested.

"Fuck you," he said, but mildly. He was thinking.

On Friday morning, he met me at the bottom of the driveway. The back of his truck was empty of buckets, but his ponytail was brushed and his cheeks shone above his beard. He wore his bling. "Two problems I can see with our new business," he said.

"What are they?" I asked.

"One, none of these fucking idiots knows that fruit tree stewardship is what's standing between them and a deeper understanding of what it means to be human."

"Two?" I asked.

"Two is volume and efficiency. We just aren't hitting enough people. You know cartoons where one character is hungry and the other character turns into a giant hamburger? That's how I feel about people's yards and fruit trees right now."

"I'm not sure I follow," I said.

"I've done some figuring," he said. "We do between one and four tree jobs a week. Sometimes we have whole weeks off when we don't have any work."

"And that's the way we like it," I said.

"But it's inefficient," he said. "If we were quick, we could be planting between eight and ten fruit trees a night."

"Rudy, I sleep at night," I said.

"We ought to be working at night," he said. "We could be getting a lot more trees in the ground. It's bad business not to."

Between Karen, Lily, Rudy, and me there was a magnetism. We women pulled away, and Rudy pushed closer. We were in orbit. Once you save someone's life you are bound to that person, or I have heard that. Karen had breathed life back into him, had nursed him back to health, Lily had drawn the curtain so he could stay on the Land Trust overnight, I'd been the one person who put up with working for him all these years, who listened to his side of the story. Each winter Rudy's plans for self-improvement failed. He hibernated for months, stayed drunk, and crawled inside himself. Each winter we were the only ones who knew whether or not he had frozen to death or, worse, flipped the coin and decided against the world. Rudy had chosen us as the only people he relied on or cared to know. I'm not saying that's friendship. I'm saying that in late October, I became an illicit fruit tree planter, stealing out at night with Rudy to shove saplings down into the soft sod of people's front yards while they slept.

Like anything, illicit fruit tree planting has its best practices. I duly noted it all down. Our shit pile from two years ago had lost its sewage smell and was growing a healthy colony of mushrooms. Rudy and I shoveled the truck bed half full of it, balanced the buckets on top, and headed for town. There, wielding shovels, we opened abhorrent lawns, filled deep holes with layers of human manure, stuck the tiny trees in, and mounded the soil back on top. I buried the end of the garden hose, and Rudy followed the hose back into the bushes along the house, found the tap, turned the water on. While we let the roots flood, we went on to the next yard.

We waited for hours sometimes, watering those fruit trees in until the soil turned to soup. While the moon rose and set, Rudy and I watched the sky, or napped on the edge of lawns, irrigating, pressing the earth down again where the water bubbled up. We didn't speak. We turned off taps. We coiled hoses. We slunk away before dawn.

At first I told myself that I went along with Rudy to keep an eye on him. I told myself the fruit trees were Rudy's only plan for staying out of that icy bed on the coal company land, the bed that tipped him toward the grave. At first I did it to mitigate his recklessness, to influence his excesses. But that can't account for the peace and thrill I felt, stalking the streets with our headlights off, turning yard after yard to orchard.

It was a small county and an even smaller town, and people knew me, and people definitely knew Rudy, and soon enough things were bound to get complicated.

"What a view, there's the sheriff's deputy," Rudy said one afternoon when we were up in the nursery shoveling manure. I leaned on my shovel, but Rudy kept right on working. The deputy parked his car at the bottom of the driveway and marched straight up the pipeline easement. Rudy and I did not confer. Rudy did not stop shoveling, but watched sideways as the deputy turned from ant to life-size struggling man, clutching his side and red in the face.

"Rudy Gibbs, we've had complaints," he said, wiping his forehead. He flung the sweat from his hand.

"Complaints?" Rudy said.

"Well, not complaints exactly. But we've been getting calls where people say things," the sheriff's deputy said.

"What things?" Rudy asked.

"They say that they don't want to take care of an apple tree, let alone two."

"But they've got to have two or they won't get apples. The trees need to cross-pollinate," Rudy said.

"You'll have to stop this, Rudy," the deputy said. "There's a slew of things I could charge you with."

"Like what?" asked Rudy.

"For one thing, trespassing," the deputy said.

"Don't you think people sort of like it?" I asked.

"Who are you?" the deputy asked.

"I'm Helen," I said. "This is my place. I work for Rudy."

"Careful now, you're telling me you're his accomplice," the deputy said.

"Accomplice," Rudy said. "I like the sound of that. Way better than employee."

"All right, you two. You've been warned. I've given folks my direct line to call at any time if there's a problem," the deputy said.

"Sad day when the sheriff's deputy arrests a man for planting trees," Rudy said. "Not that I'm admitting anything."

"Why do you have to make my life hard?" asked the deputy.

"Okay, we've been warned, I hear you," said Rudy.

When the sheriff's deputy had packed himself into his car again, I turned to Rudy, who had never paused in his shoveling. "What now?" I asked.

"You heard the man. No one's even complained."

"We could get in trouble. We could go to jail," I said.

"Oh yes," said Rudy, throwing his shovel aside. "You and your delicate sensibilities. Talk so much shit about questioning authority, private property is an oppressive construct, as long as you can safely observe us assholes from the sidelines. You fucking landowner. Typical college loudmouth. Don't think I don't notice how fast you shut up and stand back when the real shit's about to go down. Can't even shoot a gun in the air when it counts."

Sometimes I would swear that Rudy didn't notice me at all, that I was only his foil, setting them up so he could knock them down. Yet he had been watching me. I thought of the people I knew back where I came from, people like my aunt and her friends, people with strict divisions between commentary and conduct. I had left that behind, hadn't I? Where they talked, I acted. I worked so hard every day that I had to explain myself. I had to say, I did wash my hands they are just permanently that color. I labored with shovel, wheelbarrow, snare, and knife, I worked until I was an empty vessel, all spilled out, nothing left to give. I was helpful even when Karen and Lily refused to be helped. Still, what Rudy said knuckled itself into me. I had no way to reply.

Rudy saw this and softened. "Don't take it so hard," he said. "Those folks just called the sheriff to chat. They wanted to talk about their feelings. You said it best. People like the trees, but they're confused. It's like a new shirt. It's hard to spend money on one, but hell, if it just shows up you kind of take to it."

So we kept right on.

Three weeks after we had begun, Rudy shifted the truck to neutral and turned off his headlights, and we coasted to a stop in front of the principal's house. It was three in the morning. "I want to shake this guy's hand," whispered Rudy. "This is the guy who started it all. Let's give him four trees. No, six. He said he didn't want apples, so let's give him three Kieffer pears and three Fellenberg plums."

It took us nearly an hour just to dig all the holes, which was more time than we usually spent at one house without at least circling around the block. I was getting jittery, felt my bowels drop, had to squat behind the hedge. The principal's porch light came on.

I crouched with my pants around my ankles. Rudy hit the ground and lay flat, the slope of the lawn swallowing him up. When the principal stepped out in his bathrobe, green-faced in the porch bulb's unfriendly light, he blinked into the empty night. With one mind, Rudy and I waited him out. The night was with us. The shadows were with us. The sloped lawn was with us. The principal's gaze didn't linger on the six dark holes along the edge of his lawn. He didn't turn his head to see the truck in the shadow of the tulip poplar. He tracked neither Rudy's figure nor mine. He withdrew, closed his front door. A moment later the porch light went off.

I fastened my belt and crawled across the lawn to Rudy, who knelt on the grass, grinning like a fool.

"Did you shit yourself? I almost shit myself," he whispered.

"Yes," I whispered back. "I shit. Luckily my pants were down. Let's get the hell out of here."

"You can go if you want to. I'm not leaving without planting the trees," Rudy said.

"Rudy," I said. "It's time to go."

"We've got to plant the trees and then we've got to water. I am not letting these trees die just because you're a pussy." I won't bother pretending I was surprised, let alone that I considered for one moment leaving him there alone.

I buried the hose end in the roots of the first pear tree. Rudy reached into his jacket for a tall can of Natural Ice. He sprawled on the dark lawn, propping himself up on one elbow, and I sat next to him. With the patience of a high-wire act, we moved the hose from one tree to the next, and we passed the can back and forth. "What did I tell you? If someone was coming for us, they'd be here by now," Rudy whispered. We listened to an owl call, a squirrel rummage, the low burble of the water, the distant whine of a police car. Which got closer. Which careered around the corner, which pulled up behind Rudy's truck just as the porch light flashed on again, just as the principal opened his door, no longer in a bathrobe but dressed for all the night to see in a shirt and tie, wrinkle-free slacks to match.

The sheriff's deputy stepped out of his car, but Rudy's business wasn't with the deputy, and it wasn't Rudy's way to triangulate. He rose to his feet and faced the principal. "Those are prime trees you got there," Rudy said. "Should be producing fruit in five years, tops. Three Fellenberg plums. Three Kieffer pears. I know you said you didn't want apples and I respect that."

"Mr. Gibbs, I am a reasonable man," the principal said. "I am not sure what you are doing here, but I will give you the opportunity to remove those trees."

"Yeah, or what, you're going to suspend me?" asked Rudy.

"I'll press charges," the principal said.

"Charges?" asked Rudy, squeezing the beer can with one hand until it crunched. "Let's talk about charges. I'm giving you these trees free of charge. You should be thanking me." He whipped back and threw the can hard against the house. The principal ducked, but the can went wide, missed him by a mile. If it was a duel, I was Rudy's second, and it could be said that we stood, if not our ground, then on the ground. We stood on the ground, side by side, as the sheriff's deputy made haste across the lawn. "I warned you, Rudy, I warned you," he said.

"You warned me," Rudy said. "That's true. And I'm warning this fucking yuppie that he better take care of these trees or he's going to wish he did." He had time to spit on the ground before the deputy wrestled him down, shoved a knee into his back, and cuffed him.

The deputy glanced up at me, breathing heavily. "Get into the squad car, Miss Conley, if you please."

"Make a run for it," Rudy said, his face pressed into the grass.

"Be smart. I know where you live," said the deputy. I walked toward the car, but Rudy went limp and had to be dragged. His bootheels left long muddy streaks across the sidewalk.

The principal had come down to the edge of his yard to oversee the operations. He watched us sadly, with his hands folded behind him, certainly the same pose he struck while giving Perley laughing lessons. I opened the door to the sheriff's car, but thought of commentary and conduct, thought of what I'd said or done since the moment the deputy arrived, which was exactly nothing. I turned back to the principal. "Remember that they need plenty of water when they're young like this," I told him. "Gallons and gallons. Remember to mulch them before it gets cold, cover them when it freezes. Remember to prune them in the spring." It wasn't shooting the .22,

193

not even into the air, but it was something.

The squad car pulled away, with Rudy cursing and twisting in his seat, and I turned to look out the back window. I could see the principal down on his knees in his wrinkle-free slacks. He hadn't even bothered to get a shovel. He was ripping the fruit trees out of the ground with his bare hands.

The sun was coming up as Rudy and I were ushered into separate cells. They made me take off my boots and jacket, so I sat there shivering on the cement bench staring through the glass into the outer room where clerks answered phones and itemized the contents of inmates' pockets: cell phone, cigarettes, penny, baby sock, lotto card, rolling papers, rubber band, receipt, car key, stub of pencil, same stuff as people who weren't in trouble with the law.

There was a pay phone on the cell wall, and I called collect. I crossed my fingers that Lily and Karen had the landline plugged in, hoped that there was enough electricity to run it, but the previous day had been cloudy. Karen picked up on the third ring, and I heard her accept the charges.

"We already heard from Rudy," she said. "I can't say I understand or appreciate it, but I think I get the picture. So what do you want us to do?"

"I just wanted you to know where I am," I said. "There's this phone here, on the wall."

"Like I said, Rudy already called," she said. "You want us to post bail or something?"

"No," I said. "I guess not. The court probably opens in a couple of hours. Might as well just wait it out."

"Might as well," she said.

"Thanks for accepting the charges," I said.

"Of course," she said. "Call again if you need a ride." She hung up.

On our way into the courthouse, we passed a public defender with a slack suit, bowlegs, and heavy white eyebrows. He took one look at Rudy and sent that brow up three inches, seemed like he was angry until you noticed he was smiling. "System got you again, Rudy? You know she's a jealous mistress, don't like to let go," he said.

Rudy said, "Aldi, you ancient asshole, just the man I hoped to see this morning." They embraced, then looked at each other a long moment. "Wooly worms say it's going to be a hard winter," Rudy said. "You prepared for that?"

"I'm retiring," Aldi said. "Give it about three weeks. By Christmas for certain. I'm going to let those dark days come at me without the added darkness of this hell pit." He waved a hand toward the courthouse. "That should improve my mood."

Remembering me, Rudy put his arm around Aldi and introduced me as his accomplice. "This here's Aldi Birch," he told me. "Only man who truly understands me. Aldi's the one helped me out years ago, when they first locked me up in the psych ward. Tried to sue them for, I don't know, breaching confidentiality."

"Didn't work," Aldi said.

"But he tried," Rudy said.

I had heard Aldi Birch's name, of course, knew he was a neighbor of ours, knew he had a place out on Lodi Creek. But this was the first I'd seen him. He took me in from under that impressive brow and I can't say, even now, if he approved of what he saw.

Rudy told him why we were there.

"Why did you have to throw that beer can?" asked Aldi.

"These fucking yuppies deserve that and worse," said Rudy. "They deserve fruit trees. They deserve to have to take care of them."

"I think you're using the word yuppie incorrectly," I said. The men looked at me. "Young urban professional, right?" I said. I looked at Aldi for confirmation, but Aldi, so ebullient with Rudy, gazed at me like the stranger I was. I pressed on: "That principal may be a professional, but he's definitely not young or urban."

"Helen's from Seattle," Rudy said. "She's just mad because she's a yuppie, too."

"He knows 'em when he sees 'em," Aldi said, and they laughed and slapped each other on the back. We went into the court-room together, and Aldi took the bench behind us.

Then we were called before the judge, and the sheriff's deputy stood up, and between us we were charged with criminal mischief, trespassing, resisting arrest, and drunk and disorderly conduct. The deputy wiped his face, looked me up and down. "I wouldn't stay mixed up with a guy like this, nice girl like you, no priors," he said.

"I'm not a girl, and I'm not mixed up," I said. Aldi Birch and Rudy laughed at that until the judge called for order, and I'll admit I was warm with pleasure to find myself back in the fold.

We were released on our own recognizance and told to report back in a week.

"Don't worry too much," Aldi said on our way out. "Not all those charges are going to stick. I doubt they can prove you were drunk and resisting. Plead, pay a fine, do some community service, it'll go away in one year, maybe two."

"What counts as community service?" asked Rudy. "Does planting fruit trees count?"

"I wouldn't push it," said Aldi Birch. They laughed again.

"That white oak out front of your place still need pruning?" Rudy asked. "I don't think it has another winter in it, not without crushing you."

"The answer's still no," Aldi said. "Hands off that oak."

"Now, don't get defensive," Rudy said. "Call me up if you ever feel like seeing another living soul."

We swiped some thin coffee on the way out and walked back through the morning neighborhoods to retrieve Rudy's truck.

The principal's yard was empty, the six fruit trees gone, the holes filled back in, Rudy's defiant boot marks swept away. The principal, that hard worker, had even sprinkled new grass seed, though it wasn't yet noon. Rudy shook his head, and we sat in the truck with the radio on, drinking our coffee while the kids across the street screamed and beat one another, launched themselves from monkey bars onto their fellows, aimed rubber balls at one another's heads. That was if you were included.

"At least we came out ahead," said Rudy.

"How can you say that?" I asked. "Did you hear all those charges? Besides, most people got rid of the trees we planted."

"Most but not all," said Rudy. "There are now five more apple trees, three pears, and six cherry trees gracing this godforsaken town. And they're doing well. They're probably going to make it." He took a sip of coffee. "I don't know about you, but I could use something stronger. What time is it? Want to hit the bar?"

"I still have my standards, Rudy," I said.

"Of course," he said. "I've got to remember to look up bourgeoisie in the dictionary more often."

In fact, I might have gone to the bar, the day was so disarranged already, but at that moment I saw Perley across the street, leaning hard against the fence. He waved at us as if he were adrift in an open boat, our truck the only airplane in a barren sky. We went right over.

"You want some coffee?" asked Rudy, holding his cup up to the fence.

"It might stunt my growth," said Perley.

"Old wives' tales," said Rudy.

"Mama K and Mama L said I shouldn't

bother you, but can I ask you one question?" Perley said.

"Ask us anything you want, we've nothing to hide," Rudy said.

"Hold on," I said. "You can ask me one question if I can ask you one question, too."

"What's jail like?" asked Perley, his fingers curling around the chain link.

"Nothing to brag about," I said.

"Cold, no private place to pee, bad food," Rudy said. "But pretty much everyone else in there had it worse than us." Perley nodded.

"My turn to ask a question," I said.

"Okay, but only one," Perley said.

"How is it really going here?" I asked. "I mean at school."

"I told you it's fine," he said.

"Cut the bullshit," I said. "What's up with that little asshole Bexley Epps?"

Perley looked startled. "How did you know?" he asked.

"Adult omniscience," I said.

"He calls me names," Perley said. "I just can't seem to mix in that good. Don't tell Mama L and Mama K."

"I've got an idea for your community service, Rudy," I said.

"If you mean me teaching that little Epps punk a lesson, I don't think the sheriff's office will sign off on it," Rudy said.

"Pick Perley up from school a few days a week with all the chain saws in the back of the truck," I said. "Let the kids see him with you. Might just help matters. What do you think, Perley?"

"Won't count as community service," Rudy said.

"Go to the school office, they've got volunteer opportunities, mentoring shit, they always do. Sign up and make it official," I said. "It'll be like an internship."

"An internship with a man," Perley said. Rudy laughed and Perley joined in, his first real laugh since the school bus doors had closed behind him.

Karen waited until Perley was asleep before turning on me. Lily fretted beside her.

"Man internship? With Rudy?" Karen said. "So now being a man means someone who can't stay out of jail or stay sober?"

"I just think you should consider exposing Perley to a positive male role model," I said.

"Where do you pick this shit up?" asked Karen. "Positive male role model? Internship? Best practices? Is everyone like this where you come from? You think we're a fucking nonprofit out here? Anyway, you don't think that Rudy is a positive male role model."

"And you don't think that people should go to jail for planting fruit trees," I said. "So don't act like you suddenly have respect for the law."

"Perley says he likes school," said Lily. "He even has a friend. The kid from down the road. Bexley."

"Bexley and Perley aren't friends. They're foes," I said. "Bexley calls him a faggot bastard because he doesn't have a dad."

It fell on them like a blow from my hand.

"We're taking him out of school immediately," Karen said.

"But Perley wants to stay in school," Lily said, her eyes wet.

"We don't have to do everything he wants to do. We're his parents. We have to make decisions," Karen said.

"It's true that I don't think Rudy is a positive male role model," I said. "But I do think that maybe just getting Rudy and Perley together might help Perley fit in."

"I don't want him to fit in," Karen said. "I want him to tear everything apart and start over."

"Rudy is unbearable," I said. "Yet he is highly skilled and actually strangely sensitive. Also, he is reliable."

They sat with it for a moment. They looked at each other.

"He can pick him up and drop him off at school as long as he's sober," Lily said.

"He can teach him about trees, he can teach him to use a goddamn chain saw, for all I care. But that doesn't make him a 'positive male role model.' This isn't Focus on the fucking Family," Karen said.

Though our fruit tree business was essentially finished, Rudy kept the nursery going. As winter approached, he mulched the trees eight inches high, swaddled them in yards of burlap. He put a sign down at the mailbox: COME UP AND GET YOURSELF A FRUIT TREE! EXPERIENCE THE TRANSFORMATIVE WONDER OF FRUIT TREE STEWARDSHIP. GRATIS! Lily planted two Idared apple trees at the top of our garden, but other than that I don't know that he had any takers.

Rudy's request to roll out his sleeping bag in the nursery remained unchallenged and spread beyond weeks into more than a month. As it got colder, I lent him my wall tent with its miniature woodstove, and he built a platform for it, on the far side of the pipeline easement, next to his trees. I knew that feeling, the feeling of proximity after being alone for so long. Rudy didn't live with us, he lived four hundred feet away from us. To people for whom togetherness was an unfathomable riddle, to people who hovered but never drew near, to Rudy, four hundred feet was downright cozy.

7

Perley

My motto is excellence and at first I excelled at the man internship because Rudy excelled at letting me do whatever I wanted as long as he could talk a lot and drink from his cans. His truck was even louder than the school bus which I didn't have to get on that special day when my teacher heard Rudy's truck coming and said, Jesus, just get a friggin muffler. Rudy didn't get out just honked his horn and said, Hop in, twerp.

Bexley said, I thought you didn't have a dad, and I said, He's not my dad, he's my friend. He has oh about ten chain saws, how many does your dad have? I didn't let him answer I just got into the truck, real cool like a dog with a bandanna.

About that, Rudy said on the way home. Do you ever wish you had a dad?

I wish I had a chain saw, I said. I wish I

had a wizard chiseled from the very stone. But do you wish you had a dad? asked Rudy. My dad was a turkey baster, I said. Oh hell, said Rudy. Don't make me puke. I wish I could fight really bad, I said. I could teach you to do that, said Rudy. Like ninjutsu, I said, or like elfin fighting skills from the back of a wolf. Rudy said, Something like that.

We went up the pipeline past the fruit tree buckets way up into the woods at the top of the ridge, and Rudy sat with his back against a tree and he drank from his can and he made me practice my moves. Then he licked the droplets out of his beard and said, This sissy stuff where you lie down and get up really quick and do push-ups, that's not going to get you anywhere. So he taught me the uppercut the sucker punch the right jab left jab the duck and protect your balls. It's an ancient martial art, he said. Trust me, it'll come in useful. Just don't pull hair or slap like some kind of pussy queer sorry but you know what I mean. He opened another can.

My women don't drink that stuff, I said. There's a lot you don't know, he said, about your women. That's probably true, I said, but they don't drink that stuff. You're pretty fucking smart, he said, so I asked him if I could use the chain saw. Sure, he said, why not? You are a totally problematic parent, I said, I'm way too young to use the chain saw, I can't even lift it. Weakling, he said. But then he gave me the smallest one that he called the Echo and then he excelled at helping me start it and then I excelled at cutting a rotten branch in half and then Rudy excelled at saying, With a chain saw it's not about strength, it's about focus.

Focus, I said. My teacher told me I have to focus and the principal told me that I have to focus. But I can't focus, I can't do my Specials, I'm just staring out the window like, Wolfriders, come take me away. Tell me about it, said Rudy. You have to remember to resist them at all costs. I said, That sounds like Mama K. She's not stupid, your Mama K, said Rudy. But resist who? I asked. Who is Them? The teachers the jail guards whoever, said Rudy. But I told Rudy that I liked my teacher. I liked the principal. I wished I could make them happy.

Rudy said, You've got to have your tricks or they'll get you.

Like lying? I asked, and Rudy said, Call it what you want. You've got to have a way out. Take for instance when I was in jail. With the Mean Aunt, I said, and Rudy said, No. A different time, a long time ago before

207

you were born. I was honest, he said, I told them how I really felt and then they tried to make me take pills.

Like vitamins? I asked, but Rudy said, Worse than that. Pills that make you easier to deal with. But I outsmarted them, he said, and I said, How did you outsmart them? and he said, I held the pills in my cheeks. You mean like a squirrel, I said. That's right, he said. I held the pills in my cheeks like a squirrel with his acorns and then when it was safe I flushed them down the toilet. But what if the pills could have helped you? I asked. I am beyond help, said Rudy, and he opened another can, and he said, You've got to remember the tricks, you know.

Like a sucker punch? I asked, and Rudy said, No, something wily something original.

I don't know any tricks like that, I said. Shit, said Rudy, and then he gave me the jewels from around his neck I mean this totally sweet mime face that was smiling and frowning which is how I felt every day. What is this? Is this a trick? I asked. Yes, said Rudy. This is a trick, it's your bling, it will protect you, said Rudy. How will it protect me? I asked, and Rudy said, It will blow your enemy's mind, is how. And while they are confounded, you can plan your next attack.

■ ■ ■ ■

Rudy dropped me off at school the next day with the radio going so loud, the song about the umbrella and we were standing under it ella ella and the other kids looked at me in that toxic loud car, I was covered in jewels with the best music pumping and the chain saws in the back and I thought I saw them bow down.

Sauntering is what you do when you know how bad they all want to be you, so at recess I sauntered and I wasn't surprised when I saw that acorn kid watching me, hugging the side of the building, pulling his feet in and out of his red rubber boots. He crept from dumpster to fence to wood chips to tire swing until he got up close. And I wasn't surprised when Bexley cut in front of him and jumped into my face and said, What is up with that necklace? I had been waiting to accept his homage so I said graciously, It's not a necklace it's bling, and then the acorn kid said, Actually that pendant represents early Greek drama, and Bexley said, Who asked you, mongrel? and when he said that the acorn kid did this thing. All I can say is that it was highly skilled. It was optimum strategy. He put up a force field around himself which I wished he could tell me how he did it. Bexley couldn't get to him through the force field, so Bexley turned back to me and said, Where did you get it, faggot? and I said, My friend Rudy gave it to me, and Bexley said, Oh, you mean that fucking hillbilly who gives you a ride to school? That guy is a drunk and a criminal. And from inside his force field the acorn kid said, I think that pendant is actually pretty cool, and I turned on him fast like a Wolfrider. Back off, it's not a pendant, I said. Well, if it's not a pendant, what is it? asked the acorn kid like he genuinely wanted to know. It's a weapon, I said, and he said, A weapon are you sure about that? Then I summoned my elfin powers and I yelled, It's a weapon, you faggots, and I pointed it first at Bexley and then at the acorn kid, but nothing happened except that Bexley laughed and laughed until he almost fell over, and the acorn kid opened his mouth like he wanted to say something but then he closed it again and he walked away taking his force field with him.

Excellence is my motto, so when Rudy picked me up that day, I gave him back the pendant. Did it work? he said. Oh yes, I said. Yes, it was excellent. I told you, he said.

He said, Then while they're dazzled you can use your sucker punch wham bam who's the fool now, but I told him I didn't want to practice my sucker punch that day I actually just wanted to go home and he said, Fine, but I have to get my hours because he was doing community service and his community service was me.

And at home Mama L asked, How is the internship with Rudy going, and I said, Good. And Mama K said, Good? Is he drinking? Is he being an asshole? You can tell us. And I said, It's excellent. And the Mean Aunt asked, Is it helping you fit in at school better? And I said, Oh yes, oh certainly. I am excelling. At. It. And the Mean Aunt made some notes in her special binder that had everything in it that she said was for my life. She looked at Mama K and said, See, what did I tell you?

The Mean Aunt always acted like she could read my mind like she knew me best even when she said my mamas were totally delusional. But when I told her everything was excellent, which was not true, no friggin way, the Mean Aunt couldn't even tell that I was lying. Also I don't think the other kids were bowing down after all I think they were just tying their shoes. Also I felt sorry for Rudy for being a hillbilly and a criminal.

He was flanged like me and the acorn kid and he didn't even know. So it turned out that a lot of things that I thought were true were actually not true. Adult omniscience wasn't true. It wasn't true that Rudy's jewels could protect me. It wasn't true that an internship with a man could help me fit in. And all this time I thought I was Friend of Snake but that couldn't have been true because that night I rolled over in bed and the black snake bit me in the face.

I was sleeping when it happened. I was sleeping in an inky pool in Mama K's arms, and then she opened her mouth and a boy came out, a boy like me but with sharp teeth and a red tongue, and then the part of me that was made of thick oatmeal and buckskin was eaten away suddenly, like the pages of the Mean Aunt's binder eaten away by mice, and then my face had the feeling of red and purple and then I was awake and all the women in my life were around me and none of them had their shirts on and breasts of all shapes and sizes swung over my head.

Karen

I'd wanted Perley to be strange to me. I'd wanted him to be animal. I got it and I paid for it. He screamed like I'd never heard his voice before, like I'd never soothed him to sleep as a baby. He screamed like a stranger, but the worst part was when he stopped. He went slack. His voice ended. The snake was part of his face, attached somehow. I couldn't see his left eye. For once, Lily didn't cry. She wrestled Perley into her arms snake and all. She held him so close that he was tiny again, his legs and arms folded against her, that snake swinging from him. Helen, naked and wild-haired, burst in and threw herself onto the bed next to Lily, got her arms in there around Perley, too. But me, I didn't reach for Perley. Instead I clasped the snake.

I'd seen a copperhead bite before, a rattlesnake, never a black snake. But I'd read up on it at Community Health. People came in with all kinds of shit. I tried to stay prepared.

A black snake's bite is like a slap, there and gone. You treat it like you'd treat any minor abrasion. Keep it clean and dry. Put your mind to other things while your body does its good work.

But the way a black snake eats is different from the way a black snake bites.

When a black snake eats, its mouth is a conveyor belt. Its back-curved teeth haul the snake forward to engulf its prey. Once attached, it's difficult, as a practical matter, for that snake to let go.

Perley was prey too big to eat whole. He'd rolled onto the snake with the full weight of his sleeping body, trapping it. The snake struck his face, just below his left eye. It couldn't retreat, so it dug in. The snake thrashed against him. Perley hung in Lily's arms, Helen pressed him. His mouth dropped open, his eyes rolled up, gone. The odor that overtook the room belonged to all of us. "Kill it," commanded Lily, crisp and dry-eyed, but there was no way in. I had hold of the snake just below its head. I used my other hand to find the hinge of its jaw. I wedged my fingers into the snake's mouth.

My fingers worked against Perley's flesh, and I felt the snake's teeth punch holes in me, and I saw my blood mix with Perley's blood but none of it was painful until later. My task was to make the snake loosen its teeth, but the panicked creature kept pulling back. It dragged Perley's skin wide. When I finally pried the snake free and flung it at the wall, bits of its teeth remained, winking at us like pearls in an oyster. Beneath my hand, my boy's face lay gaping and raw, his horrible open eye vacant above the wound.

"Call 911," Helen said.

214

"I'm a nurse, I can handle this," I said.

"Perley, can you hear us, Perley, can you say something?" Lily said.

Perley's small voice returned from a long and lonely journey. "Madcoil," he said.

"Madcoil," I answered.

"It was Madcoil," Perley said, stronger this time, and Lily said, "I'm holding you," and Perley said, "You're holding me."

Direct pressure was the next thing, so I pressed Rudy's filthy T-shirt to Perley's cheek. He drew back, which I took as a good sign. Pain meant he wasn't in shock. "Helen, go boil some water," I said.

Helen opened her mouth, but I said, "The last thing I need right now is the benefit of your wisdom. You want to be fucking helpful? Then do what I tell you." She didn't use the ladder, but swung herself down to the kitchen. The first day I met Helen she'd been useless but for boiling water. That day, we took charge of killing her drakes, and here she was again, filling the pot and setting it on the burner while I gave her a rapid list: alcohol, iodine, tweezers, swabs, bandage. She handed it all up to me. Lily kept Rudy's shirt on the wound while I cleaned my hole-punched hands. Easily, I dressed them. Then I set to Perley.

"I can get you herbs," Helen called from

the kitchen.

"Don't interrupt," I said.

"Plantain," Helen said. "It says so right here in the Best Practices Binder."

"I don't care what you wrote down in that binder of yours," I said. "Plantain's no good if there's infection underneath. He could get an abscess. Yarrow might be the one. It's antibacterial, pain-relieving, and it'll stop the bleeding. Sage is a good disinfectant."

"Both in the garden," Lily said.

It was for Perley's body that I'd quit working as a nurse and now I took it up again. He cried. He yelled. He shuddered. I attended the body I most wanted to attend. I dug out tooth fragments, cleaned, compressed, applied salve, dressed the wound. Lily held him hard from beginning to end, murmured to him, kissed his ear, smoothed and smoothed our son's sweaty forehead. The snake had left a slick substance, some kind of rank defensive oil. It coated my arms and chest. It soaked the sheets.

Finally, when my work was done, Lily released Perley into my arms. It had been two years since she'd stopped nursing him, but as she fell back into the bloody pillows, I saw the damp circles spread from her nipples, darkening the sheet. Her new milk mingled with the snake oil.

Helen

Perley's wound looked like a human bite, all the little holes arranged around a circle, and Karen barked at me for iodine, tweezers, sage. I handed her the supplies, climbed up after them to watch. No one told me not to hover. No one told me anything, except how to help. In the morning we moved Perley down to the sofa. Karen stitched Perley up with her suture kit. Perley clung to Lily, who had gone liquid, salt dripping down her cheeks, milk leaking down her front. "The breast milk is good," Karen told her. "Squeeze some into a cup so that we can use it to clean the wound." Watching Karen push the suture through, pincer it with the needle pusher, calmly tie each graceful knot, I knew I was supposed to feel distressed, panicked even, definitely sobered. I told myself that I felt those things. But I was lying. I felt like singing.

Humming, I made breakfast. Cheerily, I clanged the pans. I melted duck fat. I unsealed a precious jar of venison. I fried extra sardines. I kept Karen and Lily full of strong coffee. I plugged in the phone and called in to work for Lily. I poured catnip tea down Perley's throat until he spluttered. No one scolded me. No one told me to butt out. I had been seven long years with these women and their child, and this was the first time we were all in agreement.

"Should we take him to the doctor?" Lily asked, wiping her eyes into Perley's hair.

"What could a doctor do that I'm not already doing?" Karen asked.

"What if it gets infected?" Lily asked.

"If it gets infected, I'll give him antibiotics," Karen said. "I can do that. Don't worry." She squeezed Lily's hand. She wiped Lily's blurred eyes with the corner of her shirt. I tried not to stare.

Perley attempted to examine his wound by straining his eyeball down toward it. This added to his new grotesqueness, eyelids half closed, eyes crossed, mouth drawn down as he tried to look at his own cheek. I brought him the shard of mirror from above the sink.

"Toxically gross," Perley said, faint but happy. "What about school?"

"You're not going to school," Karen said. "You'll stay home and rest. We need to watch and make sure this thing heals up right. We need to make sure you don't get a fever. So just settle in."

"Settle in where?" asked Lily. "I won't have him stay one more night in this house until the snakes are gone."

"Where else can he stay?" asked Karen.

"Stop crying, Mama L, I'll camp on the

218

pipeline with Rudy," Perley said.

"I won't have it," Karen said.

"He can stay in my old camper," I said. I waited to be rebuffed. Instead, Karen said, "There's an idea. But it needs a little bit of work."

"I'll clear it out," I surged. "I'll do it right after breakfast." The day was a warm wave, raising me up and tossing me toward the human family. They needed me. We were invincible. We had purpose. As comrades, we could solve any problem.

"Stay there by himself?" asked Lily.

"You can move up there with him, Lily," Karen said. "Helen and I will stay in here and get rid of the snakes once and for all." And what could be further proof of our bond but that Lily and I received this and didn't gloat? We didn't even look at each other. I pressed the coffee. Lily found a place for her head on Karen's shoulder, puzzle piece to puzzle. Karen put her arm around Lily and pulled her in close.

These days, Karen was the only one who went into the camper with any frequency. It was where she kept her tools. I opened the door, but could hardly stand up inside, could hardly move, the ceiling was so low, the walls so close. I could hardly believe I had lived here with my boyfriend, or that I'd spent a winter in it alone.

The narrow space was filled with insulation spilling out of contractor bags, double-paned windows with cracks patched by duct tape, an old screen door, metal shelving disassembled, a three-legged utility sink with mud still in the drain, Perley's old high chair, a pressure cooker with no gasket, my old bicycle, now frozen into rust. I stopped to look inside Karen's toolbox. She had tools in there that I couldn't identify, some kind of chisel set with bamboo handles, a series of finely toothed handsaws lovingly encased in leather, a heavy iron thing, half clamp, half pliers, meant for what use I couldn't say. I admit to a pang then, remembering building the house with her. She said I'd rushed her, that I'd overstated my skill. Maybe I had. I certainly hadn't asked her any questions. But history had borne me out, hadn't it? We had lived in our house for years now, and it hadn't fallen over. True, we had to work steadily to stay ahead, patching the roof, replacing stovepipe where it had rusted, adding more insulation to the walls, jacking up one side of the porch where it sank into the mud. True, most of that work fell to Karen while I worked for Rudy or gathered wild foods. But that was life. We all contributed in our own way. And if I hadn't pushed us, the house might never have been finished. There was an old saying, wasn't there? The perfect is the enemy of done. I closed her toolbox and reclaimed my light feeling. I was purpose. I was needed.

I flung open the door and raised all the small windows, packed the cold woodstove with yellowed newspapers and magazines, junk mail, cardboard boxes. I stoked the fire to dry the place out and to banish mold. I piled load after load into the wheelbarrow, hauled windows, shelves, insulation, tools, all down the path to the garden, then down through the garden to the house. There was nowhere else to put everything, so I filled our house to bursting between sofa and stove. Karen and Lily cradled Perley on the sofa while he slept, talking quietly to each other. They smiled at me as I heaped junk before them. As the day wore on, our house became the new storage shed. By evening, the camouflage camper was clear, ready to be lived in again.

I found the others around the firepit. They had dragged the bloody snake oil bedding outside and set it ablaze. They sat on camp chairs, Perley on Lily's lap, Karen pulled up nearby. They leaned into one another in the dark. Perley put his hand up to his face. Lily grabbed it and moved it back to his side. Karen turned to me. "How's it coming?" she asked, not impatient, not skeptical. Kind.

"Home sweet home," I was so happy to reply.

I insisted they borrow my old down sleeping bag. Lily carried it. Karen carried Perley, and together we made our way up the hill. The camper windows, dark for so long, showed the light of an oil lamp. The chimney sent forth a modest stream of woodsmoke. Karen set Perley down, and he approached the camper in the manner of a young prince.

"My own house," he said. "Here, I make the rules."

"Don't worry, Piglet," Lily said. "I'll sleep up here with you."

"No way," he said. "Not unless I say so."

"Someone's got to be with you tonight, at least," Karen said. "We've got to watch your temperature, and change the dressing on the wound."

"You keep trying to mess with it," Lily said, catching his hand again. "You have to stop messing with it."

"Who are the McCanns?" Perley asked, pointing to the old markings above the door.

"What does AWA mean?"

"These are the questions that plague us," I said. We squeezed inside.

Lily tended the woodstove while Karen set up a first-aid station on the low counter: herbs, salve, iodine, clean rags, thermos of hot water. Perley insisted on making the bed. When he unrolled my sleeping bag, a string of photo-booth photos fell out. He picked it up and studied it. "What's this?" he asked, handing it to me, and so I looked into my boyfriend's face for the first time in nearly a decade.

We pressed our faces to the camera. He wore safety goggles. I wore a man's fedora. We stuck our tongues out. Frowned and smiled. Kissed on the mouth. I remembered when we'd crammed into that photo booth. It was soon after we'd bought the land. To warm up, to get a little electric light, to avail ourselves of the hot running water, we'd had a night out at the second-run movie theater and arcade. It hadn't ended well, because my boyfriend had spent most of the evening talking to the ticket-taker, a neighbor of ours, forgetting, as usual, that we were supposed to be on a date. I wish I could say that he was flirting with her. At least then people would know where to aim their pity. But it wasn't that. He simply loved nothing better than to chat at length with strangers. He loved any chance to make a good impression. I rode the bumper cars and fed quarter after quarter to the mechanical claw that's supposed to pick up toys. I didn't get a toy. I didn't want a toy. I wanted my boyfriend and he didn't want me, at least not very badly. Well, the joke was on him. It turned out I didn't want anyone. Anyone but this family.

"That's him," I told Perley. "That's the man that you told me I look like. It's just that you've never seen him before."

"Was he your boyfriend?" Perley asked, scrunching up his face so that his bandage puckered.

"I'm not sure I even know what that word means," I said.

"Like how Mama K and Mama L are," he said.

"I never had someone like how Mama K and Mama L have each other," I said. "Never like that."

Karen tucked Lily and Perley into their sleeping bags, kissing them both soundly. Then she and I went back down to the house, ready to stalk snakes. But for once, there were no snakes to be found.

"Cowards," I said.

"They know that they've broken our hearts," Karen said.

"What's the thing about Madcoil again?" I asked.

"Madcoil is a snake monster that killed a bunch of elves," Karen said. "I didn't think our snakes were like that."

"What happened to him?" I asked.

"To Madcoil?" Karen said. "In the end, the elves killed him. After he'd already done a lot of damage."

Without Lily or Perley there, we didn't bother to build a fire. Karen said, "Might as well turn off the light to save power. Unless you mind?" So we sat side by side on the sofa, huddled into our coats, staring into the dark, invisible piles of our old possessions inches from our faces.

I stood up and banged my shin on my bicycle.

"What are you doing?" asked Karen, but I didn't answer. I felt forward with my hands, maneuvering around the window frames and garbage bags, down through the kitchen to the bookshelf, reached up high, felt around. I knew when I had my hands on the right book because it was sticky with grease and dust, soft with cobwebs. With the Best Practices Binder under my arm, I fumbled back to the sofa. I sat down again next to Karen, and I slid the thing over until I felt it fall into her lap.

"What is this?" she asked. "Oh shit, don't tell me."

"You should make an entry sometime," I said.

"Helen, please," she said, pushing the binder back to me. But we were both unwilling to let go of the day's good feeling. I wouldn't take the binder back.

"Best Practices," I said. "How to Treat Non-Venomous Snakebites." We sat cocooned. She didn't try to give me the binder again. I almost thought she'd gone to sleep. Finally she said, "I could consider that. An entry like that could come in useful."

"There's a right way to do nearly everything," I said. "You were perfect today."

It was dark, so I couldn't see her smile.

Lily

My Piglet had always known his own mind. On his fifth birthday, he'd said, No more, when I offered my breast. This from the boy who had asked for milk every forty-five minutes from the time he was born, even if only a sip. I'm done, he said. Roughly, he pushed me away, so I was forced to look for other parenting strategies, and I found none but holding him.

226

I found none but holding him and singing the shipwreck lullaby and saying the names I'd made for him and offering him sugar when Karen wasn't looking. Now my Piglet was seven, and his face was all fucked-up, and my breasts were full. I was as surprised as anyone, but there was no question of him nursing. He was over it.

I woke in the camper, leaking milk, stretched and sore. I don't know how long Perley had been awake, but he sat cross-legged on the bed staring at me, his wound a bright gem on his face. "What's the password?" he asked as soon as he saw my eyes open. I rolled over into the damp spot I'd made on the sleeping bag.

"Password?" I asked.

"This is my house," he said.

"Piglet, you're wounded. You need me to care for you," I said. "You're supposed to be wearing your bandage."

"I took it off so I could see my wound," he said. I reached for him, but that person, that imperious person, the apple of my eye, he showed me to the door. "It's my house and you can't come in if you don't know the password," he said. He gave me a gentle shove out onto the doorstep, and he shut himself inside the camper.

Down the garden path, the kale was bright

green through its layer of frost. My breath marched before me toward the house. No smoke came from the chimney. On the porch, Karen used one of her wooden spoons to stir a pot of oatmeal on a propane burner. Helen came out with silverware in the front pocket of her overalls.

"No point in digging out bowls," she said. "It's impossible to find anything in there. The dish cupboard is behind a stack of old dresser drawers."

"Perley kicked me out," I said.

"Kicked you out? How does his face look?" asked Karen.

"His face looks horrible except for the big smile on it," I said. "He says we can't go into the camper unless we know the password." We huddled on the porch, warming our hands over the oatmeal. I expected Karen to take the news hard, but she looked pleased. "Must mean he's feeling better," she said.

"But we need to look after him while he heals," I said.

"As long as he lets me care for his wound every day," Karen said, "I think that camper's a good place for him."

"But he's only seven. He's too young to live alone," I said.

"He's not living alone," Helen said. "The

camper's just up the hill. He's nearby. Look at it this way. He finally has his own room."

"Dignity of risk," Karen said. "It's something we talked about in nursing school. Your duty to care for someone doesn't outweigh their right to be their own person."

Under my jacket, my shirt was wet, under my shirt my breasts were tight and hard. I managed three more spoonfuls of oatmeal, then went inside the house. I dug my way through the junk museum until I found a bowl and my secret store of brown sugar, hidden inside a box of powdered milk. Outside, Karen and Helen were talking snakes.

"Snakes eat mice but what eats snakes?" asked Karen.

"Snakes are actually pretty good eating if you kill them right and don't make a mess," Helen said.

"Hey, if you cook it I'll eat it," Karen said. Not since the invention of Survival Dice had the two of them been so happy together. I slipped the sugar inside my jacket, and I took the rest of the oatmeal up the hill.

Rudy waited at the camper door, sitting on an upturned bucket. At his feet were two lemons, a taproot, an elderberry stem hollowed into beads and strung together, a glass jar of crystals, and a hot-pink plastic dream catcher.

"Helen told me what happened," he said. "So I brought my cures. Some of them I've tried, some of them I haven't. Some of them work, some of them don't exactly not work. I knocked on the door, but Perley told me I have to know the password if I want to go in."

"Perley," I called. "I brought oatmeal." The small window above the bed slid open, and Perley stuck his head out.

"Does it have sugar on it?" he asked.

"Of course," I said, handing in the bowl.

"Damn," Rudy said, taking a good look at him. "You look like a pirate lost his eye patch. Now you'll finally get some respect."

"You think so?" Perley asked.

"Let me come in and show you my cures," Rudy said.

"I told you. You have to know the password," Perley said.

"Well, what is it?" asked Rudy.

"I don't know," Perley said. "I haven't invented it yet."

I picked up the dream catcher, hot pink, emerald-green feathers stuck on with glue. "What we could really use help with is getting rid of the snakes," I told Rudy.

"Good fucking luck," Rudy said. "I know

a woman gave her house to the snakes and built another one."

"We've got to get rid of them so that Perley can move back into the main house," I said.

"I'm not moving back in," Perley said. "I'm free and independent now as a human man."

"Does that shit hurt?" Rudy asked, touching his own cheek in sympathy.

"Of course it does," Perley said. "Can I have your Sharpie?" He pointed to the marker stuck behind Rudy's ear.

"I use that to label my fruit trees," Rudy said, but handed it right over.

"We've tried everything except a cat," I said.

"You know I'm always at your service," Rudy said. He turned his bucket over, deposited his snakebite cures into it, and crashed off through the woods toward the pipeline.

We came to an agreement. Perley allowed us to administer first aid, to wash his wound, to take his temperature. He rested when we told him to rest. He ate the nourishing food we cooked. In return, we let him sleep alone in the camper. Perley used Rudy's Sharpie to make a sign that said NO

231

MAMAS ALLOWED. To that he added NO MEAN AUNT, NO RUDY. PASSWORD REQUIRED. I didn't know the password. I couldn't guess it. I didn't try.

At first the snakebite rode full sail on his face, and we couldn't look at or think about anything else. His punctured places were black and red, raised in scabs, his cheek bruised dark purple. We fed him vitamin C, spooned cod-liver oil down his throat. We changed the dressing four times a day. Four times a day, I kneaded my breasts and expressed into a cup. Then I washed Perley's wound, using a dropper to send my milk down into the sutures.

The danger of infection passed. Perley's purple faded to reddish brown. I hadn't been to work in two weeks and we needed money. It was a busy time for Helen, too. The acorn harvest was over, but she had to finish her community service hours before the end of the calendar year, and she was working long days for Rudy, trying to make back court fees. So Perley was left with Karen.

It was nothing new. From the time he was a baby, while I worked during the day, she'd stayed home to teach him all that she knew. He took to her old comics so that the two of them nearly shared a secret language:

232

sending, treeshaping, soulmate, wolf friend. He'd echo her, Practice and prepare, and if she managed to press knowledge into him, he'd be proud of it. But all the while, he'd resist her. She'd tell him to muck out the duck shed, and he'd toss his shovel in a ditch. He'd hide behind a tree, aim hickory nuts at Karen if she came calling him. She'd teach him to use live coal to hollow wood into bowls and spoons. He'd use that coal to build a fire and burn up the whole project. She'd set him to digging up multiflora rose. He'd lay aside his hoe and follow deer into the forest to find out where they slept. By the time Perley decided to go to school, the only time there was ease between Karen and our son was at night, when he slept with his head in the crook of her arm, when she licked her fingers and smoothed his eyebrow.

When I went back to work, the two of them stood together at the top of the driveway and waved goodbye to me. It looked as if they planned to stay right there waving until I got back.

But when I came home that day, it was to the corduroy sound of the handsaw, the clap of the hammer, and I found Karen and Perley kneeling in front of the camouflage camper, surrounded by scrap lumber. They bent their heads together over a piece of waxed cardboard. On it, a drawing of a table surrounded by three-legged stools, a shelf, what looked like a porch swing. The whole thing was covered over with measurements and notations. Perley wielded Rudy's Sharpie, his tongue out, concentrating. Karen's toolbox was unpacked around them.

"Mama K's teaching me tools and whittling," Perley said, barely glancing at me. He capped the Sharpie and began to arrange drill bits by size. He was wearing Karen's tool belt, cinched beyond the last hole. "We're going to make my house so sweet. It's going to have everything I need for living forever."

"The camper could use a table and chairs," Karen said. "It could use a bunk bed. A bookshelf."

"Have you been inside it?" I asked her.

"Of course she has," Perley said. "How else could we have figured out how high to make my new bunk?" He took her sheepsfoot blade from the tool belt, held it up proudly. "She's showing me how to carve spindle legs," he said.

"Mortise-and-tenon joints," Karen said. "We'll need to use the chisels."

"Does she know the password?" I asked.

They looked at each other.

"It's a secret," Karen said.

They spent their days together building, as Perley's red wound healed to yellow, as the sutures began to wear away and fall off. To Helen's unmasked joy, Karen documented her care of him in the Best Practices Binder, dating her entries, detailing the whole process. "You'll have a scar," Karen said. "But why shouldn't you?"

"Toxic," Perley said.

Rudy brought us an orange tomcat, mean and squint-eyed. It peed all over the house, but it didn't get rid of the black snakes, who'd all come back. We didn't notice them so much because of the garbage bags, the window frames, the bike, the insulation, the utility sink, the high chair, the old sleeping bags, all of it soaked in cat pee. Underneath all the junk, the snakes switched their tails and smelled with their tongues, trying to stay warm as the days turned cold.

It was mid-December, dark early, freezing by dinnertime. But our house was overrun, so we built the campfire big those evenings, and we put on our coats, and we ate our supper outside. Perley took up his nightly reports to Karen again, going over what he'd learned that day. "Cut on the outside edge," he said. "Make the line disappear." His wound had healed to where we didn't dress it anymore. His crescent scar cast a shadow down his cheek, luminous in the firelight. "For finish work, countersink before driving in your screws." He demonstrated how to use her sheepsfoot blade on a chair leg. Shadowboxing, he demonstrated his sucker punch. Karen said, "That's not sportsmanlike. Watch this." She turned a somersault over one shoulder, came up on both feet, knees bent, ready to strike.

"Where'd you learn that?" asked Helen.

"Just something I picked up on my travels," Karen said.

After, wrapped up warm in our coats, I held him. I didn't know the password, but I held him. I rocked him. I carried Perley up to the camper, where earlier Karen had stoked his fire and shut the stove down so that it would be warm when he came to bed. I whispered his name. I carried him to his door. He raised his mending face. I leaned down to kiss it. It was like going on a date, the chaste kind I had liked to imagine as a kid, before I knew what would be required of me. He waved goodbye. He went inside. He latched the door.

Perley's snake had fled, maybe to nurse its

wounds, maybe to die from them. But it wasn't in our bed, and Perley wasn't in our bed, and so Karen and I had our bed to ourselves. We hardly knew what to do. Waiting for Helen's light to go off, we lay on our sides facing each other, uninterrupted and shy. Through the partition, Helen began to snore. I took Karen's hands and placed them on my breasts, tight with milk.

"They're enormous," she said.

"They hurt," I said.

"This is a mastitis risk," she said. "Something must be done."

She put her mouth there. It was a task that needed doing. She sucked to take care of me, and it was how we found our way back to each other, her sucking, me moaning, the toothless black snake cowering and ashamed somewhere, jealous of our heat.

8

Perley

After the snakebite is when I began to live alone and that's when the real me starts. I lived in my own house and it was just my size with all the best furniture that I made myself. It was a round tin house with wheels. It was painted to look like it was the woods, real tree. My house had a label. THE MCCANN'S: STEP AWA, it said, and no one knew what that meant it was a secret and I made a secret password so no one would bother me. No one knew the password except Mama K. She was proud of me again and we did things together like we used to do. She taught me to use all her tools, the chisel the bevel the drill the Japanese saw, the tree-shaping sheep knife. Mama K was my elfin chief and I was an elf. She was the wise old wolf Nightrunner and I was Choplicker the wolf pup. We were steadfast and resolute and every night I gave her my report while she and Mama L held hands which they never used to do but now they did.

Mama L acted like any day they'd make me move back into the main house but I knew it was good that I moved into my own house because after that my women laughed at one another's jokes or when one of them said something the other two would nod their heads instead of start telling her why she was wrong. Sometimes they would smile at one another which at first I thought their faces would fall off if they did that. So even though I would always have a scar, I knew it was good that I got bit by a snake and I knew it was good that I lived alone and one day I was ready.

On the day that I was ready I knelt down at the campfire. I knelt down before my elfin chief Mama K. I said, I'm ready to go back, and Mama L was like, Oh, Piglet, not to school, and I said, Yes, to school, and the Mean Aunt was like, School, I thought you'd forgotten about school. Mama L was like, You don't have to go back to school if you don't want to, Piglet.

I want to, I said.

But Mama K didn't say anything she had her knife out and she was whittling the last leg of the chair we were building.

Then Mama L said, I called them and told them you were sick and I can call and tell them you aren't coming back.

I am coming back, I said, I have to go back.

He'll fall behind if he doesn't go back soon, said the Mean Aunt.

Then Mama K finally said something she said, Fall behind what, fall behind the regimented brainwashing schedule? I could tell she didn't think I was honorable and that all the time we had sawed with the Japanese saw and countersunk with the quarter-inch paddle bit didn't matter to her. It didn't matter to her that we were almost done whittling the legs for the chair. It didn't matter to her that she knew the password. It didn't even matter to her that I was her wolf pup and she was my wolf.

I could tell the Mean Aunt liked it a lot better now that Mama K and her were getting along because she looked at Mama K and she looked at me and then she said, You know, Perley, you do seem a lot happier not being in school.

I said, I have more training now and my power has only increased.

What I thought about was that I finally had my trick which was my new toxic face. And what I thought about was Rudy saying, Now you'll finally get some respect.

Mama K still wouldn't look at me and I could tell Mama L was worried because she kept looking at Mama K and waiting for Mama K to say something but Mama K just whittled and frowned at the campfire and didn't take Mama L's hand so Mama L started talking.

Mama L said, We respect you here, my Piglet. We respect your skills we admire you we love everything that you do. How can you prefer to go back to a windowless room instead of roaming in the woods?

But I said, Of course you respect my skills, of course you admire me, of course you love everything that I do. That doesn't prove anything. You are my women and you have to do that it's the law.

I don't have to do anything, Mama K said.

I am still honorable, I told Mama K even though she wasn't listening or if she was listening she couldn't hear me right. I just needed some time, I said. I practiced. I prepared. Now I'm ready to show them what I've got.

My wound was tight and itchy with an ache on the inside and I wasn't supposed to touch it but it felt good really good. It felt good when I stepped up onto the bus and the kids were like, Whoooaaa holy shit what's wrong with your face? and I was like, I got attacked by a snake. That's what I said. Attacked. And that word made them forget the word faggot and the word bastard and instead their brains became full of the word snake and the word attacked.

You should have seen the snake, I said, it was like a mile long. It was bigger than Madcoil even. Bexley didn't say anything just looked at me but I could tell he was toxically jealous and when we got to school there was a crowd around me on the playground and I couldn't even see the outside of it and Bexley couldn't take it anymore. I don't believe him, he said really loud. The faggot bastard is a liar.

But this other kid was like, No seriously I seen snakebites and that's definitely a snakebite but it's the biggest one I ever seen, and then this other kid was like, Dude, did you die? So why not, I was like, Yeah, I died. I died and then I came back. I have a special power. A special power? the kids asked. Yes, I said. I am Friend of Snake. Evidenced by that they live in my house and they sleep in my bed. Bexley tried to be like, Yeah, one time I got a snakebite, too, but this other kid who was his cousin was like, Yeah, and you cried like a friggin baby.

Everyone laughed and I laughed, too, it was friggin awesome. I laughed and then I got real serious and I said, I didn't cry. Which wasn't exactly a total lie. I didn't cry it's more like I couldn't make my arms let go of my mamas for an entire day, but I didn't need to tell anyone that. I felt steadfast. I felt resolute. I looked at each and every one of them in the eye. I didn't cry, I said. I. Did. Battle.

I had a feeling that the acorn kid would have been able to tell that I was lying, but the acorn kid wasn't there of course because he avoided crowds. He was like how I used to be before I was so super-popular. He was flanged. Too bad for him. I smiled sadly in a generous way because he was an oppressed minority and lucky for me I wasn't. Everything was going so well, it just kept getting better and better and I could see the kids almost be like, Sweet, can I come over? Almost, almost, they almost said it, but then I saw my nice teacher Ms. Carroll on the edge of the crowd, and she pushed her way in, and then she beckoned to me is what I would call it. She beckoned to me so she killed my dream of being carried on the shoulders of the other kids, like the conquering hero, Friend of Snake. Instead I was beckoned through the crowd of kids, and

they watched me go like I was Tyldak glid-
ing to Blue Mountain which was the principal's office.

You don't have to be afraid, honey, Ms.
Carroll said. What really happened to your
face? And the principal was like, Yes, honey,
no messing around, what's going on here,
you can tell us. It was weird because no one
had ever called me honey before and all this
talk of honey made me want some honey so
I was like, Can I have some honey? Oh,
honey, said Ms. Carroll, and she gave me a
Tootsie Pop. So I felt extremely powerful
and I didn't say anything. Are you worried
about being in trouble because you won't
be in trouble, Ms. Carroll said. You can trust
us. But I just chewed through the first Tootsie Pop and asked for another one, and then
when I had another one I was ready to talk.
It's a snakebite, I said which was easy to say
because it was true.

How did you get a snakebite? Ms. Carroll
asked.

A snake bit me, I said.

Were you unsupervised? the principal
asked. That one made me pause for a
second because it sounded like a trick. I
was supervised, I said because from the way
they said it I could tell that you were supposed to be supervised. I said, It's just that

244

I was asleep and the snake was in my bed with me, and it was my fault because I rolled over on it. I think that's what I said or pretty close. I have replayed it many times in my mind. I have replayed it like reading and rereading my comics to find out what made Ms. Carroll and the principal have those looks of disbelief and sorrow but also of what I would call satisfaction on their giant friendly faces.

9

Lily

I know it looked bad. The snow had begun. It was late afternoon. I stirred a pot of nettle stew over the campfire, hunched into Karen's overcoat against the wind and the thickening flakes. The dice were against us that week, so I worked through our stores. I added dried nettles by the handful, doused the stew with soy sauce for flavor, a cup of acorn flour for texture, a half cup of lentils for protein. My ingredients were lined up on a cinder block, and I held my coat open to shield them from the weather. I know it looked bad. We should have strung a tarp.

The dice were against us, but inside the crammed house, Helen leaned against a heap of fiberglass insulation, processing a roadkill deer by candlelight. She'd made it down to the guts, which were folded into a bloody soup in a five-gallon bucket at her feet. She meant to make thread from the sinew, pudding in the stomach sack, she meant to boil the kidneys in milk when we could get some. On the range, the deer's head simmered in the large canning pot. She meant to render the fat and save the skull. The whole mess reeked, swampy, warm iron, fat, shit, and wax, steaming up the windows.

After school, Perley had bolted straight out into the snowflakes. He wanted to check on some secret places he knew, wanted to see if the creek was frozen, barely allowed me to yank a blaze-orange hat over his ears. I'd told him to stay within whooping distance, but I'll admit that I hadn't whooped in a while. I'll admit that if my boy had fallen down a sinkhole, say, or met a rabid animal, or met a pervert wandering in the snowy forest, I might not have known. Dignity of risk. That's what Karen called it. I know it looked bad.

It might have looked worse if Karen had been home to get angry, but she had gone to answer a nickel ad for free scrap wood. It certainly would have looked worse if Rudy had been there to swagger and brag, but he was binge-drinking on the coal company land. Helen, Perley, and I were the only ones on the land that dark afternoon, and we fucked it up properly all on our own.

I took the intake worker for a Jehovah's Witness because I wasn't expecting anyone. I wasn't expecting anyone, and she came struggling down the path past the duck shed in sneakers and a long denim skirt, the hood of her sweatshirt hiding her face. The ducks ran before her, beating their wings, sounding the alarm. She swatted at snowflakes, dodged frozen lumps of duck shit. She tried hard not to touch the ground. About fifty feet from me, she waved, and I waved back. I figured I'd offer her some stew and then send her on her way, wait to burn up *The Watchtower* until after she'd gone. No need to hurt her feelings.

She made it to the campfire and she tilted her head back so I could see her face under that hood, and I saw how young she was. Nearly a kid. Then she raised up her feet, caked in icy mud, and she wiped her sneakers on my cinder block. The cinder block was my kitchen counter, my bottles and jars, my wooden spoon all lined up, but she was blind to it. She mistook it for a mud scraper. So I began to feel dread. She was not a Jehovah's Witness. She had a face like a Twinkie, cover-up caking her acne scars, lips like petals pushed together, a baby's mouth, her bad shoe scraping mud on my kitchen counter, and I won't forget how she smelled, amazing. Slapped across the face by a spring day. She was like the overgrown kid on Halloween who doesn't wear a costume. She brought me dread, and she was there to rob me.

"Are you Lily Marshall?" she asked. "The parent of Perley Marshall?"

"What's this about?" I asked, but polite.

"I'm here from Children's Services," she said. "There was a report at school." Was she nineteen, was she twenty? Was she from the college in town? There were students, I knew, eager to go into the community. They loved the community. I was the community. I'd heard of such things. I'd tried not to imagine them.

"A report at school," I said. "A report at school about what?"

"Surely you can tell me what you think there might have been a report about," she said. She was a straight-A student. She was the top of her class. She smelled amazing and I knew her voice. She was only a kid but her voice was the voice of my own mother, who would circle me with a sweet smile on her face, and then pounce. She would pounce and my grandma would have to hold her back.

"I'm sorry, but I really don't know what you mean," I said. And I didn't.

249

"Perley says he was bit by a snake in his own bed," the girl said. "We have to check on things like that." From deep within the pocket of her sweatshirt, she drew a slick rectangle, a tablet. She brought it to life. She tapped on it, her fingers red from the cold. I didn't stir the stew. I didn't tend the fire. I didn't invite her inside. She was ten feet from the house and blind to it. Blind to it the same way she'd been blind to my kitchen counter.

But this was a time for catch more flies with honey. This was a time for give the woman, the kid, whatever she is, give her what she wants. She loves me, the community. Give her what she wants and gasp for air once she's gone.

"You know how boys are," I said. "All kinds of scrapes and bites and bruises. At least he's healing well." I smiled to show I had nothing to hide. I smiled to hide my heart, struggling to escape from my chest. My cheeks broke ice when they lifted.

"You kept him home for three weeks, I understand," she said, not smiling back.

"We didn't want to expose him to all those germs at school," I said.

"Did you take him to a doctor?" she asked.

"My partner is a nurse," I said.

"Your partner?" she asked, fingers over

250

her screen.

"My partner. My domestic partner," I said the words. "Perley's other mother."

She tapped.

"Your partner's name?" she asked.

"Karen Sweeney," I said.

"But you are Perley's real mother?" she asked. When I didn't reply, she said, "Sorry. His biological mother?"

"I gave birth to Perley," I said. I wasn't an idiot. I'd heard about this. I'd heard it whispered between women, passed among families. I'd feared it. But I hadn't practiced. I hadn't prepared my comments. I had nothing to hide but that's not how it felt. Still, I tried to draw the honey into my mouth.

"I nursed that boy as long as he'd let me," I said, smiling. She looked at me. "Which is recommended by the World Health Organization," I said.

"What is?" she asked.

"Breastfeeding as long as possible," I said.

"I see," she said, tapped.

"My partner is a nurse," I said. "So she keeps up on these things."

"Is your partner the one who decided that Perley didn't need medical attention for the snakebite?" she asked.

"She's a nurse," I said.

251

"Ms. Sweeney works at the hospital?" she asked.

"She used to work at Community Health," I said.

"She's unemployed?" she asked.

"She takes care of Perley while I work," I said.

"Perley also said he lives alone," she said. "He says he lives in his own house, without adult supervision."

"Did he say that?" I asked.

"Yes," she said.

"He's definitely supervised," I said. She was a girl, I decided, a girl or not much older than one. She slipped her tablet into her pocket.

"Ms. Marshall. If you don't mind, I'd like to go inside," the girl said. "It's getting cold out here. I'd like to have a talk with Perley. I'd like to see the child's living situation."

So I had to invite her in, but what was in? There was no in, though for a moment I thought I could invent one. I closed my eyes, but when I opened them, it was still our shack facing me. There was nothing to do but lead her to it and watch her confusion. She must have thought it was a tool-shed. She must have thought it was a hollow tree. She was a girl but she was my own mother following me to the door, my mother who'd never come to visit, who'd moved to Virginia with someone she told me to call stepdad, my mother who'd never met Perley, though we sent pictures once a year, had just sent another one, the only way we ever remembered that it was Christmas.

Inside, the girl made a noise deep in her throat, put her sleeve over her mouth. I heard that gag before I remembered the smell, the steamed guts and deer brain, the boiling head, the snake musk, the cat pee, the mildew. Helen was invisible, separated from us by stacks upon stacks of old belongings. What was all this shit? Why hadn't we thrown it away? All of it worn-out, molding, broken, no use. I couldn't explain it, not to myself or to anyone. The girl gagged, a deep growl, and I showed her to the sofa. She perched on the edge like hovering over a toilet seat. I hovered over her. I folded my hands because there was nothing else I could fold.

"Can I get you anything? A cup of coffee?" I asked, but she shook her head. She took out her tablet again, shone the thing up at her face.

"Is this your primary dwelling?" she asked, rolling her finger across the screen.

"We're always working on it," I said. I struggled to remember my project, which was still sweetness, smoothness, nothing to hide.

Helen stuck her head out from behind the insulation pile. Her arms were red to the elbows, coated in blood, guts, and brain.

"Who's this? A Jehovah's Witness?" she asked. The girl looked up.

"This must be Ms. Sweeney," the girl said, and I was happy to correct her.

"This is Helen," I said. "Helen Conley. She's like Perley's aunt. She's kind of a butcher."

"Licensed?" asked the girl.

"I'm not a butcher," Helen said. "I just happen to be doing some butchering. What is this? What is this about? Who are you?"

"Helen," I said, "it's all right. She's just asking."

"Asking about what?" Helen asked.

"Asking about Perley's bite, which is healing quite well," I said.

"I don't get it," Helen said. "Are you Perley's teacher? Are you the police? You don't look like the police."

"Are you a student in town?" I asked.

"Graduated," the girl said. "With my B.A. in social work."

"Congratulations," I said. "Your mother must be proud."

"A social worker?" asked Helen. "What

254

do you want with us?"

"I do intake work for Children's Services," she said.

"Perley told his teacher about his snakebite," I said.

"Oh shit, you've got to be kidding me," Helen said.

"It's healing well," I said. "There's nothing to worry about. Kids and their scrapes." I clasped my hands together until they hurt. I never sat down.

"Where is Perley now? I'd like to talk to him," the girl said.

Helen looked at me, but I didn't say anything right away. I had nothing to hide, yet I was hiding, hiding, I was hiding him.

"Where is he?" the intake worker asked.

"There's a lot of new studies out," Helen began, "about what they call helicopter parenting. Experts are reexamining the benefits of nonintervention and free play."

"Dignity of risk," I said.

"Where is he?" the girl asked.

"He's playing outside," I said.

"Alone? In the dark? In the snow?" she asked. "Ms. Marshall. I'm asking you. Do you know where your child is?" She made to get up, but I beat her to it, lunged for the door, escaped onto the porch like fleeing a burning building.

I whooped. I whooped. I whooped. I whooped. I screamed into the woods. It was the screaming I'd grown up with, the hollers of angry grown-ups tearing past all the wolf trees at backyard borders, tearing them apart. I whooped. I didn't hear back. I despaired.

Then came Perley's whoop, and then came Perley. He bounded out of the darkness, down onto the porch, hatless and joyful, his small face red, his scar shining purple in the cold. My milk flooded. I lifted him up into my arms.

"There's someone here to see you," I said, crushing him as he wriggled free.

"I knew it!" Perley said, glowing up at me. "I knew it. I knew someone would come over to see me. Who is it? Is it Bexley?"

"It's a nice girl," I said. Perley dimmed.

"A girl?" he said.

"A woman. A young woman," I said.

"A grown-up?" he said. "Can I go back out to the woods?"

"She says you told people about your snakebite," I said, and he lit up again, proud.

"Of course I did," he said. "They asked me what happened so I told them. They love it. They love me."

"She says that you told people you live alone," I said.

"Definitely," Perley said.

"You don't live alone, Perley," I said.

"Yes, I do," he said.

"You'll have to tell her the truth, Perley," I said. "No big stories. Some people might misunderstand the way we live."

"Of course I'll tell her the truth," Perley said. "Why would I lie?"

When we went inside I kept my hands on Perley's shoulders so that I wouldn't fall down onto the floor.

I'd judged the intake worker as no manners, no good with people, but when she saw Perley, I understood why she'd chosen her line of work. Her pinched teenager face lost its reserve, her body relaxed, she dropped off the sofa and knelt in front of him, careless of the layer of filth on the floorboards. She left her tablet on the sofa.

"Hello, Perley," she said, leaning toward him. "I'm Lisa. I'm here to help."

"I was in the woods and I found a cave with deadly icicles but I never found where it ended because it's basically unfathomable," Perley said. "I can show you if you want."

"How is your face feeling?" she asked, like it was just the two of them. "It looks like you got an ouchie."

"It feels great," he said. "It feels super-amazing."

"He's fine," I interrupted. "He was outside playing, and now we're going to have dinner."

"Where?" the intake worker asked Perley.

"Outside at the campfire," Perley said. "This place isn't fit to be lived in."

"Inside," I said. "We'll eat in here tonight."

"We don't really have a house right now," Perley said.

"There's been a misunderstanding," I said. "Tell the nice girl the truth. Tell her that you don't live alone. Tell her your snakebite is healing just fine."

"Yeah," Perley said. "But my mamas still can't get the snake out of the bed. That's why I live up in the woods in a totally sweet house all by myself. I even get to have a fire up there and no one else is allowed inside. I can show you if you want."

"The snake hasn't been in the bed since the night it bit you," I said. But this, like everything else, was a mistake.

"This must be some kind of joke," Helen said.

"Helen," I said. But she bustled forward into the room, up to her elbows in gore. She shoved past me and dropped down onto the sofa above the intake worker, who drew closer to Perley. Helen pursued her, put her sticky elbows on her knees, and leaned around to peer into the girl's face. Then I understood that nothing and no one could stand in Helen's way. Goddamn it all to hell, she was going to be helpful.

"What are you, seventeen? Eighteen?" Helen asked.

"I'm a social worker," the girl said.

"Oh right, you have a B.A.," Helen said. "Four years of college. Very impressive. Me too. Can I ask you something? Who sent you?"

"The principal called our office. He's a mandated reporter," the intake worker said.

"That principal," Helen said. "Of course. That stuffed shirt. I should have known it. What's he got, a fucking vendetta?"

"We make home visits all the time, just to check that everything is normal," the girl said.

"Normal. Ha," Helen said. "Tell me. Do you have children of your own? What in the hell are you doing here bothering us?"

I strengthened my grip on Perley's shoulder. He shrugged my hand away. I clamped it right back.

The young intake worker remembered her training. She rose, reached for her tablet. "Ms. Conley," she said. "I'm here to talk to the family. Not to those who aren't in the family." She turned to me. "Ms. Marshall. It's just you and your child living here with how many nonrelative adults?"

I opened my mouth but Helen didn't give me a chance. "Nonrelative adults," she said. "Just what do you mean by that?"

"How many single adults live here?" the intake worker asked again, trying to ignore Helen.

"Just Helen," I said.

"And you mentioned Karen Sweeney," the girl said.

"Karen's my domestic partner," I said.

"Ha. Not by state law," Helen said. "According to state law we might as well be practicing polygamy up here on this hill."

"What's polygamy?" asked Perley.

"We aren't practicing polygamy," I told the intake worker.

"Or even polyamory," Helen said. "Which isn't actually illegal."

"Helen has a sense of humor. She's very good with Perley," I said.

"She's my Mean Aunt," Perley said, "and I love her."

"Of course you do," the intake worker said. "Any other adults?" she asked me.

"You might as well put Rudy on there," Helen said.

"Rudy doesn't really live here," I said.

"He's just a frequent visitor."

"Just tell them everything," Helen said. "They'll find out anyway and then they'll say you lied if you didn't tell them in the first place."

"So Rudy is a friend or a boyfriend?" asked the intake worker.

"Oh please," Helen said. "A friend. Or a royal pain in the ass, depending on what day you ask."

"He's a man we let sleep out on the pipeline," I clarified.

We all have our strategies. Mine had been to keep smiling, to try to steer us smooth, to cast a spell around us. But Helen's strategy was to treat the caseworker like a bear. To be firm. To be aggressive enough to show that we weren't afraid, but not so aggressive that the bear would charge. Follow this strategy and the bear will retreat.

So the wisdom goes, but every word that Helen said was alien and appalling to this intake girl, who was not a bear, who appeared to be made of ice-cream cake, caving in when exposed to the rank steam of our kitchen, her makeup dripping down her neck, pooling around popped zits. As she melted she resented us for it. As she melted, she became more sure of her duty.

"Who owns this place, or are you rent-

261

ing?" she asked.

"We own it in common," Helen said. "We don't really believe in private ownership."

If Helen knew so goddamn much, then why didn't she know when to shut the hell up? Instead, she opened her mouth and the whole room fell into it, window frames, bicycle, boxes, fiberglass, guts, and brains. All I could do was stand back and keep hold of Perley, dig my fingers in under his collarbone, those small caves, too small to crawl into and hide. Helen's mouth was a drain, sucking everything in, leaving us no escape.

"Wait a minute," I said. "Actually, legally Helen owns it, but she shares it with us. And actually I think I do believe in private ownership, or at least no one has ever asked me my feelings on the issue."

"It's not like this is a case of neglect," Helen said, standing up and taking a step toward the intake worker, who moved back, colliding with the rusted bike frame. "Neglect would be if we weren't doing anything about the snakes. But this is a very organized household. We have a lot of plans. And if you need proof, I have proof. I'll show you." She wiped her hands on her shirt, smearing deer guts. She stepped up onto an upturned dresser drawer and took the Best Practices

Binder down from its shelf. I watched dully, I am not proud to say. Hiding, hiding, hide him, was what echoed inside me, though I know I should have been more clever, more practical. I know it looked bad.

"There's a best way to do nearly everything," Helen said. "I don't know if you know what it's like to try to live simply, to do it yourself. I don't know if you know what it's like to live by a code, a system, to challenge yourself each and every day, to practice and prepare. But those are our watchwords up here." She handed the binder to the intake worker. The girl took it gingerly in two hands, avoiding the place where Helen's hand had been. Wincing, she sat down on the sofa.

"Open it," Helen said. "We could publish this thing. We're very professional up here, seriously. I think you'll find this very reassuring." Haloed by the steam of jellied deer brain, Helen grinned. Cobwebbed, lonely, misunderstood, the Best Practices Binder was yet Helen's ace in the hole. She'd been waiting years to play it.

The intake worker thumbed through a few pages and stopped. "What's this?" she asked. "Dump the shit bucket when it's two-thirds full?"

So Helen closed her mouth. Simply, she

263

saw what she'd done. So what? Can I forgive her? The only one I can forgive is Perley, who said eagerly, "It's my job to shovel the shit pile." He didn't say it to be mean, or to complain. He said it because we'd trained him to be proud of all that he could do.

"Excuse me?" asked the girl.

Helen rallied. "Don't worry," she said. "It's called humanure. We let it sit for two years before we put it on the garden." Maybe she even hoped to make the intake worker laugh. But the girl never wrinkled her makeup with a smile.

"Do you have a toilet?" she asked. Perley hesitated like he'd heard that one before, but the girl gave him that private smile again. "You can tell me," she said. "I won't be mad."

"We shit in a bucket," Perley said. When he saw my face he said, "I mean poop. But if you only have to go pee, just do it in the woods. Don't do it in the bucket because it starts to smell really bad. But it's okay if you have an accident. Mama L and Mama K say that a lot of times with girls especially if they've had a baby, they poop and pee at the same time. They can't really help it."

Helen looked at me, but me and speaking were no longer on speaking terms. I had seen what good open mouths had done us, and I meant to keep my mouth shut. My tongue was dead. My lungs were flat. I had no voice. All I had were arms and hands to hold my boy against me until they pried him loose.

The intake girl's fingers sped across her tablet, but with her other hand she kept turning the pages of the binder.

Helen, gone lame with desperation, said, "Let's put that away. It's probably boring. It's not finished. It's actually not even fact-checked, not completely."

The intake worker thumbed. Stopped. Read.

"What's Survival Dice?" she asked, and Perley was eager to explain.

When Perley was a baby, I'd promised to respect the mystery of him. So here he was, mysterious. I'd never noticed before how much Perley wanted to show himself to other people. He practiced, he prepared, he learned and recited each day, and somehow he believed — had we taught him this? where had it come from? — that the day would come when the world would reward him. He'd yearned for that day, and now he figured it was here.

Helen, on overdrive, pushed aside boxes, dove beneath the sink, unearthed a mouse nest and a family of cockroaches, rummaged and cursed, until, flushed and breathless, hat falling over her eyes, ratty hair coming loose over one shoulder, she rose. "Found it," she gasped. She clenched that old housewarming gift, the one from my boss at the hardware store. The economy-size, unopened, seven-year-old bottle of hand sanitizer.

"We care a lot about hygiene around here," she said. "I know you people are really big on this stuff. Am I right?"

The intake worker remained silent, frowning slightly.

"Right?" asked Helen again. She pushed forward, toppling window frames. She raised the hand sanitizer above her head. "Right? Just admit it. Please could you admit that you people love hand sanitizer? Just give me that."

"Please," the girl said. "Please calm down. I am going to leave now, and we can have this conversation later when I feel safer."

"Safer? What in the hell does that mean?" asked Helen, brandishing the bottle.

"You are behaving erratically," said the intake worker. "So I'm going to come back at a better time."

She turned to me. I stood swaying, my fingers numb from grasping my boy. "I will make my report, and you can expect that we will be in touch again soon." Then she knelt down again before Perley, her prize.

"Perley, honey, don't worry," she said. "Remember that you can tell your teacher anything that happens, okay? We are here to help you. Sometimes mommies and daddies — even when they love you very much — they need help. Or they need a break. And it's not about you, and it's not your fault."

"We don't have a daddy," Perley said.

When she left, the house fell down around us and we burst into flames.

Helen and I sat on the sofa, hands limp on our laps, deer skull bubbling, dinner forgotten. Perley sat between us, peering between our faces, the Best Practices Binder on his lap.

"I'm just glad you weren't here alone, Lily," Helen said.

"You should have let me handle it," I said.

"You needed my help," said Helen. "You couldn't even talk. You had guilt written all over your face."

"But I'm not guilty," I said.

"You needed someone to stand up for you," Helen said. "You needed an ally. Rudy says that I don't know how to stand up for what I believe in when the time is right. I've

267

been working on it. I won't be a bystander anymore."

"Being a bystander was never really your problem," I said.

"That girl had a B.A.? Well, so what? She thinks that's going to intimidate us? I have a B.A., too," she said.

"I think you're what they call an educated fool," I said.

Perley pushed the Best Practices Binder onto the floor and climbed into my lap. "I don't see what everyone's freaking out about," he said. "That girl probably never met people with such toxically cool skills as us."

"That's probably true," I said.

"I told the truth," he said.

"Yes, you did," I said.

"I think I kind of blew her mind. I think she really liked me," he said.

I smoothed his hair back and dug my chin into his fuzzy head. "Don't worry," I said. "Don't worry, my love."

"I'm not worried," he said. "I'm hungry."

"Let's eat chocolate-chip pancakes for dinner," I said. "Let's eat quickly before Mama K gets home. It'll be our secret."

"That girl was obviously totally delusional," Helen said. "It's actually really hard to take a child away from their family. They can't do it just because you shit in a bucket, or because your kid gets a bug bite."

"A snakebite," I said.

"Don't worry," she said. "Just forget about it."

"Take me away?" Perley said. "Take me where?"

"Nowhere, Perley," I said. "Don't worry."

"I'm not worried," said Perley. "And I don't think that girl seemed crazy. I thought that girl seemed nice, and pretty."

"She wasn't pretty," I said.

"She didn't look like a man. She looked like a woman," Perley said.

"She was wearing makeup," I said.

"She smelled good," Perley said.

"I noticed that, too," I said. "What did she smell like?"

"New shoes," Perley said.

"You don't know what new shoes smell like," I said.

"Then mustard," Perley said.

"Salt water," I said.

"Varnish," Perley said.

"Pepper," I said.

"She smelled like after they mow the pipeline," Perley said. "Or like when we have macaroni and cheese for dinner."

"We've never had macaroni and cheese for dinner," I said.

Helen scooped up the Best Practices Binder and held it under one arm while she made her way over to the range and turned off the burner. "People get paid millions of dollars to figure out how other people can smell and look in a way that will be completely persuasive to a developing frontal lobe, not naming any names," she said. She looked meaningfully back over her shoulder at Perley.

"Am not," he said, pressing his head up under my chin.

"Are too," Helen said. "You are a developing frontal lobe. Which is why sometimes you are seduced by cheap thrills such as makeup, perfume, and chocolate chips." She used tongs to lift the deer skull dripping from the pot. She set it to dry on a stack of old newspapers by the sink.

"Karen's going to be pissed," I said over Perley's head. "She'll say we were stupid to even let that girl in the door."

"Why tell Karen?" Helen said. "Save her the worry. It's just that asshole principal trying to scare us. He's still mad about those fruit trees."

Perley made his voice small so that only I could hear. "Was that true?" he asked. "Do you need a break? Do you need some help?"

"No," I said. "Yes. I do need help. I need

270

your help not telling Mama K about the chocolate-chip pancakes, and I need your help not telling Mama K about the nice girl," I said. "It will only worry her, and like you said, Perley, like you said, what's the point of everyone freaking out?"

Lord knows how I let him off my lap, how I pushed myself off the sofa to make pancakes. Lord knows how I could wade through the deer guts, the bucket, the brain, to lift the skillet and scrape the last cup or two of flour. Lord knows how I could do it, but I stumbled forward in my rubber boots to try. I added muddy prints to the blackened floor. I reached for the secret stash of chocolate chips. I uncapped the vanilla. And then I knew.

"She didn't smell like any of those things," I said. "She smelled like Outside."

"Holy fuck," Helen said, in immediate recognition. She'd been to the mall just like I had. Just like I had she'd cut through to the feed store at least once a month, tracking mud past the perfume counter. We never bought anything, of course, it was just our shortcut to the duck pellets. But we'd seen the advertisements, hay bales appetizing as sponge cake, glittering streams, oak trees with not one leaf out of place. We'd dodged the free samples they sprayed at you, the

271

new line of perfume that was supposed to make you smell fresh and untamed.

She tried to comfort me, upbeat until the last. "Don't let it get to you," she said. "It's just some stupid perfume. They sold it, she bought it. So what?" She handed me the skillet, but I took it without feeling its weight.

The intake girl had bought the new perfume, the perfume called Outside, whereas my sorry ass lived outside, the outside that smelled like diesel oil and sawdust, smelled like rendered guts and compost, smelled like the shit pile. So then I knew for sure that the nice intake girl would be back. I knew that she would win.

Karen

I should have been there. I was always there. Helen might be off with Rudy, Lily might be at the hardware and salvage store, but me, I'd made up my mind to quit the clinic, to bring in firewood, to lever up the house where it fell down the hill, patch rotten boards, thaw frozen water pipes, fix the duck shed, dig out drainage. I'd raised Perley day by day until he left me for that damn school. I'd made up my mind to ignore the lonely days when they came. I'd made up my mind to stay with my pack. So I should have been there. Should have been but wasn't.

I was always there but that day I saw in the nickel ads that I could take down a shed in Alexander Township. I could take down the shed and get all the wood from it, plenty to finish the chair and the bunk in Perley's camper, extra for garden beds, firewood, a new porch step. Maybe some interesting pieces to whittle into spoons, chains, skulls. Could be hardwood, sometimes you'd even find walnut mixed in. I went off that afternoon to have a look. But when I made it there, there was no there. Someone had been there before me, and the shed was gone, leaving only a shitty foundation, black from years of a coal-burning stove. I drove back, leaking oil through gusts of snowflakes, hoping stew would be ready when I got home, hoping they'd stoked the fire, maybe strung a tarp, because we were still eating outside, the house full of trash and snakes. But when I got home the campfire was out and they were all inside. I could smell pancakes and everyone was busy, I mean everyone was absorbed, I mean Lily handed me a bowl of burnt stew, but no one would talk to me.

Except Perley. Perley wasn't busy. He sat on the sofa with keen eyes, staring at me, his mouth sealed shut. He had chocolate on his face. I pretended I didn't see it. I was tired of being the villain.

"What happened today?" I asked, spooning stew into my mouth. "Did I miss anything?" But no one would talk to me.

Except Perley, who said, "Lots of stuff happened. That's the thing about days. So many things happen every day. So many things that it can be hard to remember exactly what things happened. So it's impossible to be bored which is what you taught me." Then he shut his mouth again, watching me.

"Thank you, Perley," I said. "Thanks for reminding me." I took a bite of the stew, scalded mulch.

And why even tell this part of the story, when me knowing or not knowing makes no difference? Should have been there but wasn't. I'm nothing. A non-thing. So why even talk about it? Why talk at all?

Why talk at all except to report that the sheriff's deputy showed up the next day with a teenage kid, made-up heavy as a drag queen, stinking like the inside of a funeral parlor. I stood at the door of my house but they wouldn't look at me. I talked to them but they wouldn't talk to me, because they said they would only talk to the legal parent. They said they would only talk to Perley's mother but they didn't mean me. And I heard unhygienic, evidence of neglect, criminal activity — a fucking vendetta, claimed Helen — lack of supervision, possible lack of adequate nutrition. So no one needed to tell me what had happened yesterday while I was gone. I could see what had happened. Helen had opened up her mouth and talked and talked and talked. Lily had closed her mouth and leaked water down her face. Perley had bragged. And me, why even say I should have been there, when here I was now, a ghost? A hat rack. There but not there. A wolf without a pack. Disappeared.

They wouldn't talk to me as they got Perley ready to go, so I talked to Lily, who looked like there was a phone call in her ear, a radio signal she couldn't quite make out. I don't think she knew that her mouth was open or that her eyes were wet.

"Ask them," I said, as they told Perley he could choose his favorite toys to take with him, as he said, "I don't have toys, I have tools."

"Ask them what?" asked Lily.

"Ask them where they're taking him. Ask them who we talk to. How we follow up. Ask them who we can call. How we can get him back. You're the one with the legal rights here," I said. "So ask them."

Lily said to Perley, "Don't worry, my Piglet. This is just a mix-up. Don't be afraid."

"I'm not afraid, everyone, okay?" Perley said, fumbling to unzip his knapsack. "I can spend the night by myself. I don't need you people all the time, okay? Okay?"

"Ask them," I said.

"All the things Karen said," Lily said. "How do we do those things?"

Helen said to the sheriff's deputy, "You fucking piece of shit."

"Careful," the sheriff's deputy said. "I heard how you've been behaving. You need to keep your temper."

"You're a shitbag," Helen said.

"I'm doing what's best for the child," he said. "People roaming all around this place, no one's looking after the kid, no respect for the law, fudging your community service hours, trying to game the system. You people need to figure out how to live."

"Please let me," the intake worker said, touching his arm. Not unkindly, she told Lily, "He'll go to a foster family tonight, Ms. Marshall, and we'll be in touch with you about visitation. There will be a review hearing, a reunification plan."

"This can't be legal," I said.

But they wouldn't talk to me, so I talked to Perley, who was putting my *ElfQuest* comics into his knapsack.

"Perley, you need to tell these people that it's not what they think, that you want to stay here with us," I said.

But Perley said, "I like living on my own. I'm ready to go mix in with some other people for a change. Maybe some other kids. What's so wrong about that?"

"Perley," I said. My voice was quiet. "That's enough. You need to stop lying to these people."

To these people, Helen and I were the same. We were nothing but nonrelative adults. But Perley couldn't see that. He loved the attention. He reddened with happiness every time that girl got on her knees and spoke to him in her solemn sweet voice. My kid was drunk with power. Since toddlerhood he'd savored each moment of defiance.

"This is real, Perley," I said. "Perley. This isn't a game."

"I think I'd like to live somewhere new for a while," Perley said. He looked at the intake girl. He did this weird sad smile thing, like his face wasn't his face, like he thought he was the baby Jesus. He said, "I think I need a break. I need some help."

When it's your own child, love is a dark animal, is exploding. Live forever, live forever, this love pleads. But this love knows that we were born to be wrenched apart by death. This love is not a heart shape. There's no pleasure in it. This love can quickly turn to rage. It sharpens into a weapon that is out of our control. This is what's meant by a crime of passion. My crime of passion went like this:

"You little fucking moron. You little fucking liar. If this is how you want it, then you'd better fucking go. Get out. You want a wolf pack? This wolf will help you pack."

His small shocked face. My ungainly arm, ripping his knapsack from his grasp, tossing it outside. Hoisting him up by the shoulder so that his feet brushed the ground. Dragging him to the door. Ignoring his twisted arm, his cry of pain. Tossing him out after his knapsack. Slamming the door after him. The intake worker and the deputy closing in.

I broke. And by broke I mean, How can I put it back together again? And by broke I mean, No way to fix it. And by broke I mean doomed to wander.

Perley

You can call someone a faggot bastard or you can call someone a developing frontal lobe or you can call someone a little fucking moron but I am against name-calling. I am not a developing frontal lobe. I am not a faggot bastard. I am not a little fucking moron. I am a kid and I am powerful and I am Friend of Snake. It was just we never had people over. That was a whole main part of it.

I mean we'd be driving down the road and we'd wave at every single person and at the gas station we'd trade Mike duck eggs for maple syrup and after it snowed Bexley's uncle would plow our driveway, and Frank's kids would smile at me in the IGA parking lot, and we'd stop at the mill sometimes for flour, but that was as close as we ever got. We'd wave at our neighbors on the road and I'd say why can't they come spend the night? And Mama K would laugh and Mama L would say, Piglet, they probably want to spend the night in their own bed just like you like to spend the night in your own bed. So I would feel like a fucking moron 'cause spend the night is not really what I meant, what I really meant was like eat dinner with us or go exploring or have a campfire, but they never did. The only

279

person who would ever come over was Rudy, even though Rudy was a royal pain in the ass.

Rudy asked me if I wished I had a dad but this is what I wished:

To live where no one knew me, to watch television and have it where even on a rainy day, you could turn on the light at night and not just have a candle. And where my women weren't snapping at each other all the time and trying to figure out what we were going to eat and sometimes it was gross. Plus they thought everyone was either a little fucking moron or a big fucking moron and I was like wait a minute those people haven't even had the chance to see how much they totally love us.

What I'm saying is that when that girl came over I wanted to show her my skills. I wanted to show her how prepared we were. I mean for anything. I was proud. And when she took me with her I was brave.

I was brave, but I didn't look at Mama L, just to make sure I wouldn't think about how she liked to say, Look, I found a Velvet Piglet in the woods I think I'll take care of it I think I'll nurse it back to health. I wouldn't think about how she liked to hold me and ask, Have you heard the story of the mama who cuddled her Velvet Piglet so much that his head popped?

I pushed that Velvet Piglet feeling away. I was steadfast. I was resolute. If Mama K wouldn't hear my report, I would find someone else to give my report to. The snakebite made me realize I was special and I was chosen and I would always act with bravery and meet my destiny head-on like a Wolfrider. So even when Mama K tried to pull my arm off and threw me out the door, I knew it was a test. I kept my eyes dry. Even when Mama L called my name I didn't look around.

I loved my women, of course I did. They were my family. And I loved my tin house where no one knew the password unless I told them. And I loved my home which was the Holt with places that no one knew but me, for example a cave, a cliff, a tree that was a catapult, a dead giant. There was no one I knew who practiced more, who was more prepared. And still.

Rudy asked me if I wished I had a dad and this is what I wished: to be an orphan.

So when the pretty Outside Girl asked me if I wanted to try living with another family I was like hell yes and I didn't even get in trouble for saying hell.

Helen

Perley was gone. Lily was on her knees on the ground. Her open mouth was quicksand. Her silence might as well have been a thunderstorm, for how deafening and dark it was.

Karen said, "Get up," and went to take her arm, and Lily threw her off. Karen backed up, but Lily stalked her step for step. Lily went for Karen with the back of her hand. She became a snake, springing, striking. When Karen tried to pin Lily's arms to her sides, Lily ducked expertly out of her grasp, and I recognized the training Karen had drilled into Perley. I never thought Lily had paid much attention, but she came up lightly in a crouch and she brought her hand down across Karen's face so that Karen's head whipped around, and she stumbled. Lily proceeded to wallop Karen with grim efficiency, and as she did she talked. She hadn't said a thing, but now she said all the things. She said:

"It's your fault. With refusing to build a decent house, even though you knew how. With your bullshit about perfection, about training, about practicing and preparing. With him sleeping alone in that camper, with not getting rid of the snakes, with the shit bucket, with no groceries, the wild foods. Survival Dice. Fucking Survival Dice."

I stood back, not saying, For the record a lot of those ideas were mine. I didn't know where to begin. The beating continued. She said:

"It's your fault. With the way it's always us versus them, we haven't had people over since that fucking housewarming party when we first built this shithole, no friends. It's your fucking fault. It's your fault. With throwing him out the door, swearing at him, almost dislocating his fucking arm. He's our child, for fuck's sake. He's seven."

And Karen just took it. She put her hands up to protect her face. She crouched to protect her gut. But other than that, she offered herself so that Lily could beat her.

I certainly did not intervene. In fact, if anyone asked me what I thought, I might have said that Karen had it coming. I saw my own fists in Lily's fists. My taste buds chimed with the sound of impact.

When Lily had exhausted herself, she stood heaving over Karen. Her hair hung in her face. Karen was a mess, nose bloody, shirt torn open.

"Do you feel better?" Karen asked. Her voice was full of love, unguarded, the way I had never heard it. Lily just stared at her.

"Baby?" asked Karen. I had never heard her call Lily such a thing ever before. I had never heard her call Perley that, even when he was an actual baby. But Lily was unmoved. She appeared to not be in the same room with the two of us. Her anger had subsided, giving way to the next problem, the vast one. Perley being taken was the world, and standing on the world, you can't see the beginning or end of it. You can't tell if it's round or if it's flat. So Lily was mystified. You could see it in her face. She never answered Karen. She just said, "I have to get him back. I have to figure out what to do. I have to think." And she walked out the door, leaving the two of us standing there.

I brought Karen some plantain to stanch the bleeding. I brought her a glass of water. I opened my mouth, but she put her hand up.

"The best thing that you did in the last ten minutes was to not open your mouth. You're on a winning streak, so just don't," she said.

"Okay," I said.

"I said shut the fuck up," said Karen. She reached beneath her torn shirt, felt her arm, and winced. "That woman is effective," she said. She crushed the plantain and stuffed it into her nose. She looked at me. "Don't think I don't know what you want to fucking say," she said.

"What?" I said.

"Shut up," she said. "You want to thank me for taking the half of the beating that was meant for you. I know it. You and me might be like oil and water but half that shit Lily was saying she could have been saying to you. You and me are the same, right? I might not like it much, but I admit it. The odd one out here is Lily. Too bad I don't date butch girls. You and me basically belong together. We're two of a fucking kind. This fucked-up house? The wild foods? The preparations? Perfection? You want to talk about perfection? The Best Practices Binder? The motherfucking Best Practices Binder?"

"I don't think that it's fair to blame everything on the Best Practices Binder," I said.

"I told you I don't care what you fucking think. Where's the binder?" said Karen.

"What?"

"Where's the fucking binder? No, don't say anything, I told you to shut the fuck up. I'll find it."

She went around the kitchen, pulling apart shelves and drawers. I had hidden the binder, worried about a return visit from the intake worker. I could see a corner of it sticking out from behind the bread box. I tried to edge in front of it, but Karen saw me. She reached behind me and grabbed it. "I should have done this a long time ago," she said, and she took the binder and left the house, so I went after her. I saw her plunge down the hillside to the creek, which was full and ferocious from the melting snow. She flung the binder in. It fell like a dead bird. From between the hard plastic covers its pages, feathers, flew up and out, coated the creek, and floated away or got caught in the elderberry. The binder itself was tossed up and grabbed by the milk-chocolate water. I saw it kiss a crushed beer can, snag and then loosen from a birch branch, sink again, drown. I saw Karen stand on the bank, her back to me, holding her torn-up arm. For once I didn't say a thing.

■ ■ ■ ■

PART III
GALL OF THE EARTH

■ ■ ■ ■

10

Perley

If no one will invite you over but you want to go over then you want to go over then you have to find your own way over. The pretty Outside Girl gave me candy like eating a blue princess, and we went. But we didn't go very far. We probably could have got there way quicker just by going through the woods instead of along the road but it was night and it was snowing and when we got there a woman turned the porch light on it was an old woman. The Outside Girl said, Come on, Perley, don't be afraid. I won't say I was afraid. I will say that I was alert. I will say that the Outside Girl held my hand and led me up onto the porch and she said, This is Grandma Barlow, and Grandma Barlow said, You'd better come in where it's warm, my son, and the Outside Girl gave me a little push and she and I went into the house and Grandma Barlow came in after us and she shut the door and she blew her nose into her night-gown. She said, Welcome, and I looked at her better. She was a giant old woman with gray skin like an old magazine with writing on it that I couldn't read, yellow hair like big tin cans, and silver flowers everywhere I mean all over her nightgown and the Outside Girl said to her, Sorry we got here so late we had some trouble over there took longer than I thought I'll be back in the morning and we can do the paperwork and talk things over. Then the Outside Girl knelt down to me the way she liked to do and looked deep into my eyes like she saw in a movie which I am not allowed to watch and she said, For now, Perley, get some sleep. Then she squeezed me so that her smell would never leave me and she left through the front door, and when she left I knew I probably had made a mistake. I was not afraid, I was alert, but I would just as soon have been at home with my Mama L. I would just as soon have been giving Mama K my report. I would just as soon have been leeching acorns with the Mean Aunt, but instead I was in this weird house with Grandma Barlow and she said, Tonight it's the pull-out bed 'cause Altemonte's already asleep, and there's no need to wake him. I didn't ask who Altemonte was and she lifted the cushions on the sofa and like magic a bed sprang out and there was a blanket that smelled like flowers floating in soup and I climbed under the covers with all my clothes on and Grandma Barlow said, I'll bring you some hot milk that will do you good, and she left the room and she came back with a plastic cup. I didn't like the smell, I didn't like the skin on top, but I drank it anyway because she was watching me and then she said, We'll chat about it all in the morning, my son, just holler at me if you need any little thing, the bathroom is at the back, and she switched off the light and left the room and I was alert. I tried to orient myself. I sealed my eyes shut and imagined every turn the car had made on the ride over, just to make sure I could find my way back, and when I could see my way back to my women, I fell asleep. I didn't dream about Mama L and I didn't dream about the Mean Aunt. In my dream it was just me and my Mama K. She was the old wolf and I was the young wolf but we were also elves riding on wolves. We were on a quest. It was the quest we would one day go on together after we had been through all of our trials and tests, of which this was one. I was up to it. I was invincible. As far as anyone knew.

When I woke up the old snow grayly

slushed against the windows which had plastic stapled across them so you couldn't see all the way out and the soup blanket curdled me and I had to pee so bad but I knew that if I moved the day would begin and I wasn't ready for that, I needed to think. Then came coffee grinding in the kitchen and I heard Grandma Barlow talking to someone it was the Outside Girl back again. I heard their voices back and forth and soon I heard coffee go glug into a cup and they were in there talking about me. Everyone was talking about me ever since I got the snakebite and became super-popular and famous. So I just flexed my whole body really hard and held my pee which was one of my toxic skills and I listened.

Of course I can take another one, said Grandma Barlow. Of course I can.

The Outside Girl said, And I thank you for it, we appreciate it, the agency does.

I'm here to comfort them, Grandma Barlow said.

And you do, said the Outside Girl.

Grandma Barlow said, But some things, there's no comfort. Losing your baby.

He's not a baby, he's seven, said the Outside Girl.

Altemonte's eight and he's still my baby, Grandma Barlow said. Altemonte's mama's a grown woman and she'll always be my baby. There's no words for it, is what I'm saying. I feel for Perley's mama.

When she said that, I felt for my mama, too. I felt for her so that I almost followed the map in my mind right back home, but then the Outside Girl talked about me again. She said, Perley's been through a lot. Which sounded like a quest so I just held on to my pee harder and I kept listening.

We'll put together a reunification plan, of course, the Outside Girl said. But they've got a lot of work to do. He's mostly been left to take care of himself. No proper nutrition. No adequate housing. Snakes in the house.

What kind of snakes? asked Grandma Barlow.

Black rat snakes, said the Outside Girl.

It certainly is hard to get rid of those, said Grandma Barlow. Everyone around here knows that.

Did you see that bite mark on his face? asked the Outside Girl.

Looks like it's healed up good, said Grandma Barlow. That scar might fade in a year or two.

They don't have a toilet, said the Outside Girl.

Grandma Barlow said, My own parents

293

shat in a hole in the ground. They always had two holes, so that when one filled up, they'd just move the seat over and fill the next one.

Things just aren't right over there, said the Outside Girl. Perley's struggling at school. No dad around. They don't even know who the dad is, or they won't say.

Grandma Barlow said, When Altemonte's daddy comes around I lock the door and get the gun. You should see him, black as tar and bigger than this house. I ain't racist, you understand, you know how much I love my grandbaby and he's brown as sugar. I'm just saying when it comes to daddies sometimes you're better off without one.

Perley's mom has random adults living over there, said the Outside Girl. Involved in criminal mischief, just petty stuff, you understand, but no environment for a child. No adequate supervision.

I heard more coffee go, a sizzle, a chair scraped, I smelled a frying smell and my stomach sparkled, but I knew my mission was to remain stealthily incognito, and to hear Perley's family get talked about with so much sad loving horror and even though it sounded like a different person, a different family, actually Perley was me and Perley's family was my family. I touched my snakebite scar, felt it tingle. It better not fade in a year or two. It better not. I almost dribbled but then I remembered to flex and I flexed.

Grandma Barlow said, Everyone deserves comfort but in the end there's no comfort. We'll all be separated, especially from our children. I've got no words. Jesus can help, but then again sometimes there's nothing can help. I know what I'm talking about. You take my Marg. She bore Altemonte and it was like she'd gone to war, she never was quite the same. Never enough money. Then there were pills, and not the healing ones. The forgetting ones. After that the fighting ones. And always hungry for more. Oh, for years.

How's Marg doing? asked the Outside Girl. She's working now?

Pipelining up north, said Grandma Barlow. Where all our kids seem to end up. This land here is like a funnel. Far from home, no job for a woman if anyone asked me, but she never did. Then again she works so hard I don't think she has time for the drugs so that's something. Sixteen-hour days. Don't even go to church on a Sunday. Sends us money, that's true. Got a letter from her this morning. So many kinds of pain. I'd like to get that boy in there some comfort, his mama, too.

Speaking of that, said the Outside Girl, I'll make an appointment for him.

The sooner the better, said Grandma Barlow.

I can pick him up at school and drop him off here again afterward, said the Outside Girl.

I just don't want to see him in pain, is all, said Grandma Barlow. Missing his mama. Nothing worse.

Actually, said the Outside Girl, he wanted to get out of there. He wanted to come with me.

Underneath the covers in my elfin cave my pee swelled up and pressed and pressed. All the grown-ups acted like I was on one team or another team but none of them knew I was only on my own team. I was living by my wits. I was questing. I just kept on flexing.

No matter what the Outside Girl said about me wanting to go over, when I heard her talk about the shit bucket and the snakes and the no dad, I got the Velvet Piglet feeling really bad and I started thinking maybe I'd had about as much of a break as I needed and I was really ready to go back to my women. Then I had to pee so bad I knew I would not be able to make it to the bathroom so I threw the covers off of me and I saw a plant in a pot in the corner of the room and really soft, flat-footed and silent as Cutter and Skywise, I aimed my privates in there and watered that plant, all the while looking over my shoulder and I heard the voices in the kitchen stop. I got my pants up just in time and I heard Grandma Barlow call to me, My son, come on in. So skilled was I that they never knew I peed in that plant even later when I kept on peeing on it until it yellowed and then it died.

The kitchen was not like ours, a mad science lab, but instead had lace curtains on the windows and a clock radio and a picture of Jesus on the wall smiling sadly at you and pancakes on the griddle and Grandma Barlow gave me one. We don't have syrup but we have plenty of sugar, she said, and heaped it on. The Outside Girl picked up her purse from the back of the kitchen chair and she finished her coffee and set her mug in the sink even though she said, Do you want me to wash this? and then she put on lipstick that was the color of frosting and she said, This is a good place for you, Perley. I'll see you again soon, to take you to an appointment, she said. Don't I have to go to school? I asked, but she said, It's an adjustment period. When it's time for your appointment, I'll write you an excuse. You will like the appointment, Perley, it's with a counselor, a nice person who is there to help you. And I knew about the Wolf Council where they make important decisions just by being together with their minds and their yellow eyes, and afterward they stand in their pack on the hilltop and they howl at the moon, so I was like, Sweet, and I kept eating my pancake and looking at the next pancake which was also on the griddle and the Outside Girl zipped up her hoodie and left.

Grandma Barlow sat down across from me and she leaned on her elbows and said, You are welcome here, Perley, and you are safe here. You'll soon see there is a way we do things, with chores and the like, you will catch on, and I was like, Yes, ma'am.

But seriously this was not the way I envisioned it would be to go over or to mix more. I mean, the pancakes were good, but it was just me and one old lady. When I imagined going over I thought it might be a place with like an obstacle course and a PlayStation and a cool dad that smoked cigarettes inside the house and Diet Pepsi to drink. So I was like, Are there any other kids here? Yes, said Grandma Barlow. My grandson, Altemonte, who is only a year older than you. Where is he? I asked. Is he still asleep? Oh no, she said, he was up hours ago. He's out in the woods, that boy's mostly in the woods. When she said that Altemonte was mostly in the woods I said, I know all about the woods I know a mushroom you can eat that smells like licorice but doesn't taste like licorice. Oyster mushrooms, Grandma Barlow said. I know, I said. She said, There's plenty in the woods back there on them ash logs in the springtime and in the fall but not now not in the winter. I know, I said. She said, Why don't you go find Altemonte and tell him to come have some breakfast and tell him I'm making pies today and tell him there's a letter from his mother?

So then I was in the woods again, out back of the house which now I could see was really a trailer, a big one, with lavender paint and a cement patio. The more I kept moving away from it the less I was a Velvet Piglet because I could see that this was woods like our woods with the same winter weeds, stalks of greenbrier, and spears of blackberry and goldenrod all frozen and soaked brown, and the same trees, sugar maples and tulip poplars and beech trees and even one or two walnuts, and I kept walking deeper, I walked so far that I couldn't see the trailer anymore. I knew that if I walked far enough I could just walk right home anytime I was ready. That made me feel better. Just knowing I could go home anytime I wanted made me feel like I wasn't ready to go home, at least not yet. I had to find out more. I had to discover my mission. I walked deep into the woods and I didn't see any grandson but I started to see other things. Signs. I saw willows bent over and tied together to make a hut and I saw a pile of stones arranged in a tall tower and I saw an arrowhead sitting on a churned-up pile of clay and then I saw this other kid a chubby kid with red boots and he was the acorn kid from school who turned out to be Altemonte.

He saw me and stopped what he was doing which was twisting joe-pye weed into a knot like a secret.

He said, You're that snakebite kid.

You're that acorn kid, I said. And you can call me Friend of Snake.

You're the new one come to stay with my grandma? he asked. Did they make you come stay because of that snakebite?

Did you make all this stuff? I asked.

What stuff? he asked.

The willow hideout and the stone tower

and the arrowhead, I said.

You think I can make an arrowhead? asked Altemonte. He started twisting the joe-pye again. He said, Obviously an Indian made the arrowhead, probably a mound builder that used to live around here but vanished and no living person knows why.

Okay, I said, but did you dig it up and put it on that churned-up clay as a sign?

Maybe I did, Altemonte said. Or maybe it was someone else.

Who else? I asked.

Maybe it was me, said Altemonte. But then again, I'm pretty busy.

Me too, I said.

Busy how? asked Altemonte, and I said, I know Brazilian ninjutsu and I know how to get out of most police holds.

Really? asked Altemonte. Then how did they make you come here?

How come you're an oppressed minority and your grandma isn't? I asked.

Is it true what the other kids say that you're retarded? asked Altemonte.

Where's your mom? I asked Altemonte.

Where's yours? asked Altemonte.

I asked you first, I said.

She's working so she can send money home, said Altemonte, but I don't care.

Your grandma said there's a letter from

her, I said. You better go inside and read it.

You think I want to read that letter, I don't want to read it, you faggot bastard, he said. So I said, At least I'm not a mongrel. He looked at me like I was a science experiment and I just looked right back at him the same way, and neither of us cried, we just stood there looking. Sorry, I said. I'm sorry, too, he said.

It's okay, I said, I actually am retarded maybe I think.

You're probably just spastic which is slightly different than retarded, said Altemonte.

I'm totally problematic, I said. I don't even have a dad.

Oh that, said Altemonte. You think those other kids have dads? Plenty of them don't have dads. You've got two lezzies for moms which everyone knows is against god but my grandma says hate the sin not the sinner.

She's the one takes care of you? I asked.

Altemonte said, She thinks she takes care of me but I take care of her. She bakes like twenty pies per day and always says it's dinner at two in the afternoon. I take care of her by eating so many pies. If I didn't eat those pies she'd cry her eyes out. That's how come I'm so chubby.

Do you have a dad? I asked.

Sure I do, Altemonte said. Who else do you think taught me how to be in the woods and twist joe-pye and find arrowheads? He comes over and knocks real loud and tries to come in. But he took bad pills my grandma said, so she tells him to go. So he goes. That's what grown-ups are good at. Leaving.

Not my grown-ups, I said. Not my women.

Oh yeah? he said. Then how come you're here and not at home with them?

My women didn't leave me, I said. I sounded it out to see how it felt. I said, It was the other way around. It was me who left them.

Altemonte looked at me to see if I was lying but I wasn't lying. Cool, he said. I kind of hate grown-ups. Grown-ups are hypocrites.

I wanted to ask him what a hypocrite was but instead I asked him, What was that thing you did when Bexley called you that name? Because even though it was the name I had just called him I didn't want to say it anymore.

What thing? he asked.

That thing where you put up a force field, I said.

Oh that, he said. That's just something I

303

invented. In my laboratory. He opened his arms toward the forest. It's not perfect yet, though, he said. I'm still tinkering with it. Someday I'm going to make it into a fire-bomb.

When they call you names, how come you don't tell the teacher? I asked.

How come you don't? he asked right back, and I didn't say that it was because I knew if I told on Bexley then he would never be my friend and Bexley's way would never be my way. Somehow I knew that Altemonte had a different reason that would maybe make my reason seem like the reason of a little fucking moron. I said, I asked you first. And he said, Because it wouldn't make things better if I told the teacher, it would only make things worse, where do you think Bexley learned it from? What about your grandma? I asked. Altemonte said, Yeah, one time I told her and she just said those kids are ignorant hicks you better pray for them, but I could tell it just made her feel bad and I don't want her to feel bad because it's just me and her. We're all we've got.

Altemonte finished tying his joe-pye knot and wrapped it around a grapevine. Anyway, he said, Bexley and the other kids aren't even real to me, and so I was like, What's real to you? and Altemonte said, I could

304

show you something if you want. Sure, I said. We have to go pretty far back in the woods, he said. In case you're scared. I'm not scared, I said. I'm toxically skilled. I'm part wolf part elf. Altemonte looked at me. Come on, then, he said.

He turned around and started walking, and I followed him. We went down a slope, deep in icy leaves and muddy slush, we went back up the other side, pulling ourselves hand over hand over tree roots, climbing up loose sandstone, we went so far I thought we might have to forage for our food, and finally Altemonte stopped. Get down, he said. He was breathing really hard and he pulled me down behind a blackberry thicket. Be quiet, he said, and he pointed through the leaves until I saw it. A stone house. A stone house with a chimney built out the back. But a really small house. A really small stone house like only big enough for someone like an elf or like me or like Altemonte. And I whispered, Whoa, sweet, toxic, did you make that? And he denied it. He denied that he made the stone house but who else would make it, a gnome? And he was like, Yeah, a gnome.

So then we were friends, and shared similar enthusiasms.

Helen

For once, I didn't say a thing. But it's not that I couldn't think of a thing to say. I had plenty to say. First of all, butch? Was I butch? Why, because I cut my own hair and didn't smile all the time? Wasn't it sexist to put a label on that? Second of all, Karen and me alike? Was that true? During the fist-fight — simply put, the beating — I hadn't interfered. But Karen was right. Now, when I imagined myself as part of the fight, I imagined being beat. Me and my big mouth. Me and the Best Practices Binder. The hand sanitizer. I knew I deserved it.

Karen was right. But not about everything. For example, she thought she knew what I was trying to say when I kept interrupting her, but she didn't know. In fact, I wasn't trying to say anything. I was trying to ask a simple question, and not even one that I already had an answer for. One simple question: How are we going to apply direct pressure, stop the blood, and get Perley back? But every time I opened my mouth to ask it she told me to shut the fuck up.

In the days after they took Perley, Karen and Lily staked out opposite territories on the land. Karen stayed in the house. Though I also slept there, kicking the blanket on my side of the partition, Karen refused to speak to me or to anyone. She didn't sleep. She took the .22 down from the rafters and paced the floor, stalking snakes. In the morning, I swept up exploded skins, scattered mouse meat, split snake hide. She'd grin darkly at the wall.

Karen didn't sleep but Lily made up for it. She moved into the camper, password or not. Perley's new bunk still smelled of sawdust, still waited to be sanded. Lily crawled into it and fell into a sleep so deep and resolute I knew she must be dreaming up a plan to get Perley back, or else how could she just drop out?

As for me, I climbed up and down through the garden, beating the trail back and forth between the two hemispheres. I delivered food, nutritive and fortifying, iron-rich stews and mushroom broths, ignored. I kept both fires going. I used my five senses and in the heavy air I heard wailing, saw bleeding, smelled vomit before I saw it, didn't step in it, tasted despair and felt its companion, inertia, settle over our camp. But besides sleeping and shooting, I saw no action. None that was discernible. Karen shot and Lily slept and I was the one who was there to receive the envelope, thick as the phone book, delivered to our mailbox three days after Perley was taken. From Children's

307

Services, it said. To Lily Marshall.

I knew I should take it to her, or to Karen. I knew it was their right to read what was inside and show me if they wanted to. But I figured I owed them. I had helped get them into this mess and the least I could do was to help get them out of it. So I ripped open the envelope without even hiking up the driveway first. Inside: Rights and Responsibilities. Notification of Ninety-Day Review. Visitation. I had to catch the last piece of paper before it floated down into the drainage ditch: The Reunification Plan.

The reunification plan was a graceful document, custom-made just for us. Tailored to our particular situation. Communicating generously its fervent desire to help us meet solid goals. We had ninety days to do it. Ninety days until the first review hearing. The reunification plan was a list, and a short one. Lily Marshall must:

Exterminate snakes and other vermin in dwelling.

Show proof that child is receiving adequate and consistent nutrition.

Show that there is adequate, consistent, and hygienic housing for child.

Show proof of adequate and consistent adult supervision of child.

Not allow child to be supervised by per-

308

sons who have been convicted of crimes.

Install septic system.

Simple enough. Simple except that every reunification plan suggests a disintegration plan, and I could see ours. I could see us fall apart. I would get that starved look, become shrill, talk nonstop with no one there to listen. Karen would take off on her own with a shotgun and a hair shirt, give up the English language. Perley would be somewhere in this very county yet a world away and instructed not to look at me at the grocery store. Because if Karen didn't have any legal rights to him, what rights could someone like me have, a nonrelative adult, a petty criminal whose name was no less than the Mean Aunt? Only Lily would win. A world record for staying in bed the longest. I saw us far-flung, saw me alone, me in jail with no one to call but Rudy. And then I thought of Rudy.

So in my stunned fear, I fought through the woods, my hands and face all torn to hell from multiflora rose, and I came out on the pipeline. I found Rudy pruning in the frozen nursery, beer in hand. When I told him what had happened, he took a long breath, sloshed around what was left in his can. He scratched his red nose, pulled his beard. I shoved the reunification plan at him

309

and he closed one eye to study it, left a brown thumbprint on the ecru page.

"Persons who have been convicted of crimes," he said. "That's you and me, I guess." He chuckled.

"That's all you can say?" I asked.

"What do you want me to say?" he asked.

"They can't do this," I said.

"Oh, they most certainly can," he said. "They do this all the time."

"We need a lawyer," I said.

"Don't know that it would help," he said.

"What about your lawyer friend? Aldi Birch?" I asked.

"What do Lily and Karen say?" he asked.

"They haven't seen this yet."

"You opened Lily's mail?" he asked. "For sure that's a crime, or at least bad manners."

"They won't talk to me. They won't talk to each other. Lily won't wake up. Karen won't put down her gun. They won't do anything. They won't eat."

"You've probably been feeding them raw stinging nettles or rancid acorn flour or some shit," Rudy said.

"Nettle is good for their circulation," I said.

"Maybe if you hit them with it," Rudy said.

310

"The acorn flour is not rancid," I said. "It's quite fresh. They need fortification."

"Okay, whatever," said Rudy. "First things first, they need to eat."

"I can't believe that you of all people are trying to tell me anything about eating," I said. But Rudy downed the last of his beer, pocketed his truck keys, and took off down the pipeline.

"Where are you going?" I called after him.

"Where do you think I'm going?" he said over his shoulder. "I'm going to McDonald's. Goddamn if you don't need a man to get anything done around here, all this hand-wringing."

So the world had gone mad, there was no assistance, and what could I do, I brought the envelope down to the house and handed it to Karen. Her split lip was still mending. The bruise around her eye, a monocle. She looked aristocratic, that sickly. She didn't put down the gun, but sat on the sofa and read the reunification plan with a nothing expression.

"So what?" she said, which was actually talking to me, which was a start. "It's not even addressed to me. There's nothing I can do."

"You could talk to Lily," I said.

"Lily won't talk to me," she said.

"If I were you," I said, "I'd go beg forgiveness by the door of the camper, not roam around with a gun like a fucking psycho."

"Well, you're not me," she said.

"Lily could change her mind," I said.

"I know that woman way better than you do," Karen said. "I'm not going to beg."

"Are you going to get a lawyer?" I asked.

Karen sat with her slack swollen face, gun across her lap. "Lily would have to do that. She's the biological mother," she said. "I have no rights. I'm nothing. I'm less than nothing. I'm lighter than air. I'm a hole in the fabric of the universe. I'm shit."

"Oh, stop bragging," I said.

Rudy came in holding a paper sack with grease dripping through. He closed the door against the cold, as if it weren't cold inside, too. When he saw Karen's black eye, he opened his mouth to say something, but I shook my head.

"Perley's up on Sand Ridge at Elsa Barlow's place, heard it from the mailman," he said. "I went over there to check it out, peered in the window. Sure enough, he's playing video games with her grandson, killing people, whatever. Fine for now."

"He's not fine. He's been kidnapped," Karen said.

"That woman's a saint," Rudy said. "I

went out with her daughter a couple times. Then she decided to have a baby with some colored fellow, leaving me childless as usual."

"Rudy," I said. "You can't call people colored fellows."

"What?" he asked. "When did that news get handed down?"

"Are you joking? Circa the civil rights movement," I said.

"If you think the civil rights movement is over, you're the one who's out of touch, not me," he said. "Anyway, Elsa Barlow's some kind of a Christian mystic and a part-time math teacher. A pillar of this community."

"Just what we need," Karen said.

"Now do you believe me?" he asked. "The state is trying to destroy you."

"You got that from me. There was never a time when I didn't believe that," Karen said. Then she said, "What's in the sack?"

"I brought dinner," he said.

"I told you they aren't eating," I said.

"You don't know a thing," he said. "In times of trauma, you bring fast food. It's designed so that even people who aren't hungry will eat. You'll smell this and your body will start eating even while your mind and heart are not eating." Karen was already reaching for it.

"Hold on," I said, intercepting the bag. I scraped some dried nettles out of my pocket, reached into the sack, unwrapped a Big Mac, and tucked a few leaves inside. Even though the nettles were dry, they still stung my fingers a little, and the stinging comforted me. I handed the burger to Karen. "Rudy knows a lawyer," I said.

"Not that it'll do a damn thing," said Rudy.

"How do you know a lawyer?" asked Karen, tearing into her burger.

"How do you think?" I asked.

"From being a criminal and a pain in the ass," Karen said.

"He helped me out years ago," Rudy said. "We've been friends ever since."

"You think he'll talk to us?" asked Karen, sauce squeezing out the sides of her mouth. She bit a ketchup packet.

"Of course he'll talk to us," I said. "A guy like that knows Rudy's the only man who can keep a tree with a hollow heart from falling and crushing all his diplomas." Why my show of baseless confidence, I couldn't say, only that I felt a powerful need to keep Karen in some kind of motion. The motion of chewing leading to the motion of talking and thinking and getting up, leading to the motion of shaking off the fear and confu-

314

sion that kept us bolted in place. "He'll do whatever Rudy asks him to do," I said.

"I was asking Rudy, not you," Karen said.

"Helen doesn't know a damn thing about it," Rudy said. "What I'll say about Aldi, I hate lawyers and I don't hate him. He's a decent man. He's like me."

"How reassuring," Karen said.

"He's the only other man I know around here gets as dark as I do when it's dark out. Hides out most of the winter. Might be hiding out right now, come to think of it. We could call him up. If he's talking to people, he'll talk to us. He might try to help. Not that it'll do a damn thing," Rudy said.

Karen swallowed the last of her burger. She reached into her mouth and pulled out a nettle leaf, delicately folded it inside the wax wrapper, tossed the wrapper toward one of the overstuffed garbage bags but it rolled under the sink. "Not that it'll do a damn thing," she said. "But let's go get Lily." She set aside the .22. She held up the greasy bag, weighed down with another burger, another envelope of fries. "Hell," she said, "maybe she's hungry."

The camper smelled like giving up had made a nest for itself. Lily slept on Perley's bunk, which was too small for her. Her long black hair was matted. She had dried crusted stuff on her face.

"I'll wait outside," Rudy said, taking the McDonald's sack from Karen and backing out the door. Karen hauled Lily up to sitting, but Lily twisted away.

"Don't touch me," she said, pulling the sleeping bag over her head. Karen looked at me. "What did I tell you?" she said. "This isn't going to work."

"We're going to get Perley back," I told the sleeping bag. "We're going to see a lawyer."

"We can't afford a lawyer," Lily said, but she poked her head out.

"That's true," Karen said.

"We'll figure that out," I said. I wiped Lily's face with a corner of the pillowcase. She closed her eyes against it like an irritated toddler. Karen handed me a bottle of aloe vera, left over from the supplies she'd brought up to treat Perley's wound. I rubbed it into Lily's face, which she tolerated. "You want me to brush your hair, too?" I asked, but she took the brush from me and gritted her teeth as she worked out the snarls. When we emerged from the camper, Rudy stood up respectfully and offered her some fast food. She took it without a word, didn't look at it, didn't eat it. Down the steep driveway, she kept ahead of us, chin raised high, McDonald's bag firmly grasped in one fist, completely alone.

Rudy said, "Karen, how's your truck?"

"Still leaking oil," Karen said.

"I've been meaning to fix it for you," Rudy said.

"I can fix it myself," Karen said. "Anyway, it's drivable."

"It's on blocks," I said.

"We can take mine," Rudy said.

At the bottom of the hill, Karen cut in front of me so that she could wedge herself in next to Lily in the cab. Rudy drove, and I slid myself in against the window, ear and cheek pressed flat.

Karen said, "Baby."

Lily said, "I'm not a baby. My baby's gone."

Karen said, "Baby, Rudy knows where Perley is."

"Well, then let's go get him back," Lily said.

"It's not that simple," Karen said. "It's foster care. But it's good that we know. That we know he's okay."

"He's not okay," Lily said. "He's been kidnapped," which was exactly what Karen had said, but as soon as Lily said it you could see that she'd woken herself up a little. She reached up and twisted her hair under her baseball cap. You could see her thinking, If they kidnapped him, then what's to stop me from kidnapping him right back?

Karen said, "Rudy knows the woman he's staying with. He says she's kind."

"From what I remember about Elsa Barlow," Rudy said, "she's strict about Jesus but she indulges in some downright paganism when the timing's right. She loves pies, Lite-Brite Marys, and mathematics. She's a nurturer. Rest assured she's stuffing that boy full of food, letting him watch all kinds of TV. She likes to comfort people, and if she can't do it in one way she'll do it in another."

"We've got to go get him," said Lily.

"Let's see what this lawyer has to say," I said. "It can't hurt to talk to him."

"It could hurt," Lily said. "We don't know yet."

"Let's just wait until we've been to his office," I said.

"We're not going to his office," Rudy said.

Aldi Birch sat on a metal folding chair under the biggest white oak I'd seen. There was also a yawning tin and vinyl garage, wide door open to the winter, but the tree was the main show. The oak menaced the garage, its roots levering up the foundation, its bare branches lunging over the roof. The thing must have been over a hundred feet high and the trunk more than four feet across. Aldi smoked, bare head against the tree's trunk. At the courthouse he'd worn a baggy suit, but now all he had on was an enormous hunting coat over an undershirt and a loose pair of pajama pants, drawstring hanging. He stood to meet us, letting the end of his cigarette fall to the frozen ground. His bushy eyebrows came together to try to figure out who we were, and I could see now, more than I'd seen in court, how damn old he was. Bent way over. Legs bowed like he was walking on willow trees. Last few wisps of iron hair blowing in the wind. I wondered again what he thought of me. Rudy parked the truck, and we got out to face him.

Aldi beamed when he saw Rudy and me, but closed his mouth when we told him why we'd come. Those eyebrows met his hairline. He felt around in the pocket of his coat until he found his glasses, and then he reached for the reunification plan. He read it and sighed.

"Which one of you two young ladies is Lily?" he asked. She stepped forward. The aloe, meant to make her look dewy and vulnerable, had frozen to her face and was scaling off.

"Black rat snakes?" he asked. She nodded.

"Fucking impossible to get rid of," he said. "And what, you shit in a bucket, is that it?"

"It's not a crime. It was good enough for my grandma when she was a girl," Lily said.

"Sure, plenty of folks around here still have outhouses," Aldi said. "But then again, it doesn't look too good when added with all this other stuff. Look, I've been defending poor folks in this county for forty years, not that it's done much good. If you don't know by now, you're poor, you're fucked. By the system, I mean."

"See?" Rudy said, shaking Aldi by the shoulder. "That's my man."

Aldi beckoned us toward the garage. Inside, a big-bellied woodstove, a chicken coop running the length of one wall, lit up with heat lamps. Broiler chicks teemed. The business card thumbtacked to the wall read *Aldi Birch JD, Public Defender.*

He wanted to hear from us, our beginning-to-end, all the details we cared to include. He took notes. He especially wanted to hear the story from Lily, but I helped her with the places she couldn't remember or if she remembered it differently from me or if she paused at all to think. Even Rudy weighed in, letting Aldi know about the run-in with the principal, the man internship, the community service hours. Only Karen kept quiet. On the drive over, the way she was talking to Lily all soft and low, I thought she'd finally got reasonable. But something about being in the presence of the lawyer made her go weird again. Draped across a folding chair, she seethed in the corner and rubbed her black eye, one big foot tapping like she couldn't wait to get out of there. When Aldi asked who she was, she said, "I'm no one. I'm invisible. Just a fly on the wall."

"She's Perley's other mother," I said. "Lily's partner and co-parent." But she just chewed on her lip.

"Co-parent," Aldi said, raising one eyebrow. He made a note of it, then looked at Karen. "Someone got to you pretty good," he said. "What happened to your face?"

"You just said it," Karen said. "Someone got to me pretty good."

When we had finished telling the state of things as we saw it, he set his notebook on his knee. He took off his glasses and rubbed his eyes.

"You let Perley sleep in a bed with a snake?" he asked.

"We moved him into his own place as soon as he got bit," Lily said. "To protect him."

"Don't you think seven is a little young for a kid to be living on his own?" Aldi asked.

"Dignity of risk," Lily said, glancing at Karen, who didn't glance back.

Aldi said, "I'm not sure there's much here to defend."

"Whose side are you on?" I asked.

"I'm looking at it from the standpoint of the court," Aldi said. "In this state, it doesn't take much. Poverty itself can be an emergency order."

"Some teenage girl is squeamish around human shit, that's supposed to be my problem?" said Lily. "That doesn't prove Perley's not safe at home. Just because he was playing outside when she got there, that doesn't prove we don't take care of him. Don't they have to prove it?"

"It's between a car wreck and a criminal case," Aldi said.

"What does that mean?" I asked.

"All they have to do is show clear and convincing evidence that the state should have custody," Aldi said. "Which, with the snakes in the house, the plumbing thing, and these other odds and ends, it looks like they can do."

"We need him home," Lily said.

"Where's his dad?" Aldi asked. Lily opened her eyes wide. Karen gave an ugly laugh.

"He's got two parents. Karen and Lily," I said. "That's enough. That's all he needs."

"Can't say I entirely understand it," said Aldi. "In my day, if you were like that you just kept it to yourself and they called you a confirmed bachelor." He looked at Karen and Lily, but Lily just kept her wide eyes on him. Karen folded her arms and glared, but she didn't say what was on her mind.

"Hell," Aldi said when it was clear they weren't going to say more. "He's probably better off with two moms anyway. Oh, when I think of my mother, how I wish there were two of her. I couldn't get enough of that woman. She cared for me and cared for me. She and I preferred each other. My dad, that man — I'm not sure where he ended up, but I have to assume he is burning in hell. That's what gets me through the day. At least if there had been two of my mother she could have outnumbered him. She could have got to him before he got to her."

"They're being unfairly targeted for being lesbians," I said, waiting for Karen and Lily to come in strong, to stop this sullen teen-

323

age act. "Obviously."

"Very hard to prove," Aldi said. "And also, technically legal."

"Unconstitutional," I said.

"Out of my pay grade," Aldi said. "Unless you want to take this to the Supreme Court."

"We do," I said.

"Fuck you, Helen," Karen said. She had been leaning back in her folding chair, tipping it against the chicken coop, but now she let all four of its legs down hard on the cement floor. "Fuck you, and fuck the Supreme Court. We want Perley back. The fastest way possible."

"Honestly?" Aldi said. "I think the fastest way is to wait for the ninety-day review. From a legal standpoint, the reunification plan is pretty reasonable. I don't think there's any real sticking point there. I mean, you could fight it, file a motion, say it's an unfair burden to make you put in a septic system. But quickest way to get the kid back? Probably get the toilet."

"Ninety days?" echoed Lily.

"You might just have to be patient," Aldi said.

"Patient," said Lily. She was gone again, scanning the horizon, out there somewhere on her own.

"I know Elsa Barlow," Aldi said. "The woman's a saint."

"So we've heard," Karen said, glaring.

"From the paperwork, it looks like you'll be able to have supervised visits with Perley starting in two weeks."

"I don't get supervised visits," Karen said. "I don't get shit."

"I'm not saying it's fair," Aldi said. "But fair don't count in this fucking system." This time, no one clapped him on the back. Rudy, leaning against the garage door, kept his hands in his jacket pockets, ponytail in his mouth, eyes on the floor.

"What happens if we don't measure up by the ninety-day review?" asked Karen. "Putting in a septic system, that's money we don't have. Damned if I know how we're going to rid the place of snakes."

"They'll give you a year to get the kid back," Aldi said. "After that, the state takes permanent custody."

Rudy spit his ponytail out and stepped forward. "I don't get your meaning, Aldi," he said. "Are you going to be our lawyer or aren't you?"

"Sounds like he can't help us," Karen said. "Just like we thought." She stood up.

"Now, hold on," Aldi said. "I'd be happy to do what I can, but I don't see that there's much I can do."

"You know I hate lawyers," Rudy said, "but I wonder if it might count for something just them knowing we have one."

"Could be something to that," Aldi said. "We could send around a retainer agreement. Tell them not to talk to you without they talk to me first."

"Can't afford it," Karen said.

"Won't charge you for it," Aldi said.

"That's not what I was driving at," Karen said.

"We'll come to something," Aldi said. "I'm not making promises. Seems like you're just now hearing the news everyone else already got."

"We heard that news," Rudy said. "You're poor, you're fucked. Well, we're not poor."

"One thing I've noticed, no one thinks they're poor," Aldi said. "It's always somebody else."

"We've got resources," Rudy said.

"Glad to hear it," Aldi said. He pulled himself to his feet and went for the chicken feed.

Suspension shot, we bumped down the pitted driveway, past a beleaguered dog, and turned onto the road, and Karen put her hand on Lily's knee. Lily removed it. Karen said, "Baby, what are you thinking?"

Lily said, "Kidnapping."

"No kidnapping," Karen said.

"Why not? We know where the Barlow place is," Lily said.

"Where would we fucking go?" asked Karen. "To your family? They'd turn us in. We'd lose him permanently. We'd have nothing. No. We might hate it, but looks like the lawyer's right. We need to be patient."

"My provider," Lily said bitterly.

"We can't do anything crazy," Karen said.

"What will I tell Perley when he asks me why I didn't come and get him right away?" Lily asked. "All these amounts of time, you're talking about them like they mean something. Two weeks. Ninety days. It's the same to me. All I hear is way too long. This Elsa Barlow doesn't mean shit to me. I need Perley back now. I needed him back yesterday."

"Okay, but we need to think this through," Karen said. "You heard Aldi. We've only got a year to get our shit together, tops."

"You're not listening," Lily said. "I'm not worried about what's going to happen in a year. I'm worried about what's happening now. If it's been a year and I don't have Perley back, it won't even be me you're looking at, I'll be someone else."

"Aldi's a good man," Rudy said. "If he says he'll help us, he'll help us."

"We can't afford to pay a lawyer fee just to say we have a lawyer," Lily said.

"We're not going to pay him, we're going to trade him," Rudy said.

"Trade him what?" asked Karen.

"Did you see that old white oak? I've had my eye on it for years now. It's about to come down hard. It's got included bark," Rudy said.

"What does that mean?" asked Karen.

"In this case, it means that water damage has built up over time in the crotch of the trunk, there where it splits." Rudy steered around a bloated deer carcass, fishtailed, recovered. "I've spent years avoiding that oak tree," he said. "Too hairy. Be the hardest job I've ever done. It'll probably kill me. Or more likely you, Helen. Well, probably both of us. But we'll do it."

"But Rudy," I said.

"We have to get the kid back," Rudy said. "When I leave things up to you women you just talk about your feelings and can't make decisions. You're all so self-aware, and it doesn't make any damn difference."

"But Rudy," I said, "Aldi might just take us on pro bono."

"Fuck charity," Rudy said. "We'll take down the tree. Needs done anyway. It's about to crush his place. Won't make it through the winter. We'll do it for him and he'll get Perley back for us. That's how it will be."

"I'll help," Karen said.

"You're not trained," Rudy said. "Helen and me will do it."

"Kidnapping, kidnapping," Lily said, staring straight ahead.

Karen

Rudy blazed straight up the pipeline toward his nursery. I figured Lily would go back to the camper, but she followed us up the driveway to the house, which made me regret, like Helen said, roaming the place for days like a fucking psycho instead of making it nice in case Lily decided to stop by. It was not nice. It was cold. There were mouse pieces. There were snake guts. Lily didn't seem to notice. She dropped the Mc-Donald's bag on the sofa, sat next to it, and began to thumb through the visitation paperwork. Helen went to the stove and started cooking something rank and mysterious. So I called up Frank, hoping I could get reception without having to climb the ridge. Frank, fuzzy, listened with sympathy but nothing like surprise. "They'll take everything they can sooner or later," he said. "Never should have sent him to school." Then he said, "Septic, huh? Probably set you back fifteen grand or more. I could ask around."

"You're breaking up," I said, and hung up fast. Of course, there was nothing to do but tell Lily and watch Helen's eager face set to goddamn problem-solving.

"Fifteen thousand," Helen said, turning up the burner. "That's half of what we paid for this place." Lily set aside her paperwork and looked at me like I was the one charging the money.

"Where are we going to get it?" she asked.

"Could we borrow it?" asked Helen.

"From who?" I said. Lily closed her eyes and reached out to me. My heart jumped until I realized she was only reaching for the phone. I handed it to her.

"I'll call my mom," she said, voice dry and quiet. She stepped out onto the porch.

She hadn't talked to the woman except Christmas cards since she'd run away at sixteen, the year her grandma died. A moment of teenage indiscretion, maybe born of having the wrong kind of crush again and again. She made it all the way to New York City, stayed with a high school friend, another queer who'd made it out. She came home, but by that time her mother had left for Virginia with some devout stranger, so there was never time for reconciliation. They believed that she'd had a child out of wedlock, which is the phrase they used on their Christmas cards, but they believed it was their duty to love him anyway. They'd never mentioned me.

Helen stirred and sprinkled, I shoveled snake off the floor, tried to build up the fire, and soon Lily came back in with eyes as wide as the dinner plates Helen was covering in groundhog stew. Holding the phone away from her as if it were vermin, Lily carried it to the bucket we kept beneath the sink to catch the overflow from leaky pipes. She dropped the phone in, listened thoughtfully to the splash, cocked her head as it hit bottom. To the ceiling, she said, "Lost that child out of pernicious irresponsibility. He's probably better off in foster care. Let this be a lesson. God has a plan."

I plunged my arm in up to the elbow, scooped the phone out, buried it in a jar of rice. Lily watched me.

"What's the point?" she asked. "There's no one we really need to talk to. What would we talk to them about?"

"You need to eat," Helen said, pressing a

plate into her hands.

So Lily ate up all the groundhog stew on her plate, then turned her attention to the cold Big Mac and finished that off, too, nettle leaf and all.

Then she threw it all up.

"You need to lie down," I said, stooping to clean up her vomit. "I'll clear off the couch. Just give me a minute and I'll find you a pillow."

But she was already out the door.

Helen waited a respectful nine seconds before saying, "It's a setback. But we're not defeated."

"We might as well move," I said. "Fifteen thousand dollars."

"You're not moving," Helen said. "We can get the money. Maybe I could take out a mortgage on this land."

"Hey, Bank," I said. "We'd like to take out a loan on a submarginal piece of land. Too steep to farm. The house ain't worth shit. Oh, and there's a pipeline down one side of it. Great idea, Helen. Let me know how that goes."

"We're going to figure this out," Helen said.

"How'd you get thirty thousand dollars?" I asked.

"What?" she asked.

"You said that's what this land cost," I said. "How'd you get that kind of money?"

Helen looked embarrassed. "My uncle died and left me some, not all of it. Like I told you, my boyfriend paid off the rest working up north."

"In one of those camps," I said.

"He did what he had to do," she said. "It was a job." She saw my face. "You better not be thinking about that," she said.

"It's not right that you and Rudy are paying for this lawyer," I said. "Perley's my kid, I should pay."

"We're not paying," she said. "It's a trade."

"I'm not providing anything," I said. "And everyone knows this is all my fault, beginning with the way we built this house. It's different for you, because you didn't know any better. But I did. I knew how to build. I saw every mistake we were making, but I just stood back like a fucking ghost. Telling Lily we should bide our time, that we would fix it later. I'm what people mean when they say good-for-nothing."

"Your self-loathing isn't helping," she said.

"I'm not helping," I said. "Rudy won't even let me help take down that tree."

"You should go back to nursing," Helen said. "You never should have quit that in

333

the first place. All this time, Lily working for minimum wage, and you with a nursing degree. It doesn't make sense."

"Please, Helen," I said. "Please tell me how I should make money. You're the one with a B.A. Why aren't you sitting behind a computer somewhere, raking it in? You've got all the lingo. Why don't you help revitalize Appalachia or whatever the fuck? Or fucking graduate school. You could probably get a stipend just for studying Rudy."

"A stipend? Are you serious?" said Helen. "You have no idea what that world is like. You should see my aunt. You know she has a Ph.D. in philosophy? She's selling clothes online. After years of adjuncting at a community college. Bill collectors will probably show up at her funeral. I make more by the hour doing tree work. But not as much as you'd make nursing. That's good steady money."

How could I tell Helen what I could barely tell Lily? I couldn't go back to nursing after Perley came. I couldn't go back to the clinic to have the truth forced on me: Everyone was just parts waiting to fail. Perley's body, precious to me, wasn't precious, or even special. No one was special. Every time I closed my eyes, I saw again and again all the ways we could get bad news. I wasn't strong enough to face that every day and then come home and face Perley. Now that the bad news was actually here, I didn't feel any stronger.

But I wasn't going to tell Helen all that. It didn't matter, not now. Even if I decided to go back to the clinic today, after seven years out of work, it would be too late.

"It's steady money, all right," I said. "Too steady. You think I haven't done the math? Too slow and steady for the ninety-day review."

"It would help," she said.

"It's not enough," I said. "It's not enough for a septic system. It's not enough for a lawyer. It's not enough when things go wrong."

"You're not going off and leaving, not right now," she said. I sprayed vinegar, wrung a dishrag.

Fifteen thousand dollars. That sum of money made me know I was a useless piece of shit. Didn't have it in savings. Didn't have it on the horizon. Didn't know anyone who did. Like not asking for help on the house, didn't want to admit to any of these assholes that I couldn't provide for my own family. And anyway, how did I know they were my own family if I couldn't provide for them? As I'd always suspected, I was bound to be alone. Lily wouldn't talk to me. Perley at every turn chose the Mean Aunt and even the ice-cream cake intake worker over me. The law said I was a nonentity. Might as well be a nonentity somewhere I could be useful. Fifteen thousand dollars. Maybe if I had that, I could buy my way back in.

Next morning, I cursed my leaking truck, cinched up my hood, and started walking to town. Got about halfway, a good three miles and an hour through the cold, when Rudy pulled up next to me in his truck. "Where the hell are you going?" he asked. "Do you need a ride?"

"I'll accept it," I said. "I guess I'm going to the library."

"The least you could do is let me buy you breakfast first," he said.

The dive bar on the edge of town looked closed but was never closed. Inside, the place was warm and dark, heat vent blasting, pool table in the corner, beer signs dim, no other customers. We sat at the bar and Rudy ordered a Natural Ice from a sleepy bartender, one for me too, though I hadn't had a drink in years. He asked for peanuts, but was informed the peanuts didn't come out until 4:00 p.m.

"Sorry about that," he said. "I could have sworn they had free food."

"Shouldn't you be hibernating by now?" I said. "We usually don't see you until spring."

"This year I've got the nursery," he said. "It's doing wonders for my mental attitude. Keeps my paranoid fantasies at bay. Makes me less defeatist. Still staying low-level lit, though. When I've got the money." He sipped foam. I followed suit. The deeper I got into the glass, the better it tasted.

"Septic's likely to cost fifteen thousand," I said.

"Shit," Rudy said, and I suddenly loved him for the simple fact that he was neither Lily nor Helen.

"Just out of curiosity," I said, "what would you do?"

"You know how people do it around here when they need money fast," Rudy said. "They go north."

"Right," I said. I'd just wanted to be sure.

"Plenty of work on those rat crews," Rudy said. "High turnover. Get sick, get hurt, get attacked by some male. There's a reason they call them man camps. It's no place for a woman, but you probably don't care about that. That probably makes you want to do it more." He ordered another beer. "And a cup of coffee," he said to the tender.

"What the hell do you know?" I said. "It's the only way I can think of."

"Have you told Lily?" he asked.

"Lily won't likely forgive me," I said. "But then, she also won't forgive me if we can't get Perley back. Might not forgive me no matter what happens."

"Speaking of curiosity," he said, licking the foam from his mustache.

"Better not," I said.

"I just have to ask," he said. "What about Perley's dad? Why not hit him up for some money? Surely he owes you."

"Perley's dad?"

"That deadbeat's out there somewhere," Rudy said. "Right? I mean, how did Lily get pregnant?"

"So that's what you're after," I said. "How long have you been wanting to ask us that?"

"Possibly seven years," he said. "Give or take."

"What do you want, beginning sex ed?" I asked.

"Could help," he said.

"Lily's high school friend overnighted us semen on ice," I said. "Suspended in some special fluid. Finally, it took."

"So that's how you people do it," Rudy said.

"End of conversation," I said, pushing my stool back. Rudy took no notice.

"Does this high school friend have any money?" he asked.

"Rudy, get off it. He's the donor. He's not Perley's dad," I said.

"But legally?" Rudy asked.

"Suddenly you're so into the law," I said.

"Just spitballing," Rudy said. "I mean, what's this guy like?"

"He's not like us," I said. "He's like, he's a high-powered gay in Manhattan."

"High-powered? You mean he's rich," Rudy said.

"Rudy," I said. "We sent the guy some photos when Perley was born. That's it. He doesn't want any other involvement. Neither do we. That was the deal."

Rudy said, "I get it, I get it. You don't want to ask this guy for anything. I mean, shit, he could come on the scene at any time and claim Perley's his kid and he wants equal time."

"You have no clue what you're talking about," I said. "Trust me, he really loves the childless life. He loves his tiny dog. His apartment, everything's white, not that I've ever been there. Plus, he grew up around here, never wants to come back. His slick friends probably don't even know about his humble origins."

"Damn, if it was my kid, though," Rudy said. "I'm just saying. I'd want to protect myself."

"I'm not worried about it," I said.

"Then you're a stronger man than me," Rudy said.

"Drop it, Rudy. Right now, that's the least of my worries," I said. "And it's none of your damn business."

"Okay," Rudy said. "Enough said. Thank you for indulging me."

But I couldn't make it through the rest of my beer, just sat there tipping it back and forth in the glass. This guy, this semen contributor, he probably had more legal rights to my kid than I did. We had worked hard to build a life and now I was seeing how fragile it was, how fragile it had always really been. I tried to picture this high school friend, who Lily hadn't seen since she was sixteen, her one jaunt to the big city. When she agreed to have a baby with me she looked into my face, smiled slowly. There's this guy I know, she said. Old friend, but I swear now that I think about it, he looks like you. Same coloring. Same bridge of the nose. Almost you could be twins. Let's call him up. And over the phone he was agreeable, he was happy to hear from

Lily, happy that she was in love. This is my good deed, he said. This is how I'll get two scoops of raisins on my Kellogg's Raisin Bran. Oh lord, that kind of joking, ripping off old commercials, I hoped that wasn't genetic, I hoped Perley wouldn't inherit that.

Rudy pushed his pint glass away. He tipped back the last of his coffee, redid his ponytail, stepped down off his stool.

"Library, is it?" he said. "I don't have all day."

"It's nothing to worry about, Rudy," I said. "We haven't heard from him in five years, maybe six. He's the one told us he doesn't ever want kids."

"Sure," Rudy said. "But still, you never know. Suddenly this guy gets baby-crazy. Seriously, I've had bouts of it myself. His biological clock starts ticking and he comes after you, and then what? He's the dad. I mean, how rich is he?"

"He has some kind of stock market job," I said.

"Oh yeah, this rich asshole," he said. "This yuppie is going to take your kid. If we can get Perley back in the first place, that is. Yeah."

"Yeah?" the beer sat in my empty stomach, the warmth of the bar drained away.

"Shit's fucked," Rudy said, waving to the tender and holding the door for me. "One thing I've noticed is that rich people don't seem to get themselves into these situations."

We drove in silence to the library. He kept the engine running as I climbed out. "I hope it helped to talk about it," he said.

"Sure," I said.

"I'm always here for you," he said. "You women are my family."

"Thanks," I said.

"What time you need picked up?" he asked.

"I'll walk home," I said, though what was the point of hating Rudy if all he was telling me was the same shit I was already telling myself?

I hunched over the library's PC, feeling sleazy, as if I were looking up pornography, not oil field jobs. The website listed roustabouts, oilers, excavators, drivers. Low-end seventeen bucks an hour, high-end thirty. From the plastic cup next to the computer I grabbed a scrap of paper and a stub of pencil meant for recording Dewey decimals. I did some basic arithmetic. In ninety days, with no days off, at twenty bucks an hour, working twelve hours a day, sometimes more, I could make more than twenty thousand dollars. The no breakfast, the beer in my stomach rose. My mouth watered. It would be enough to buy a septic system. Enough to pay a lawyer. Enough to get Perley back. Maybe even enough to stop me from thinking about some rich guy in Manhattan. Enough to pry myself out of invisibility, to show that this was my family. I was the provider.

I started filling in the fields: Karen Sweeney, address, DOB, then I got to résumé. Résumé, shit, I barely had one besides working as a nurse and a couple of under-the-table construction jobs. Dishwashing in high school? Apple picking in Wenatchee? Odd jobs on the road? None of that shit applied. And how did people get jobs, anyway? By knowing the right person, that's how.

It was a long shot, but what the hell? I logged in to my old AOL account. I went to the search field and scanned, and it came up right away: the email that Helen's old boyfriend Shane had sent me nearly a decade ago, back when I lived on the Women's Land Trust, and he was working as Rudy's ground crew. Rudy'd had some short-lived plan about upgrading his business. He'd been fascinated by email but refused to use it himself, so Shane had been scheduling jobs, sending invoices. He'd responded to my query about clearing the ash out back. Shane's email said, Sure thing. Me and Rudy'll be there Sunday at 2 p.m. Eight years later, I pressed reply.

All these years, Helen had said she had no idea where Shane was. She said she didn't know where he went when he left her. She said she'd never heard from him again. She'd never tried to contact him. When Shane left, Helen had missed him at first, then changed her position to good riddance. As if to prove she'd learned her lesson, she hadn't dated anyone since. I felt like I was cheating, I mean I felt like I was having an affair, I mean contacting Shane was so easy. I sat there browsing the oil field jobs page, clicking back and forth to my in-box. Within five minutes, Shane had written back to me. Ten minutes later, I had a job.

Karen Sweeney, he wrote. Good to hear from you. I've been wondering about all my old friends down there. You ever hear from Helen? He wrote, You should see me, I'm living on steak and shrimp. I got in early with this industry and I've been making it pay ever since. You should see the new pipeline they're building, he wrote. Supposed to stretch all the way down to Louisiana. He wrote, Sure there's openings. There's always openings. Sure, you should come up. I'm glad you asked. Roustabout on a pipeline crew. Pays twenty-two bucks an hour, twelve-hour days, sometimes more. You're supposed to have some experience but I'll vouch for you. I always like to help out friends.

He'd vouch for me, but he barely knew me, hadn't talked to me in eight years. Last time Shane saw my face, Rudy was on the ground and Shane was running, scared and ashamed. That shame had made him leave town. Now we were old friends? But that's how Shane was, I remembered it. No one was allowed not to like him.

He wrote, When can you start?

The job was a few counties away, about four hours north. I'd traveled thousands of miles but never bothered to go up that way. Why go see a bunch of cornfields close to home? Now what you heard was that the cornfields had gone to drill rigs and flares lighting up the sky so it was never night.

I typed back, I'll start as soon as I can get there.

I pressed send.

The first time I saw Lily, she was working at the hardware and salvage store, wearing overalls two sizes too big for her, a pencil stuck behind her ear. A knockout with hair all down her back. I couldn't really talk when I looked at her, so I bought something I couldn't use. What did you come in for? she asked, pointing her sharp chin at me, and I didn't know what to say. I was building the cabin out at the Land Trust. I'd come in for a box of screws, but Lily, or her hair, or the way that her oversize clothes hinted at grace and heat beneath them, all this made me want to make big purchases. So I said, A piece of furniture. She blinked and then laughed. We do sell that, she said. We do sell pieces of furniture. I laughed, too. I said, How about beds? You got beds? Later I would tell this story as if it were all by design, as if I had game. But I had no game. None. Zero. I was terrified. I asked, You got beds? and was suddenly so embarrassed I could hardly continue existing. The last thing I wanted to do was come on to this woman. When I looked at her I didn't want to come on to her. What I wanted was for her to come with me. To come with me and come with me. I wanted to be with her like being alone. As unending as that.

But Lily held my gaze, and she took me to the beds section. I asked which one she liked the best, and she said, This one will do. But it's for two. Are you looking for a single or a double? She never stopped looking at me. I couldn't believe how outrageous this was. Faced with the possibility of getting what I wanted, I faltered. Never mind, I said. I'll buy a sink. A utility sink. She sobered up. Her eyes got wide. I'm sorry, she said. I got the wrong idea. It's fine, I said. Just show me the sinks. She did. I bought the biggest utility sink they had.

Halfway home, I realized I'd forgotten the screws. I went back the next day. Lily just smiled. The next day it was a saw blade, then caulk, then hinges for the door, and finally Lily said, You know, you've come in every day this week, and I said, Do you want to see what I'm building? And she said, You live out on that separatist land, right? And I said, Do you want to come over? And she said, Yes. At the Land Trust, I led her toward my bed, which was really just a camping mat rolled out on the floor, but she pulled me the other way, out behind the cabin. She led me to that utility sink, no legs on it, half sunk in the mud. It's big enough for two, she said, and she laughed. She insisted that we stand in it while we finally kissed and kissed and took each other's clothes off one piece at a time, those giant overalls filling half the sink, her hair hiding her dark nipples, the line of down descending her belly, and I followed that line and what I found was ready for me and so deep, and we did make it to the camping mat, eventually. But for a long time, what we liked best was to find funny places to do it in, places that would make us laugh until it felt too good to laugh, the utility sink being only the first of them.

I left without saying goodbye to her. That last long day, I fixed the oil leak on the truck, got it down off the blocks. I mucked out the duck shed, even though it was mostly frozen. I hacked away at the shit-covered ice. I spread fresh straw. I fed the ducks scoops of corn. "Lay," I commanded, knowing they weren't likely to do so for another month at least. Next, I hauled arm-fuls of firewood onto the porch. Helen came out to watch me. "What are you doing?" she asked. "Where are you going?" But I knew she knew. "This is the green stuff," I said. "Dry it around the stove before you use it. You don't want creosote buildup."

Then I took a load of firewood up to the camper. I let the wood fall, thumping against the tin wall. Inside, I heard Lily stir. What was I supposed to do, goddammit, visit her in a dream? I stacked the wood, pulled a tarp over it. I stood outside the camper door, listening. She turned over. Exhaled. I never knocked. I didn't say goodbye to Lily. But all the same, I let her know I was leaving.

Lily

Dignity of risk is how I'd defend myself if I could, how I'd defend myself in court if they'd let me, how I'd defend myself to Children's Services if they'd listen. I'd defend myself to anyone who'd ask, but no one asked. Our neighbors didn't need to ask because without asking they were on our side. Frank said, That's why my children don't have birth certificates, even. My boss from the hardware store said, Take as many sick days as you need to. Deirdre said, Janice and I saw a drone. Bright lights. They're always watching. The mill operator gave us some flour. Mike held his hat and said, When your boy comes back he'll be different. You make one mistake. Of course, they didn't say this directly to me, because I was sleeping. But they told Helen, and Helen stood outside the camper door and told me.

Dignity of risk. I wanted to believe it. But when I woke in the dark, or in the late afternoon alone, then I said into the musty silence, Unfit. Then I said, Guilty, guilty,

guilty. If your baby had met a rabid animal he would have been bit, a sinkhole, he would have been swallowed. And look, he was bit. And look, he did fall into a sinkhole. He's in a sinkhole now. Swallowed up. And there's nothing you can do.

The lawyer, nice man, said, Wait. But I don't like the man who tells me to wait. Never have. So even though Helen and Rudy and Karen tried to act like there was hope, like it was good to have a lawyer on our side, I knew that this lawyer wasn't worth waking up for. My mother's voice said, You deserve this. I shut it out. My grandma's voice said, Girl, you need to get your behind out of bed and get to work. I shut her out, too. Helen would stand outside the door, telling me the news. I tried to listen. I tried to reply. I kept meaning to eat, to feed myself, to build my strength, to take action. I kept meaning not to sleep, but it didn't take. I slept.

Before you have a kid, life is full of work that ends. But your kid is born, and that's it. There's no off hours. It just goes and goes. You'd better hope there's no end. In the seven years since Perley had been born, the work of my life was nothing much, just to get my boy through his day, food, clothes, ailments, snakebites, hurt feelings, unanswerable and relentless questions. Each morning I woke up ready. I was a parent. I was always ready. And now that was over. That's what it is to lose a child. There's no one to care for. There's nothing to do. The work just stops.

Helen, Karen, Rudy, these people were bargainers, grasping for anything they'd give us. Two weeks. Ninety days. One year. For me it was all or nothing. So for a while there, I admit, it was nothing. I refused to put numbers on the days. I let time go by. I turned and turned in bed alone. I turned away from strategy and action. I turned toward that word: unfit. I was pincushion and pins, sticking myself once for each mistake, turning porcupine.

One morning, Karen came to the door. She thought I didn't know but I knew. I heard her stack wood. I heard her stand outside. I heard her not knock. I waited her out. I knew when she left. I went outside to pee and I found her note sitting on top of the woodpile, stuck to the tarp with a button cap.

She wrote, I'm leaving. She wrote, I found work. She wrote, I'm leaving because it's the only way that you and me and Perley can be a family again.

I knew how her mind worked. I knew she

351

was trying to pass this off as pack leadership. Maybe she could fool herself, but she couldn't fool me. She was running. The stranger in her had finally won out over the wolf pack. I knew where she was going. Where did anyone in our hills go when they ran out of options? They joined one of the crews in the oil fields up north, drilling or pipelining or wherever the jobs were that season. They called them rat crews because they weren't union and they'd do just about anything to get the job done. They lived in one of the camps that were all men, the boomtowns that sprang up, and they made money and sometimes they got sick or had accidents or did things they weren't proud of, and people said it was dangerous to be a woman up there, but woman or man, they always made money. They always came home with money.

She wrote, I'm leaving so that I can come back.

I've forgiven Karen plenty, but I can't forgive her for not understanding that leaving so you can come back is bullshit. For not understanding that just because I didn't have time to talk to her, just because I was catching up on sleep, that didn't mean I wanted her gone. For not understanding that leaving is nothing special. Leaving is just leaving. Staying is the hard thing.

When Perley was two, he learned to say, I love you. He would say, I love you, and Karen and I would stop what we were doing to pick him up and spin him around, to kiss his fat face. Then he would say, I love your eyes. He would say, I love the snake. I love the stove. I love the Mean Aunt. I love the sofa, the house, the sun, the snow, the rain. I love boogers. I love poop. I love pee. I love stew.

At the bottom of the note, Karen wrote, I love you. But I didn't care. I let the woodstove take it.

11

Perley

Altemonte watched me unpack my stuff on the top bunk which was now my bunk, which all it was was my *ElfQuest* comic books. Real casual and cool, like maybe I didn't even care, I asked him, Have you read *ElfQuest*? No, he said, and so I Frisbeed one down onto the lower bunk which was his bunk. I flicked him one that had an album at the back where you can look at all of the elves up close in totally saturated full color. Skywise, Pike, Cutter, Strongbow, Redlance, Leetah, Nightfall, Moonshade, and he looked at it, he inspected every page. This is pretty sweet, he said. Then I told him about my house, about the MCCANN'S: STEP AWA. I said, Me and my Mama K built it up with all the top furniture like a total bunk bed and even a table and chairs and we're going to make a porch swing even though it doesn't have a porch and I'm pretty good with tools, plus no one knows who the McCanns are or what AWA means, it's a mystery that plagues us from basically ancient times. And he said, I know what AWA means, AWA stands for All Worship Alte-monte, and I was like, You wish. Then Alte-monte looked at my comic book again and he said, Who do you think would win between a flaming arrow and a flaming axe I mean if an elf was shooting it or a dwarf was throwing it? I felt bad for him, but I had to say, You can't be an elf you're too chubby. And also, they don't have elves that are African-American, which is what Ms. Carroll said to call him. He asked, Are the elves American? Which I had to admit I didn't know so I said, Am I American? And he said, I don't know are you? And I said, Are you? And he said, I'm not sure but I don't think so, and I said, Why not? And he said, Because I've never voted for the president. And I said, Me neither. Then he said, You think I even want to be an elf? And I said, What else would anyone want to be, unless it was a wolf? And he said, I could be a dwarf which can make things out of metal while what can an elf do but be all graceful. I said, But who even cares about dwarves? So he showed me this book he had called *The Hobbit* that didn't have any pictures and that never exactly said if the dwarves were chubby or African or American it just said that they lived in Middle-earth and that they had these toxic axes and other sweet fighting skills and they liked treasure which me and Altemonte totally did, too. Flaming arrows, I said. Flaming axes, he said, so we stuck with that and played double-crossing pretend where none of the other kids could tell we were playing pretend which they would not allow us to do without creaming us.

I mean at school.

Because one thing about school is I wasn't really popular anymore. The kids knew that I was a foster kid. When Ms. Carroll had borne me aloft to the principal's office, I had stopped being Friend of Snake and instead become Stupid Abused Neglected Kid. I knew it, I knew all the words even though I didn't see the need to use them. My first day back, Bexley came up real close to me and I crouched, ready to throw a flaming axe at his face, but he just said, My dad said to leave you alone 'cause you're going through some stuff. So I said, It's okay, you don't have to leave me alone don't leave me alone please, and Bexley said, My dad said. And then he left me alone. Everyone left me alone. Actually I was totally alone except for Altemonte.

Whatever, said Altemonte. Half of them are foster kids, too. The agency places kids at my grandma's house all the time.

What kids? I asked, feeling like I was getting stabbed with the flaming sword of jealousy, but Altemonte said, Mostly just kids who don't care about Middle-earth or dwarf weaponry. They don't stay long.

Altemonte wasn't that popular, either, and thus I learned a life lesson which is that true friendship, acorn collecting, and flaming axes might be all that is left after you try and totally fail to be cool. I learned that I'm into having one true friend and that friend is Altemonte. Every day we pulled on our ears, so our ears would stick out more and kind of be accentuated but we would still be incognito. We collected acorns and filled the hollow places beneath tree roots. We silently existed as elf and dwarf. We felt that no one could see us.

So now I knew. I knew that my mission and my destiny had been to meet Altemonte. I kept searching my comic books to see what the elves would do, or if the wolf pack council knew a way I could take Altemonte with me. Because now that I had met him, and now that I had accomplished my mission, I figured what was to stop me from bringing him home.

I mean, here I was living with him at his house, but I'd just as soon he come live with me in the All Worship Altemonte camper. There was plenty of room for both of us and I would gladly tell him the password. Hell, I would make up a new one just for him.

But when I brought it up, Altemonte backed away from me and said, I don't want to live at your house, this is my home, I want to stay here with my grandma, and Grandma Barlow heard him and came in from the kitchen and pulled Altemonte into her lap and she said, Perley, I can only do what I can do. I can't make miracles, so you can't go home, not just yet. And you can't take Altemonte, he's my tiny baby.

I'm not a tiny baby, Altemonte said, but he snuggled in close.

But I need you here with me, my pie, Grandma Barlow said.

Grandma Barlow could only do what she could do. And what she could do was bake pies. And teach math, and cover us with quilts, and fill us with pancakes, and prop us up in front of a video, and furnish us with a PlayStation, which we could throw flaming axes across the screen right into the forehead of the bad guy, and she did all of this to comfort us.

She held Altemonte in her lap and I watched them and I didn't think about how it felt to be in Mama L's lap. Altemonte pushed his head up under her chin and I didn't think about what it felt like to push my head up under Mama L's chin. I just watched them and tried to think about pancakes and pies and flaming axes and elves and bad guys and foreheads. Grandma Barlow said, Altemonte, it's time for your medicine. She took a bottle from her pocket and reached for a water glass. The pills were blue and looked like nail polish. Altemonte closed his eyes and swallowed. Grandma Barlow watched me watching. These pills make my boy feel better, she said. It might be they could make you feel better, too.

At school, the principal kindly called me into his office again and I went in and we smiled sadly at each other. The Outside Girl was sitting in a chair and she stood up and I smiled sadly at her and she said, Perley, I'm here to take you to see a counselor, remember we talked about it? I remembered the wolf pack council and she drove me into town. I thought she'd drive me past our driveway so I could make sure it was still there. She was going that direction, but she swerved at the last minute and took a different route.

The counselor wasn't a wolf pack he was just a guy with a soft voice and a pancake face all smooth and golden. He asked me some questions about making friends and leaving the classroom without permission, and about the tablet and about not completing my Specials. I try to complete my Specials, I said. I like to look at them on the tablet but it's like I can't really see them. It's like I look at the screen and my eyes start to blur does that ever happen to you?

No, Perley, that doesn't happen to me, he said. It sounds distressing. Which was a word I loved, like being shipwrecked, like the lullaby Mama K and Mama L used to sing, so I was like, Distressing. Yes. Totally distressing.

Then the counselor asked, Are there other times that you are distressed? and I wanted to help him so I said, Sometimes I can't sleep. The pancake counselor said, Because you are worried about a snake biting you? I stayed quiet, but my scar spoke up. The counselor asked, Is that why you can't sleep? So I just said, Can I have a pancake? I could tell it wasn't what he wanted me to say, I mean he probably wasn't even thinking about his own face and how much like a pancake it was, but he smiled again and he asked me, Are pancakes your favorite food? I said, Mama K says I'm not allowed to have a pancake or any cake. I am allowed to have pemmican arranged in the shape of a cake. But sometimes Mama L makes me pancakes when no one's home and Grandma Barlow makes us pancakes whenever we want, me and Altemonte. The pancake counselor said, I'm sorry to say I don't have any pancakes, but you may certainly have pancakes later.

So it was a successful distraction and I didn't have to tell the pancake counselor why I couldn't sleep. I didn't have to tell him that lately I almost started to fly out of my body, I almost sent myself out like the special power that Savah of the Sun Folk has because I missed my Mama L so bad, and I missed Mama K, too, and the Mean Aunt and Rudy, and I didn't want to tell the pancake counselor that, because I touched my scar and it told me, Use your tricks. Dazzle him.

Afterward, in the waiting room, which had *Blue's Clues* and this giant baby with a bottle that couldn't walk but just sat there looking, looking, the Outside Girl extended her hand and received a piece of paper from the pancake counselor. I saw it all happen. And we stopped at the CVS on the way back to Grandma Barlow's. And that night when Altemonte took his blue nail polish pill I got to take one, too, and then we had pancakes for dinner. Which were good. Eating pancakes was like eating my pillow which I had always wanted to do, but knew wouldn't be as good as it looked. And that was funny, because two days after I took the pill I noticed that the pancakes tasted like that. Like my pillow. Like nothing. Like a cardboard person eating a cardboard cake on the PlayStation. And anyway, my stomach started hurting and I didn't want any more pancakes.

After dinner that night, Grandma Barlow said, Altemonte, it is time to write a letter to your mama, and his face went wrong. Why should I write her when she went off like that, what's she got to do with me? he asked. You watch your mouth, Grandma Barlow said. It's to make money to feed you that she went. She's working a job and sending the money home and someday you'll do it, too. I'll never do it never, said Altemonte. You'll do it and you'll consider yourself lucky when you do, said Grandma Barlow. What about my dad? asked Altemonte. Your dad ain't no better and he might be worse, Grandma Barlow said. Now do you want to find out quick about the misery of life or will you write the letter? What should I write? said Altemonte. Write her about your day about school about the pie I fed you about the arithmetic you're learning, said Grandma Barlow. Altemonte wouldn't show me what he wrote but worked at it with furrowed brow. What about me, I asked, should I write a letter to my mama? You're going to see your mama real soon, my son, said Grandma Barlow. You've got visitation with her next week. With Mama K or with Mama L? I asked. With Lily Marshall, Grandma said, which sounded like a movie star or like someone I didn't know. Grandma Barlow said, Your mama must be Delia Marshall's granddaughter. That woman always did do things her own way. She was my mother's great friend, and you should have heard those two telling the world what to do. Some things haven't changed, women are still doing the talking, and still no one bothers to heed what we say.

After I started taking the blue pills with Altemonte, my special powers increased. I mean all the background noise died down to zero and when we played the PlayStation I could beat the levels, and at school I could do my Specials and I could read the tablet, and I started getting like one hundred percent. I wasn't super-popular anymore but I didn't care, I was like a ninja. A ninja isn't super-popular. A ninja is just a ninja. A wolf is just a wolf. Elves and dwarves aren't super-popular. They are entities.

I said to Altemonte, I am so focused, I am so clear, let's climb out the window. So we did. And we went to the stone house.

At the stone house the moon smacked down off the chimney, blinding us. We crept inside. There was only enough room for two people, those two people were me and Altemonte. What should we do now? I asked, but then we both knew. We both knew at the exact same time. Altemonte said it out loud. I mouthed the words right along with him. We should dig a hole. We should dig a portal to the elf world, to the World of Two Moons or to Middle-earth, whichever world we got to first. So we did. We used sharp stones and sticks. We scraped at it and burrowed, and carried red clay out of the gnome house in our hands cupped together.

That was the first night but it became the second and the third. We were so sharp, we were so focused, I was like, How will we know when we are finished? and Altemonte was like, We will probably see some kind of light I imagine. We have to make it extremely deep. When the time comes, we will know.

My brain on fire became a goblet. My

brain became the wizard statue chiseled out of the very stone that is holding a crystal ball.

The only downside was that my tongue tasted like I ate the pan instead of the food inside the pan, and my stomach felt like I swallowed the dish and the dishwater. First I pooped like ten times, and then for a week I didn't poop at all. But I didn't tell anyone.

I went to see the pancake counselor again and when he asked me how I felt, I said, I have found my soulmate he is Altemonte. We recognized each other. The counselor said, Don't rush to big decisions, where did you learn the term soulmate? And I said, sometimes elves just look at each other and they just know that they will be side by side forever and there's no denying it. It's like what Mama L and Mama K are, I said, except it should make them fight less, but they fight anyway, and the Mean Aunt fights with them, too, whose soulmate is I don't know Rudy I guess. The pancake counselor was like, Sounds like things were pretty hard at home, and I was like, I think the wolves have soulmates, too, but only with other wolves not with elves exactly. And also when you recognize someone their soul name comes into your mind, but you're never supposed to say it out loud, and then the pancake counselor interrupted me and said, Would you like to see your mother? And I was like, Mama L or Mama K? and he said, Your mother. And I said, Mama K doesn't want to see me. She told me to pack up and go. The pancake counselor said, You don't have to worry about her. I want to know if you want to have a visit with your mother, Lily. And I couldn't swallow and when you can't swallow you can't talk so I couldn't talk. I was worried that the pancake counselor could see the Velvet Piglet under my clothes.

I mean, me and Altemonte were making a portal to the elf world which was a place for wolf councils and axe throwing, which was a place for flaming arrows where our brains would finally fit in. I didn't want this pancake face to see me cry, which was against my training from Mama K. The pancake counselor said, You can tell me the truth. But I kept my mouth shut.

The truth is a story my women told me from when I was a baby: Where is Rudy? my women would ask, and I would point to Rudy. Where is Auntie Helen? they would ask, and I would point to the Mean Aunt. Where is Mama K? they would ask, and I would point to Mama K. Where is Mama L? they would ask, and I would just stare and stare. I couldn't point her out. I couldn't find her. I couldn't find her because she was me.

The truth is that someday I will see Mama K again, and I will say, I did what you told me to do. I made you proud. I went on a quest. I went on a survival mission. My mettle was tested. I followed the protocols. I used your training. I was intrepid. I was tough. I had stick-to-itiveness, and they never saw me sweat. I will tell Mama K this, and she will catch me up into her arms and throw me like she did when I was so small that it's only a half moon in the corner of my eye and a pair of hands and a splinter wedged in. She will be my elfin chief. I will give her my report and she will kneel before me and touch me gravely on the forehead the way a noble old wolf would touch foreheads with a bold young pup. You have done me proud, Perley, she said. You are my Perley. You are mine.

So of course I couldn't tell the truth, even though the pancake counselor sat staring at me with kind and sorrowful eyes. Instead, I was the lowest line on the eye chart, that silent, that small.

Lily

You have a child and then you wait for the day when he'll call you a hypocrite. You wait for that day. He'll use it even before he knows what it means. He'll love how it feels on the tongue, how it sounds coming out. It sounds like an animal, like a prehistoric mammal reptile. It sounds familiar, but bad. He wants to use it against someone, and unfortunately, you're all vulnerable. Helen, for example. Claims to be so antiestablishment but then she goes around using words like best practices and optimum and internship, words that come so directly from the establishment that no individual could have invented them. And Karen. Swears by hard work and a strict do-it-yourself ethic, but anyone can see how lazy she is. She just wants to whittle and let nature take over.

Me, I almost let myself believe I was safe from the word hypocrite. After all, I was the one who loved sweets, and sometimes I sneaked Perley sweets, too. But I'd brought Perley up to be fearless, and now here I was, so afraid I couldn't open my eyes. I'd brought Perley up to be free, and here he was, captured, and I wasn't doing a thing, not a thing but lying all day in the dark, warm with terror and regret.

The piece of mail Helen slipped under the

door said visitation. The word inside my head was hypocrite. The lovely combination was what got me out of bed, helped me read the address on the letter, delivered me to that address on time.

We met in the park along the two-lane highway to town. Years of driving the truck or riding my bicycle along this road, I'd seen that park a million times. But I'd never seen anyone there. I'd never once brought Perley there to swing on the swings or to brave the tall slide. Now I knew why. I knew why the swings sat empty and the slide was covered in pine needles. It was the visitation park. People knew to stay clear of it. Somehow, I'd known, too. Parents played with their children here as a performance, while some social worker sat on a bench nearby, watching. Maybe people stayed away to give undone families some privacy. But more likely people knew the truth. Trouble is catching. If you played with your children at this park, an ordinary day might suddenly become a visitation day. You'd find yourself alone at the end of it, your kids waving to you from the back of the social worker's car. Pariah Park. Fear Park.

But fuck that. Who cares about the park? Who cares about it when Perley was in it? He stepped out of the caseworker's Camry and came toward me like he was still a baby, pigeon-toed and tumbling. He cut through the frost-covered grass of Pariah Park, and I thought, Let's just live here. You're here, I'm here, what else do we need?

But all I said was, "Perley."

Perley said, "Mama L." But when he was four feet away from me he stopped. He just stopped, like I was behind a pane of glass. He stopped and looked at me. And I saw he'd changed. It had only been two weeks, but he was different. Something in his eyes. I'll know you anywhere, my boy, I'll know you by your toes, by your pinkie fingers. I'll know you. I wanted him to come closer, but I didn't know how to make that happen. So I sat down in the grass. There was a thaw that day. The temperature was climbing toward fifty, but the ground was hard and cold. I killed ice crystals sitting on them. Perley pushed back his hood. He gazed at me without smiling. His breath made hard quick clouds.

I said, "I love to see your face every day. Are you all right? Are you hungry? Are they taking care of you? Will you come home soon?"

The caseworker, that child-woman I refused to recognize, came up behind him, swinging car keys. "That's an inappropriate question, Lily," she said. "And it's a lot of pressure on Perley. If I were you, I'd use visitation time to play together, not to ask him when he's coming home. Let me assure you, the home he's in is a perfectly good one."

Perley took a step closer to me. He was wearing clothes I didn't recognize, the hood attached to an unfamiliar puffy coat. His blue jeans were stiff, cuffed at the ankle. "Where's Mama K?" asked Perley.

"She had to go to work," I said.

"She doesn't go to work," Perley said. He looked at me sideways. "It's probably that she doesn't want to see me."

"She does want to see you," I said. "She went to work to save money to bring you back home," I said.

"That's enough," the caseworker girl said. "That's really enough. It's not appropriate to talk to Perley about details of the case, especially when we don't know the outcome. It's not fair to him. The swings in this park are some of the best in the county, really state-of-the-art. You've got one hour. I'll go sit on that bench over there."

Perley and I walked over to the wood chips. His body was shielded from me beneath the enormous coat. I couldn't even hold him right. I wasn't sure if he wanted me to. He sat on the state-of-the-art swing. "You'd better push me," he said, so I pushed him.

"I'm sorry. I'm sorry this is happening to you," I said.

"What I think is weird is that there's nothing you can do about it," he said, like observing an unusual insect. "I mean, even though you're my own mama, and you always promise me that you'll find me and bring me back again, that you'll know me by my toes, actually they just took me away and there's nothing you can do, right? Or do you just not want to?"

"Of course I want to," I said. "I'm trying."

"Really?" he said.

I thought of how much time I'd spent sleeping, forgetting time. I gave him an extra big push, so that the chain went slack at the top. The white sky glared at me.

"What is it like, where you're staying?" I asked.

"It's nice," he said. "I made one true friend. His name is Altemonte."

"This is a mix-up, Perley," I said. "A mistake. You'll be home soon."

"Do you and Mama K still love each other?" he asked.

"Yes," I said.

"Do you still fight all the time?" he asked.

"Well, like I said, she's not home right now," I said.

"Does she want me to come home?" he said.

"I told you," I said. "She's saving money to bring you back."

He thought about it.

"Ransom," he said.

"Ransom," I said.

"She's on a mission," he said.

"Right," I said.

I had let the swing slow until Perley's toes dusted the wood chips. The caseworker, on her distant bench, looked up from her phone. "You'd better keep pushing me," he said.

So I began a fearful pushing. I stood behind the swing, circled my arms around him, then dug my feet sideways into the sawdust, hauled him backward, and let him fly up into the air. It got aerobic, difficult, strained. I couldn't say if he enjoyed himself. I couldn't say if I did. But when I pulled him in close to me I began to understand the change in him. It was the change I'd seen in his clear eye, with a pupil like a pencil point. When I held him around the waist, he was thicker somehow, not so most people would notice, but this one had been part of my body. So I knew, I knew, but I didn't know what I knew until I pulled him in close and I smelled him. This boy who'd always smelled like pitch and yeast, smoke and yogurt, yarrow and graham crackers even though we didn't let him eat graham crackers. Now there was something else. Now there was metal and chalk.

"What do they feed you?" I asked as I hauled him backward, his head up against my chest.

"Pie," he said. I let him fly.

"What else?" I asked as I dragged him to me again.

"Pancakes," he said. He flew. I drew him back.

"And?" I asked.

"Medicine," he said, and I watched him arc away from me, far gone as a bird.

I went home furious and for the first time full of energy. I didn't even look at the camper. I stormed to the pipeline, where Helen and Rudy were in the nursery bent over buckets, bickering and pruning. I ignored their obvious pleasure at seeing me out of bed.

"I want to go see Aldi Birch," I said. "They've got Perley hopped up on some kind of meds."

"Oh, that's typical," said Rudy. "Of course they do. You all are babes in the woods."

"We'll take Rudy's truck," said Helen.

Aldi's place was all closed up, the cavernous garage locked up tight. There was no answer when I knocked. "He gets like this in the winter," Rudy said. "He gets real low. Sometimes you don't see him for a month or so." I turned to go, but Helen said, "This is bullshit. He said he'd help us." She put her whole arm into it, beating on the metal door. No answer. Rudy found an old two-by-four leaning against the side of the garage, and started whaling on the door with that. "Come on, asshole, open up," he said between swings. "Come on, we know you're in there." Aldi Birch opened the door.

"I'm drunk," he said.

"You're not drunk," said Rudy. "That's just an excuse."

"I'm useless. You'll have to forgive me. I'm in no mood to talk," Aldi said.

"Then don't talk, just listen," Rudy said. I described the situation.

"He says he doesn't even know what pills they are. He doesn't even know what the diagnosis is," I said. "I asked the caseworker, but she won't say."

"It'll be hard to find out what pills they have him on," Aldi said, not inviting us in.

"This is pretty common, and sad to say perfectly legal."

"What did I tell you?" Rudy said.

"When kids go into foster care around here, first thing they do is diagnose them with something. Probably hyperactivity or something like that," Aldi said. He still hadn't opened the door all the way, but spoke to us through a narrow opening. All we could see was his nose poking out. We couldn't even tell if he was wearing clothes or not.

"He's not hyperactive," I said. "He's perfect."

"I'm in no position to argue with you," Aldi said.

"I'm his mother. I decide if he needs medicine or not," I said. "Don't they have to notify me? Who the hell are these people?"

"Like I said, Elsa Barlow's probably just doing her best," Aldi said. "I'm not saying it's right."

"What can we do?" I asked.

Aldi sighed, rubbed his face. "I'll file a motion," he said.

"A motion? A motion about what?" asked Helen.

"A motion to make them release the information about the diagnosis and the meds," Aldi said.

"When are you going to file it?" I asked. "Today is February nineteenth. They took Perley on February fifth. That means it's fourteen days Perley's been gone. That leaves seventy-six more days until the ninety-day review, which is on May sixth." They all stopped and looked at me. I was back on the calendar again. I was awake now and I was counting. "We've wasted enough time already," I said.

"I'll file it first thing in the morning," Aldi said.

"They ought to be thrown in jail for this," I said.

"The ones that belong in jail are rarely the ones you see in there," Aldi said. He began to close the door. Rudy stuck his foot in, forced it back open. "You're not dropping out on us," Rudy said. "I know how you get in the winter. You'd better not disappear. You're going to help us. You promised you would."

"First we file the motion," Aldi said. "Then we can try to prove that it's a frivolous diagnosis. But there are no guarantees. And it's going to take time." Polite, he used his own foot to move Rudy's out of the way. Firm, he closed the door.

On the ride home, Rudy said, "I taught

377

Perley a lot of tricks, you know. During the man internship. I told him about pills. He's wily."

"He's a child, Rudy," Helen said.

"Still," Rudy said. "Could be he gets out of this thing all on his own."

When we got home, Helen said she'd make acorn casserole for dinner, but I said I wasn't hungry. Rudy said I was welcome to take out some of my anger on target practice up in the nursery, but I told him maybe later. They watched me walk back to the camper. I knew what they were thinking. Don't go back to sleep. Please don't go back to sleep. I might have told them to save themselves the worry. I might have told them I would never sleep again.

It's a good thing Karen was gone, it's a good thing I was alone, because if anyone had looked inside the camper that night it would have been a demon they saw, a demon in the dark with glowing eyes drying out. Aldi Birch could go ahead and file a motion, but I wasn't going to wait around for any motion. My own motion had finally begun. All night, I fed the fire. I stared at the woodstove until dawn. I ground my mind against the flame.

In the morning, light snow fell. Barefoot, I stepped outside to pee. Fox tracks circled the camper. Ducks cackled down at the shed. I let the cold stab up through my feet and into my legs. I'll know you, my boy, I'll know you by your toes. You can roam, but I'll find you and bring you back again. By that time, I had made my plan.

12

Karen

I took the Greyhound to points north. As a young whittler, I would have hitchhiked, but the problem with hitchhiking is that people pick you up because they want company. You have to talk to people, and I didn't want to talk to anyone. I wanted to be alone. I knew that where I was going it was likely to be all men, and not men I wanted anything to do with. And I had a setting for that. Most women have it, definitely most queers. A setting where I sealed myself off. So it would probably be about the same as being alone. Which is what I deserved anyway.

When I boarded the bus it was night. Our part of the state was all hills and water, was like a jungle the way wild grapevines grew and big leafed trees closed in. Sandstone, red clay, no flat land, people farmed anywhere they could, shoving a few seeds down into the sediment on top of a boulder, the cattle grazing down in the valleys. But I traveled north away from all that, and in the morning the red winter showed land flat and hard and even, cornfields and long gray highways, road signs you could see coming a mile away. Soon the fields of silage gave way to towers, drill rigs, well pads, containment ponds, lights and lights and lights. The sky above was mud.

The bus pulled into the Greyhound station on the edge of town, people smoking outside, large men, brown skinned or dark, white men with red faces, all in work clothes. The only woman I saw worked the ticket window. Then I saw Shane. He was leaning on a silver SUV, brand-new by the look of it. He'd lost some of his hair, but what was left of it he still wore long and wavy, tucked into the collar of his shirt. He brought a cigarette to his mouth, which wasn't a habit I remembered. Other than that, he looked about the same, his quick face, unfailingly friendly, eager to share all the information he had. He saw me through the bus window, stubbed out his cigarette, brought out his old grin, showed a couple of new gold teeth, raised his arm so high in the air he lifted himself off the ground. If he'd lost a few teeth over the years, hell, so had I.

Shane took my knapsack, hugged me, gave me a careful kiss on the cheek, looked to see who might've noticed. He ushered me into his car, closed the door, switched on the heated seats so I felt like I'd pissed myself. "It's good for you to be met here by a man," he said. "It's good for them to see you're friends with me. You can't be too careful."

"Sure," I said. He pulled out of the Greyhound lot.

"I hate to say it, but these people are scum," Shane said. "Trust me, it's a fucking free-for-all."

"You've been here all this time?" I asked. "Nearly ten years?"

"You kidding? I certainly haven't been in this shithole the whole time," he said. "At first the company sent me all over. Seriously, the industry's spreading, even out to the coast. I loved the travel, but now more of the jobs are union."

"Why not join the union?" I asked. "Better pay."

"It's who you know," Shane said. "There's a ten-year waiting list to get in. Anyway, I'm management now."

"For rat crews," I said.

"Call it what you want," he said. "But I've learned a lot. This industry's not so bad, no matter what all the greenies say. And I'm one, too, you know I am. Recycling, planting trees, solar power. I love all that stuff. But this is bridge fuel. It's better than coal, that much I know. Management's good money, I don't have to get my hands quite so dirty, saves my back. Anyway you shouldn't be talking union. If this was a union job you couldn't just show up like this. No way. I'm doing you a favor. Glad to do it, too."

"Thanks again," I said, wondering how many more times I'd have to say it.

"When I started, things were more tame," Shane said. "But now it's big-time. I don't even want to tell you what I've seen."

"I'm pretty good at taking care of myself," I said. We drove past mini-marts and motels, camper parks and more cornfields, diners and lots where large yellow pieces of equipment waited side by side. I counted the number of women that I saw, but hadn't even got through the fingers of one hand before Shane looked at me quickly, then cut his eyes back to the road.

"How's Helen?" he asked. There was no way I could match his bald chattiness. I was already tired. So I doubled down on my

Greyhound setting. It had served me well this far. Why not leave it to Shane to do the sharing?

"Fine, I think," I said.

"I looked her up a few years ago when I was out in Seattle," he said. "Thought I'd buy her a beer, you know, for old times' sake. But her aunt told me she's still living on that damn twenty acres we bought." He shook his head. I didn't say, I'm living on that damn twenty acres, too. I didn't say anything.

"I can't imagine what she's doing for work," Shane said. He waited.

"She's working for Rudy," I said.

"Rudy?" Shane said. "You've got to be kidding me. That guy is such a phenomenal fuckup."

"Well," I said. "Some people stay. Some people go."

He glanced at me. "Is she with him?" he asked.

"None of my business," I said, but for some reason I didn't deny it outright.

"That woman," he said, "she never stopped talking, and now I have all the time in the world to think about the things she told me." He looked over at me again as he said that, maybe thinking he'd get sensitivity points. I kept my face quiet. "It's good

384

to see you, Karen," he said. "I've missed you."

I figured he and I must have different working definitions of what it meant to miss someone. The man hardly knew me. Helen had been all torn up about him when we first met her, but if you asked me he was one of those guys who strove so hard to make a good impression that it made you want to deny him the satisfaction.

"You in trouble, then, or what?" he asked.

"I'm not in trouble," I said.

"You don't have to talk about it if you don't want to," he said. "But it seems like if you weren't in trouble you'd stick to nursing. Good high-wage job. Not many of those down where you're from."

Here I was, far from home, talking with someone who knew me but didn't know Perley, the best part of me, the part of me I'd ruined. I'd hoped to avoid talking to Shane or anyone else about the details. I kept it as brief as possible. "Government says me and Lily have to put in a septic system or lose our kid. Where am I going to get that kind of money quick?" I said. If Shane was surprised, he didn't say anything about it, adding to the list of things I was surely meant to be grateful for.

"Boy or girl?" he asked. Just for a moment, I thought he meant me.

"Boy," I said. "Seven years old. What about you? Any little Shanes running around somewhere?"

"I hope not," he said. "I'm dating here and there, nothing serious. I've got a friendship with a woman who runs the motel you'll be staying at. She's from down in the hills, too."

"You booked me a room?" I asked. "Better be cheap. I'm here to save money, not spend it."

"Only place cheaper is where the guys stay," Shane said.

"I'll just stay in the cheapest place," I said.

"You don't want to stay out there," he said. "It's dangerous for a woman. I told you. Don't be stubborn about this."

We passed a Walmart Supercenter, then came up over a rise to rows and rows of container units, back and back and back, all white and beige, laid out neatly in a grid like refrigerators on the moon. It took me a minute to see that each container had one window, and an aluminum door. I guess you could call these signs of humanity. It was a ghost town this time of day, everyone at work.

"That's two hundred people," Shane said. "All men. No wives, no children. And they're bored. And they're lonely. You don't want to be staying out there."

"If you're talking about rape," I said, "I know plenty of people wouldn't get bored or lonely enough to rape someone."

"Hey, you're preaching to the choir here," he said.

We pulled up in front of a fetid motel, meant to be seafoam green. The office out front flashed a VACANCY sign, and there were shacks lined up behind it, uneven cement pathways running between them, brown grass, hardened black snow by the curbside. If it wasn't a step up from the moonscape, at least it looked as cheap.

I waited outside while Shane went into the office and brought me back a key. He said he'd pick me up at 5:00 a.m., said don't worry about breakfast he'd bring me an egg sandwich, said he'd bring me coffee, too. I just kept saying thank you until he drove off.

I found my assigned shack, worked the key. A bed with a broken spring, a stained chair, the smell of sweat and cigarettes, a swipe of grime across the window, sticky sink, a hole in the wall the precise size of a fist. But unlike home, the place had plenty of electricity and hot running water. I took a shower forever. I let the water scald me and I thought of Lily. I thought of Helen and Rudy. But of course mostly I thought of Perley.

He must have been four or five, one of those endless afternoons we were together while Lily was at work, endless until they ended. We'd been digging drainage, and he was lobbying for macaroni and cheese for lunch. How do you even know about macaroni and cheese? I asked, putting a hard-boiled duck egg in his hand, pulling his muddy boots off, sitting him down on the sofa. Macaroni and cheese is like magic, I said. You're not going to grow up to be some kid who thinks the food comes out of the box, magic, the water out of the tap, magic, the house you live in. Remember, if you're not the one who did the hard work, someone else did. Never take that for granted. Magic? asked Perley. Like the elves? Like Redlance shaping trees? Like you do? Or like Leetah healing people? Like how you used to be a doctor? A nurse, I said. You're missing the point of those comics, Perley. The elves don't rely on anyone or anything else except each other. They're ready for whatever comes up, I said. He knocked his egg against his head, pulled a face. Magic, he said. Did you hear me? I said. Okay, he said. I heard you.

Just don't take anything for granted, I said. Except me.

And look at us now.

Up here, the ruined fields yawned from me and I used that open space to think. My boy's skills weren't magic, they were hard-won and he'd learned them from me. It was simple as knowing someone best. I knew he'd always wanted to go on a mission. So he was on his mission. And I was on mine. We'd trained each other for this moment. That's what I came to, in that filthy bathtub in the shale fields, in that shower, the hot water like a miracle. That's what I tried to focus on. Because of course every thought of Perley came with an equal and opposite non-thought. I thought of his skills, his tree climbing, arrow shooting, acorn curing, squirrel skinning. I thought of how I'd shown him how to whittle with my sheeps-foot blade. I thought of his martial arts, his swiftness, how good he was at hiding him-self. I thought of his damn elves riding on their wolves. I thought of that instead of thinking about how he looked on the other end of my arm as I threw him out the door, his knapsack sailing over his head, his bewildered newborn face, instead of think-ing how I'd failed him.

I meant to call home. I meant to let Lily

know I got in safe. Even if she refused to talk to me, I meant to talk to Helen, to ask her to deliver the message. I meant to head toward the office to ask Shane's girlfriend if I could use the desk phone. I even pulled back my curtain to see if the office light was still on.

Instead, I saw that someone had built a campfire. Out in the stubbled fields, past where the cement pathways ended, big blaze, embers tossed up. Quiet voices, figures moved in the flicker.

I almost went toward it.

Didn't.

I let the curtain fall back. What would I say to Lily anyway? She was pissed. She wanted kidnapping, instant action with no thought to future consequences. I'd preached patience, strategy. The last time I'd done that, back when we were building, we'd ended up in a house whose front door didn't even seal, didn't seal the state out, didn't seal Perley in. So what did I know? I had nothing to report. I'd call her when I'd had a chance to prove myself. I'd call her when something had changed.

Shane picked me up before sunrise. He said he had good news.

"I told you there were jobs as roustabouts,

390

but I got you something better," he said, handing me a paper cup of hot coffee as I took my place on the heated seat. "You'll be working in the control room, foreman position. Sorry. Forewoman. Below me, of course, but above the crew."

"What's the control room? Foreman of what?" I asked.

"Pipeline site for now. Later maybe a drill rig. It's a small crew. They're cleaning up where the pipe got laid. You just sit in a trailer, you look out on-site, you're surrounded by cameras that show everything, so you can keep track of it all at once, and if you see anything's off, you tell someone. Or make a report. Easy."

"What happened to the last foreman?" I asked.

"High turnover," he said.

"I think I'd rather do roustabout," I said. "Digging, hauling, that I can do. I think it would show pretty quick if I'm foreman for something I don't know anything about."

"This shit's easy," he said. "You can learn it in a day. Besides, it's a job a woman can work by herself, so keeps you safe. And the pay's better. Twenty-five bucks an hour. You should be thanking me." So I thanked him.

We drove through flat land stickered with drilling equipment, derricks, cranes. No

391

signs of human habitation but for one house. One red house with a white fence and a garden outside, the beds resting under straw for the winter, its only neighbors tanker trunks. A skinny dog stretched, chained to an autumn olive bush.

"Who lives in that house?" I asked.

"One old guy wouldn't sell out," Shane said. "Didn't matter. The company sued him. Still lives there, but he couldn't get a cent. Should've moved to greener pastures like all the other lucky bastards who lived around here."

"You don't believe that, do you?" I asked.

"I used to be into all that back-to-the-land stuff," Shane said. "But I grew up. You know it was me who paid off Helen's place? I was too stupid to put my name on anything, even. Walked away without anything. Funny thing is, I got the better end of the deal. I mean, look at Helen, chained to that muddy hillside. Come on. There's more to life."

"Seems like you've changed," I said, but I had to remind myself again that I'd never known him all that well to begin with.

"A living's a living," Shane said. "If you don't think so, why did you come?"

The job site was a dingy yellow excavator next to one of those beige container units, piles of mud and rubble, stacks of pipe lashed together, heaps of dark gray felt — filter bags, said Shane — and bales and bales of straw, for containment, he said. All of it enclosed behind a chain-link fence with a flimsy lock. A black pickup truck idled outside the gate. Shane waved. "That's your crew," he said. "Glad to see they're early." He got out to slide back the gate. We rolled in, and the truck followed. Shane handed me a set of keys. "Now you're the foreman, you can let everyone in and out. Don't need a manager to do that," he said, magnanimous.

Shane and I stood in the cold, finishing the last of our coffee, as the pickup parked next to us. "Indians," Shane said. "Shawnee. They don't really like outsiders, but they do a good job, they won't give you any trouble. It takes all kinds, is my philosophy. You've just got to stay friendly. Watch what I do."

The crew piled out of the king cab, all of them zipped into stiff black coveralls, woolen caps pulled low, faces pinched from the cold. They handed a thermos among them, stamped their boots. And one of them was a woman. I didn't know where to look, so I looked at the sky, where a circling bird looked majestic until I realized it was just a damn turkey vulture, first thing to remind me of home.

"New foreman," Shane told the crew. "Karen, meet your crew, unless you met last night at the motel?" It was way too early in the morning for such shining cheer.

When none of us said anything, Shane pointed his index finger at each of them in turn. "Lawrence, Jay, Marie. Marie'll be running the excavator, Jay is oiler. That makes Lawrence the roustabout. These folks are known for good work."

Jay looked me up and down. "First time I've been on-site with two women," he said. "Should get a picture, must be historic. Even if she is the foreman."

Marie didn't smile and I didn't smile. But we looked at each other. We looked at each other and if the others were hoping to witness something like sisterhood, they weren't going to. Not friendship, either. Just your basic scrutiny.

"Karen's experienced," Shane said. "You don't have to worry about that."

"Didn't say worried, said historic," Jay said.

"But you all know the ropes, so make it easy on her, okay? I know I can count on you," Shane said, doling out his generous golden smile. He checked his phone, clapped his hands. "It's go time," he said.

They turned to the truck bed for their hard hats.

Inside the container unit, I asked Shane, "How come it's all Indians on a crew?"

"Preference," Shane said, and I didn't ask whose. "The company likes to hire them to make sure we don't get caught with our pants down, trampling sacred relics or whatever. Someone wants to make a fuss, our ass is covered."

He showed me the surveillance screens, showed me the safety protocols pinned to the wall, showed me how to take pressure readings, showed me spill monitoring. "Not that you'll have to do any of that stuff," he said. "Right now it's mostly just containment, cleanup, keeping an eye on the personnel." He logged in to the computer, gave me the company password. "Classified information," he said. "They don't give it out because of domestic terrorism." He laughed. "So don't go spreading it around."

"To who?" I asked. "Doesn't look like I'm making any fast friends." Shane punched me lightly on the shoulder. "I've missed your sense of humor," he said. He told me to call him if I needed anything at all.

He was right. The job was easy. I sat on my ass in the trailer surrounded by cameras, the big computer staring at me from a folding table in the corner, coffee going all day, space heater buzzing. I wore my insulated coveralls for no reason, so I unzipped them to get some relief. I even took off my boots, which stank. My hands ached to whittle, and I searched my pockets before I remembered I'd left my knife in Perley's camper, next to the chair we'd nearly finished. So I watched the screens.

There wasn't much to see. The day was bright and hazy, one of those winter days that fools you into thinking it's warm until you're out in it, but on the black-and-white screen, the crew moved through an electric blizzard, private as the ultrasound I'd seen when Perley was just a cluster of cells. Marie moved the excavator back and forth, flattening the mounds of rubble and mud, moving bales. Lawrence and Jay handled shovels, levered rocks out of the way, laid filter bags, spread straw. On the screen, the three of them didn't look Indian. Marie didn't look like a woman. But what did that mean, that they all looked like white guys? Like Rudy or Shane? Did Rudy and Shane look alike? What did I look like? No mirrors in the camper, not even one in the motel. Helen sometimes talked about white people, or whiteness, as she called it. Like most of the stuff she'd learned at college, it didn't seem to add up to much besides her sucking air out of the room and saying in a complicated way what everyone already knew, that the ones in power weren't giving it up anytime soon. Helen was as pasty as I was, but she talked about whiteness like she wasn't part of it, like she was just watching the rest of us assholes from the sidelines. But how did I talk about it? I guess I didn't. I guess I didn't think of myself as white unless I was around people who weren't. I guess coming up north had made me into a woman again. At home I thought of myself only as some fierce raptor parent, a vessel of lessons and principle, a weight on the ground that worked and whittled with my head down. On the screen in front of me, humanity was a disorganized jumble, and if I wasn't sure how I was supposed to keep an accurate eye on it, I figured that for twenty-five bucks an hour, I could figure it out. I was getting what I wanted, a chance to prove my family belonged to me and that I belonged to them. The loneliness was as insulating as a layer of snow.

I was almost dozing when the quiet woke me up. The excavator had stopped. I leaned forward and squinted at the grainy monitor. The crew was gathered in front of the machine, closed in a tight knot. Then Jay and Lawrence stepped back, and Marie walked out from between them with her arms held out in front of her. I couldn't see what the hell was going on, so I moved to the window. Marie passed beneath it, not looking up, and I saw that she held a snapping turtle, scooped out of hibernation, its shell crushed in the middle. The turtle's legs kicked slow responses to its spine's final currents. It beaked around for something to bite. Marie walked over into the scrub grass, past the tower of excavated clay. She knelt down and let the turtle roll to the ground, waited through its last spasm. She took a cigarette from her pocket, peeled back the paper, and let the contents fall near the broken animal. Jay and Lawrence waited at the machine, leaning on their shovels. Marie rejoined them, and swung herself back up into her seat. The excavator rumbled up again. The whole thing had taken maybe three minutes.

Was I supposed to do something? I looked at the list of protocols on the wall, but I didn't really read it. Instead, I turned back to the screen, embarrassed by my own curiosity. I kept watching, but nothing like that happened again.

I ate lunch by myself, a ham sandwich Shane had bought me. On the screen, I watched the crew climb into their truck to eat with the heat going. Then I had to pee, and no one had said anything to me about that. So I went out and stood near the truck, but the crew didn't look out at me. Inside, I could see them laughing and talking, passing the thermos around. Finally, Lawrence opened the door and said, "Was it something you wanted?"

"Is there somewhere to take a piss around here?" I asked. Jay laughed, Lawrence blushed, but Marie rolled her eyes.

"Just pop a squat any old place," she said. "You'd think they'd provide porta johns. If I ever see that, I'll let you know."

So I squatted behind the trailer. When I opened the door to go back inside, Marie's voice stopped me. "Hey, foreman," she called, rolling down the window. "Thought you was experienced." Laughter from the cab. There was really nothing for me to say. Marie wasn't waiting for an answer. She'd already rolled up the window. I hid myself in my container.

Shane picked me up at the end of the day, bringing me a burrito wrapped in foil. Marie threw her hard hat into the back of the truck, tossed Jay the keys, climbed in next to Lawrence. I thought I could feel her watching me as I closed the door of Shane's

SUV, I thought I could feel her wondering, but maybe it was my own eyes I felt. Maybe I'd become the watcher of myself, finally split in two.

That night, I went to the campfire. I don't know why. It was clear I wasn't wanted, but there was something about Shane — the word Helen would use was obsequious — Rudy would say fucking sycophant — that tainted my loneliness. I couldn't tell what he wanted from me, approval, verification, but I was struggling under the burden of whatever it was. I told myself I could take anything for twenty-five bucks an hour, but when I counted how many times I'd already said thank you, how many more thank-yous might be in my future, I felt like sleeping under the bed instead of in it.

So, without thinking what I would say when I got there, I walked empty-handed into the circle of light. Lawrence and Marie wrapped gloved hands around beer cans, Jay sipped a Mountain Dew. They'd been laughing, but when I stepped from the shadows, they stopped. Then Jay laughed again. "Foreman," he said. "Thought you'd be tired of staring at us by now."

"Pretty cold to be standing around outside," I said, what an opener.

400

"If you don't like it, you could always go back to watching us through the window," Jay said, crunching on ice. "Or did you come here to point at us again? One, two, three little Indians." He thrust his can forward, big exaggerated smile, a perfect Shane. Marie laughed, her can hiding her mouth, but Lawrence passed a beer my way.

"Where are you coming from?" he asked.

"From down in the foothills," I said. "Local."

"You ain't local," Jay said.

"More local than the Louisianans," I said. "The West Virginians. The Texans. At least I'm in-state."

"In-state? What's a state? Don't know that word," Jay said. "Must be something white people invented."

"Don't mind him," Lawrence said. "That's one of the ways he has fun."

"Fuck you, Lawrence," Jay said. "You don't want to see me have fun. Only locals around here are the Miami and the Shawnee, and most of them are in fucking Oklahoma."

"Shane told me you were Shawnee," I said.

"He probably did tell you that, didn't he?" Jay said.

"We're from farther north," Lawrence

401

said. "Great Lakes."

"Shut up, Lawrence," Jay said. Marie still hadn't said anything, though she'd stopped laughing. Was she bored or was she angry? She shifted from foot to foot and leaned in closer to the fire so that the flames warmed the angles of her face. I opened my beer and drank for a decent amount of time.

"Aren't your people against these pipelines?" I asked.

"Our people. I love it," Jay said. "Let me ask you, what about your people?"

"Who are my people?" I asked.

"Exactly, who are your people? I don't know. The redneck hillbilly bull-dyke people?" Jay said. Marie smiled.

"That's not fair," Lawrence said. "It is true, we do have a people and white people don't have a people and they feel so sad about it. You've got to just leave them alone or they'll start crying, you know that." Jay raised his Mountain Dew can, winked. Lawrence turned back to me. "Short answer to your question is, I got to feed my kids. What about you. You got to feed your kids?"

"I do," I said.

Jay reached into the back of the pickup and levered out a hunk of poplar, thunked it down onto the fire to make the embers explode. "This pipeline shit might be a fresh

402

hell to your family," he said, "but we already got this shit going through our land. Hell, whenever something like this comes through you can be damn sure they go for our homes first."

"Probably hit the hillbillies next, though," Lawrence said. "So that's one thing we got in common." But Jay wasn't interested.

"What I like about white people," he said, "is they're always feeling sorry for us. And I'm like, Listen, you poor white-trash motherfucker, this pipeline's coming for your family, too, so you can save your pity for your own kin."

"Oh yeah?" I said. "What about you? I hear you're bought by the company. You're the pipeline's Indians, paid to give them your sacred blessing."

Marie came for me hard. She plunged straight through the fire, her right arm gleaming backward. She crushed her beer can into my face so that I fell back out of the firelight, cracked my head on the truck bumper as I went down, felt the sharp aluminum dig open my cheek. Marie stood back. "Say it again, you fucking cracker, say it again," she said. Lawrence and Jay stood watching. I raised myself to one elbow, but Marie kicked my arm out, so that I stared again at the dull stars above, dimmed out

403

by flaring. Marie's spit hit my shoulder. "I ain't no one's fucking Indian," she said.

Probably that was my cue to leave, but all I could manage was to sit up, to sit up and pull myself back near the fire, look into the flames, touch the blood on my face. Strictly speaking, I wasn't against feeling shame, no more than I was against feeling loss, irritation, anger, isolation. Better than saying thank you to Shane all damn day. Lawrence passed me another beer.

"But what were you doing out there today, with that snapping turtle?" I asked.

"None of your damn business. We were talking to the ancestors, not to you," Marie said.

"It ain't what you think," Lawrence said. "Shane says, You find bones or shards, just let me know so I can bring in one of our archaeologists to verify its authenticity. Yeah, right."

"I don't take that money," Marie said. "I make my money operating machines, not whoring. If you didn't notice, I got actual skills."

"I got skills, too, Shane just won't let me use them," I said.

"Right. Got to protect the white lady, make sure she's got walls around her," Marie said.

"No one's ever called me a lady before," I said. I held my beer can to my cheek, cooled the bloody gash.

We drank in silence. I could lie and say it was a companionable silence. I could tell the truth and say it was better than talking to Shane. It was the kind of silence that said, Why the hell don't you leave? The why wasn't rhetorical, the why was a question with many possible answers, none of them quite good enough. But I stayed until finally Marie said, "It's true, you know. What the guys are saying. It's coming for your family, too. You said you live in the foothills?"

"Down near West Virginia," I said.

"So think about it. Where do you expect that pipeline is going?" she asked.

"I'm not worried about it," I said. "We've already got a pipeline going through our place. Been there since the sixties. It's never given us any trouble. We've even got a nursery out there. Fruit trees." I heard myself refer to Rudy as we, nearly felt it to be true.

"Yeah, those old pipelines," Marie said, "the ones that are out of use, they're repurposing them. Going to start shooting all this new high-pressure gas through there, whole new level. Jay, what's the statistic?"

"Blast zone of two miles, could be," he

said, "anything goes wrong."

"How far is your house from the line?" asked Marie.

"I don't know," I said. "Maybe four hundred feet?" She nodded.

"Yeah, but me, I wouldn't worry too much about that," Lawrence said. "Thing that worries me is leaking, especially with those old lines, the ones the company calls vintage. My family drank from a well. The industry came around. Can't drink from that well no more."

"We've got a spring," I said.

"Like I'm saying," Lawrence said.

"What do you mean by a blast zone?" I asked.

"What does it sound like I mean?" Jay said. "Damn, we knew you was white trash, but are you stupid, too?"

I let it go, instead paid attention to the fault line I felt, the tremor. The pipeline was my own spine.

"What makes you so sure it's going through my place?" I asked.

"Common sense," Marie said. "They're sending this stuff all the way down South, down to ports in Louisiana to sell overseas."

"But how do you know the exact route?" I asked.

"We don't," Lawrence said. "They don't

let just anyone see that. No way. They don't want people to know where they're putting this shit. Not until it's a done deal and it's too late for anyone to do anything about it."

Marie watched me. "But you, working in that control room," she said. "You probably got a password or something. You could probably find out a lot of stuff."

Before dawn, Shane pulled up with coffee and doughnuts. Walking out to his SUV, I almost ran into Marie. She pushed past. "Special friend of the boss, huh?" she said over her shoulder. "Must be nice."

"It's not what you think," I said. But maybe it was.

I bent down to Shane's window. I thanked him for the coffee, he said no problem, I thanked him for the doughnuts, he said my pleasure, I thanked him for the ride, he said of course, I told him I wouldn't be needing a ride anymore, he didn't say anything. I said, "I can ride with the crew. You gave me the keys, remember?"

"Did you ask them?" he said. "They like to keep to themselves, you know."

"It just makes sense," I said.

"What happened to your face?" he asked. I left him sitting there.

When I knocked on the truck window,

Marie cracked it. When I asked for a ride, she didn't say no, she didn't say yes, she just held open the truck door, and leaned forward so I could wedge myself back into the cab. Lawrence passed me the thermos, but Marie said, "Don't give away all our coffee, asshole."

"It's all right, I got my own," I said.

"Doughnuts, too," Marie said. "That Shane. What a gentleman."

"I'm over it," I said.

"I bet you are," she said. Jay turned the radio up, and we rode to work listening to Springsteen, the only boss Jay said he could stand.

That day, swaddled away inside my buzzing container, I used my classified password and I found the pipeline map. It looked like a restless worm, a parasite writhing across five states. Or it didn't. Or it looked like something innocent, banal, businesslike. Or it didn't even look like a pipeline at all, it looked like a timeline. The construction had already begun, and it was moving fast. You could see it on the map. The red line was where they were working. The green line was where they hadn't got to yet but meant to get to soon. The red line pulsed farther south each day.

I scrolled down until I could see our county, the lines folded tightly together, layer on layer to signify the hills. Then I moved my finger along the screen until I found home. There was our twenty acres, which barely existed. In some people's consideration it didn't exist at all. But if I squinted I could just make it out, the ridgeline, the camper, the ducks, the garden, the house, the sugar maple trees, the old tires, the truck leaking oil, the scrap metal pile, the creek, the acorn barrels, the used condoms by the side of the road, Helen, Lily, even the damn snakes. I couldn't see Perley. What I could see was that lime-green line, and where it cut through. Not to the right of it. Not to the left of it. Marie was right. They planned to aim that high-pressure gas straight down the center of Rudy's nursery.

13

Helen

By the big saw, Rudy meant the Husqvarna 394XP, with the bar so long that it pulled him to the ground. To use it, he had to brace it against his thigh. We stood in the early morning cold with Aldi Birch. The three of us gaped up at the ancient white oak dwarfing Aldi's garage. "We'll use the big saw when it comes time to fell it," Rudy said. "But we'll start small, way up top, limbing. We'll take it down in sections, take off some of the weight, make it a little shorter. It'll take us a while. Maybe a week. Maybe more. I've been thinking and not thinking about this job. Probably for years now."

First thing that morning, the judge had rejected Aldi's motion. Airless with defeat, Aldi had called Rudy's phone to let us know. I'd gone to tell Lily, fearing what the bad news would do to her. But she'd been different since visitation. She'd been ablaze

410

with industry. She went back to work at the hardware and salvage store, and each day she rushed home to haul truckloads of trash to the dump, to scrap the scrap metal pile, rake up duck shit, scrub the house with vinegar and even bleach, empty mouse traps and re-spring them, throw out unlabeled cans and jars. To say she'd woken up would be an understatement. In fact, she'd stopped so much as sitting down, unless it was to throw herself down onto the sofa and take up her new hobby, knitting. She'd returned from one of her junkyard trips with bright balls of yarn, awful colors, garish pink, chartreuse, royal purple, all of which she turned into scarves, hats, gloves, slippers, but mostly scarves. Small garments, I noticed, garments made to fit a seven-year-old. Not only that, but she'd begun to collect pastel plastic eggs, the kind you pay a dime for and turn the dial on one of those dispensers. The eggs accumulated in her knitting basket, unmentioned, as if she didn't owe me an explanation, as if she didn't owe me anything at all. She didn't talk to me much. She rejected my offers to cook for her, instead ate stewed venison cold from the jar. She sang the raucous shipwreck lullaby under her breath while looking at me with unfocused eyes, the

411

corners of her mouth slightly upturned, a smile that reminded me of Karen's. When I told her that Aldi's motion had failed, she nodded. The look on her face said nothing would ever surprise or shock her again, least of all any such thing as a court proceeding. She bent over the scarf she was working on and counted her stitches. Then, with no explanation, she began to unravel the yarn, winding it and winding it back into the ball, so that before my eyes the scarf disappeared.

Rudy and I packed up the chain saws, the pole saw, the ropes, gas and oil, and drove straight out to Aldi's place. We had to pick the lock on the garage, feel for the light switch. The place smelled like chicken shit, hundreds of birds teeming in their warmed crates along the wall. Rudy peeled Aldi off his cot behind the woodstove. I was getting sick of coercing people out of bed. Rudy wrapped Aldi's coat around him and pushed him out into the rude winter. It was time to encounter the white oak. This was our way, to get to work. It was the only honest antidote we knew.

"You don't have to take down that tree," Aldi said, swaying next to us.

"You're going to help us get Perley back," Rudy said.

"Looks like I can't do much," Aldi said.

"You'll do what you can," Rudy said.

"Sure," Aldi said. "But what I can do I'll do for free."

"Don't talk like that," Rudy said.

"I'm the one should fell it if anyone should," Aldi said.

"You can't do it. You're too old and you'd immediately kill yourself," Rudy said.

"It's a suicide mission no matter who does it," Aldi said.

"A trade's a trade," Rudy said. "We'll do it. We'll do it and you'll sit out here and keep us company and work on the case."

"In this fucking cold? You must be crazy," Aldi said.

"Helen's going to build you a fire," Rudy said.

Rudy set his anchor line and clipped into his harness, while I found the woodpile out back. Aldi grumbled, but I brought him a canvas camp chair, warmer or at least softer than his metal one, and I bundled him into it, layering him up with the musty coats I found heaped behind the door. "At least bring me my briefcase," he said, once I'd stoked the fire high and hot. I found it beneath the cot, stuffed the scattered papers back in, dropped it in his lap.

Rudy spent all morning up in the tree, pruning branches and lowering them down

413

to me with the Port-a-Wrap. He didn't even come down for bathroom breaks, but delighted in pissing from the heights, calling for Aldi and me to look out below, but what he really meant was look, and I didn't.

We didn't generally work in the winter. In the winter, Rudy would all but disappear and I'd try to get by on what we'd made over the spring, summer, and fall. I wasn't used to working under so many clothes, two pairs of socks, heavy gloves, woolen long underwear, heavy coveralls, a wool hat under my hood, a hard hat on top of that. I could hardly move. I was cold and overheated at the same time. I dragged brush, used the 346 to cut it to firewood length, saved the skinny ends for the chipper. Aldi rustled his papers and asked for Natural Ice, which I brought him from the cab of Rudy's truck. He watched me, his eyes watering against the woodsmoke. "Are you a man or a woman?" he asked.

"I guess that's supposed to be a joke," I said.

"I mean, if I didn't already know," he said.

"I'm working," I said.

"I can see it," he said. I kept dragging brush, throwing my saw forward to start it, but I felt strange. Not bad and not good, just strange. I felt strange and then it occurred to me that Aldi admired me. That his question, awkward and rude, was an attempt at flirtation. Worse, I knew how I should feel about it, but I found that I didn't. I didn't know how I felt about it. I kept working, but when he looked at me, I looked back.

At lunch, if it could be called that — Natural Ice, cold hot dogs, and potato chips, to which I added acorn patties I'd hurriedly wrapped in foil that morning — we leaned in close to the fire.

"I saw a save-the-whales documentary once," Aldi said. "There was this little kid who said, Why would anyone want to harm the whales? The whales are so friendly. But that doesn't seem to capture it, does it? Now, who do you think told that child that whales are friendly?"

"Whales? Friendly? That's a laugh," Rudy said. "That's just the kind of ridiculous eco-hippie nonsense we can do without."

"Certainly whales aren't friendly," Aldi Birch said, but he directed his comments to me. "Friendly doesn't really come into it. Or more to the point, why should we care if they are friendly or not? Is that what we want from whales? Friendship? It's like asking if this white oak here is friendly. It's not friendly, in fact it will likely fall on me.

When I die, it won't shed tears. It's not friendly. It's over one hundred years old, is what it is."

"If it's a day," Rudy said.

"Now you've pruned it, you could just leave it at that," Aldi said.

"Don't worry about a thing, Aldi," Rudy said. "We'll take care of it."

"The fact is," Aldi said, "I don't want that oak to go. If that oak goes, I might as well go with it."

"Aldi," Rudy said. "I respect your feelings on this. You know me. You know I don't like to drop hardwoods. I don't. As a rule, I won't do it. But that oak is going to go anyway, and it's going to take out your garage right along with it, broiler chicks, woodstove, all of it. One more big storm. Sorry, old man, but you can see as well as I can. It's coming down one way or the other. We're just its guides."

"That oak has been there all my life," Aldi said. "Used to shade out my granddad's barn, now it shades that garage. I remember when the hollowness came to it. It was a lightning storm, and the water's just poured in ever since." He looked at me again, as I realized I had been waiting for him to do. "I was your age, maybe a little older."

416

"How old do you think my age is?" I asked.

"I'd put you about twenty-eight or so," Aldi said.

"Closer to forty," I said.

"The older I get, the younger people look," Aldi said.

"But you see my point," Rudy said. "Better I do it than one of these fucking Asplundh guys."

But Aldi was still looking at me, and I could see that his eyes were wet. I found that I wanted to touch him, to pinch his shoulder just a little, feel that fragile bone, but I knew that would embarrass both of us. Still, when Rudy was back up in the tree, I added another log to the fire.

"You got kids?" I asked him.

"One son. Grown," Aldi said. "He steers clear of me. We don't get on. When I remember that man as a baby, I wish that baby was still around. I could have stayed near that baby forever. But now, most adults I don't care for."

"I know what you mean," I said. "I had an uncle who made me feel like myself, but he died and now it's just my aunt. We hardly know what to say to each other. I haven't made it back to visit in years. It's hard to see the point."

"That's it? No man? No kids of your own?" he asked.

"Perley's about as close to having a kid as I'll ever get," I said.

"You miss him?"

"I try not to get too attached to people," I said. "No point in being disappointed. But Perley, he decided for me. He decided for me that he and I were attached."

"Some things are impossible to argue with," Aldi said.

"We're going to get him back," I said. "They won't get away with this."

"What about you and Rudy?" asked Aldi. "I took it you two were going together."

"Rudy and me? No way," I said.

At the end of the day, Rudy rappelled down to us, fumbled in the cold to unclip his harness. He clanked over in his spurs to stand by the fire while I coiled his rope.

"She's powerful, like a basketball player," I heard Aldi say.

"Helen?" Rudy said. "Anyone clumsier, I haven't met them. That's how come I don't let her climb."

"All the same, I like the way she moves," Aldi said.

"Back off," Rudy said. "She's not interested."

"I'm way too old for her anyway," Aldi

418

said. "But there's someone out there she'd be happy with."

"Helen hates that kind of shit," Rudy said. "Trust me." It was true. This kind of thing generally made me want to puke, but somehow I kept listening. I wasn't sure what I wanted, but somehow, I wasn't sure I wanted Aldi to stop.

I daisy-chained the loose end and came back to the fire. "Don't worry," I told Aldi. I put my hand on his shoulder, a gesture that was as awkward as I'd imagined it would be, so I took my hand away. "We won't take the tree down without giving you a chance to say goodbye."

Rudy looked from one to the other of us and frowned.

On the ride home, he said, "Aldi doesn't like women, if that's what you're thinking."

"He likes me," I said.

"He's my friend," he said.

"I know," I said.

"Me and him go way back," he said.

"I've been wondering how it is between you two," I said.

"What do you mean?" he asked.

"I've never heard you talk to anyone the way you talk to Aldi Birch. No gratuitous swearing. Minimal bragging. You treat him with such care. You treat him like your own dad."

"My dad can eat shit and die," Rudy said. "My dad isn't worth licking the shit off of Aldi Birch's boots. In fact, probably my dad and Aldi's dad are together somewhere eating the devil's shit."

"So much shit," I said.

"I don't treat Aldi Birch like my dad," he said. "I treat Aldi Birch like Aldi Birch, an old man in pain like someday I will be an old man in pain. If you haven't noticed, I don't have too many friends, and so when I get a good one I try to keep it."

"Self-awareness!" I said.

"Fuck you," he said.

"You know what he asked me when you were up in the tree?" I said. "He asked if I was a man or a woman."

"Don't let it get to you," Rudy said. "You're obviously a woman."

But Rudy didn't get it. I liked that mismatch. I liked that Aldi Birch liked that mismatch, too.

I came in the door peeling off layers. Lily was knitting a brick-red tam-o'-shanter, around and around. She set aside her needles to hand me a large square envelope. "Something addressed to you not to me for once," she said. It was the kind of envelope I had recently learned to flinch at. This one had been sent all the way from Texas. Lily watched me open it.

Inside, the cover of the glossy pamphlet was worth framing: fields of red clover at sunset, farmlands tucked in beneath gentle pink clouds. Stamped across the sky were the words: An Interstate Natural Gas Facility on My Land, What Do I Need to Know? I skimmed the FAQs. Are Pipelines Safe? Can the Pipeline Company Use Eminent Domain? The answer to both questions, according to the beautiful pamphlet, was Yes. I searched for something specific to our twenty acres, but didn't find it. Folded inside the back cover was a letter from someone called the right-of-way agent. The letter began by saying that the pipeline company had recently decided to abandon certain parts of the line and to repurpose others. It ended by saying that the company strove to be a good neighbor and to provide safe, clean, and reliable energy to the nation's consumers and industry. The many pages in between were a jumble of docket numbers, parentheses, and blurry zoomed-out maps.

"Anything important?" asked Lily, needles clicking again.

"Hard to say," I said. "It's got something to do with the pipeline."

"Is it about that helicopter?" she asked.

"Could be," I said. I handed Lily the pages. She put down her needles and leafed through them.

"It looks like they're going to be repurposing pretty soon, whatever that means. Maybe in the spring," she said.

"I'll ask Aldi about it," I said. "His place is right on the line, too. He might've got the same mail."

Lily handed the letter back to me. "Couldn't be any worse than what went through there before," she said. She began to unravel the red tam-o'-shanter.

"Still," I said, "might be good to find out." I put the glossy pamphlet, the letter, the pile of maps and numbers back in the envelope. "Have you heard from Karen?" I asked, since we were on the subject of interstate communication. She didn't bother to answer, just raised her eyes to me like, What do you think?

"What about you?" she asked. "Has that lawyer had any more bright ideas?"

Heat came to my face. "Look," I said. "That man. He's. He's damaged. I'm not sure how good he's going to be getting Perley back. His talents might lie elsewhere. I can't explain it except to say we might need to focus on cleaning this place up rather than expecting any legal miracles."

"Helen," Lily said. "What do you think I've been doing these past few weeks?" She swept her arm out over the room. It was still cramped. It was still sloped. It was still drafty. But it was empty of junk and scrubbed clear of mold. It smelled of Lemon Pledge and creek water. A merry fire rippled in the stove, boxes of brand-name food were stacked unopened on the shelves, the bucket beneath the sink had disappeared, the leaky pipes had been patched, the pissy tomcat had been banished, the spiders, wasps, and mice, if they were there, knew better than to show themselves. Lily and I were the only animals to be seen. "Look at this," Lily said. She reached into the bib of her overalls, and carefully pressed open the reunification plan so that I could see where she had begun to check off items, one by one. "I think we can do this," she said. "Besides the septic system."

"And the snakes," I said.

"I haven't seen one since Karen left," she said.

"That's because it's winter," I said. "They're hibernating. If I lifted up the floorboards right now, you'd see them curled up sleeping together in a cozy ball."

"The review won't happen until the spring," she said. "They might have moved outside by then. They're really the worst in the fall."

"We can't depend on that," I said.

"I'm doing my best," she said.

"So then you've given up on kidnapping," I said. I wasn't gloating, exactly, but I was glad to be right.

"Kidnapping is leaving and then leaving again," Lily said. "It's always on the run. They want to push us out. Well, I won't let them. I don't want to leave. I want to get Perley back, and I want to stay."

The tam-o'-shanter was gone. Lily tossed the brick-red ball into her knitting basket, where it rolled down to settle among the plastic eggs.

"Where did you learn to knit?" I asked.

"My grandma taught me," she said. "She also taught me to hot-wire a car. But it's been years since I've done either one."

I put the envelope from the pipeline company on the kitchen counter, intending to take it to Aldi. Later, with her newfound efficiency, Lily filed it among the cookbooks. Later still, I moved it to the drawer underneath the silverware. This is one way of saying that it got buried beneath other shit, including our lives, and it wasn't long before we forgot all about it.

Pushing forty, and suddenly I knew what it meant to give someone the eye. For all his swagger, Rudy was essentially a prude, and maybe I was, too. Maybe we both could have taken tips from Aldi Birch, the old goat. Aldi knew how to admire me, was the first person to admire me in a long time. I could tell the way that I bewildered Aldi Birch was what he liked, and I liked bewildering him. None of it made sense. I mean he was old, one might even say infirm. He was not attractive, not in any conventional sense. But what was I? A braided rope. A well-seasoned tarp. Aldi looked at me. I imagined myself near him and then I was near him.

For Rudy, my ground work tended to be hurry up and wait. While I waited, I began to do things for Aldi, small things. Two days into the job, more broiler chicks were delivered. I helped Aldi carry the box into the garage, watched while he sliced open the lid. Inside, the chicks massed. Aldi and I knelt shoulder to shoulder, scooping one chick after another under the heat lamps. One at a time, I dipped their minute beaks in a pan of water, then set them in the fresh sawdust Aldi laid down.

Aldi was gentle with me. He patted me on the thigh and for some reason I didn't mind it. I touched him and he wasn't embarrassed. When I say I touched him, I mean that I helped him up from his chair. Or I rubbed his diabetic feet. "You don't have to do that," he said.

"I want to," I said, and I did. Always, I could tell he had pain, and not just the physical kind.

Rudy may not have liked it, but Rudy was up in the oak.

Many evenings, we'd stay on after the work was done. No reason not to, I told myself, not much waiting for me at home. When Karen had been there, it always seemed that Lily was the one I'd rather be on a desert island with. But now that she and I were on that desert island, I found it hard going. I can't say that I missed Karen, but I can say that she made more sense to me than Lily did, even if Lily had decided to stop maundering and start cleaning. With her knitting and unraveling, her collection of plastic eggs, her glassy eyes, Lily hadn't saved a place for me. She hadn't even asked me to help her work through the reunification plan. I'd been trying to help her for years, and now it seemed she'd found a way to help herself. Well, good for her if she didn't need me anymore.

So Rudy and I stayed at Aldi's, later and then later. We'd begin by having a beer after work, then Rudy would say that he'd better stoke Aldi's woodstove before we left for the night, so we'd move inside, into the smell of those tiny chickens. We'd pull ourselves into the glow of the big-bellied orb. From beneath his cot, Aldi would draw out a jar of sassafras root, still with the red dirt clinging to it, and he'd pass those roots around, and we'd chew on them. That and Natural Ice would be our dinner.

Making a study of it, I understood why Rudy loved Aldi so. Put simply, Rudy talked so I didn't have to and Aldi talked so Rudy didn't have to. Aldi talked about his time in the service, about his wife walking out on him, about the morphine. Later, when he was deep, deep in his cups, Aldi would talk about what his dad had done to him. Rudy listened to Aldi talk, listened to that misery, and he'd nod his head and lean into the light of the stove, and sharpen his chain saw as the hour grew late, and he'd never say a word. Aldi didn't need him to. They understood each other. These were men who took breaks. They took breaks from life, long hiatuses of evil lowdown opting-out. They lay in bed for months, took the winter off from being human, and then reentered the community when it suited them. They knew that each time people, people like me, would welcome them back, sometimes in spite of ourselves. One was old and one was almost young. Rudy with his beard and his fruit trees, his *Count of Monte Cristo,* his chain saws, Aldi with his chickens, his briefcase, his willow legs.

We never slept over. No matter how late we stayed, Rudy always tightened the chain back onto the bar, packed up his file, patted Aldi on the back, and said it was time to get going, that we had hard work to do tomorrow.

We never slept over and I can't say I wanted to. But I sat near to Aldi, those long nights, I sat on the side opposite him so that I was in the shadow of the woodstove, where Rudy couldn't see, and I slipped my hand into Aldi's hand, and we kept the pressure on.

One night, Aldi said, "So here we are, Rudy, both of us out of hibernation for once, and the deep midwinter, at that. Is it just this thing with the kid that's keeping you awake?"

"That and my fruit tree operation," Rudy said, his saw disassembled before him so he could clean each piece.

"Got you in trouble once already," Aldi said.

"It's what keeps me out of trouble," Rudy said. "If I could only get folks interested. You and me, Aldi. Neither of us loves much, but we both love trees."

"You don't love trees any more than I love the fucking county prosecutor," Aldi said. He was well into his second six-pack of Natural Ice, but still we hadn't noticed when he'd turned mean. Through all of it, he never let go of my hand.

Rudy said, "Now what are you talking about?"

Aldi said, "I might be old but I'm not blind. I can see what's happening to my oak."

Rudy said, "You might not be blind, but you sure are paranoid." He tried to laugh it off, but Aldi wasn't laughing.

Aldi said, "You're like the rest of them, you're no different."

"Aldi, we've been over this," Rudy said.

Aldi said, "Biggest job you've ever done, huh? A way to get your rocks off. Get a bunch of firewood for free."

Rudy began to collect saw parts by the handful. He said, "I don't have to sit here and listen to this." He tried to capture the unbridled vim he'd use on any other person, but instead his voice softened. "Free firewood? Aldi, you're keeping all the firewood. I'm doing you a favor, Aldi. I'm doing this for your own good."

Aldi said, "That's funny. First you told me you were just holding up your end of the bargain. Remember that? A trade's a trade?"

Rudy swiped his tools into his bag, shouldered his chain saw, stuck his ponytail in his mouth, and walked out.

Aldi yelled after him, "I won't burn a stick of that wood, not a stick. You can keep it."

He gripped my hand so hard I feared something was broken. "Helen?" he asked. "Am I wrong?"

"Aldi," I said.

"You know what I mean about the tree," he said. But I didn't know anything. For years, I had known everything, and it hadn't exactly been working out. Knowing hadn't fastened Perley to us, and it hadn't brought him home yet. Knowing never made anyone love me. With Aldi, I had been trying out what it might be like to hold his hand without understanding why, to sit in the dark and not know a thing.

"Are you going to stay?" Aldi asked, and then I knew I would disappoint him.

430

"I'm sorry, Aldi," I said. A finger at a time, I freed my hand.

At the truck, Rudy was waiting.

The last night with Perley we hadn't known it was the last night. He went to sleep with chocolate chips smeared on his face and then his moms and me whisper-fought through the walls. The last night with my boyfriend, all those years ago, I hadn't known was our last night, even though he tried to tell me. The last night before cancer took my uncle, I hadn't known it and neither had he. That night, we watched TV, for Christ's sake, we didn't say the things that needed to be said. Always expecting it is the same as never expecting it. There's no way to be on guard.

After that evening, Rudy and I kept showing up to work, but Aldi stayed inside his garage. Sometimes the curtain at the side window moved. Sometimes we'd even see his face. But when he looked out at us, it wasn't the look he'd give to a stand-in son, nor to the object of his surreptitious affection. He watched us as if we were the enemy.

The oak had begun to look shorn, bare, vulnerable, a naked thing against the sky. Aldi's garage was exposed now, bright beneath the unforgiving winter glare, somehow huge now that the oak had shrunk.

One day, Rudy lowered the final branch. The saw shrilled down to silence. He descended, unclipped. We loaded our equipment into the truck.

"We've got to tell him," I said.

"I know it," Rudy said. "But I don't want to be the one." So I knocked on Aldi Birch's door. I didn't expect him to answer and he didn't answer.

"Tomorrow is the day, Aldi," I called. "Tomorrow we'll fell it. I promised we'd tell you."

Nothing.

"Do you want to say a few words?" I tried again.

Aldi opened the door and walked up to the oak. Though diminished, it was still massive. Aldi leaned his head against its trunk, laid his palm flat on the bark. "It's like she's already gone," he said. "What is there to say, anyway? So long, old friend. So long, self. The older I get, the less people there are that are older than me."

He had lived his life in a landlocked state, but Aldi walked back toward his garage like he hadn't yet found his land legs. Rudy worked his hard hat around and around between his fingers. He spat out his ponytail. "Aldi," he said. Aldi stopped. He stood on the threshold without turning around.

"You know I'm good, Aldi, the best around," said Rudy. "But still."

"What is it?" asked Aldi, not turning.

"Still. Just. Maybe no need for you to be in that garage when we fell the thing. Just plan not to be home tomorrow," Rudy said.

"You're going to drop it on my garage?" asked Aldi.

"I want it safely done," Rudy said. "You can understand. I just want some insurance."

"Insurance," Aldi said.

"This isn't entirely risk-free," Rudy said. His voice was high and uncertain, the voice of a boy. "Look, I'm leveling with you the way I wouldn't with most people, Aldi. It hasn't happened yet, a tree doing major damage, but still. This isn't about you. I wish you would stop taking it so personal. I'd tell the same thing to anyone."

"Tell them what?" Aldi asked. He still had his back to us.

"Tell them to stay the hell out of the way," Rudy said, but Aldi still wouldn't look at him.

Rudy's hard hat slipped from his hand and bounced once on the frozen ground. I had never seen him lack confidence in a job, not even when we had felled acres of yellow pines, notoriously unpredictable and deadly.

Then, he'd just been irritated, but now he was sick.

Aldi reached for the doorknob.

"Wait," Rudy choked, and moved fast. He reached into the back of the truck and tore the corner off the box of Natural Ice, turned it over to the blank side. He reached for the pen he kept in his pocket. He bore down hard with the nib on the cardboard, his face clenched and sweating into the cold air. Something was glittering at his temples, could have been tears. When he had finished, he read aloud, "I Aldi Birch have been told ahead of time that I should not be on the premises when this motherfucking white oak goes so help me god I have been warned by my friend Rudy Gibbs that the thing might do some damage, and I will not hold Rudy, my friend, accountable should an accident occur, because he fucking well told me ahead of time." He held the cardboard out to Aldi.

"Sign this, please," he said, doing his best to close up his face, to steady his broken voice. "Liability."

Aldi, ghastly white, signed it, then slammed the door in his face.

The next morning, as Rudy and I rolled up out of the darkness, we could see the crooked gesture of the ancient oak on the long approach, a giant middle finger shoved up into the sky, black against the rising sun. It looked as big as if we hadn't spent a week and a half shearing it down, as if we'd never touched it at all. At Aldi's place, the garage door was closed, curtains drawn, no smoke from the chimney. Aldi's old sedan was nowhere to be seen.

Rudy arranged the ropes and his harness, hauled out the 394XP for me to put gas and oil in.

"There's no way he's in there, right?" I asked.

"Don't know, don't care," said Rudy. Without looking at me, he reached into his back pocket and held the cardboard piece high. "Got what I need from that stubborn idiot. Superstitious. Fucking sentimental. High-and-mighty educated man, looking down on the guy who's got to do the shit job for him. Doesn't want to get his own hands dirty. He's got to keep them clean so he can wring them and be all saintly." He almost sounded like himself.

"When's the last time you ate?" I asked.

"Don't start with me," he said.

"I brought you some breakfast," I said. "Pumpkin seeds. They're good for men."

"What the hell does that mean?" he asked.

"They're good for your prostate," I said.

"At a time like this, I'd rather have a fucking cheeseburger," he said. "Or almost anything else."

Rudy pitched the end of the bull rope up into the tree, tied the bowline. Down at the pond, I wound a cow hitch around an old stump, hooked up the come-along. When I came back up the hill for the rope, Rudy said, "I want you to stay clear of the area. We might have taken a lot of weight off this thing, but don't be fooled. It's big and it's hollow and it could go anytime." I went back down to the pond and scoped an escape route, which meant being ready to swim.

Rudy took the big saw in both of his hands, and approached the tree like an outmatched fighter. I heard the saw whine. I saw him send the bar through. I began to pump the come-along's handle, keeping the rope taut so that the tree would fall the direction we wanted it to go, away from the garage. The plan was to aim the thing down Aldi's front lawn, running toward the pond. We would spend a day or two bucking it up and stacking it.

The oak was a fifteen-ton mousetrap waiting to go. The saw blade worked, and the oak sent up a wail, creaking and groaning, so great was the pressure. I worked the handle back and forth, and the shriek of the tree rose up so that I couldn't hear Rudy call to me. I heard no signal from him. Soon I could hardly hear if the saw was working or not. I saw his yellow hard hat shiny like a thumbtack against the base of that mass, that force of tree. The tree drowned everything out. The way I knew something was wrong was that the rope went slack.

The rope went slack, and the white oak began to fall, but it was happening much sooner than it should, and it was not going in the right direction, and for some reason I could see Rudy too well. He was close to me when he should have been distant. He was meant to be on the ground, but he was rising into the air, and his saw, the 394XP, was flung from him, a dandelion from its stem.

I didn't understand, and then I understood.

Instead of breaking at the hinge where Rudy had opened it, the weight of the tree had pulled its roots up out of the earth like a primordial creature waking up and opening its mouth. Rudy, standing at the base of the tree, was carried up with the root ball. He rose into the air, his arms wheeling backward, his saw disappearing into the new cavern in the earth. Rudy was up, ten feet up, fifteen feet, more, before he pitched forward and came careening down the trunk of the tree as it fell. He skidded off the trunk and rolled to the ground. But the tree kept moving. The trunk hurried toward him. He was lying down and it was the white oak's plan to lie on top of him. I was also a tree, rooted where I stood. It's true there was no time, no real time to act, but in my dreams again and again I step forward and I catch the oak tree just in time. I catch it, and Rudy rolls free.

I did not catch the oak.

Instead, there was silence, a frozen frame, a pause where there should have been a crash. The world regained itself so I could look at it again.

When I did, I saw that Rudy had not been crushed, but lay panting, nose nearly touching wood. The uppermost spire of the trunk had got caught up on younger oaks that grew next to it, a tangle we had hoped to avoid by felling it at an angle. The massive oak hung suspended in the air. As I would have it in dreams, Rudy rolled free.

He let out a string of curse words and yelled to me, Get back get back get back.

"I am back," I yelled. "You get back," and we both ran. We ran to the knoll at the head of Aldi's driveway. We dropped to the ground and just breathed in and out for a while.

"What a mess," he said. "We shouldn't go near that thing again. You couldn't pay me."

"What about your chain saw?" I asked.

"She can have it," he said.

"She?"

"The Mother Earth," he said.

"What are we going to do?" I asked. "We can't leave the tree hanging there."

"Okay, but check it out," Rudy said, and pointed. I looked at the oak. The upper part of the trunk clung to the lower part by only a foot of wood, all twisted out of shape. The upper section of the trunk was ready to break free. When that foot of wood gave way, it would swing like a deadly pendulum.

"I guess if Aldi were in there, he'd have come out by now," Rudy said. "I'm glad he signed that piece of cardboard."

"It's going to crush his garage, isn't it?" I asked.

"Or we could get lucky," said Rudy.

"Too bad we didn't do this on purpose," I said. "It's really a thing of beauty, I mean if it were a trap for our enemies."

"Shut up, I'm thinking," Rudy said, and we sat in silence. "What do you think?" he asked.

He had never asked me that before.

"I could shoot it," I said. "I could shoot that foot of wood."

"You?" he asked.

"I'm a pretty good shot. We've been practicing all winter," I said.

"No way," he said. "I fucked this up. I better take the shot so that we can say I fucked it up from beginning to end."

"But it was my idea," I said.

"But I'm your boss," he said.

"You're probably in shock," I said. "Haven't you heard of zebras shaking and shaking until they regain their equilibrium? I mean after a lion attack? You just almost got crushed to death."

"But I've never felt better," said Rudy. "I feel like I've been sleeping for the last five years and I just woke up."

"That's not a good time to shoot a gun," I said. "I'll shoot, and you should shake."

"Shake?" he asked. "Like, on purpose?"

"Yes," I said. "Like a zebra."

"Okay," he said, which was another thing he had never said to me.

"Do we have a gun?" I asked.

"Of course," he said.

He went to his truck, folded back a tarp, and took out his shotgun. He handed it to me. He passed me my ear protection.

"Stand back," I told him.

Rudy stood back.

"Shake," I told him.

And he began to shake and fling himself around and make a noise like, Yayayaya-yayaya, and I put on my ear protection, and I aimed at that foot of oakwood, and I sprayed Rudy's cut with shot, reloading from Rudy's box of shells. I sprayed it until the cut gave way, breaking the trunk in two. Then the lower part of the trunk, freed from the weight of its upper half, levered itself up into the air and rocked back on its roots, closing the creature's mouth, sending up clouds of dust and leaves, sealing Rudy's big saw down into the earth forever. Just like that, the oak stood straight up again, the jagged stub gaping upward, its roots back in the ground. The top half of the tree tore through the underlayers, clawing its way to the ground with the noise and the weight of an avalanche. Thunder. It hammered debris down on Aldi Birch's roof, but it missed the garage. By less than two inches, but it missed. Rudy whooped and began to laugh, and I dropped the gun and jumped up and down many times, hollering, until I fell backward to the ground. Rudy threw himself down next to me, and we lay there looking into the forest and into the sky and then we turned to look at each other.

My heart was still and blank. I felt no regret and no loneliness, no worry about Perley or about the future, no attachment to anything except to the narrow escape from death.

Rudy and I looked at each other. He was propped up on his elbow, my hands were behind my head. I noticed for the first time his Adam's apple, nearly hidden under all that hair, his eyes the same stupid color as mine, gray with an orange ring. We looked at each other.

Then we heard the yell.

Here we are dealing in matters of scale. We had been so focused on the sheer girth and weight, the incomprehensible muchness of Aldi's ancient oak, that we had failed to notice how heavy and destructive a normal oak tree branch can be. When the old oak was freed, it had torn a branch off one of the younger oaks. It was this young branch that punched a hole in Aldi's garage roof, that dealt Aldi Birch a glancing blow to the left hip as he stepped out his door.

14

Perley

I'm not a little fucking moron. I know whose boy I am. I am Mama L's boy which I knew when she pushed me on the swing and it was never the same after that. It was never the same after that to ride in the Outside Girl's totally sweet Camry, or to eat pancakes at Grandma Barlow's, or play the PlayStation. It wasn't even the same to be with Altemonte. I knew I needed to harness my skills and find the right tricks to get home, and I knew I needed Altemonte to come home with me even if he himself didn't know it yet. And I knew that I had to prove to Mama K that I was worth the ransom, and I knew that if I used my skills to get us home again then Mama K, my elfin chief, my noble wolf, would claim me.

All of which was really no problem because me and Altemonte, our brains were superior, we were digging a portal to the elf world, which who could do that but a boy genius or two? Our motto was excellence.

But the trouble with portals is that when you open one you start seeing portals everywhere.

At first I liked that my brain was a crystal ball held in a chiseled wizard's hand, but then the crystal ball started showing weird stuff.

Sometimes when I looked through the crystal ball it wasn't a portal into the elf world. Instead it was a hole. The hole was deep and its sides were made of dirt and stone, you could see the tree roots sticking out the side, you could see how deep it went into the ground, and below that was the blank universe, and the world became slippery and slanted and I was sliding down into the hole and I had to fight and fight and fight to stay out.

This could happen anytime. This could happen at school during my Specials or when Grandma Barlow showed me math equations, or when Altemonte threw a flaming axe at my forehead or when I shot a flaming arrow at Altemonte's forehead, and especially it would happen when Altemonte and I were digging with our hands in the gnome house our portal to the elf world. One time we were digging and I had to stop and crawl out of the gnome house really quick and lie down with my face in the snow and Altemonte came out and said, Are you okay? and I said, Yes, and Altemonte said, No, you're not, what is it? And I said, Nothing, and he said, Do you want to stop digging? And I said, No way are you kidding we are almost to the World of Two Moons we have to join the Wolfriders in the battle at Blue Mountain there's no time to waste.

I knew that Altemonte missed his dad really bad even though he acted like he didn't and I knew he missed his mom, too, even though he said she was a hypocrite and I knew that Altemonte acted like he didn't know anything at school when actually he knew more than the principal and the teacher put together and I knew that Altemonte's favorite plant was gall of the earth because it had the dwarfest name and I knew that one time Altemonte tried drinking cooking sherry and it made him throw up and then go right to sleep and I knew that Altemonte liked to gnaw on unripe pears like a deer eating a tree but I did not know how to ask Altemonte if he was being tipped into the death portal, too.

But one night when we lay in our bunks waiting for Grandma Barlow to come give us our medicine and turn out the light my scar murmured, it glimmered. I was like, Altemonte, and he was like, What? And I was like, Wouldn't it be so toxically sweet to find out what would happen to our brains if we stopped taking our medicine?

But I've always taken my medicine, Altemonte said.

Why? I asked.

My grandma said I have to, he said. She said that before I took medicine I was like a lethal weapon.

I want to be a lethal weapon, I said.

But my grandma won't let us, Altemonte said.

I said, I heard about this top-secret ninja spy who wouldn't swallow his pills. Instead, he saved them inside his cheek like a squirrel, and then he flushed them down the toilet.

So that night Grandma Barlow came in and gave us each our blue nail-polish pill and then she said, Good night, my boys, just holler if you need any little thing, and when she was gone I lowered my hand down between the bunk and the wall, and Altemonte slipped his pill which was all sticky and wet into my hand. And I jumped down from the bunk and went down the hall to the bathroom, and I dropped the pills into the toilet and then I aimed my stream of pee on them to make them sink to the bottom of the bowl and then I flushed. It felt like espionage that dazzled, like the kind of trick that could get me home again, and Altemonte and I were so excited we couldn't sleep but stayed up all night fighting about which was best, the World of Two Moons or Middle-earth, and who could make the best sound of flames with only our mouths, and this was the kind of fight that I could have forever with extreme joyfulness. And in the morning, Grandma Barlow sizzled pancakes and set them down before us on the table, and then she set down a cloudy water glass between us and there were two blue pills floating in it, and they were dissolved but they weren't all the way dissolved they looked like rotten teeth.

They didn't flush, she said.

Yes, they did, I said. I made sure.

They came back up again, she said.

Then Altemonte started crying and he said, I'm sorry, I'm sorry, I'm sorry.

Then Grandma Barlow said, Altemonte, think of your mama. Think what you're doing to her. She's up there working and she's saving money, and Altemonte, she's doing it for you. Last time she came home to visit, you wouldn't even go to her. And now this. You're just making more pain.

And Altemonte said, I'll go to her, I'll go to her, Grandma. I looked at Altemonte and at his snot which was totally gross and amazing, and I wished that I could cry the way that he could cry.

It was my idea, I said. It was my fault.

Grandma Barlow said, Where's your pain, Perley? You've been willful ever since your visit with your mama.

I'm ready to go home, I said.

That's not in my power, she said.

I'm starting to feel more powerful, I said.

Grandma Barlow sat down at the table with us and she pulled Altemonte into her lap who was still crying and she reached for my hand across the table and then she prayed which I can't remember all the words but it didn't sound like she was mad.

When she was done praying she started talking. She talked the way she would sometimes, where she would basically clasp me and Altemonte, she would clasp us but it didn't really feel like she was talking to us. She just talked and rocked Altemonte on her lap and he stopped crying and buried his head in her nightgown which she was still wearing even though it was morning and my mouth watered remembering what burying your head in someone's nightgown could be like.

So many kinds of pain, she said, which was something she loved to say and then she said she knew what a real family was supposed to look like, one man one woman and their children all alike, lined up one two three searching for eggs in the coop. But you hardly ever saw that family anymore, Grandma Barlow said, that one man one woman children all alike. She rocked Altemonte and she held my hand and it felt so good like a giant marshmallow. Then she said the world was rotten to the core it surely was. She said, There was the man at your door saying that they could take your kid and take your house if you weren't careful and the only way to make money was to work for the same people who said they could take your house, and people were sick, seemed like every week she heard of a new person with bone cancer, people younger than her, people who should have been old-timers but would not make it to old-time status, and it was hard to know what to do or who to blame. And the pastor said to pray so she was praying. That's what Grandma Barlow said but I said, I'm not sick and Altemonte's not sick, so maybe we don't need to take that medicine.

So Grandma Barlow stopped rocking and noticed me again.

It's those damn snakes, isn't it? she said.

I am Friend of Snake, I said.

That may be, she said. But you can't go home until the snakes are gone.

My mamas have tried everything, I said. They can't get rid of them.

I'll bet there's one thing they haven't tried, Grandma Barlow said.

Then she told me about the ritual.

Then I made her tell me again. Then she told me again. Then I said, Wait, hold on, and I went to my bunk and I got one of my comic books, and then I came back and I asked for a pencil and then I made Grandma Barlow tell me one more time, and I wrote down what she told me on the inside cover of *ElfQuest, Book One: Fire and Flight*. I wrote down what she told me word for word.

That week Mama L pushed me on the swing again and the Outside Girl sat far away pretending not to watch us. We chose the swing with the noisy rusted chain. That way we could talk. Mama L said, Tell me about Mrs. Barlow.

She's basically the nicest, I said. She totally loves god. But still, I'm not her boy. Altemonte is her boy.

Mama L said, Piglet, you're my boy. My

boy and Mama K's boy. I promise that I'm doing everything I can to bring you home.

When? I asked.

Soon, she said.

Does Mama K have the ransom yet? I asked.

She's doing everything she can, Mama L said. She's working very hard.

She threw me, I said. Out, I said. She threw my knapsack. She hurt my arm.

Does it still hurt? asked Mama L.

No, I said.

She loves you and she didn't know what to do, Mama L said. She was scared. But I don't want you to be scared.

I'm not scared, I said. That's not it. The way I feel is another way.

What way? she said. Tell me, Piglet.

I almost told her about the death portal the hole the blank universe but I didn't want to scare her so instead I just said, I feel like a picture out of focus, like there's one me and two mes and three mes and I can't move the way I want to. Like I don't know how I feel until after I felt it. I don't want to eat my food even though I'm allowed to eat all the pancakes I want.

I saw that I'd scared her anyway.

You should stop taking those pills, Mama L said.

I kind of knew what she meant, I wasn't a fucking moron. I kind of knew or else why would I have tried flushing the pills down the toilet, I kind of knew but there were one me two mes three mes, and at least one me got mad at Mama L for telling me what to do. Mama L telling me to stop taking the pills was actually a supremely easy thing for her to tell me.

I said, The pills make me super-smart.

She said, You were already super-smart.

I said, The pills make me so I can do my Specials.

She said, I don't care if you can do your Specials.

I said, That's why they took me away. You have to care about stuff like that.

She said, That's not why they took you away.

What about Altemonte? I asked.

What about Altemonte? she asked.

He takes the pills, too, I said. And he's my best friend. Our motto is not only excellence but it is also loyalty. The same thing's wrong with Altemonte that's wrong with me. He misses his parents and he's looking for the elf world but it's very hard to find it. He collects acorns.

I don't know about Altemonte, Mama L said. But I know about you. You are my

Velvet Piglet and you don't have to take that medicine.

Yes, I do, I said.

No, you don't, she said.

You don't know, I said.

Yes, I do, she said.

No, you don't, I said.

Perley, I am your mother and I want you to stop taking that medicine, Mama L said in a new voice that made her sound like Mama K.

But I was equal to it. I said, You're not in charge. You don't know anything. And then I said, You're a fucking moron and not only that but you're a hypocrite, too.

And Mama L sucked in so sharp I thought that I had accidentally shot and killed her which was totally not what I meant to do, I just meant to tell her that she didn't even know about the spy and the squirrel and the toilet and the cloudy water glass and about Grandma Barlow talking so much and praying and Altemonte crying and saying sorry and how amazing his snot was. Mama L was telling me what to do like it was all so easy but actually it wasn't easy at all. She wouldn't even give me a chance to tell her about the snake ritual because she was so busy thinking she knew everything. But actually it was me who knew everything.

The Outside Girl basically ran as fast as she could over to us. I didn't think she was pretty anymore. I didn't think she smelled good. Now when she talked to me I wanted to tell her, You and the pancake counselor should get married and have a big wedding and you should invite me but guess what I won't come, I'll burn the invitation. But I knew it would be rude to say that so instead I pretty much didn't talk to her.

She stopped the swing from swinging by putting her glove on the rusted chain.

Switch swings, she said.

Why? asked Mama L.

This one is too noisy, she said. I'm supposed to be observing you, but I can't hear what you're saying to each other and Perley seems upset.

I'm not upset, I said, which was actually a lie but it was the kind of lie I was totally okay with because in another way I was telling the truth, and the truth was, Leave us alone.

Switch swings, she said. She was the one in charge which is what I had been trying to tell Mama L.

We switched swings. The Outside Girl didn't go back to her bench, she stayed near us. She took her tablet out but I wanted to tell her it wouldn't keep her warm. I wanted to tell her that to keep warm she should build a fire. I could even have shown her how to do it with a bow drill because I knew she didn't have any matches, but by now I knew she wasn't interested and when she pretended to be interested it was a trick but it was a trick that didn't dazzle me.

I sat on the stupid frozen swing and Mama L didn't push me she just stood behind me with one hand on my shoulder like she forgot where we were. I didn't tell her to push me, because I was tired of telling her to push me and also I was tired of being pushed.

The Outside Girl looked up and said, If there's a problem we can try again in two weeks. It's supposed to get cold again. If it's snowing, we could meet inside the Center.

Mama L said, There's no problem. Why would there be a problem?

The Outside Girl said, Ms. Marshall, you and Perley both seem upset.

Mama L said, Of course we're upset. Perley's been kidnapped. If we weren't upset, we'd be dead.

The Outside Girl said, This visit is over. Perley, your mama is tired. We can see her again next time. It's time to say bye-bye.

But then Mama L said, Can I have a project with him?

And I was like, A project?

And the Outside Girl was like, A project?

And Mama L said, I want to teach him to knit.

I just sat on the swing kicking my feet. My scar made noise on my face and I knew it was telling me what would happen next. Which was that the Outside Girl just kind of wrinkled her nose like a bunny which I think is something she practiced in the mirror to make herself look cute.

Mama L said, It's an activity Perley and I could do together, besides swinging, on visitation days.

The Outside Girl said, Isn't knitting for girls? But Mama L said, Knitting was invented by ancient fishermen making their nets.

Yeah, I said, even though it was the first I'd heard of it, but right then I knew that being an ancient fisherman was probably almost as good as being an elf.

The Outside Girl leaned down to me on the swing and looked meaningfully into my eyes and asked me, Perley, would you like to learn to knit?

And even though I had never thought about knitting before and even though I didn't really believe that Mama L knew how to knit or at least I had never seen her knit,

456

of course what I said while I looked mean-ingfully into the Outside Girl's eyes was, Hell yes.

So then Mama L reached into her coat and brought out this yarn that was the color of kings and queens I mean it was purple like a cape and the Outside Girl said, Maybe this would be a better activity for next time when we're at the Center where it's warm, but Mama L said, We have another hour. Legally. My lawyer will file a motion. And the Outside Girl was like, Ms. Marshall, there is no need to be angry. Knitting sounds constructive. I'm supportive of knit-ting. It sounds like a Strength.

Then Mama L made me sit down with her on the bench but I thought, If she is really just teaching me how to knit how come she is breathing in such an organized way? My elf sensibility began to speak to me via my scar and Mama L pulled me close and handed me the yarn it was a knot.

This is a skein, she said. The first thing that you have to do is wind the skein into a ball. Find the end, so I found the end. She said, And what do you wind it around? What is at the center of the ball?

My finger? I asked. A marble? An acorn?

Or anything, she said. Then she reached back into her coat and she brought out a pink plastic egg, the hollow kind for Easter candy that I am not allowed to have. What's inside? she asked. Candy, I said. Nope, she said. There's nothing inside it. She looked at me hard. She said, It's empty.

So I wound the skein of yarn around the hollow plastic Easter egg, wound it around and around until the skein disappeared and a big purple ball sat in my lap.

The pink egg was its secret center.

The Outside Girl sat next to us on the bench, watching us like a totally unskilled spy who didn't even know how to spy. I know how to crochet, she said, and then Mama L sounded just like the Mean Aunt and she said, Aren't I supposed to get some time alone with him? I mean legally, which was basically her new favorite word. The Outside Girl looked hurt which was weird and she said, I'm just doing my job. I'm trying to defuse the tension. I'm trying to be an advocate for Perley. Did it ever occur to you that I'm not your enemy, Ms. Marshall? But Mama L said, No, that didn't occur to me, and she threw a flaming axe at the Outside Girl's forehead or that's the kind of look she gave her. The Outside Girl moved to the next bench, but she was still close enough to hear what we were saying.

Mama L took a breath. Are you cold, Perley? she asked me. Yes, I said. Are you too cold to learn to knit right now? she asked. No, I said, because something about the way that Mama L held that yarn so solemnly, so royally, made me want to knit so bad. Mama L took out two gleaming needles like Bilbo Baggins's dagger. Her fingers flashed and there were loops up and down. Then she taught me this rhyme, In through the front door, Round to the back, Down through the garden, And off pops Jack. Every time she said And off pops Jack, she put a loop on the other needle and pretty soon I could do it, too, because I am a genius.

But there was a problem. I knew that Mama L wanted to tell me something besides Down through the garden, besides And off pops Jack, I knew that she wanted to tell me something that she couldn't tell me with the Outside Girl sitting right there listening and totally wishing she could be our knitting friend when all she could do was crochet and who even cares about crocheting, no one even knows who invented it, I could actually hear the ancient fishermen laughing at her. But still, we were under heavy surveillance.

So I said to Mama L, Send.

What? she asked.

Don't you remember *ElfQuest*? I asked.

Of course I do, she said. I read those books with Mama K before you were born. Didn't like them all that much, but I read them.

Whatever you want to tell me, just send what's in your mind to my mind, I said. I'll hear you. I'll understand what to do.

And even though she was the mom and I was the kid, she did what I said. She sent to me. She sent me a story. And at first the story I received was just the story of knitting but soon it was the story of hollow eggs and soon it was more.

By the time Mama L had finished sending, I had knit five rows, and dropped most of my stitches, and the visit was over for the day. The Outside Girl smiled at us even though I could tell she felt left out. We really do like to try to keep families together, she said. I am so glad to see you and Perley doing well. I can tell you have a real bond.

Which was true.

Knit, purl, knit, purl, knit, purl, knit, purl. Ancient fishermen invented it and I got really good at it so fast, and I showed Altemonte how to do it, too. That was one project. But there was another project, too. Each night I would unravel the ball of yarn, down to its hollow center, and I would open the plastic egg, and I would spit my pill into it, and then I would close the egg and I would wind the yarn back around the egg but not all the yarn. I would spend two weeks knitting something, a square, a scarf, a pot holder, a swatch Mama L called it. And at visitation, I would see Mama L, and I would say to her, Trade you. And when I said, Trade you, she would give me a new color of yarn with a new plastic egg empty in the heart and she would take my leftover yarn, with two weeks of soggy blue pills inside where no one knew or heard.

Altemonte kept taking his medicine. He said, I promised my grandma. I said, But what about the death portal? Altemonte said, What happens to me is different than what happens to you. Maybe it's because you're slightly spastic. Maybe someday I'll stop, he said. But not today. But our motto is excellence and loyalty, I said. He said, Sometimes you say that things are our motto when really they are just your motto, and I said, But don't you think excellence is important? And he said, I don't really know what excellence is, it sounds like something the principal would say. I asked, What about loyalty? Don't you think loyalty is important? And he said, I think it's important that you are on your quest and I am on mine. I said, But Altemonte I want our brains to be the same. And he said, But Perley our brains will never be the same no matter if we take medicine or not. But don't you even have a motto? I asked him. Altemonte said, I guess if I had to have a motto it would probably be trust.

Trust is the same as loyalty, I said.

No, it's not, he said.

Yes, it is, I said.

No, it's not, he said. Then he said, I won't betray you. I'll even help you.

So I had to do the project without him.

The first visit the yarn was purple and the second visit the yarn was gray with flecks of emerald green, and by the third visit, when the yarn was yellow like a goldfinch, the death portal had begun to seal. I could taste Grandma Barlow's pies, I could taste her pancakes, and the wizard had dropped the crystal ball and disappeared, and the crystal ball had shattered and inside it was my old brain back and my old brain was a mushroom it was a drum it was a fist that opened and closed.

Lily

I've stopped trying to defend myself. I won't claim that I was a good parent, only a parent in love.

If I couldn't kidnap Perley back, I could kidnap the pills. Instead of moving from bottle to hand to mouth to throat to gut to bloodstream to brain, now they moved from cheek to plastic egg to yarn ball, and then, when I smuggled them home, the pills moved deep into a hole in the ground, out in the woods, buried and forgotten, so that even I couldn't find those small deposits of metal and chemical, sulfur and chalk.

When Perley told me to send, I almost scolded him. Oh lord, I thought. *ElfQuest.* Always ready to show me I'm not good enough, and now it's because I can't read minds. I almost told him, This isn't a comic book, Perley. This is real life. But then I thought, Why not? We were the same body once. Why shouldn't we be able to see inside each other? So I willed it. I wouldn't let it not work. I wouldn't let doubt in. Half by code, half by mind reading, Perley and I embarked on our great project. I sent to him, mama elf to baby elf. He received.

Each visitation day, as March turned to April and the maple sap ran in the trees and the hills churned toward spring and toward the ninety-day review, Perley and I sat side by side in Pariah Park, stitching and winding and talking, fingers flying, the caseworker watching jealously from the side-lines. She'd begun to bring her own handwork, a crocheted purse that she said she'd been working on for years. I didn't offer her a word of encouragement. It was her job to stay cheerful, not mine.

Eventually, she began to sit farther away, so finally Perley and I could speak almost freely again, though Perley insisted that sending was an easier way to talk to each other.

One day he said, "Did you hear that?"

"Were you sending?" I asked.

"Yes," he said.

"I didn't quite get it," I said. "Try me again."

"I asked you where you put it," he said. He looked toward the caseworker at the other end of the park, who was half turned away, absorbed in some uninteresting crocheting challenge. Still, Perley lowered his voice. That was one way my boy had changed. He'd gone from guileless to crafty in more ways than one. "Where do you put the medicine," he whispered, "after I give it to you?"

"A hole in the ground," I said, and Perley flinched. That was when he told me about the death portal, about the grave he saw sometimes. "I don't see it so much now," he said. "Now that we're doing our project. But I don't want it to come back. I don't want to fall down that hole."

"Piglet, you won't," I said.

"How do you know?" he asked me.

"Because," I said, "I dig the holes, and then I put the pills down there, and then I fill the holes back up, and then I pat the earth down over them, and then I make a mixture of milk and earth and moss and I pour it over the place I dug, and where I pour this milkshake more moss begins to grow, and mushrooms, and soon no one can tell where that hole is, not even me. It's not a hole anymore. It's healed."

He thought about this, his fingers still working. That day he was knitting a blue mitten, just one. It would never meet its mate. It would be unraveled. He asked, "Does Mama K know about our project? Will she come home so I can give her my report?"

"When Mama K comes home I will tell you right away," I said. "You'll be the first to know."

Perley said, "Can I still come home even though I'm different now?"

I said, "You're my same Velvet Piglet."

Perley said, "I'm changed. I'm Velvet Piglet, I'm elf, I'm dwarf, I'm wolf, I'm spy."

I said, "And me, I'm your mama, again and again and again."

Perley said, "I don't want to come home unless Altemonte can come with me."

I said, "Bring him."

The visit after that, the redbuds were on the trees. It was the beginning of April, thirty-four days until the review hearing. Perley brought me one of his comic books. He handed it to me at the end of the visit, when we traded yarn, gray-green for ocher. "Check the last page," he said, before climbing back into the caseworker's car.

At home, I opened it.

ElfQuest, Book One: Fire and Flight:

Catch two snakes. Behead. Skin. Clean. Brine for at least two hours. Bring a pot of water to a rolling boil. Slide the snakes in. Parboil for ten minutes. Drain and cool. Say your prayers and thank our heavenly father. Once you've eaten both snakes bite for bite, the power that was theirs now belongs to you. You can tell snakes what you want them to do, and they will do it.

And a note:

This ritual was handed to me from my mother Sissy Barlow and her sister May, and they say it came from their grand-mother.

I heard my own grandma's voice in it.
I heard the Best Practices Binder in it,
too.

I heard my own grandma's voice in it.
I heard the Best Practices binder in it,
too.

15

Helen

While Aldi lay in the hospital, Rudy and I stretched billboard canvas over the hole in his roof. We battened it down. We bucked up the oak. We chipped the long limbs. We raked. We swept the sloped lawn. When we brought Aldi home, Rudy lifted him into the truck, careful of his injured hip. He stopped at the pharmacy to pick up Aldi's prescriptions. He detoured through the drive-through to get Aldi some fast food. But never once did he speak to Aldi, and never once did Aldi speak to him. Never once until I had settled Aldi onto his cot, furnished him with sassafras root, a jar of nettle tea, and a six-pack of Natural Ice. Then Aldi said, "Tell Lily I've done all I can, and I'm sorry I couldn't do much. I only hope I didn't make things worse."

"It was good to have someone in our corner," I said.

But Rudy said, "What the hell did you mean by it, Aldi? Hiding out in here that day? You hid your sedan, for fuck's sake. Old man, I know you got a death wish, but don't make me do it for you. You want to make a killer of me? You want to kill me too?"

Aldi turned his face to the wall.

"We'll be back soon to see how you're getting along," I said.

Rudy was stewing, but that didn't mean he didn't come along with me to bring Aldi food most days, venison hot dish, sardine-and-dandelion fritters, butternut squash stuffed with acorn meal and dried chicken-of-the-woods mushrooms that I soaked in broth. We left it at his door. He wasn't showing his face. We knew he was on hiatus. We knew, during these times, that Aldi became a husk. We knew he wanted to heal alone, to make it through what was left of winter in his own way.

Rudy knew it better than anyone, but it didn't soothe him any. When the redbuds came onto the trees, we got a job taking down a cherry, which pissed him off. The clients, a young couple who taught at the university, asked us to slice the cherry into rounds and build a flight of steps through their garden. Rudy barely waited until they were out of earshot before losing it. "I'm not their fucking trained Ewok," he said.

"Come on, Rudy," I said. "They're respecting the whole living system. They're keeping the tree as part of the landmass."

He looked at me with deep contempt.

"I'll show you a fucking landmass," he said. "I'll fucking spread my shit evenly over every one of these steps. I'll save my hair and fingernails and make a fucking mosaic, if that's what these goddamn hippies want."

I put my head down, went for my ear protection.

"That's the trouble with people," Rudy went on. "No one knows how to live. No one knows what friendship is. Goddammit. Me and Aldi Birch go back years, and now he won't talk to me? Fuck that."

"We dropped a tree on him," I said. "And then you blamed him for it."

"Don't be a bitch," said Rudy. "You want to get fired?"

"Why don't you call him?" I said.

"Why doesn't he call me?" he said.

"If you don't call him, maybe I will," I said. "I know it's his way, but all the same I get worried about him, all alone in there."

"What about me? Don't you ever worry about me?" asked Rudy.

I looked at him. Briefly, that moment

came back to me, when we'd lain side by side after the tree fell, when I'd noticed the iron oxide color in his eyes. I didn't like him any better now, but I remembered it. "That's an interesting question," I said. "Yes, I'm always a little bit worried about you. But also, I'm worried about myself when I'm around you, which is why I like to keep my ear protection on."

Rudy rolled cherry rounds down the hill, heedless of tender violet shoots. I used a shovel to dig out benches for stair steps.

He said, "Just don't butt in for once. I'll call him."

"What are you going to say?" I asked.

"None of your fucking business," Rudy said. "I'm going to say, I'm sorry I crushed your hip. I'm sorry about the oak. I'll tell him I'm sorry."

But then he didn't. He looked at his phone. He drank a Natural Ice. He didn't call.

Rudy didn't call Aldi until the last time it snowed.

It was March, and we'd thought the snow was past, had even unswaddled fruit trees, tilled up a few garden beds, prepared to plant peas. But that final snow came down wet and thick, burning coltsfoot blooms, turning redbud flowers brown. First thing

471

in the morning, when the roads were still clear, I brought Aldi pancakes with pemmican spread on top. I went to pin a note to his door, knocked just on the off chance. No answer. A snowdrift had gathered against the undisturbed heap of food we'd left him. Now it was three days' worth. No light behind the window curtains. I looked up at the chimney. No smoke.

At home, I found Rudy holed up in his wall tent, lounging in his long underwear, wool socks propped on the woodstove. He was eating chili out of a can.

"I'm just back from Aldi's place," I said. "You need to go over there with me."

"Get off my back," Rudy said.

"It doesn't look good over there," I said.

"It's the winter. Aldi's sleeping it off. It never looks good," Rudy said.

"I don't like it," I said. "You said you were going to call him. You should have called him."

"I called him," Rudy said.

"No, you didn't," I said.

"I'll call him now," Rudy said.

He called. I paced. Rudy's bling, dangling above the woodstove, grinned and grimaced at me. Rudy put his phone down. "No answer," he said.

"We're going over there," I said. "Get up."

"You can go if you want to, but I'm not going," Rudy said.

"Rudy," I said. "You told me not to be a bystander. Well, this is it. You either show the fuck up, or you check the fuck out."

"I'm checking the fuck out," Rudy said.

"I'm taking your truck," I said.

"Snow's getting worse," Rudy said. "Don't be a hero."

"I'm not a hero," I said. "But I'm going over there."

"If it makes you feel better, I'll call him again," Rudy said, dialing. "This time, I'll even leave the bastard a message on his answering machine."

It didn't make me feel better. I didn't wait to hear what sort of message Rudy would leave. I slid and stumbled down the pipeline, barely able to see five feet in front of me. I pushed the snow off of Rudy's windshield. I got in and turned the key. I backed up so fast the tires spun out, and I almost hit Rudy, who had followed me. He got a running start and vaulted himself into the bed of the truck as the tires found purchase. He turned his back firmly toward me, and we pulled out onto the snowbound road.

My heart numb, my stomach rotting out, I parked the truck at the bottom of Aldi's driveway. No way the tires would make it up to the garage. We walked. The big tin building had settled deep and silent into the snow. It was dark. I didn't focus, not fully, on what I might find inside. I kept focused on Rudy instead, my irritation a constant comforting motor. Rudy hiked grimly next to me. He was the one who picked the lock, shouldered the door open, pushed us into the gloom and the stench that told me I was right.

We found Aldi Birch's body, his shattered leg splayed off-kilter, his face mostly gone, his gun nearby.

We stood. We stood. We sank. We sank. Rudy said, "I'm going to puke," and he puked. "I'm going to shit," he said. For that, he made it to the bathroom. Me, I was all stopped up. I didn't stop looking at what had been Aldi. I didn't stop looking at the mess he'd made. Not stopping looking was the least that I could do.

Beside the upturned cot, the answering machine was blinking red. His family, it occurred to me. The next thing to do is contact someone, isn't that right? What about his son? I pressed the flashing button, so when Rudy came into the room he heard his own voice playing back to him.

Pick up the phone, asshole. Pick up the phone. I've had it with this. You've got to talk to me. You're my brother, my father, you're all I've got. Pick up. You motherfucking asshole. Pick. Up. The. Phone. Or wait. I get it. You've offed yourself, haven't you. You've finally pulled the trigger. You're lying there dead on the floor. You've blown your own brains out. Well, if that's what you've done, then hear this. I will never forgive you. In fact, I'm coming over there. I'm coming over there and when I get there, you crusty motherfucker, I will kill you all over again.

Rudy's message cut out. The chickens teemed, hungry. We would feed them, but not yet. It was very cold. We sat side by side on the floor, where it was coldest. "Aldi," Rudy said. "How could you? How could you leave me?"

But the first feeling that came to me, when feeling came back, rushed in strong and undeniable, from no source that I knew. His choice. He can do this if he wants to. It's a mystery. It's his mystery.

We didn't want to call the sheriff. We knew Aldi hated the sheriff. We knew he wouldn't want to be dragged to the funeral home, manhandled by a bunch of strangers, but we couldn't see what else to do. So we called, but before the sheriff came, we unplugged the answering machine and we hiked it down to the truck. We buried it beneath the chain saws.

When it was all over, when our statements had been taken, when the ambulance — why did they need a fucking ambulance? — had come and gone with Aldi's body, when we had fed the chickens and waded back down through the dripping, warming slush, we sat in the truck dumbly.

"What now?" Rudy asked.

"Where should we go?" I asked.

"I don't want to be separate," Rudy said.

"Me neither," I said. "I don't want any more separation."

"I want the opposite of separation," he said.

"What's that?" I said.

"What's that?" he said.

"Take me home," I said. "Go fast."

I can't explain what happened next except to say that the opposing magnetism that for years had pushed Rudy and me decisively apart turned around and sucked us toward each other. I was near him so hard, I was against him and he was against me and then I was caught because he had always been against me and I had always been against him, but this was a different kind of against. We didn't need to talk, because we'd spent years talking and we knew everything. We knew we were no good for each other. We knew we were built for lifelong loggerheads. We were grieving so hard, we were grieving so bad, we were so hard for each other. I don't remember why we didn't just fuck right there in the truck, and I don't remember how we made it home, how we pulled each other up the pipeline and into the wall tent. Rudy kicked aside his boots and dirty socks, his multiple editions of *The Count of Monte Cristo,* that classic tale of revenge, his yards of burlap, shoe grease, chewing tobacco, lamp oil, the chili can. He threw his wool army blanket onto the floor. He pushed me or I pulled him down onto the blanket. Whatever it was it felt violent, rough, and clumsy, two people who hadn't done this in a while. Can I fuck you now, he said, can I fuck you? I said, You'd better. He said, Fuck, you don't let me go. I'm not, I'm not, I can't, I said, and we didn't feel the cold and we didn't feel the snow and we didn't feel the heat from the fire and when two bodies come at each other that hard they reach terminal velocity and liquefy upon impact and we did.

And when he was inside me, I felt Aldi Birch, saw his exploded caved-in face. But also, I saw before that explosion, saw his eyes beneath his brow, his willow legs, felt the ways he and I had petted each other softly, as if we were only touching ourselves.

Karen

I had something to report. I had a reason to call home. High-pressure fracked gas, a whole fresh hell, was on its way to our place, would be shot through the repurposed pipeline beneath Rudy's nursery, would flow alongside the spring. I thought of vintage pipe, fissures, seepage. I thought of what Jay had said. Blast zone of two miles. I spent long days in my container Googling pipeline spills, leaks, explosions. The industry said things were fine, of course they did. But pretty much everyone else said things weren't fine at all. I needed to warn Lily.

When Lily and I got together, she said I seemed experienced, a woman who knew what she wanted from life. But if it had been left up to me, we'd still be standing awkwardly in the hardware and salvage store. All I'd known how to do was bring home a utility sink and come back the next day. Lily did the rest. She made me understand that the only reason I'd built a cabin at the Land Trust was for her to live in it with me. Pretty soon she was packing me sandwiches and apples for my shifts at the clinic, patching the tire of my bike so she could ride it to work, catching my eye at interminable Land Trust meetings while Deirdre strummed her guitar. We slept outside together as often as we could. We held on to each other. We stayed side by side. Lily took my terror and confusion and translated it to love, or to going through life together, whichever came first. I needed to hear her voice. I needed to call home.

Needed to but didn't.

If I called home, Lily would say, You'd better be able to rewind the tape. You'd better be able to replay the scene so that this time when you grip Perley's thin arm, when you hoist him harshly, you don't throw him out the door. Instead, you swing him into your arms. You hold him tight. You tell him why you did it. You tell him what it means. You tell him that you're bringing him home.

She would say, Well? Do you still think we should be patient?

I didn't call.

Instead, I spent the rest of February and March paralyzed in my container, my eye on the classified map. I watched that green line turn red, watched it creep farther south, watched it go under waterways, hide itself in the marshes and wetlands, plant itself next to the poor and vulnerable, cruise like a smart missile straight toward my family. I knew if I called Lily, I would have to say out loud how bad it was, and if I admitted to her how bad it was, then I would have to tell her what we were going to do about it, and when we were going to do it, and how the hell was I to know a thing like that?

Marie and Lawrence liked to talk about the zombie apocalypse. It passed the time at lunch, when I joined them near the pipeline pit or in the truck cab to eat bologna sandwiches. It passed the time around the campfire, where I sat smoking cigarettes, which I'd taken up to replace whittling. There was a lot to do to prepare for the zombie apocalypse, especially because, according to Marie and Lawrence, these particular zombies would know how to operate heavy machinery. Therefore, they said, it would be of primary importance to disable all equipment so that it would be useless to the zombies. There were many ways to do that, and Lawrence and Marie went over each one in detail.

"Gallon of water in the fuel tank or oil filter," Lawrence said, adding a log to the fire, popping the top off a beer. "Done. That thing ain't running."

"Oh right," Jay said. "The zombies are after you, and you have the presence of mind, let alone the time, to fill up a jug of water. Ain't going to happen."

"So just grab a couple handfuls of sand," Marie said. She sat on a cinder block, her gloves off, fingers wide over the flames. "Send it straight into the crankcase, or better yet, the intake."

"What about battery acid in the radiator?" Lawrence suggested.

"There you go again," Jay said, swinging Mountain Dew. "Where are you getting the battery acid? You've got to use what you have on hand."

"So you bring a turkey baster," Marie said. "Use it to suck acid out of the battery, then down it goes into the fuel system."

"That's right," Lawrence said. "You've got to have your zombie apocalypse kit ready. Turkey baster, crescent wrench, water jug, flashlight."

"With a red lens," Marie put in. "Remember, zombies can't see red lights."

"What else you got in this kit of yours?" asked Jay.

"What about sugar?" I asked into the smoke. I shook out a cigarette, passed the pack to Lawrence.

"Sugar?" asked Lawrence.

"Everyone knows putting sugar in an engine is the worst thing for it," I said, using a twig from the fire to light up.

"Oh, everyone knows that, do they?" asked Jay.

"You do hear that," Marie said. "But it's bullshit. Don't know how that rumor got started."

"The zombies probably started it," Lawrence said. Jay and Marie laughed.

"Sugar in an engine's no good. At most, it'll just clog the filter," Marie said, turning her palms.

"But as long as we're bringing food, a box of quick rice is worth including," Lawrence said, exhaling smoke. "Empty that down the radiator. Or a potato in the exhaust pipe."

"No one's mentioned my favorite," Jay said. "Fill a condom with crushed walnut shells and fine sand, any abrasive will do. Drop it in the crankcase. Zombie drives the thing about thirty miles when the condom disintegrates, and that's it. Engine's completely destroyed."

"I've never heard of zombies that could drive," I said. "I thought zombies just ate

483

brains and lurched around. The thing that's scary about them is that they just keep coming."

"Oh, these zombies can drive," Marie said. "They can drive and they just keep coming. And only we can stop them. That's why we've got to be prepared."

"Practice and prepare," I said, lighting another cigarette from the end of my first one. "Back home, those were our watchwords."

"Practice and prepare for what?" asked Marie.

"Hard to say now," I said. "Looking back, I might as well have just rolled out of bed and done the first thing that came to mind, for all the good my plans have done me. Hell, maybe all along it was the zombie apocalypse we were preparing for, and we just didn't know."

"Good a thing to prepare for as any," Lawrence said.

"One thing you can count on anyway," Marie said. They raised their cans. I raised mine, too.

By that time we weren't enemies, I don't think, but I wouldn't say we were friends, either. I knew how many kids Marie had, but not her kids' names, knew what she thought about her ex-husband but not her current one. I knew Lawrence had it bad for a woman wouldn't give him the time of day, didn't know why he had it so bad for her. I knew that Jay had an older son in jail, younger one played high school football. I didn't know who he talked to for so long on the phone during cigarette breaks. They knew about Lily, knew my kid got taken, knew about my lonely days because they were looking at them. They didn't know about *ElfQuest,* about whittling, about the wolf pack. They didn't know how small Perley was, how little he weighed when I'd wrenched him up by the arm. They didn't know his shut-down eyes when I tossed him out into the snow. I listened to them and they listened to me, but we didn't ask one another too many questions. Even when Jay fought with Lawrence, even when Marie'd had enough of both of them, still I was always the one on the outside.

So when Jay didn't show up to work one morning, Lawrence and Marie just said he had to go up north to see about his family, didn't explain more than that.

"I guess I'll call Shane," I said, heading for the trailer. Lawrence stopped me.

"No need to call Shane," he said. "We'll just work shorthanded until Jay gets back. Shouldn't be more than a few days. It's no big deal."

"I don't think we're supposed to work shorthanded," I said.

"Supposed to, nothing. This isn't a union job," Marie said. "I don't want to work with whatever prize white guy Shane decides to send us."

"What, now you're racist?" I said.

"Call it what you want," she said. "Mixing hasn't ever done me much good. When I'm pipelining I try to stick with Natives, even Natives from other tribes. Just seems to work out better that way."

"All white people aren't bad," I said.

"All white people don't have to be bad," Marie said. "Just the right white people at the right time."

"How bad could it be?" I asked.

"Probably pretty bad," Marie said.

We have to decide when to take action. Some people decide never to take action at all. Some people look back on a jumble of uncertain floundering and cast the right frame around it so that they can remember doing the right thing when it counted. I'll try not to revise. Each day, I needed to call home, but each day I walked past the motel office and I never once went inside. I didn't know what the hell to do about the pipeline, but I knew Lily would tell me I should pack up and leave. And when it came down to it, I wasn't prepared. I wasn't prepared to pack up and leave. Not yet.

Why should I? If the pipeline was time-sensitive, well then so was the ninety-day review. So was my mission of making money fast. And anyway, one look at that map and it was clear that they'd already put the line through everyone else's homes, so who was I to protest? I wasn't going to give up a decent job, my one good chance to get Perley back, just to stage a futile fight against the company, which I probably wouldn't win. Like I said, I Googled it, goddammit. Alone in that trailer all day, I Googled it and I found out that people all over the continent were fighting these pipelines, Indians were, white people were, hell, even Hollywood celebrities were. But they weren't winning.

And now here Marie and Lawrence were, asking me to do them a favor, to go against protocol when they still barely gave me the time of day, treated me like I was their own personal General fucking Custer or some shit, wouldn't even tell me where Jay was or when he was coming back.

If I couldn't win against the pipeline, I wanted to win something. I had a strategy. If I kept my job, I could win my family back.

Wait and see.

So Marie climbed into the excavator, Lawrence grabbed a shovel, and I went into my private trailer and called Shane. I told him, We're shorthanded over here. But I'm just letting you know. Don't worry about us. We'll make do until Jay comes back. We don't need anyone else.

By lunchtime, the new guy was there.

Cameron. Long blond hair, tattoos crawling up his neck, handsome like a ferret. The three of us just stared up from our bologna while he introduced himself. "This must be a mistake," I said. "We don't need anyone else."

"No mistake," he said, gray eyes flickering past me to rest on Marie. He gave her a long appraising look, but she just scowled back. He said, "Never fear, Tiger Lily. Let me show you what I can do with this baby." Then he strode right past where we were eating to swing himself up into the cab of the excavator.

"What the hell is that?" Marie asked, throwing down her sandwich. She got to her feet, and Lawrence and I followed.

"Looks like the foreman here called Shane," Lawrence said.

"You called Shane?" asked Marie.

"Shane would have found out anyway," I said.

"I guess now we'll never know if he would have or not," Lawrence said.

"This is my job we're talking about," I said. "I'm not here to make friends. I'm here to make money and go home."

"You want to do your fucking job, foreman?" Marie said. "Tell that bag of dicks to get out of my excavator."

But when I did, Cameron said nice and loud, "Shane told me I'm up in the seat."

"Like hell," Marie said. "That's my machine."

"Princess, it's the company's machine," Cameron said. "None of this belongs to me or to you."

"Well, foreman, what do you say?" Lawrence asked me.

"She ain't the foreman," Cameron said. "She's just Shane's old girlfriend or something is what, even though she's ugly. But I ain't picky."

"Everyone just wait a minute," I said. I went into the trailer and called Shane. "What's the idea?" I said. "I tell you we don't need anyone else, and you send us the biggest asshole in the state?"

"Calm down," Shane said. "Cameron's a character, all right, but he's harmless."

"You'd better come down here," I said.

Ten minutes later, Shane's SUV pulled through the gate. He got out with a nervous grin, his wavy hair all brushed. "Folks, please," he said, "just work it out."

"I ain't no oiler," Marie said.

"Marie, you've got to understand," he said. "Cameron's experienced. I switched him off another crew to fill in short notice. He's been up in the cab. Can't very well put him on the ground. He's doing us a favor."

Cameron sat smiling in the operator's seat, waiting it out.

Shane turned on me, and now his gold teeth were nowhere to be seen. "Karen," he said. "You told me you were shorthanded, so I sent someone to fill in. Now you expect me to come down here and deal with some petty conflict? What am I paying you for? To sit in that trailer all day and do nothing?"

I didn't know what he was paying me for, and I'd hoped it would never come up. Cameron smiled down at us. Shane pursed his lips to conceal his teeth. Lawrence watched Marie. Marie watched me. Whatever my strategy had been, whatever I'd been practicing and preparing for, it wasn't this.

I said, "Come on, Marie. Ease up, okay?

It's just until Jay gets back."

She met my eyes like murder.

That night at the campfire, Lawrence and Marie wouldn't talk to me, wouldn't pass me a beer, wouldn't take the cigarettes I offered, nothing.

"It's not my fault," I said. "Shane's an asshole, you saw it."

But they picked up talking about the zombie apocalypse like I wasn't even there.

"Fire might be the best way," Marie said. "Thorough."

"Like a Molotov cocktail?" Lawrence said. "Way too dangerous. End up blowing yourself up instead of the zombies."

"Haven't you heard of delayed ignition?" Marie said.

"I don't trust it," said Lawrence.

"If you pour brake fluid over swimming pool cleaner, the mix ignites after fifteen minutes," Marie said. "That's plenty of getaway time."

"And if Jay were here, he'd say, where'd you so conveniently come across that swimming pool cleaner?" Lawrence said.

"Add it to the kit," Marie said.

"Right next to the quick rice and the potato," Lawrence said. They bumped cans. I sucked on my cigarette.

"Fuck it," Marie said. "What I really want to do is to take a crossbow, stand way up on a hilltop overlooking one of these sites, and shoot flaming arrows. One. Two. Three. Four. Down into gas tanks, one after another, right where it counts. Watch the whole fleet go up in flames. Beautiful."

"Score one for humanity," Lawrence said.

"Zombies zero," Marie said.

Me, I was no zombie, but I didn't quite feel like part of humanity, either. When I stumbled to bed, too many beers, not enough conversation, I was more wretched than a ghost, but I was a ghost.

But what did it matter? I stayed on the job. I stayed while March turned to April. I stayed while Marie and Lawrence continued to drive me to work but ignored me as neatly as slicing off dead skin. I stayed while every day Cameron ran the excavator and Marie and Lawrence worked on the ground. I stayed while every morning Cameron propositioned Marie, saying, I'd make your knees knock, Tiger Lily, and Marie saying, Fuck off, douche-bag, and Lawrence saying, You heard her, you need to stop, and Cameron saying, Hey, can't blame a guy for trying, and me saying, Okay, people, let's get back to work. I ate lunch alone. I watched the computer map. I watched the green line go red. I hid in my trailer and I watched the crew on the monitoring screen and tried to imagine I was far away from it all, that everything happening out in the yard was of only abstract interest to me. I was making money. I'd made almost enough. I'd spend the bus ride home figuring out what to say to Lily and, most of all, what to say to Perley when I saw him again. My mission was almost complete.

Then one morning toward the end of April, Cameron swung the boom of the excavator down and glanced Marie in the head with the corner of the bucket, a ton if it was a pound. If it had hit her square on, it would have killed her. As it was, it split her hard hat in two pieces, easy as opening a grapefruit. Marie was knocked out cold.

When I burst out of my trailer, Cameron stood up in the machine to meet me. "You want to fucking talk to me, dyke, I'll kill you, too," he said. I grabbed him by the leg and hauled him out of the excavator, went for him with whatever was on hand, which happened to be a pipe wrench. Backhanded him across the face with it while Marie lay out next to us. Now there were two of them on the ground. I turned nurse, considered triage, went to check on Marie first. Lawrence was already there, holding her head on his lap. There wasn't any blood, the hard hat had done that much, at least. She opened her eyes, focused them. I unlaced her boots. She could wiggle all her toes. She could say her name when I asked.

"That motherfucker is going to pay," I said.

"You sure are ignorant," Lawrence said. "No one ever pays for anything. The people that should pay don't pay. And the more people like you interfere, the more we're the ones paying."

I thought of Helen, how eager she'd been to tell me and Lily we should take our case to the Supreme Court. The rage I'd felt at her I hadn't bothered to explain, not even to myself. Still, I said, "He won't get away with this."

"You're the reason he's here at all," Marie said.

Lawrence said, "It only gets worse from here. We're going home. We can pick this up again somewhere else."

Behind us, Cameron was laughing. He pushed his hand against the blood on his face, one of his eyes wouldn't open, but he had climbed back up into the excavator to watch us. "You clocking out, Tiger Lily?" he asked.

"We can fight this bastard," I told them. "There's a camera in the trailer. It caught everything on tape."

"Makes more sense to fight the zombies," Marie said.

I called Shane, and he showed up quick, looking stressed out.

"What happened?" he asked. Not me or Marie, not Lawrence. He asked Cameron.

"She's such a fucking slut," Cameron said, thumbing toward Marie. "Hardly walks away to pee. I could tell you the color of her panties. She's probably fucking Big Chief over here, and the fucking dyke, too." He raised his voice to me again. "You think I don't know, just 'cause you have long hair? I can tell. I have amazing gaydar. And I'm very accepting."

"You're crazy, Cameron," Shane said. "You're fucking crazy. You can't talk like that. Get the hell out of here." But Cameron stayed where he was.

"You okay?" Shane asked Marie. He tried to help her up, but she shrugged him off. She laced up her boots and got unsteadily to her feet, leaning on Lawrence.

"He hit her with the bucket. I saw it," I said.

"Fucking dyke attacked me with a wrench," Cameron said.

"Cameron, you asshole," Shane said. "What the hell is your problem? I told you to go the fuck home." Cameron just kept smiling.

"I told you, Shane. I ain't no oiler," Marie said. "I should be sitting up in that seat."

"This is not about that," Shane said. "You know how these guys are, fragile egos, think with their dicks. In the future, do you think you could go farther away to pee?"

"Oh please," I said. "Shane, you don't provide porta johns. Fucking Cameron pees on any rock, pees on the fucking pipeline, for god's sake."

"Practically pees on me," Marie said.

"Well, like I said," Shane said, "it's Cameron's fault. He got out of hand. He's got mental problems. Don't worry. He's off the job."

"We can report this," I said.

"We?" Marie said. "There's no we."

"We've got to fight back," I said.

"Oh, I'll fight back, all right," Marie said. "But not with you. I can take care of myself, foreman. You need to pull your head out of your ass." Lawrence helped her to the truck. They didn't look back. I watched them drive away. Cameron still sat in the excavator, chuckling high and reedy in his throat.

"Go home, Cameron," Shane said wearily.

"Please just go home, okay? I'll call you."

When it was just Shane and me I said, "I'm still reporting this."

"Who are you going to report it to?" asked Shane.

"I saw what happened," I said. "Including sexual harassment, assault, everything. He's not getting away with it."

"Be careful, Karen," Shane said. "There's two sides to every story. Remember, you hit him in the face with a pipe wrench. Drew blood. Not that I don't admire it."

"You want to see what that asshole did? I'll replay the tape," I said, but when I dragged Shane back into the trailer, there was nothing to replay but snow, though I pressed and pressed buttons, rewound and rewound again. Shane stood behind me in the doorway.

"You motherfucker." I turned on him. "You fucking coward."

"It's not me," Shane said. "It's the system."

But I wasn't finished. "You think I don't remember?" I said. "When Rudy was lying out under that ash tree, near death, you just stood there. You couldn't do a thing but leave the county, left Helen on her own with barely anything just as winter was setting in. And she'd been depending on you. This

497

here's the same shit, only it's way fucking worse."

"You don't know Helen like I do," he said. "You don't know what it was like to live with that woman."

"Oh, I do," I said. "I do know what it's like to live with that woman."

"You think I should have just stayed with her all these years?" he asked.

"It's good enough for some of us," I said.

"She never stopped talking," Shane said. "Only other person I know who talks that much is Rudy."

"At least she shows up," I said. And of course I was thinking, Sometimes too much. Sometimes the woman shows up and shows up and shows up and you end up thinking, Please don't show up this time. Just maybe sit this one out. Still, I found myself defending her to Shane in the way people defend their family. I'm the only one who has the right to despise this person.

"I'm not a coward, I'm pragmatic," Shane said. "Everyone makes compromises, Karen. Even you."

"What happens to Marie?" I asked, already knowing the answer.

"It's up to her," he said. "She still works, if she's willing to. I just find a better place for her."

"What about that fucking guy?"

"Cameron? He still works, too," he said. "They won't work together, of course. Everyone needs a job. You think you're being a hero, but you're pissing against the wind, and you're never going to change anything anyway."

But Shane was wrong. I didn't think I was a hero. I thought I was a nothing, a nothing person. But I'd run out of patience. My mind had cleared the moment I held that pipe wrench in my hand.

I turned down his offer of a ride. I made it back to the motel and I looked for Marie, but she was gone. The fire ring had been scattered. The low plain drew back like the apocalypse had chosen that place to touch down.

Still, I wasn't quite finished. Before Shane had a chance to change the locks, I used my set of keys one more time. I walked back to the crime scene, took me two hours. The sun was setting as I rolled back the fence, slipped inside the trailer. I didn't turn on any lights, just felt for the computer switch. I held my breath, but my password worked, the pipeline map flickered onto the screen, and I followed the red line with my finger. Construction had reached Muskingum

County, only two counties north of our place. It stopped just outside of Zanesville. There, the red ended in a blinking purple icon, and when I checked the key at the bottom of the map, to see what that icon meant, I learned that a compressor station was being built there, ten acres with a turbine to pump fracked gas south.

I logged out, locked the door behind me. I threw the keys as far as I could into the scrub grass, past the snapping turtle shell bleached in the sun.

I figured I'd walked this far, I could make it another mile to the Walmart. It wasn't busy that time of night, not even anyone at the door to greet me. I grabbed a basket. It took me a while to find the swimming pool cleaner, but when an employee asked if I needed help, I said, Just browsing. I hit the auto department next, found brake fluid no problem. In hardware, I added a crescent wrench. A flashlight in the camping section. My last stop was kitchen supplies. Turkey baster. I felt the cash in my pocket, carefully stored up all this time. Still not enough for a septic system. On the way to the register, I guess I got lost. I circled back past the protein bars, knelt behind the sunglasses display, and dumped the entire basket into my knapsack. Then I held my breath and walked out.

I thought for sure someone would come after me, but no one did. I kept along the road until I felt the straps of my pack digging into my shoulders. It was finally time to go home.

Now that I was headed there, I could find no reason to call. Anything I had to say to Lily, any news there was for me to hear about Perley, it could wait one more day. I couldn't believe I'd stayed away so long. This time, I wouldn't take the Greyhound. This time, like in my youth when I thought that knowing old songs and glorifying hoboes would free me of my high school self-hatred for wearing everything used, for wanting to marry a woman, I hit the on-ramp, and I stuck out my thumb.

First ride I got was from a tanker truck driver. He said he was going all the way south with gallons of oil field waste to inject underground in our valley. It was 2:00 a.m. when we made Muskingum County. He could have taken me all the way home that night. But I asked him to drop me off near the river, the one they say people used to cross to get to freedom. Figured I'd have a look around.

Lily

So many false thaws, I didn't believe in spring that year until the asparagus. Every morning in April new spears, green, purple, and white. I broke them off and brought them to Perley at Pariah Park. We gnawed and knitted and hoped for superhuman strength. In six days it would be the ninety-day review.

I wasn't sure how much Perley knew, and I didn't want him to be nervous. I didn't want him to get his hopes up, and most of all I didn't want to let him down ever again. Our new project was going so well, what was the use of reminding him that we weren't in control of everything?

But in my breast pocket, the reunification plan was soft and worn, pressed open and refolded again and again, marked and underlined, lists made in the margins. The house gleamed. The dice were gone. I'd done everything I could do to prepare, but everything I could do still wasn't a septic system, and everything I could do didn't account for the snakes.

Which had come back in force now that it was spring.

The snake behind the woodstove, the snake among the dish towels, the snake in the drawer with the rolling pin and the measuring cups, the snake on the bookshelf, the snake behind the sofa, they were all there, faithful as the redbud and dogwood, the fleabane and mayapple. As fast as I shoveled them outside, they returned, sunning themselves beneath the windows like satisfied cats.

If it had been a hard winter for everyone, it had been a hard winter for Helen, too. I knew it hurt her when I tackled the reunification plan on my own. I knew she wanted to know what I was up to with the plastic eggs, with the piles of yarn. She always wanted to be central to any plan. She'd probably figured that with Karen gone, she and I would become an unstoppable duo. But when Karen had left, I'd discovered that acting alone was the only way I could act. I couldn't expect Helen to understand it. And then when that lawyer passed, it knocked something out of her. She was the one who found him. She didn't say much to me about it, but for weeks, she didn't come home. She didn't say where she was sleeping. When she finally wandered into the kitchen one morning, looking sick and distracted, I thought I had the perfect thing to offer her, to bring her back to herself. I finally needed her.

But when I showed her the snake ritual, carefully recorded in Perley's awkward hand, she glanced over it, then handed the comic book back to me. "I don't know," she said. "Sounds hokey. Sounds like more stealing from the Native Americans."

"This isn't some new-age crap," I said. "This is the kind of shit my grandma said her Irish grandma did when she wasn't praying the rosary."

"You don't know," she said.

"You don't know either," I said. "What I'm wondering is, what if it works?"

She took the book back from me, looked at it again.

"Why do you need my help?" she asked. "It seems like you've been making out just fine without me lately." I might have resisted such fishing, but for once my own need met hers.

"Even if I could eat one snake," I said, "I could hardly eat two. And anyway, you're the one knows how to skin them and clean them."

When I mentioned eating snakes, Helen looked green and shut her mouth quick. When I mentioned skinning and cleaning them, she said, "When we met, you and Karen were the ones showing me how to butcher animals."

"Seems like we've switched places," I said. She smiled, satisfied that I'd say so.

"It's easy," she said. "It's like cleaning a fish."

"If it's so easy," I said, "it'll be easy for you to do it."

"We'll do it together," she said.

In spite of everything, it felt a bit like butchering old pets. I chose the sofa snake and the woodstove snake, the boldest, the easiest ones to catch. Helen held the sofa snake by its tail. It arced and sent musk, crimped up. She lowered it, and as its head neared the floor, the snake thrust itself horizontal and offered its neck. I swung the butcher knife. Then we did it again.

I took one headless snake, and Helen took the other. She showed me where to find the vent and we sliced up from there. We worked our paring blades to separate the threads of muscle tissue and peel back the skin. Six inches down, Helen gripped her snake's body, and pulled off the rest of the skin like rolling down a sleeve. She nodded to me and I unsheathed mine the same way. I found clothespins, and we hung the gleaming skins in the windows to dry. We scooped out the neat tube of guts, and dropped them in a bucket next to the heads. While Helen rinsed the bodies, I brought down the big mixing bowl and poured salt into water, watched the small storm it made, the cloud dissolving. We added the snakes, pale pink as quartz. We left them to brine.

It was a fine evening, clear, with rain on the horizon. The ramps blushed deep green on the banks of the creek. I built a fire outside and filled the canning pot. Helen and I sat out in camping chairs, watching the pot boil, which you're not supposed to do, but she still wasn't as talkative as usual. I tried to ask her about Aldi, but she just shook her head. "There won't be another one like him," was all she could say. I offered to make dinner, but she grimaced.

The water was just beginning to steam when, over by their shed, the ducks set up their watchdog chatter, and Helen and I turned to see Karen come home.

She came down the path, long and tall as ever, hands stuffed in her Carhartt pockets, a rolled-up newspaper sticking out of her knapsack, loose braid fraying, hat pulled low to make it clear she wasn't betting on what kind of welcome she'd get.

When she saw us, she stopped, and it helps when you haven't seen your someone in ages, it helps when they catch you unawares, it helps when you haven't been rehearsing. It gives your body a chance to be the smart one.

From underneath her hat, she said, "I didn't make all the money. I made most of it. I made enough to get started. But in the end I fell short."

"You idiot," I said. "It doesn't matter about the money. Don't you have anything else to report?"

"I guess you've seen this," she said, pulling the newspaper from her pack. She sidled close enough to hand it to me. I looked it over, and passed it to Helen.

"Compressor station inoperable near Zanesville," Helen read aloud. "No injuries, but machines disabled, thousands in damages. Arson suspected. Pipeline construction delayed. Damn," she said. "People could have been killed."

"You read the thing," Karen said. "Whoever it was waited until after hours. The site was deserted. Not a single human was injured."

"Too bad that kind of thing doesn't create lasting change," Helen said.

"On the other hand, what does?" Karen said. She sat down next to me.

"Is that up where you were working?" I asked, some kind of feeling in my stomach.

"Not even close," Karen said. "I was way farther north. But I can say this. I can't condemn or condone what that person did, but I can understand what may have driven them to such an act." She took a pack of cigarettes from her pocket, shook one out, and lit it. I didn't say anything, just watched her lean forward and pick up a stick of firewood, not walnut like she preferred. White oak. Watched her turn it over in her hand. I took her sheepsfoot knife from my pocket, handed it over.

"I found it in Perley's camper," I said. She set her blade to wood. Smoke met smoke. Shavings sparked into the fire.

"Karen," I said. "Welcome home. You're just in time for the ritual."

When we put the snakes in the pot to boil, they came back to life, or that's how it looked. Headless, they rose. They twined out of the steam, lunged from the pot and down through the fire, out over the stones toward us. Their skinned bodies blanched white, they twisted, hissing mouthless in their dance of death.

Helen said that their spinal cords were sending dead letters, but I'll say that the spectacle helped me with the part of the ritual where I was meant to find the words to pray. Heavenly father or not, I was all in.

When the snakes were once and for all still, we rinsed them of earth and ashes. We ate them with knife and fork.

All except Helen.

"Why aren't you eating?" I asked.

"When you figured out you were pregnant with Perley," she said, "what tipped you off? Just your garden-variety missed period or were there other signs?"

"Helen," I said.

"It's too early to know," she said. "But I know."

Karen laughed. "I've missed a lot," she said.

"Aren't you going to ask?" Helen said.

"Ask what?" I said.

"If I'm going through with it."

"Are you going through with it?" I asked.

"Yes," she said. I ran around the fire and hugged her. She said, "Aren't you going to ask if I'm worried, if I'm worried about being a single parent and being so fucking old?"

"No guarantees," Karen said, "but most

likely you'll be fine."

"And you're not a single parent," I said. "You've got us, and Rudy's been dying to have a kid."

"Right," Helen said. "Dying to drink lukewarm beer while the kid uses his chain saw. Wait, how did you know it was Rudy?"

Karen and I looked at each other, then back at her.

"Well, anyway," Helen said. "It's over now."

"Does he know?" I asked.

"Don't push her, Lily," Karen said.

"He knows I'm pregnant," Helen said. "He's excited. He actually pumped his fist in the air and said something like, Who is the man? But we're not going to be together. It just wouldn't work."

"Took you so long to try it," I said. "Might as well give it a go."

"Rudy doesn't want to," Helen said. "He said it doesn't feel right after all. He says what brought us together was just the grief, that and shock from losing Aldi. He's still all fucked-up from that." I put my hand on Karen's shoulder. There was still so much she didn't know. Helen went on. "He says, I don't know if it's such a good idea, you and me."

"What about you?" I asked. "Do you want

to be with him?"

"Oh, I don't know," Helen said. "Not really." Then she shook her head. "But I probably would've kept it up. I mean, it's not like I love the guy, and I definitely don't like him, but my body — goddamn, I could have done it all day. For a long time, I wondered what had happened to that part of me, where it went, if it ever existed. Now I can locate it. It's not Rudy, it's that feeling. That sex thing. The world's in color, that's what people say, and it's true. I'll be honest. I've been masturbating like a teenager for weeks. Then one day the cramping started. I'd get off, and then waves of pain, like menstrual cramps, except my period won't come. I've never known anything like it."

Eight years in a shack together, hearing every single thing through the walls, and never had there been such an outpouring between us. We'd always been private in that way, or shy. Eager for details, curious though I was, I blushed and looked away. But Karen, a nurse, was unembarrassed by vocation.

"Actually, the uterus always cramps after orgasm," Karen said. "It's just that when you're not pregnant, you can't usually feel it." She thought one more minute. She lit

511

another cigarette, got back to her piece of white oak.

"I guess I'm carving another baby spoon," she said. "I guess we'll have to make the house bigger."

18

Karen

I wasn't afraid of the flames. I wasn't afraid afterward, as I emptied my zombie apocalypse kit into the river. Through it all, I felt a cold and bitter joy. I wasn't afraid until I made it home, came down the path, and saw Lily. Her black hair, her sharp chin, her open eyes, it wasn't just Lily I was looking at, it was Perley, too. I saw everything I'd set out to protect, and everything I'd risked. Then fear rose in front of me like a wall and knocked me back. Seeing Lily made me remember things, how chatty the tanker truck driver had been, how Shane would have found by now that I'd cut out. What other loose ends wasn't I thinking of? How long would it take for them to find me? What would they do? I had no way of knowing, and those were the wrong questions anyway. Helen was wrong when she talked like any of us knew what created lasting change. Those words came straight out of a can, it wasn't even her own voice saying them. I'd whittled down past all that. I didn't know if I was right or wrong, wily or a fuckup. All I knew was that after days and months of grim confusion, I'd arrived at the compressor station in Muskingum County with a certainty that I hardly recognized as mine. Against that, what was fear? I did my best to push it aside.

I wasn't planning on talking to Lily about any of that. My plan, which I'd come up with on the final hitch home, when I'd kept my mouth shut and pretended to sleep against the window, was simple. To tell Lily I hadn't saved enough money. To tell her I was sorry I left. To beg forgiveness. Not to say Sorry but, or Sorry and. Just to say sorry.

But she wasn't interested.

First of all, she wanted me.

She invited me to bed, which was itself a surprise, more so even than the house, clean as I'd never seen it. She'd even built a small bed just for Perley, partitioned off in the corner. I hardly recognized the place.

I didn't remove a stitch of clothing. I even kept my boots laced up. I lay there like a board next to her. But as soon as we heard Helen's even breathing, Lily's hands were everywhere relieving me of all that. "It's not because I'm not mad at you," she said. "It's because I need it."

"I need it, too," I said, and I got in under the covers. When she touched me, she was delayed ignition, she was Marie and Shane and even Cameron, all that mess, and when I touched her, I was the old-timers and the ones who'd done her wrong, I was rich and from Manhattan and poor as shit from right here, I was the sap running in the trees and the arrowheads that get churned up when big threatening work is done. We didn't finish for a long time.

When we did, I raised myself to one elbow, kept my hands in her stream of black hair fanned on the pillow.

"The pipeline might be delayed, but they mean to come here," I said.

"We got something in the mail," she said. "Is it bad?"

"It's worse than they say," I said.

"What will we do?" she asked. "Where would we go?"

"We're not going anywhere," I said.

Then Lily told me about Perley, about Aldi's failed motions, about Grandma Barlow, about Pariah Park, about Perley's stiff new clothes, his newfound guile. She told me that he'd made a friend, a real one this time. She told me about the blue pills, the knit-

515

ting, the yarn, the eggs, the holes. She told me about closing the holes.

"Perley's sound," she said. She clasped her hands behind her head. "He's smart and he's strong. He's prepared. He's your son, even though he still insists he's an elf or a wolf."

"He's my son, all right," I said.

"He asks about you all the time."

"What do you say?" I asked.

"I don't know what to say," she said. "Next week's the review hearing."

"Sorry about the money," I said. "I tried."

"I know," she said.

"We'll call Frank about septic in the morning," I said. "Maybe we can work something out. I can go back to nursing. I can pay the rest off over time, I can —" But Lily waved me off.

"You have to talk to Perley," she said. "That's what's important."

"How?" I asked. "What will I say?" This was where my plan ran out.

"You're good at figuring things out," she said. "So figure it out."

I fell asleep holding her. I dreamed of sumac trees and woke to the full moon staring at me through the window. I didn't even try to close my eyes against it.

In the dark kitchen, I found the bucket

with the snake guts, the two blind heads. Needed burying. My flashlight was drowned in Muskingum County, sunk with the crescent wrench and turkey baster, the bottles of pool cleaner and brake fluid, emptied and then filled again with rocks. But I didn't need a flashlight. I had the moon. All the way to the back of the acreage, silver striking each leaf, I kept walking. I found the old goat path, gullied and pitted, crisscrossed with blackberry. I climbed up to the ridge. The buds stood on the dark trees, misformed elfin ears. The remnants of a peach orchard persisted below me on the coal company land. I could have buried the offal anywhere, but I kept walking. The bucket glowed white as new blossoms. I walked until the moon set, until the sky changed color on its way to morning. I wasn't on any trail. I was looking for the right place.

Perley

Once I stopped taking my medicine I didn't want to dig the portal in the gnome house anymore. Instead of digging under the ground, I wanted to go over the ground. I stood outside the gnome house and gazed nobly using my super-sensitive wolf vision to see beyond the next ridge and Altemonte came out and said, What are you looking at aren't you going to help dig? And I said, What's the farthest you've ever ranged? and he was like, You mean from my grandma's house? This is the farthest. And I was like, I predict that we can range even farther because we have extremely strong legs, and we basically never get tired even though we stay up all night. The fact is we probably could range farther than we could dig and we could get to the elf world sooner. So Altemonte said, You want to range, okay let's range.

So after that every night we ranged farther. The first night we made it to an ash log with oyster mushrooms on it and we picked the mushrooms for Grandma Barlow and Altemonte marked the log with a knot of joe-pye and then the next night we had our destination. Our destination was that joe-pye ash log and when we found it again we went a little farther. During the day, Grandma Barlow would say, Where did you find the oyster mushrooms and I knew that Altemonte didn't want to lie to his grandma, so I would say, After school down by the creek, that's where.

We ranged farther each night. Every night Altemonte tied a knot of joe-pye to a tree so we would know where we'd been and where we'd go next.

On the night of the full moon our super-sensitive wolf vision was at its height. We ranged so far that the color of the sky confused me. I said, Altemonte, look at the sky, it's all pink. We've finally made it to the Wolfriders' land, to the World of Two Moons, or maybe to Middle-earth. But Altemonte said, I think the sky is that color because it's morning and the sun is rising. We'd better go back before my grandma wakes up.

But then I saw my cave.

It was the cave I had discovered just before the Outside Girl took me away, except then it had been winter so its mouth had teeth which were icicles, and now it was spring so the cave had a mouth of puffball mushrooms and a red eft crawled out of it like the cave had a tongue, and once I saw my cave I saw everything else too. The oak tree with the split trunk and the sandstone like a star from outer space and the burned-out elm stump where I sometimes found morels and the sassafras that was a catapult. What is it, Altemonte said, you look like you have to pee or something. I told Altemonte, This cave means that I am home. Altemonte said, You told me you lived in the All Worship Altemonte camper not in a cave, and I was like, That camper isn't far. I know my way from here.

I pictured every step, first the hollow beech tree, then the ditch that the ducks liked especially to shit in when they roamed that far, then the sharp turn downhill where one time but not again I saw a snapping turtle, then the jagged hickory, then the trees of heaven that Mama K liked to cut rings around, then the worn-out peach orchard, the oak tree where the Mean Aunt and I shook acorns, the goat path, and then the roof of the house and then the house, then the smoke from the chimney and then the chimney, then the firepit and then the fire, and then the mamas and the Mean Aunt. They were knitting and whittling and skinning and waiting for me.

I said, Altemonte, if we run we can make it home before breakfast but actually I was already running. Home beat so loud in my ears it was a while before I noticed Altemonte wasn't running with me. I ran back. I could see Altemonte's red rain boots sticking out of my cave, so I crawled in next to him. He was chewing on joe-pye. I said, What happened, did you hurt your ankle? Do you need me to make you a splint? I can carry you on my back. He said, You know that if you go home the police will just bring you back to my grandma's house again. You can't go home until the police say you can. I said, Altemonte, I don't care about that. I know how to get out of most police holds. I know how to battle like a ton of enemies. Altemonte said, I knew you would say that. That's why you're my best friend. Extreme joyfulness then took over my body and I said, It's okay if you hurt your ankle don't worry, I'll make you a stretcher out of pine boughs, wait here while I find some pine boughs. But Altemonte said, This is a deciduous forest so there aren't any pine boughs. I didn't hurt my ankle. I'm not going with you.

Back a long time ago when I was still trying to be super-popular at school, the Mean Aunt said, Perley, if your friend jumped over a cliff would you jump over a cliff? and I was like, Definitely. I said, If my friend jumped over a cliff, one of two things would be the case. Either they would be proving to me that jumping over a cliff is super-toxically amazing, so of course I would join in, or else, if it was my true friend that jumped over the cliff, I would be so lonely that I couldn't bear it and I would jump over, too. Maybe I would catch my true friend in midair and then I would grab a tree branch and I would save us. But even if we both fell together to our deaths it would be better than being alone without my true friend. The Mean Aunt got all sick at that. No, no, she said. That's not what a true friend would want you to do, she said. I should hug you, she said, but I'm covered in beaver intestines so just act like I'm hugging you. All right, I said, hugging myself.

And now I actually had a true friend which was Altemonte and I'd thought that I'd finally discovered what my mission was and what my destiny was. I'd thought my mission and my destiny was to find Altemonte and to bring him home with me. But now I knew I'd been wrong. My mission was way harder than that. It turned out that my mission was to find Altemonte and once I'd found him to leave him again.

I knew it, but still I had to try to not know it.

So I was like, Altemonte, you're just jealous because I live in my own toxic house and I get to run a chain saw by myself. But I knew it wouldn't work. Altemonte didn't get jealous, because it's like he hadn't heard of jealousy. If a kid tied a string to a horsefly, Altemonte would be the next one to do it only because it looked fascinating, not because he thought it would make him popular. He knew he was flanged, but he had more important things on his mind. Like he said, he was pretty busy.

He sat in my cave and pulled his knees up to his chin. He said, This cave has orcs and goblins probably fighting to the death down in its very bowels at this exact moment. He said, I won't tell anyone where you went I'll just say I woke up and you were gone. He said, I'll hide your knitting.

I said, You can keep my comic books.

He said, I'll give you my force field.

I said, But you need your force field.

He said, We can share it. And he cut off a big hunk of it for me, and I put the hunk of force field in my pocket for later. It was so honorable that you could almost forget I was going to see him at school and you could almost forget that maybe it was true what he said about the police and about who was in charge. Maybe it was true but we both knew there were more important things in life.

We crawled out of the cave. The sky of Middle-earth or of the World of Two Moons or of home was light and Altemonte and I shook hands as befitted our stations and then I kissed him on the lips. Make haste, he said. The last thing that I saw before I ran was Altemonte tying a knot of joe-pye, marking the tree next to our cave.

I pretty much was flying, past the hollow beech tree, past the duck-shit ditch, sharp turn downhill, no snapping turtle, trees of heaven, acorn-shaking tree below me, then oh. A shadow.

A shadow in the trees. A step. A step not my step. I slowed, but didn't stop. I listened. I remembered what I knew. The wolf pack may be near, hunting. If you're just a dog they will try to trick you into running with them, and then they'll kill you. I had to be smart. I had to show the shadow that I was a wolf, too. A little wolf, like Choplicker. But who could be walking out here on the ridge, who but a wolf, an elf, an elfin chief? Who else would know the way? I passed through the peach orchard no peaches. I paused again, sniffing the air, tracking it. Here it came, bigger than me, down the logging road, skirting the side trail, swinging something gleaming white by its side. I ducked behind the hickory. My scar shone, smarted. From the silence, I knew the big wolf knew me.

"Perley?" she said.

So I, brave little wolf, stepped out.

ACKNOWLEDGMENTS

So many friends, family members, mentors, neighbors, loved ones, and worthy adversaries had a hand in helping this book come to be — reading and responding, nurturing me and challenging me. Thanks to the many cantankerous arborists in my life, including Nate, Alex, and Jeff. Thanks to Davey McNelley, Jordan Pepper, and Brian Bors for talking to me about social work. Thanks to Tessa Evanosky for the snake ritual. Thanks to Talcon Quinn and Caty Crabb for teaching me so much about the plants and animals in the Ohio hills where we live. Thanks to Dave Baer for describing a career as a public defender. Thanks to Sammy Douthwaite, whittler. Thanks to Noah Gershman for the dice games. Thanks to Ann Tagonist for many wild ways and for helping me understand suturing. Thanks to Liz Badger for the illicit chocolate exchanges and for more than I can ever say.

Thanks to Rhonda Rose, whom I called to ask how an excavator works and heard much more than that, whose stories and passion led the novel to be deeper and truer. Thanks to readers of very early chapters and drafts who helped me strategize ways to continue the writing: Zakes Mda, Rachel Glaser, Sara Jaffe, Anna Grace Keller, James Miranda, Patrick O'Keeffe, Elspeth Vance, and Zach Ballew. Thanks to Bianca Spriggs and Ghirmai Negash for asking necessary questions, whether or not I could answer them. Thanks to Eric ffitch, for forcing me to have an internet presence. Thanks to Jenna Johnson, whose instincts as an editor seem almost like magic to me. I am so glad we worked on this book together. Thanks to Claudia Ballard, who somehow knew how to patiently and calmly steer this book to just the right home. Thanks to all of you who told me your snake stories — snakes in your linen closets, in your drawers, under your tables, in your chimneys, and, yes, even in your beds. Thanks to water protectors and pipeline resisters, and to all those fighting domination in creative, bold, and steadfast ways. Thank you to Cusi Gibbons-Ballew, Nector Vine Ballew, and Amos Dell Ballew: I never knew 'til I met you what love oh love could do.

ABOUT THE AUTHOR

Madeline ffitch cofounded the punk theater company Missoula Oblongata and is part of the direct-action collective Appalachia Resist! Her writing has appeared in *Tin House, Guernica, Granta, VICE,* and *Electric Literature,* among other publications. She is the author of the story collection *Valparaiso, Round the Horn.*